POLITY AGENT

Neal Asher was born in Billericay, Essex. He started writing SF and fantasy at the age of sixteen and has since had many novels published. He now divides his time between Essex and a home in Crete.

By Neal Asher

Cowl

Agent Ian Cormac
Shadow of the Scorpion
Gridlinked
The Line of the Polity
Brass Man
Polity Agent
Line War

Spatterjay
The Skinner
The Voyage of the Sable Keech
Orbus

Novels of the Polity
Prador Moon
Hilldiggers
The Technician

Short Story Collection
Runcible Tales
The Engineer
The Gabble

Novellas
Mindgames: Fool's Mate
The Parasite

NEAL ASHER

POLITY AGENT

An Agent Cormac Novel

TOR

First published 2006 by Tor

This edition published 2010 by Tor
an imprint of Pan Macmillan, a division of Macmillan Publishers Limited
Pan Macmillan, 20 New Wharf Road, London N1 9RR
Basingstoke and Oxford
Associated companies throughout the world
www.panmacmillan.com

ISBN 978-0-330-52139-0

1 3 5 7 9 8 6 4 2

A CIP catalogue record for this book is available from
the British Library.

Typeset by IntypeLibra Limited, London
Printed in UK by CPI Mackays, Chatham ME5 8TD

www.panmacmillan.com to read more about all our books
and to buy them. You will also find features, author interviews and
news of any author events, and you can sign up for e-newsletters
so that you're always first to hear about our new releases.

Acknowledgements

Again thanks to everyone involved in bringing this book to the shelves, including my wife Caroline, my parents Bill and Hazel, Keith Starkey, and those working at Macmillan and elsewhere: Peter Lavery first and foremost, Rebecca Saunders, Emma Giacon, Steve Rawlings, Liz Cowen, Jon Mitchell, Liz Johnson, Chantal Noel, Neil Lang, and many others besides. In *The Skinner* I also acknowledged all those excellent people whose names stretch through the alphabet from Aldiss to Zelazny, but there's others inside and outside the SF field who require a further mention because of their influence on my writing. Here's a couple: Iain M. Banks and Richard Dawkins – one for the drones and one for the genes: Oscar speech territory warning – OK, that's enough for now.

Prologue

The Polity is, in terms of human history, a huge and unique political entity. Under the benevolent rule of artificial intelligences it is ever-expanding in the galactic disc. Many see it as a precursor to Utopia, possibly eternal. However, during its initial expansion, artefacts of ancient alien civilizations began to turn up, and to the dismay of the Utopians we've since learned just how small is our dominion. Slowly, evidence has accrued to show that three distinct alien races occupied our portion of the galaxy before us, and now they are gone. It's depressing; reality often is. So, ignoring the other two for the moment, let me concentrate on one of those races. What do we know about those we have named the Jain?

Well, very little. The few artefacts remaining of their civilization date back prior to five million years ago, when the Jain obviously became extinct or disappeared. We don't know what they looked like, though there is some suggestion they might have been hot-world aquatic. We do know their civilization extended over many star systems, and that they possessed the technology to move planets and reform ecologies in ways as yet untried here in the Polity. We do know they used a highly sophisticated nanotechnology. But frankly, everything else claimed to be known about them was opinion and speculation, until recently.

The general consensus among experts was that the Jain were warlike and that their own technology wiped them out. The few fragments recovered of this 'Jain technology' are sealed in a self-destruct room in the Viking Museum on Luna. But why this consensus? Conspiracy theorists have it that the AIs know a lot more than they are telling, since their search for further artefacts of this kind absorbs a substantial portion of the Earth Central Security budget. Whichever way you look at it, recent events have shown that the dangers represented by Jain technology have not been underestimated.

The idea of a 'Jain node' was a product of one of the wilder theories until a few years ago – the whole technology of that alien race contained in something small enough to drop into one's pocket. There ensued a scramble to discover such an item, but none were found at the time and the theory fell into disfavour, its proponents dismissed as nutjobs. Unfortunately the Jain node has recently proved to be a reality, and a rather unpleasant one at that.

Earth Central Security has not been forthcoming about the events surrounding its discovery, but there are still planetary systems under quarantine, and many unsubstantiated rumours of megadeath involved. However, I did manage to get something from a nameless source concerning a Jain node and the purpose of the technology it engenders.

It seems a node will only react to a living intelligent organism, which will then become both its host and its master. The nanotechnology propagating from this relationship is mycelial in nature, and capable of penetrating all our present technologies. Horribly, it seems able to take control of living beings in the same way. Godlike power, you would think, but, no, it is a poisoned chalice. Unless he manages to exercise total *control, the user will end up being the used, the technology continuing to spread and destroy while he, the host, is absorbed as merely a component of it. Even managing to control it and evading such fate is not enough, since Jain tech is programmed, like an annual plant, to go to seed, and in the process tears its host apart in order to create more Jain nodes, which in turn will be spread to further hosts. The opinion of my source was that this diabolical creation serves one purpose only: genocide.*

– From 'How it Is' by Gordon

Over the centuries, the huge *Celedon* station's original shape, like a spinning top five miles across, had become shrouded by accretions. Now near the end of its journey and its useful life, it was slowing from one eighth of light speed on this particular edge of the Polity sphere because the stars here were dispersed and intergalactic space lay beyond. Its controlling artificial intelligence, Celedon, viewed those aboard through its many camera eyes. The resident and transitory populations had been dropping away for some years simply because they had come to realize there existed so little of interest out here. The usual tourists still arrived, but after taking a look around they soon departed. Various corporations still maintained offices and factories in the rim units, but their number decreased steadily and no new ones had established a foothold here in the last two decades. Even the low-grav and vacuum-adapted outlinker humans, living here from the beginning, were starting to trickle away to more lively stations. There were now many empty rooms, deserted corridors and concourses, and Celedon, having shut down three of the five runcibles aboard simply because these extra instantaneous gateways in from other destinations were no longer required, viewed with chagrin the prospect of the next two boring decades before the station reached its final destination.

Eventually Celedon would put the station in orbit around a star already selected, and there it would remain forever as a static outpost of the Polity. The AI had yet to decide what then to do. Perhaps a massive expansion project might spark a renewal of interest: the station could be opened out and enlarged and bases established on the single Venusian world orbiting the selected sun. Maybe that same world could be terraformed? Those options were all available – or Celedon could itself abandon this structure that was the body into which it had been born, and leave it to the control of subminds and automatic systems. Certainly some of its own subminds would be glad of the opportunity for independence, and a chance at expansion of both their capacity and responsibility. As it mulled over these possibilities, the AI was casually watching a group of children playing a game of zero-G handball, when the information package arrived through runcible C.

'Ah, three impossible things before breakfast.'

'What's that?' asked a drone located in the embarkation lounge of that runcible.

Celedon turned its attention to the individual concerned: an independent drone, fashioned in the shape of a spider, that the AI had itself employed at the inception of this station. The drone had originally been manufactured as part of a strike force for clearing enemy stations during a war between the Polity and some particularly vicious aliens named the Prador. Celedon remembered sending it to the same lounge five years ago to oversee the closing of that area, and that it had put itself into shutdown mode ever since. It rested on the wide expanse of blue carpet moss, its shiny motionless legs forming a cage around its main body, then those legs slowly started unfolding.

'The three impossible things are these, Arach. I just received a message sent through a runcible that is not due to go online for eight hundred and thirty years; from a location the ship containing the components of said runcible has a hundred thousand light years yet to travel before reaching; from a runcible technician who should still be in coldsleep aboard said ship.'

'And you're telling me this why?' Arach asked.

'The information package arrived through Runcible C. You were merely woken by a safety protocol, and so chanced to overhear me. You may shut yourself down again if you wish.'

'After hearing that?' The spider-drone danced in a circle, its eight eyes emitting an infernal glow. 'You have to be kidding.'

Arach, Celedon remembered, had expressed a degree of boredom before shutting itself down. Not unsurprising considering its antecedents.

Celedon returned its attention to the package received. The U-space coordinates were correct and the runcible signature correct. The AI opened the package and quickly scanned the information it contained, then, realizing the seriousness of the situation, it diverted a full third of its capacity to studying the data more closely, before sending a copy, via Runcible D, to Earth Central – the Polity's ruling artificial intelligence.

'Hostile contact protocol Starfire,' the distant Earth Central AI replied.

Celedon immediately contacted its drones in the three

shutdown runcible lounges: the spider itself, the fly, and the pill bug – all erstwhile products of that ancient war effort. 'Runcibles coming back online. Open all lounges and direct all humans to the runcibles, immediately. You may use non-fatal coercion. Fly, your area is to remain zero-G. Stand by.'

The AI observed lights coming on in the various empty lounges, doors opening, and the nascent shimmer of Skaidon warps growing between the bull's horns of Runcibles A, B and C. In lounges B and C, Celedon turned the gravplates back on, bringing various objects clattering to the floor. At the same time it put up on all bulletin boards, EVACUATE STATION, ALL INCOMING TRAFFIC IS ON DIVERT, and sent the same message to all personal coms and augmentations, or by voice in private quarters.

'The sender chose this station for a reason,' Celedon observed.

'Certainly,' EC replied. 'It is the least visited and the most uninhabited.'

Inevitably, the station's residents sent thousands of queries. The most hysterical were from the outlinkers who had made this place their home for a hundred years, for, being zero-G adapted humans, where they might be evacuated to could be a problem. The transient travellers, however, were soon packing their luggage, if not obediently heading towards the runcibles. Celedon itself noted a group of three tourists, who had been exploring a deserted part of the station, now being shepherded towards Runcible C by Arach, the spider-drone. Though they objected loudly, they were moving fast, especially after Arach informed them what *non-fatal coercion* could mean, and began lasering the carpet right behind them.

'Least collateral damage by feedback from a time-inconsistent runcible connection?' Celedon suggested. A runcible connection between the past and the future was considered impossible by many humans. The AIs new better.

'Precisely,' Earth Central replied.

'So you wish me to fully connect?'

'Yes, but only to Runcible A, and not until you are positioned in low solar orbit with all preparations made that the protocol implies.'

'Of course.'

The AI maintained its link with Earth Central while making those preparations. Internal scans showed that the original station structure remained as sound as ever. However, expanding that scanning process, the AI found that many of the additions accumulated over the years were not designed to withstand what must ensue. Celedon recorded, formatted and loaded 200 subminds to 200 skeletal Golem and assigned them to expediting the evacuation of those additional structures, making the ones constructed over the rim fusion engines a priority, and then observed the skinless androids, like chromed skeletons, come marching out of storage. It assigned system subminds already initiated to fielding the queries and protests from established residents and companies, then turned its own attention to the outlinkers.

'Chief Engineer Draesil,' it said, watching the man through the multiple eyes of a welding robot.

The man was tall, painfully thin, his skin coloured and patterned like the flesh of a kiwi fruit. His hair was black and he wore a tight body garment covered in pockets and strapped-down tools. In this zero-G environment he hung with one arm hooked through a wall loop, peering about himself at the activity of his multicoloured kind.

'What the hell is going on?' he asked, his gaze focusing on the nearby robot.

'Your people must evacuate the station as quickly as possible.'

'Yes, I think I kind of understood that, but why? Buffer failure or fusion breach?'

'Neither. This station will be undergoing fusion acceleration burn in fifty-three hours. Though many of those aboard would be able to survive the forces involved, your own kind would not.' Outlinkers, being adapted to low gravity, were fragile.

'You still haven't told me why,' Draesil snapped.

The AI felt a moment of chagrin. It had noted over its long years of stewardship of this station how humans readily trusted AIs until orders from such entities impinged directly on their lives. Then they started voicing questions and doubts about the abilities and motives of intelligences a thousand times more powerful than any unaugmented human. Thus, in moments of catastrophe, when hard decisions needed to be made quickly, all AIs included in their calculations a human death toll governed by a factor called 'pig-headedness'.

'A hostile contact protocol has been ordered by Earth Central. You and your people must all proceed immediately to Runcible Gate A, which will remain a zero-G area, with whatever belongings and personal effects you can carry. All resulting pecuniary losses will be reimbursed.'

Draesil bowed his head. 'What's coming through?'

'I cannot discuss that.'

'And where are we going?'

'You will be transmitted to another station's low-G section. Should it be possible after this crisis, you may return here to me. Otherwise alternative station space will be provided.'

Draesil nodded and pushed himself away from the wall, speaking into his collar comlink as he tumbled freely through the air. 'This is the real thing, people. We have fifty hours to get out of here. Grab your stuff and head for Runcible A.'

Celedon then turned its attention to other matters, glad that at least the humans in this small section of the station had become someone else's headache. Seven hundred and thirty people had already gone through the runcibles. The lounges of D and E were becoming very crowded, but now the spider and the pill bug arrived and began directing people to the monorails which would take them around the station's main disc to the other runcibles opening up. The alacrity with which the crowd obeyed those drones, Celedon put down to atavistic fears: few humans would be inclined to disobey the orders of an iron spider with a leg-span of three yards.

Now, the engines. The main fusion engine lay along the axis of the station, protruding into space below it, so was free to fire up at any time, but Celedon needed to utilize the rim engines now. It observed one area, positioned over one of those four engines, now clear of human occupants, and Golem in the process of leaving too. Celedon began closing the airlocks, but then, after noting something through its cameras, reopened a lock and sent one of the Golem back inside. It shortly returned carrying a large fat cat under its arm, which it handed to a distraught woman who came running back to collect it. Celedon emitted a silicon sigh and closed the final airlock.

The rim engines were of an old design fuelled by deuterium and tritium microspheres. Their tanks were full of liquid deuterium and tritium talc, and had been so for a hundred years. Diagnostics detected no faults, therefore this particular engine stood ready to ignite, but not yet. The *Celedon* station possessed a slight spin, not for centrifugal gravity, that problem having been overcome long ago with gravplates, but to fling away any docked spacecraft – though the last one of those had departed thirteen years ago. Checking with an astrogation program, the controlling AI, Celedon, waited the required twenty-two minutes and seven seconds.

Now.

Deuterium droplets sprayed into the freezer chamber, where they froze, and next were electrostatically coated with tritium dust. A ring of injectors then fired the resultant microspheres into the main chamber. Once a sphere reached the chamber's centre, it was captured in a twenty tesla magnetic bottle, then briefly enclosed in a hardfield case, open on one side and with just enough gaps in it to allow access for the beams of high-intensity stacked gallium-arsenide lasers. The lasers fired, igniting fusion, then this process repeated a hundredth of a second later, and kept on repeating. The resultant helium plasma contained less than .00001 isotope contamination, but was still dangerously destructive.

White fire stabbed out of the open side of the hardfield box, and then out of the layered ceramo-carbide combustion chamber. It cut through rooms previously occupied, converted walls, floors, ceilings, coffee tables and sofas to incandescent gas, and blasted out into vacuum. Spearing out from the station edge, it burned red-orange. Air exploded into space, wreckage followed. The conglomeration of structures peeled away, burst asunder, was flung away by the station's spin. Celedon noted fire alarms and systems coming online, and going off just as quickly as they collapsed. And then *Celedon*, the station, slowly began to tilt.

Shutdown.

The fire went out. In two hours' time a stabilizing burn would be required from rim engine 4, which gave the Golem plenty of time to clear out the last sixty people still within its vicinity. Gazing internally Celedon observed the outlinkers releasing themselves from wall-holds after acceleration ceased. They had not liked that sensation at all, but it made them move much faster towards Runcible A.

Celedon separated out one of the many communications sent to it and replied 'Forty-seven hours' to Draesil's query. Shaking his head in annoyance, the man himself followed a group of outlinker children through the runcible.

Two hours later, the AI initiated the stabilizing burn. The station now pointed directly at what was, by a very roundabout route, its intended destination. Forty-five hours after that, with the station finally emptied of fragile organic life, Celedon turned on the main fusion engine, and shed the accretions on the station's surface like an old skin. Then, after a three-hour burn followed by a shutdown, the AI again used the rim engines to adjust the station's attitude before reigniting the main drive. Now, rather than pursue a long curving roundabout route to the destination sun, the station took the most direct route possible taking into account its original velocity. The journey commencing would take three years, but this would not matter to the original sender of the information package. For once Celedon initiated full connection to the sending runcible, the time *there*, in the future, would not have changed at all.

Deuterium and tritium canisters arrived through Runcible D and the skeletal Golem manhandled them to the monorail train, out of which they had already torn all the furnishings to convert it into a fuel transporter. While they ran this extra fuel down to the main engine, Celedon watched through the eyes of the hundreds of maintenance robots swarming in the sector of the station containing Runcible A. That sector, shaped like a wedge with the tip cut off, was originally devised to be ejected from the station in the event of catastrophic runcible failure. However, over the years, bulkheads had been removed, doors added, its internal structure changed. Supervised by Arach, robots brought out sheets of ceramal-laminated composite from a factory located in the central spindle, to deliver to other robots who powder-welded them into place. Still other robots cut through any structural members Celedon calculated to be unnecessary, leaving only those necessary under the five-G deceleration down towards the green sun. To those remaining structural members holding the sector to the station, Celedon sent Fly to attach planar explosives. These bombs would generate a disc-like explosion which would sever the retaining members nicely.

'The *Jerusalem* will be joining you in seventy-three days,' Earth Central informed the AI abruptly.

'Should I wait?' Celedon enquired. 'I'm only fifty-one days away from achieving low solar orbit.'

'You should indeed wait. This will give you time to complete your preparations.'

'My preparations will be completed by the time I achieve low solar orbit.'

'No they will not,' EC replied, and followed that pronouncement with an information package.

Celedon scanned the package, learning only now about certain recent events in the Polity and the Jerusalem AI's involvement in them. Necessarily it both reviewed and looked towards updating many security procedures. Ejecting the A sector of the station was just part of this adjusted hostile contact protocol. The original package had made it aware it must prepare itself for the possibility of attack by Jain technology – a particularly nasty subversive technology left lying around by a long-dead alien race – but now this extra information made it realize *precisely* what that could mean. As much as an AI could be, Celedon was scared.

First the A sector: station spin alone would not be enough to eject it fast enough. After Fly finished placing the planar explosives, Celedon sent the drone to place other explosives around the inner spindle bulkhead. Once the sector detached, these too could be detonated. The air from inside the sector would then blast out, driving it even further from the station. Fortunately this sector also had a rim motor, which was self-contained but for the controlling optic feed. Fly severed that feed and installed a module to enable that motor to be activated by radio.

'So I must accept the possibility of Jain-controlled humans?' Celedon idly asked EC.

'You must, so take what precautions you can.'

Celedon allowed itself the equivalent of a wince. Doubtless Jerusalem would deal with the problem, should Jain technology board the station via that route. The station, and Celedon itself, would certainly not survive the experience.

The corridor running directly from the runcible, through an airlock into sector B, was already ready. Celedon therefore directed Fly and a hundred Golem to start building an isolation area in B. Necessarily, the surrounding areas were hardened to worm and viral attack, so the AI's only access would be via narrow-band voice and video transmission routed through five relays, all of them outside the station, all of them rigged for detonation, and targeted by masers on the rim. Sector A, however, the AI now isolated but for its link to Arach, and to runcible control, which was utterly necessary. The AI felt that the risk of Jain subversion of itself through the former communications route to be outweighed by the inherent risks of not knowing what was going on. The safest option, of course, would be to not allow initiation of any full transmission from that future runcible. But Earth Central commanded and Celedon obeyed. Obviously, further vital information might become available from that transmission.

Fifty-one days later, *Celedon* fell into orbit around the green sun, some distance inside the orbit of its one Venusian planet. As the temperature climbed, the station's AI routed heat through superconducting cables to thermal generators on its dark side, where gas lasers then emitted it into vacuum. On the sixtieth day a solar flare arched below, and the side of the station turned to the sun became too radioactive to support human life. But the AI had foreseen this possibility. The A sector, containing Runcible A, now lay away from the solar furnace, and would only be turned towards it at the last possible moment. Precisely on time, on the seventy-third day, Celedon detected a U-space disturbance a million miles out in space, as the titanic *Jerusalem* folded into existence: a spherical research vessel three miles in diameter with a thick band around its equator containing everything from legions of robotic probes up to U-space tugs and grabships, and weapons.

'Arach, you will remain by the runcible. When the evacuees come through, take them immediately to Isolation in B,' said Celedon.

'Great, thanks,' said the spider-drone.

'Jerusalem?' Celedon sent.

'Whenever you are ready,' replied the AI in the massive ship.

Low energy ion motors on the rim set the station turning. Celedon initiated connection to the source coordinates of the original information package, and routed power into the runcible's spoon. The Skaidon warp extended, tentatively linked, then made full connection. Suddenly the drain on the station grew huge: more power required, then even more. Shutting down the lasers, Celedon routed through power from the thermal generators. It then began shutting down other systems and rerouting additional power from the station's many fusion and fission reactors.

'It seems there is also a direct thermal drain,' Celedon observed.

Between the bull's horns of the runcible, the warp turned blank white, and from it cold propagated throughout the station. Frost crystals feathered across the floor and up the walls.

'Yes, as expected,' Jerusalem replied.

'Entropy?' Celedon suggested. 'This link to the future a definite confirmation of the universal slide into lower energy states?'

'No, a confirmation of the vast energy requirement of this runcible link. It is already out of control, and the phenomenon is localized but dispersed. Observe the planet. Observe the sun itself.'

Celedon focused various instruments where directed. The planet, a blue sphere, was now striated with lines of red cloud. Thermal analysis revealed that its entire surface temperature had dropped one degree. In the surface of the sun, directly below where the station orbited, a black spot formed and spread.

'Ah, hence the hostile contact protocol Starfire?' Celedon suggested.

'The hostile will most certainly try to keep the gate open, and certainly try to acquire the technology surrounding it. We will close this gate, severing the link, and the energy will have to go somewhere.'

'Erm . . . how localized is this phenomenon?'

'The radius of the sphere of influence from each runcible extends for the spacial distance between them. The energy drain drops in a near-to-straight line to zero from centre to circumference.'

Celedon could only make an estimate based on the entropic effects on nearby objects – the sun, the planet – and the result it came up with appalled it. This was why, even though AIs knew how to make a time-inconsistent runcible link, they pretended otherwise. The energy requirement increased exponentially and could not be controlled. The link drained energy directly from the space around each runcible gate, and would keep on doing so until surrounded by dead worlds and dead suns. Shutting down such a link resulted in all the absorbed energy exploding from one gate – the one still open, since it was impossible to close them both at the same instant – in the form of a blast wave of subatomic particles forced from the quantum foam. The mathematics involved was esoteric even for AIs, but they calculated that closing such a link, formed between planets ten light years apart with a time inconsistency of a year, even after only a few seconds, could result in the obliteration of one of the gate worlds, and the fatal irradiation of all life within a sphere of nearly a light year. These two gates lay 150,000 light years apart, the time-inconsistency at 830 years, and now the gate had been open for three seconds. And people came through.

Celedon observed, via runcible control, five humans falling through the Skaidon warp, then another five, then another three. There should be another forty-seven humans – and one other. Through Arach's senses, the AI studied the humans. They bore no visible sign of Jain infestation. Five of them wore the overalls favoured by runcible technicians; there was a four-person Sparkind team, two human and two Golem; the rest obviously civilian scientists, diplomats and crew, all augmented, some of them to haiman level, which meant they were both human *and* AI. They were all armed, their clothing dirty and ash-smeared. One of the haimans carried a large lozenge of crystal encaged in black metal – probably the AI Victoria from the ship of that name on which they had been passengers.

'That's all of us, shut it down as soon as you can!'

shouted one of the overalled figures – a woman with wide green eyes, cropped dark hair and skin as black as obsidian. Celedon identified her as Chaline Tazer Irand, the technician in charge of setting up the runcible in the Small Magellanic Cloud, 830 years in the future.

'Where are the others?' Celedon asked through Arach, as that drone shepherded these people towards Isolation.

'Dead,' the woman replied, her face exhausted of expression. 'At least I hope so.'

'The Maker?'

'He wants to die with his kind,' she told him tightly.

Now something else tried to come through. Celedon denied it permission, it being nothing the AI recognized – neither human nor Maker – and tried to shut down the runcible. In response to this, a deluge of information packages came through the gate, many of them opening automatically, and the gate simply would not shut down. Despite the precautions it had taken, the AI saw it could not hold out against this attack. Wormish fragments of code spilled into the gate's processing spaces and began attempting to assemble.

'Jerusalem?'

'Are you asking for permission?' the other AI enquired. 'You know what to do.'

Though couched in verbal terms, this communication lasted only a fraction of a second. Long seconds dragged thereafter as the AI waited until the evacuees reached the quarantine airlock and bulkhead doors closed behind them. This gave the attacker enough time to subvert the systems controlling gate maintenance and diagnostics. Since a selection of robots, ranging from the nanoscopic up to ones the size of termites, carried out internal maintenance, this meant the attacker now controlled physical resources. Time for Starfire.

The planar explosives detonated as one, severing thousands of structural members. The slow spin of the station caused sector A to part company with it. The sector tore out the s-con and optic cables linking Celedon to the runcible, but in the last few seconds the AI lost control of it anyway. A radio signal detonated the next explosives, taking out the spindle-side bulkheads. Air blasted out into space. Debris and ice crystals reflected the green light of the sun. The station shuddered, that one severed segment departing it like a slice from a cake.

As calculated, the segment began to turn. Transmissions now came from it – viral attacks on the station itself. Celedon immediately shut down all its subminds, and anything else that might be vulnerable to subversion. Keeping only a few hardened cameras pointed at the departing object, the AI waited until it turned nose down to the sun, then sent the signal to start its rim fusion engine. Helium plasma briefly washed over the station as the parted segment accelerated down into the gravity well. Then it shuddered. Whatever had been trying to get through the runcible was now inside. Minutes passed, then there seemed movement on the surface. Focusing, the AI observed bright writhing objects breaking through the outer skin. As pieces began to break away, Celedon fried them with masers. The segment's new occupant realized its danger and swiftly shut down the drive, but the segment lay deep into the sun's gravity well now, and metal began to ablate away from it as the sun's heat impacted. Finally it plunged into the furnace right beside the black spot. A U-space signature denatured. There came a burst of Hawking radiation as that runcible went out.

'Observe,' said Jerusalem, the moment Celedon reinstated coms.

From the point of impact a pattern of hexagons began to spread. It held definition for a while, then began to break apart, and finally disappeared. Celedon surveyed the damage to its station, its body, then ignited one of the remaining rim engines to pull itself away from the sun. The damage was severe, but a mere mote compared to what must have happened at the other runcible involved.

'In eight hundred and thirty years,' Jerusalem said, 'and a hundred and fifty thousand light years away from here, there will be an explosion of such magnitude it will cause a chain reaction between close suns. The Small Magellanic Cloud will probably be sterilized of all life, and probably most other forms of self-organizing matter, as was the intention.'

'Jain technology.'

'Yes, precisely. Of course we will not see the light for a very long time.'

1

Earth Central Security and the AIs are parsimonious in supplying the details, but I now know that one Skellor – a biophysicist with terrorist Separatist affiliations – did somehow manage to obtain a Jain node. I will be brief here with the salient details, since I don't know how much time I have before ECS gags me.

Aware of the node's dangers, Skellor settled down to study it in a secret Separatist base, trying to discover how to control the resultant technology in a way safe for the host. His eventual solution was to use a crystal-matrix AI augmentation – death would be the result of a human direct-linked to such, but the Jain tech could support human life in this situation while through the aug the human could exercise strict control over that technology. However, before he finished his researches, it was a solution he was forced to use untested when ECS agents came to capture him.

Evading them on the ground, Skellor managed to board their dreadnought Occam Razor, *kill its AI, and use Jain technology to seize control while the ship was in transit. He killed most aboard, but the agents themselves escaped the ship, fleeing to the out-Polity world of Masada. Skellor could not allow knowledge of what he had become to reach the*

Polity, so he pursued them, intent on killing all witnesses. At Masada he burnt out a cylinder world, mentally enslaved thousands, killed tens of thousands, and came close to rendering that entire world to ash. But again the agents escaped him, leading him into a trap at the smelting station of Elysium, where giant sun mirrors were used to destroy the Occam Razor.

The end? No, not really.

Skellor was tenacious, and escaping the dreadnought in its ejectable bridge pod, he again began to grow in power. He then resurrected a killer Golem called Mr Crane, and cut a bloody highway across space. ECS subsequently closed in, using improbably large forces to contain him. But perhaps it was because the Jain tech was now beginning to pursue its own final purpose, that ECS managed to finish him. Riddled with Jain nodes Skellor was finally trapped aboard an old colony ship in a decaying orbit around a brown dwarf sun, into which the vessel finally crashed.

Which goes to show that even godlike power is subject to gravity. One man, one Jain node: nearly a million dead. I'll get more detail down later . . . I hope.

– From 'How it Is' by Gordon

Cormac kept his eyes closed and remained very still, expecting something to start hurting at any moment. When no pain became evident, he opened his eyes to observe the tangle of limbs and implements on the underside of a pedestal autodoc, just as it swung aside. The last he remembered, Jain technology had been crawling around inside his head, busy rewiring it, then the rest of his body had caught up with that damage by experiencing ten Gs of acceleration.

Right . . .

He licked his lips and tried to work up some saliva in his dry mouth, then announced, 'The *King of Hearts* AI sends its regards. It wanted you to know it did not acquire any nasty Jain technology, so there's no reason for you to chase after it and blast it into component atoms.'

'That was remarkably quick,' replied a voice just hinting at the massive intellect behind it.

'That you, Jerusalem?' enquired Cormac.

'You already guessed that,' replied the disembodied voice of the AI that controlled the titanic research vessel *Jerusalem*.

Underneath Cormac, the surgical table slowly folded upright, moving him into a sitting position. Peering down at himself he saw that he wore a skin-tight garment, his hands similarly clad, and the pressure around his face and head confirming that no part of his body remained uncovered.

'Very strange pyjamas,' he observed.

'Cell welding, while wonderfully efficient, does have its limitations. Also, your spacesuit was breached and you lost nearly half your skin to vacuum freezing. This garment assists regrowth while allowing you to move about unhindered. It is my own invention.'

Cormac glanced around. He lay in a typical ship's medbay. The pedestal-mounted autodoc had now retreated into an alcove beside a bench extending from one wall, which held a nanoscope, a chainglass containment cylinder, genetic scanner and nanofactory unit. By the bench stood a chair on which lay a familiar design of notescreen.

'Where's Mika?'

'Sleeping.'

Cormac nodded and swung his legs off the surgical

table. Now moving, he could feel the wrongness. He felt tired and weak, parts of him began to ache, and something felt odd about . . . everything.

'What did you need to do to me?'

'All relevant information is available to you via ship server. Why don't you find out from there?'

A test perhaps? Cormac closed his eyes and sought mental connections via his gridlink. In something almost like a third eye he observed the optical cues for connection, but felt no actual linkage.

'I'm offline.'

'Yes, the damage to your brain was severe, and to remove Jain filaments from it and run a counteragent through would inevitably cause even more damage. I downloaded you, then reloaded you after I finished making repairs. Your link, because of the possibility it contained Jain informational viruses or worms, I completely wiped and reformatted. I similarly screened all your memories and thought structures.'

Cormac felt a clamminess.

Am I really Cormac now?

But there seemed no particular advantage in asking that question. Using his third-eye blink reflex, he cued the various channels of his link in turn and felt them reinstate. Now he could download data in just about any form to his link, either to view in his visual cortex, or so that it became part of memory – the mental component of physical skills, languages, the recorded experiences of others. In the link itself he possessed the facility to create programs: perceptile, search, analysis, logic trees . . . the list was only limited by his imagination, and his imagination need not be limited while he could link to so many sources of knowledge and experience within the human

Polity. He opened a skeletal search program, altered its parameters to suit his requirements, and transmitted it to the nearest receiver. It came back with a report he scrolled up in his visual cortex. The report itself was overly technical and detailed, so he ran it through a filter to provide him with the gist:

> *Spinal reconnection in 2 lumbar regions; extensive bone welding of 116 fractures; the removal of 1 kidney, two thirds of the liver, 2 yards of intestine, 350 ounces of cerebral tissue; extensive cell welding in all areas; currently undergoing nanocyte repair and genetic reversion regrowth . . .*

'I *thought* I felt lighter,' said Cormac. 'Tell me, how much of my memory is still true?'

'I reconstructed what I could, but perhaps ten per cent is missing.'

Cormac began walking round the surgical table.

Holes in my body and in my mind. Great.

Eventually he came to stand before a wall dispenser for disposable surgical clothing. Using the controlling touch-screen he selected a paper coverall, removed it from the dispensing slot and donned it over the garment he already wore.

'What about my crew . . . and the *Jack Ketch*?' Cormac asked reluctantly.

'Jack, the ship's AI, is safe, and Thorn and Fethan are presently on Cull. Cento and Gant are dead.'

'Gant?' he asked – he already knew about Cento.

'Gant was terminally infected by a Jain informational virus that supplanted his mind. Thorn therefore destroyed him. There is, however, a back-up copy of him on Earth.'

Cormac grimaced. 'The situation now?'

'As you must have already surmised, Skellor is now just a pretty pattern on the surface of a brown dwarf sun. I have one Dragon sphere held in custody, and the planet Cull now has been granted provisional membership of the Polity while search teams locate, remove and isolate any stray items of Jain technology still there.'

Cento probably formed part of that same pretty pattern on that brown dwarf. Only pure luck had saved Cormac from the same fate.

'You are currently in orbit of Cull?'

'No, I am currently six hundred light years away.'

'What?'

'A rather knotty problem has arisen.'

Without cerebral augmentations Thorn could only view the memory in VR and absorb it by repetition. Fethan however, being a cyborg, loaded it directly into his mind so it became part of his memory.

'What am I seeing here?' Thorn asked, the VR representation freezing all about him.

'The planet Osterland,' Fethan replied, standing at his left shoulder. 'Cold, about the orbit of Mars around an M-type sun, gravity one point two, plenty of water ice, but completely lifeless until fifty or so years ago. They used designer bacteria, biomass transfer through a cargo runcible, then an orbital mirror to heat the mix. Deciduous trees, with support ecologies, were planted right from the start, and are still being planted by agrobots.'

'Trees?'

'That was just the personal preference of the haiman in charge. He could have used fast growing slime moulds or adapted fungi to increase biomass. Instead he chose trees.'

'Interesting, after what happened here, to discover a haiman rather than an AI in charge,' Thorn noted. *Haiman*, he thought, *an amalgam of human and AI –* which meant this place was ruled, partially, by a human. And humans had never made trustworthy rulers.

'I wouldn't read too much into it – there's not a lot of difference between the two.'

Thorn nodded and took another pace forwards on the platform that extended out from the town lying behind him. He already knew that this platform would become, or had become, a jetty, as the space below it filled with water directed down great canals from the planet's melting poles. Walking in someone else's footsteps he finally came to the market located on the platform. Drizzle washed cold against his skin, for a storm approached from the northern outflow.

A dirty hand with chipped fingernails gripped his jacket. 'I got some good stuff that ain't on display, my friend,' said its owner.

'Like what?' he asked . . . only it was not Thorn asking, but the recorded memory.

She was shabby, angry: one of those losers who came to a new world to start a new life and discovered that a change in location did not change what they themselves were. On the whole her goods matched her appearance. But then the memory persona noticed something else.

'What's that?' it asked, pointing.

'This is real coral, from the Barrier Reef on Earth.'

Thorn himself then spoke, and the representation froze again. 'Do you reckon she knew what it really was? That this was a setup?'

'Buggered if I know,' Fethan replied. 'Someone will have to ask.'

'How interesting,' said the persona, speaking from Thorn's mouth. 'All right, how much do you want for them?'

'You'll have to buy the whole carton,' she replied. 'Twenty shillings.'

'I don't want that egg thing, so I'll give you ten.'

The memory faded, with the buyer returning towards the spaceport with his purchases.

'A bargain,' said Thorn. 'Let's back up to that stall again.'

He walked backwards to the stall, turned and placed the plastic carton down, and was in the act of taking back the ten-shilling chainglass coin when the representation froze again.

'Just one piece of the Jain tech coral would sell for millions on the open market – if it even got there before an AI like Jerusalem snatched it,' said Thorn. 'The Jain node itself would start in the billions, and go on up from there, if it was actually possible to buy or sell such items. In reality the planet would end up under quarantine, and the buyer and seller would be mentally dissected by forensic AI.'

'Ah, but who knew about Jain nodes *then*?' asked Fethan.

'End scenario,' ordered Thorn abruptly.

At once Thorn was in darkness, and could feel nothing. Then, as the nanofilaments of the VR booth detached from his brainstem and withdrew from his head, he felt cold and stiff. The booth's door crumped open before him and he stepped out onto the acid-etched floor. Fethan, standing to one side, an apparently old man with snaggle teeth, a mass of ginger beard and thinning hair topping a wiry frame clad in an envirosuit, detached an optic cable from the end of his right forefinger and allowed it to wind back into the wall. He then took a thimble of syntheskin from his pocket and pressed it into place over a metal fingertip that served as a multipurpose plug. Thorn eyed him meanwhile. Fethan was a cyborg, since he retained his own brain and spinal column flash-frozen and bio-gridded in a ceramal case inside him. He was not like Gant: the mind of a soldier loaded to a Golem chassis. But Thorn did not want to think about Gant right then.

'So, how did you obtain this recording?' Thorn asked.

'Courtesy of Jerusalem. Apparently there was some bleed-over from Skellor to Cormac while they were linked. Jerusalem copied it while putting Cormac back together.'

Thorn surveyed his surroundings. A large hole had been burnt through one wall by the projectile saliva of a monster called a droon, then ripped open wider when it had crawled inside. The ceiling was missing, peeled back, from when the droon broke out again like a nightmare jack-in-a-box. This VR chamber was one remnant of a ship called the *Jack Ketch*, on which Thorn had arrived here on the planet Cull. He walked to the opening, stepped through and glared round at the arid landscape. Just within sight lay dusty pieces of carapace that were the remains of a sandhog the droon had killed.

'And what exactly are we supposed to do with this piece of Skellor's memory?' He glanced up as a craft, shaped like an 'H' made from copper cylinders, drifted overhead. 'This place is still under quarantine, and both of us have been in contact with Jain technology.' Gant, the recorded mind of Thorn's friend, once resided in a Golem chassis but, when they eventually found him, a Jain tech virus had turned him into something else. Thorn and Fethan had destroyed this object.

'Jerusalem wants you to track this woman down.' Fethan rejoined him. 'And I think your ride just arrived.'

The H-shaped craft drew to a sudden halt above them, then began to descend. A hundred yards from the ground, it extruded four three-toed feet and, when it finally crunched down, one of them kicked away a nearby rock in seeming annoyance. Thorn estimated the craft to be 150 yards long and half that wide; a fully AG lander of the kind used for transporting dangerous cargoes. One strut of the H contained the ion drive, and possibly its controlling AI – though such ships were usually telefactored – and crew quarters if necessary. The other strut was a cargo pod, and the ship possessed the facility to blow this away from itself. Thorn was unsurprised when the circular end of the cargo pod opened and extruded a ramp like an insolent tongue.

'Taking no chances, but this is an insystem ship, so where or to what is it carrying me?' he asked as he began walking towards it.

Moving beside him, Fethan shrugged and made no comment.

Thorn glanced at him. 'So you definitely are staying.'

'I'm needed here.' Fethan grimaced then removed something from his pocket, weighed it in his hand for a moment then tossed it across. Thorn snatched it out of the air and inspected it. It fitted in his palm, a five by three by a half inch cuboid of burnished metal, coppery, its corners rounded. Along one end of it was a row of ports, nanofibre and optic, designed to interface with just about any computer known, and probably many others unknown. It was a memstore.

'It don't say much, but it might come in handy,' said Fethan.

'What's inside?'

'It's what killed that Jain tech construct down here, and what helped to kill Skellor in the end: a hunter-killer program constructed by Jerusalem.' He patted his stomach. 'I carried it inside myself for some time. I don't *need* it any more and I don't *want* it any more.'

They reached the ramp and paused there. Thorn held out his hand and they shook.

'Stay well, Thorn,' said Fethan, 'and try not to let that bastard Cormac get you killed.'

'You stay well, too. It's been—'

'Yeah, interesting.' Fethan pulled his hand away and gestured towards the ship. 'Get out of here.' He turned and began walking away.

Thorn thoughtfully pocketed the memstore, then entered the cargo pod. Behind him the ramp immediately began withdrawing back into the floor. He spied just one acceleration chair bolted to one wall – there were no other facilities.

'Spartan,' he commented, then grinned to himself. He had, after all, himself been a member of the Sparkind who based their ethos on those ancient Greek warriors.

After he strapped himself in, the take-off was abrupt and sickening for, though the whole ship lifted on grav-motors, the pod itself contained no compensating gravplates. Sitting above the gravity-negating field he became immediately weightless. Strapped in his chair, and without a view, there was no way of telling how fast the ship was rising, or even if it rose at all.

Many space travellers, Thorn knew, had their temporal bone and its related nerves surgically adapted to enable them to shut down any physical response to signals from their inner ear. Others used drugs to dampen the effect. Sparkind, however, were conditioned to control their reaction, so Thorn merely clenched his teeth and held onto his breakfast. Within seconds he brought the disorientation and nascent space sickness under control, and relaxed. He remembered once watching one of the Cull natives being sick over the side of a balloon basket, prompting a subsequent conversation with Fethan about his own Sparkind conditioning.

'Those must have been messy training sessions,' Fethan had observed.

'It was all carried out in VR and thus the sickness was just potential sickness to us trainees. Gant used to . . .' Thorn trailed away. Gant was dead – again. He had continued, 'It is just a matter of you deciding at first what is up and what is down, then finally deciding and accepting that there's no up or down. Drugs and surgical adaptation disconnect you too much from realities, especially if you're caught in a fire-fight aboard some tumbling ship with fluxing gravplates.'

'Tough training, then?'

'Yeah, you don't get to become Sparkind without logging five years of combined virtual and actual combat training in similar rough situations.' He glanced at Fethan. 'The two are deliberately combined so you don't get disconnected from reality. Troops fully trained only in VR develop a tendency to feel that what they then experience in actuality is something they can later unplug from. Makes 'em sloppy, and very often dead. What about you? I know very little about you.'

Fethan grinned and scratched at his beard. 'I worked for Earth Central way back before you were born, and even before memcording of a human mind became a viable proposition. I crashed a lander on Earth's moon, after my passenger threw a grenade into the cockpit and, when I survived that, tried to decapitate me with a garrotte.'

'Nasty person,' Thorn opined.

'Memcording wasn't possible for a whole mind then, but partial recordings could be made. That bugger had overindulged in black-market memory copies made from the minds of imprisoned killers. The lander hit the ground but held together. Next thing I knew, everything was dark and EC was yammering at me non-stop. What was left of my body was too damaged to restore – oxygen fire. My choices were that dubious memcording technology of the time, or flash-freezing of my brain for storage, or installation in an android chassis – or death.'

'Obviously you chose the android chassis.'

'Yeah, my nasty passenger survived the crash and escaped. He'd set the fire. I later caught up with him on Titan, where he was making a dog's dinner of his new career as a serial killer. I hauled him outside the dome with me and dropped him down a surface vent. He'd frozen solid by then, so broke apart on the way down.'

Thorn nodded to himself, then after a long pause had said, 'Enough of this macho bonding for now?'

'Yeah, I reckon,' Fethan had replied.

Now sitting in the cargo pod, Thorn smiled at the memory of that conversation. He would miss the old cyborg, but at least Fethan remained alive, which was more than could be said for certain other people Thorn missed. His smile faded, just thinking of them.

Some time later he felt the acceleration from the craft's ion drive. This lasted for an hour, next came abrupt deceleration, followed by various clonks and bangs from outside, then an abrupt restoration of gravity and a loud crump as the craft settled.

As Thorn unstrapped himself, the end of the cargo pod opened and the ramp extruded. He walked to the end of it and peered out into what he immediately identified as a spaceship's small docking bay. As he stepped down the ramp he saw that only the cargo pod lay inside the bay, after being detached from the rest of the craft and transported in by the telefactor which now slid into an alcove of the nearby wall.

A precaution against Jain infection, obviously.

Ahead of Thorn a line drew itself vertically through the air, then from it unfolded the holographic image of a woman. Her hair and her skin were bone white, but her eyes black. She wore something diaphanous, barely concealing her naked body. Speaking, she revealed the red interior of her mouth.

'Welcome to the *NEJ*,' she said.

'Hello, Aphran,' Thorn replied to this recording of a dead woman, then added, '*NEJ*?'

'The *Not Entirely Jack*,' she replied, and grimaced.

Of course the AI aboard this ship would not be 'entirely Jack', for Jack was now tangled up with the absorbed personality of Aphran herself – one time Separatist and enemy of the Polity.

Cormac rubbed his wrist as he watched the screen. *Celedon* station seemed clear of Jain infestation, and now manoeuvred away from the sun. But as a precaution it would remain partially quarantined for some years to come. Earlier he had watched the thirteen evacuees towing themselves up the telescopic boarding tube extended from *Jerusalem*. One of the Golem in the group carried a lozenge-shaped block of crystal caged in a partial skin of black metal – the AI of the long-range spaceship, the *Victoria*. But Cormac's attention focused on a woman clad in the distinctive blue overall of a runcible technician. By now the thirteen were through scanning and installed in an isolated area aboard this great ship. Shortly he would go and speak to one of them.

Through his gridlink he selected another of the row of subscreens displaying along the bottom of the main one and enlarged it. This showed three of Celedon's drones moving into an isolated area aboard *Jerusalem* – old independent drones leaving the station to now work for Jerusalem. But, there was nothing more for Cormac to learn by watching. Now he must do what he did best. He stood and scanned around the room provided for him. He needed no more than what lay inside his head really, so turned to the door.

Outside his cabin Cormac considered the phrase: *Levels of contamination risk.* Even after Jerusalem scanned his body down to the cellular level, removed Jain filaments and injected nanite counter-agents to clear up the residue, he remained a risk. So the recently installed corridor outside his cabin stayed empty, and linked his cabin only to the isolation area containing the evacuees.

'Is she ready for me?' he asked generally as he strode along.

'She is, and you will find her here.' Jerusalem transmitted a map directly to his gridlink. Now, in less than a second, he became fully familiar with the layout of the immediate area, as if accustomed to strolling here over a period of weeks. At the corridor end he turned right and came to an iris door. It opened for him onto a shimmer-shield. He pushed through this as easily as if stepping through blancmange. To his left a chair stood positioned before a chainglass screen which was optically polished so as to be only just visible. This intersected a table, on whose far side, on the other side of the screen, stood another chair. The woman, with obsidian skin, green eyes and cropped black hair, had exchanged her technician's overall for a loose thigh-length toga of green silk, cinched at the waist with a belt of polished steel links. She stood as if waiting to be given permission to sit, but he knew that unlikely.

Chaline.

She had accompanied him while on the planet Samarkand after a runcible disaster there – her job being to set up a new runcible. An alien bioconstruct called Dragon, consisting of four conjoined and living spheres each a nearly a mile across, subsequently arrived there to create mayhem – or rather just one of its spheres arrived. Dragon aimed to murder one of its own makers who had come to Polity space to seek it out. The destruction of the original runcible had been Dragon's attempt to prevent that 'Maker' leaving Samarkand. To avenge the deaths it caused on that small cold world, Cormac killed that lone Dragon sphere with a contraterrene bomb, whereupon the Polity took on the task of ferrying the Maker back to its home civilization. He had not known Chaline volunteered for that mission to the Small Magellanic Cloud, but was unsurprised. She would have relished the challenges of setting up a runcible so far from the Polity. Of course, a further complication, now he intended to interrogate her, was that for a brief time they had been lovers.

'So what the hell happened?' he asked, sitting down.

Also sitting down, Chaline crossed her legs and smiled. 'As ever direct. Hello, Ian, how are you? I'm fine by the way, if a little tired.'

Cormac sat back and smiled as well. In a mild voice he observed, 'You know how I have little time for the social niceties. I have lived a hectic life since we last spoke. I've lost friends and nearly lost my life. Your sarcasm might be acceptable if we were here meeting as old friends and exchanging pleasantries. The truth is that neither of us ever contacted the other after Samarkand, and there was nothing to stop me thinking that I would not be seeing you again for the best part of a millennium.'

'A point.' Chaline nodded. 'A definite point.'

Cormac sat forward. 'This is not about points, as you well know.'

'Then why am I here talking to you?'

'I want to hear your story.'

'Then why not just download it?' Chaline tapped a finger against her temple. 'You know I'm gridlinked. I already uploaded recordings of my every relevant memory to Jerusalem. We don't need to have this conversation.'

Cormac replied, 'I prefer to hear everything directly, while I'm looking into the face of the speaker. Cerebral uploads can be tampered with. This meeting, though crude, can reveal so much more to the right observer.'

'You don't trust me? This will be compared to what I uploaded?'

'It's not that.' Cormac shook his head. 'In situations

as serious as this it's all about information: quantities of information to be processed, assessed. Jerusalem, like any major AI, can create extensions to itself: subminds, telefactors,' he shrugged, 'whatever, but they remain only extensions. It likes those humans working for it to do their own thing: that way something unforeseen by itself might be revealed. It has agreed that I should interview you directly.'

'Kind of it to allow you such a free rein, but I doubt anything will be revealed here that the AI does not already know.'

'But something might, and that's the point.'

Chaline snorted. 'Shall we get on with this then?'

'Jerusalem did inform me that a time-inconsistent runcible connection was made – something I'd never even heard of until that moment – but why the hostile contact protocol?' He studied her keenly. 'Obviously it was to defend us against Jain technology, but how did Celedon know that?'

Chaline grimaced. 'We sent an information package through to Celedon. You can't just open an out-network runcible connection without the receiving runcible AI agreeing to it. It's a security protocol. Surely you were already told this?'

'I am to hear the story direct from you. If I were to already know all the facts Jerusalem knows, I would only be asking you questions that are utterly predictable to it.'

'Ah, so you must approach this without the constraints of foreknowledge, like a Stone Age man trying to operate a personal computer.'

'Not quite the analogy I'd choose.' He smiled grimly. 'Now, I've been allowed access to all the logs concerning the preparation for the voyage. The ship was called the *Victoria*, after an ancient sailing ship in Ferdinand Magellan's fleet – apparently the one first to circumnavigate Earth. Tell me, other than at Samarkand, did you have any contact with the Maker before boarding that ship?'

'None at all, as that's not my province. I build runcibles . . . Cormac, you know that.' She grimaced and looked sideways towards the floor. 'Of course that changed when we got underway. It changed for all of us.'

'Tell me about that. Tell me about the Maker.'

The sun seemed hatched from some cosmic egg, with pieces of its own shell orbiting it, glimpsed briefly in thick clouds lit from within by that solar orb. The Cassius gas giant, in its own orbit close enough around the sun for molten iron to rain from its skies, supplied those clouds as carefully positioned antimatter blasts gradually demolished it. Some of those eggshell fragments were a 100,000 miles across. The matter converters at their edges were the size of small moons; sucking in the miasma of the gas giant's destruction, slowly laying mile-thick composite laced with a balancing web of gravmotors and superconducting cables. But this, after a century, was just the start: a scattering of bricks on a building site, a pile of sand, a sack of cement. The project downtime was estimated at a million years, give or take a few hundred thousand. You could think in those terms when you were an AI and immortal. The humans and haimans working the project just comforted themselves with the thought that they were part of something . . . numinous.

From within the cowling of her half-carapace, situated within her own interface sphere, Orlandine observed the scene with her multitude of senses, processed the continuous feed of data through her numerous augmentations, then focused on one of those scattered pieces. This particular fragment of the nascent, fully enclosing Dyson sphere was diamond-shaped, 160,000 miles long and 100,000 wide. She analysed stress data as the first matter converter – something resembling a squat ocean liner with a mile-wide slot cut into its stern – detached. She focused in closer, observing the swarm of surrounding ships, the *Pseidon* poised like a titanic crab's claw, collapsing scaffolds of pseudomatter winking out. A storm of ionization glowed between converter and fragment, trying to draw it back, but the converter's massive drive engaged, throwing a ten-mile-long fusion flame above the plain of composite, and it pulled away.

'Are we within parameters?' asked Shoala.

'We are,' Orlandine replied.

Shoala tended to verbalize when nervous, but being haiman for only twenty years he was yet to fully accept what the term implied. Perhaps they were all like that, else they would not so often sever their link with their carapaces for spells of 'human time'. None of them yet accepted they were truly haiman – a combination of human and AI – and still believed the carapaces just complex tools rather than integral parts of themselves.

'Then this is it,' Shoala said, 'another complete section of the sphere. We should celebrate.'

Ah, human time again, thought Orlandine. 'And how should we celebrate?' she asked.

'Loud music, alcohol, and drugs are traditional,' Shoala replied.

Orlandine noted that their exchange was now on open com, and picked up on a subchannel that twenty-seven agreed with Shoala's assessment, whilst only two demurred. She decided, as an overseer, she must attend the celebration.

'The Feynman Lounge in two hours, then,' she said, and disconnected. At least this interval would give her time to catch up on her news groups and messages. Initiating subpersona one, she gave it a watching brief over the newly completed fragment of the sphere, then turned her attention to her personal inboxes. Fourteen hundred messages awaited her attention. Subpersona two began whittling those down while she called up the various news items it had earlier starred for her attention. Rather than direct-load them to her central self, she speed-read them into a mid-term memory, and learnt much of interest.

ECS did not bother to conceal that the Polity was gearing up for a possible conflict. Such activity, of course, being impossible to conceal, what with some of the big stations and zero-G shipyards, mothballed after the Prador War, now up and running again. And even the most idiot analytical programs could detect the rise in production and the diversion of resources into military industries. But the nature of the threat itself remained unknown to most. Cover stories abounded about the possibility of some major action on the part of a loose alliance between Separatists and the alien entity Dragon, two of whose spheres remained unaccounted for. Orlandine guessed otherwise, and news stories she uploaded, concerning an out-polity world called Cull, further confirmed her conjecture.

A Dragon sphere had been captured inside a USER

blockade (leaving now only one more unaccounted for), and the Separatist and biophysicist Skellor was killed. She had not even known he escaped the destruction of the *Occam Razor*. But the rest of the signs there – nothing actually being stated outright – allowed her to realize what lay underneath this particular cover story. The previous stories she studied all subtly related to it: the huge damage wrought on the space community *Elysium*, the news filtering back from an out-polity world called Masada. The subsequent 'protective quarantine' of all those same places. None of the stories sufficiently justified the scale of the AI reaction in each situation. Some other worrying element remained missing, and when she inserted that element, it all made sense. Skellor had clearly obtained possession of a Jain node and used it – hence the quarantine, hence the movement of big guns into each area, and hence events unfolding in the Polity right now.

In her position of Overseer of the Cassius project, Orlandine was allowed limited knowledge regarding Jain nodes. The initial source of this knowledge, however, still remained concealed from her. She knew these nodes contained compacted Jain nanotechnology that activated upon the touch of intelligent technical beings. She knew they then grew organic technology, and that the intelligent being affected became both host to and master of it – the level of each state dependent on other unknown factors. It was hideously dangerous because initiated thus by a host, this technology could proceed to access and control any other technology both physically and informationally, seizing control, wreaking destruction, growing and taking over anything or anyone else with which it came into contact. The AIs had told her this much, because Jain technology represented to the project one danger of which she must be aware. She was glad to have been made aware. Very glad.

Orlandine opened her eyes. It was all getting rather messy out there. ECS agents would be rattling around the Polity like disturbed hornets, and at some point they might find a trail leading to her, though she had not yet done anything seriously wrong.

She closed her eyes again and turned her attention to the messages coming through her subpersona's filters. Many were messages from other haimans scattered around the Polity: some requesting information, some offering it – the usual constant exchanges. One message from her mother, back on Europa, concerned updates of family news and veiled queries about her work, her life. She had not actually seen the woman in thirty years. However, her mother remained persistent and proprietary because of her own choice way back to adapt Orlandine genetically to the newer haiman technologies. Orlandine felt herself to be mature enough not to reject such contact outright, but still assigned the message to a subpersona for reply. Then her attention fell on one message with no personal signature – strange that it managed to get through. After preparing due safeguards, she opened it and found just a single line of text:

'They will learn about the gift.' – a secret admirer.

Just that, yet Orlandine began shaking, sweating. Did she think there were no consequences attached? Using carapace hardware, she brought her physical reaction under control. Thereafter she tried to analyse why her reaction had been so extreme. Shortly she realized why: she must act now, or not at all. Two courses of action stood open to her: confession and acceptance of consequences, or one other option. She flicked up a list of pros and cons, and left subpersona one to analyse them. The vague result depicted graphically, with much dependent on extraneous circumstances of which she could not be aware. She ran programs then to analyse an optimum 'must do' list for each suggested course of action. Studying those lists, she finally accepted that she had already made her decision; not through logical analysis but at a level more primeval than that. And it did not involve confession. It concerned what she was, a haiman, and why she originally chose to remain such.

She paused and cleared all information feeds into her mind, which in itself was not confined to that lump of organic matter in her skull, took a slow clear breath, then called up a memory of Shoala during *human time* and relived it. He was, on such occasions, a thin-faced individual with blond hair plaited down close to his skull, and a love of dressing in Jacobean fashion. Such attire – the lacy collars, earrings and embroidered jackets – concealed what he truly was. Naked, he revealed a tough wiry physique, interface plugs behind each ear and running like a line of glittering scales from the base of his skull down his spine, nutrient feed ports in his wrists and on either side of his belly, and structural support sockets for his carapace evident over his hip bones, at each rib down either side of his back, at his collar bones, and with a final pair concealed underneath his plaited hair.

By shedding her own clothing, Orlandine revealed her own carapace linkages to be mostly located in the same places, but of an entirely different design. Her body too was as wiry, but her skin purplish black and utterly hairless. The interfaces behind her ears and running down her spine were just closed slits positioned over s-con nanofilament plugs – their final synaptic connections inside her body being electrochemical rather than electroptic. She did not possess structural support sockets, rather nubs of bone protruded from the same points – keratin skinned – and her carapace limbs terminated in clamps that closed over these. Her nutrient feed ports were the same as his, but she did not need to use them so often as Shoala since, prior to a long session in a sphere, her body was capable of putting on fat very quickly, and of storing the required vitamins and minerals in her enlarged liver.

In both cases their sexual organs were standard format, and came together in the usual manner. But this was how haimans *began* sexual relationships. Cyber-linked orgasms and sensory amplification came later, when they trusted each other more, for that was *personal*.

Orlandine now skipped the virtual pornography, for she could already feel an anticipatory wetness around her suction catheter. And because she decided not to view this start of her relationship with Shoala, she realized she had already made her decision about that as well.

'That's a Prador spider thrall,' said Shoala, after the sex together, pointing into the glass-fronted case. 'What are the stones, though?'

Hidden in plain sight, thought Orlandine, as she sat up and swung her legs off the rumpled bed. She stood and walked over beside him, running her finger down the hard edges of the plugs in his spine.

She pointed at a wine-red sphere. 'Star ruby. It's natural – from Venus.'

'The metallic ones?'

'Ferro-axinite, but with weak monopole characteristics.'

'And that?'

Orlandine peered into the case at the egg-shaped object he indicated. She decided this time to tell a half-truth – maybe later she would reveal all to him. 'Something quite possibly Jain. There are what look like nanotech structures on the surface. You notice the cubic patterns? One day I'll get round to investigating further.'

He turned to her with a raised eyebrow. 'Is it listed?'

'It is – and I've two years in which to commence study. If I haven't got around to it by then, it must be passed on to Jerusalem – the AI whose purpose it is to investigate such things.'

One lie turning into a larger lie.

'And the display case is secure?'

'Yes, but this is low-risk level. It was previously scanned and threat-assessed.'

And yet another lie.

Orlandine allowed this memory to fade, and then abruptly deleted it. Now the only copy of it lay in the organic part of her brain. After a pause she accessed her private files and studied the lists of other things concealed there. Many of them were products of her personal study of the Jain node, yet she had so far only uncovered two per cent of its secrets, and most of those related only to the physical nanotechnology on its surface. What she now wanted concerned the subversive programming aspects of that technology. The contents of one file would be enough, since the receiver of that file trusted her implicitly. Checking the sphere map she saw he had yet to shed his carapace and depart his interface sphere.

'Shoala, I'm sending something over for you to take a look at.' She copied the file into a message titled 'Sexual Electronics Part VII' – it was their private joke.

She knew he received and opened it the moment the channels to his sphere began opening to her. Through a visual link she saw him lying back, his eyes closed. He began shivering. How far was she prepared to go? The viral attack isolated his sphere, but in a way that would not be picked up by the others. Now viral monads formed chains, deleting stored information, wrecking memories, trashing files and overwriting them time and again, so nothing could be recovered.

He opened his eyes. 'Orlandine?'

Her throat tight, she squeezed tears from closed eyes. This was so wrong: virtual murder. A haiman encompassed more than the organic brain. It was that, true, but so much more running in crystal-etched atom processors.

'I'm so sorry,' she said.

'Why are you doing this?'

'I . . . I cannot give this up. It's too much . . . It's what we all seek.'

Of course, the memories of that Jain node, and the lies she told about it, were from *human time*. It was not something wholly stored in crystal. It also rested between *his* ears.

He was mostly gone now, just the human part left. Orlandine blocked the signals he was desperately sending to detach himself from his carapace, and she herself began to isolate and control its systems. Into the positional map for its structural supports – the insectile legs of the louse-like carapace – she introduced a half-inch error, and cancelled the pressure-sensitive safeties. Now she stood on the brink and, stepping over it, there would be no return. What she had done thus far would be defined only as an assault, though a serious one for which, if caught, she would certainly lose her haiman status and be subject to adjustment. She sent the final instructions and forced herself to watch.

His carapace retracted its 'legs' from the sockets attached to his ribs, hip bones, and head, then repositioned them half an inch up, and reinserted them. No sockets lay waiting where they reinserted. The two on his head pressed against his skull above his ears, one slid off tearing up a flap of scalp, the other pushed his head sideways until it too slid off, ripping more skin. The eight ceramal legs, mispositioned either side of his torso, penetrated between his ribs, puncturing his heart, lungs, liver. The two over his hips stabbed into his guts. He vomited blood, then coughed out more, his arms and legs thrashing. Arterial blood foamed down inside his carapace in steady pulses, until after a moment he hung limp, blood dripping to the floor.

Orlandine stared. Now, if they ever caught her, she would be mind-wiped. Best to make sure that never happened. The subversion program she had sent could destroy itself, but there would be something left: fragments that might easily be identified as a product of Jain technology. She used that same program to locate his back-up power supply – a head-sized U-charger that ran on an allotropic and isotopic liquid pumped through vanadium-silver grids. She inverted his external power supply and fed it all directly into that charger. The trick was to make sure it drew no more than his expected requirement, but that would be enough. Now less than an hour remained before the charger overloaded and his interface sphere became radioactive wreckage.

Time to go.

2

The moment the Needle, *testing the first U-space engines ever built, dropped out of realspace during its test flight out from Mars, time-travel ceased to be merely a possibility and became a certainty. The moment the first runcible gates opened it became an uncomfortable reality. Travelling through U-space it is possible to arrive before you leave, or even a thousand years after, yet physically unchanged. And when time travel was tried, it took many months to clear up the wreckage. Don't let any of those still scared of the realities we face nowadays – those still hanging on desperately to their belief that the universe functions in ways they can easily understand – try to convince you otherwise. Go ask runcible technicians and watch them squirm, query AIs and view the incomprehensible maths. But if we* can *do it, why aren't we doing it? We could nip forward and swipe lottery numbers, we could nip back and stop loved ones dying. Yeah, just like quite a few centuries ago we could bring together a couple of plutonium ingots to start a camp fire. Those who understand the maths stare at infinite progressions and exponential factors and know we are just not ready to start throwing around that kind of energy. Time travel is dangerous, cosmic disaster dangerous. Using it for anything less than the aversion of a cosmic disaster equates to using a fusion drive to travel from one side of your house to the other. You'll certainly arrive, but there probably won't be anything left of your house when you do.*

— From 'How it Is' by Gordon

Thorn, apparently standing a mile out in vacuum but actually ensconced in VR aboard the spaceship and seeing through a remote camera, studied carefully the *Not Entirely Jack*. The vessel was one of the new Centurion-class attack ships. It bore some resemblance to the *Jack Ketch* in that its main body bore the shape of a cuttlefish bone, however here the weapons' nacelles rode either side of the ship's nose and another nacelle protruded below its stern. The ship's skin constantly bloomed with colour like some ancient screensaver, but with those colours seen on polished steel as it is being heated. With omniscient vision he then surveyed surrounding space. Numerous other ships orbited the nearby planet, and many had already landed; this was no more than to be expected considering the possibility of Jain technology being scattered over its surface. But the strangest sight in this system was the organic moonlet at bay. Thorn focused in on this – increasing the magnification of his vision many hundred times beyond what would be possible with his naked eyes.

The dragon sphere hung stationary in the ether, as if backed up against the green-blue orb of the ice-giant planet. Two dangerous-looking ships, similar to this one, patrolled around it like attack dogs. One large old dreadnought, of a similar design and provenance to the *Occam Razor*, hovered with all its weapons trained on the alien entity, and not even that was enough.

Thorn did not know precisely what the metallic object

stretching around a third of Dragon's equator could actually do, but its purpose was evident. The entity was under arrest, imprisoned in some way – perhaps the only way possible for restraining a sphere of living tissue nearly a mile in diameter and capable of travelling through space like any Polity ship. The metallic band was its manacle. Dragon, who Skellor came here to find, had also been caught in the trap sprung on that criminal.

'It seems a shame to leave,' said Thorn. 'Things are still pretty interesting around here.' He reached up, turned off the helmet projection with a tap of his finger, and lifted the VR helmet from his head – it had not been necessary to go to full immersion for this last look around. Unstrapping himself, he stepped down from the frame, then turned to watch as it folded itself together and disappeared discreetly into the wall of the chamber.

'I take it we *can* leave?' he added.

Jack, the ship AI, replied, 'There is a thousand-mile-wide passage through the USER blockade. The twelve gamma-class dreadnoughts guarding it have been instructed to let us through.'

'That's good.'

The blockade of USERs – underspace interference emitters that prevented ships attaining FTL travel – positioned a hundred light years away from this point in every direction, prevented any other ships getting close. It illustrated more than any other precaution how seriously Earth Central considered the threat of Jain technology. But as he left the VR chamber, Thorn spied four figures loping along the corridor away from him, and wondered about Earth Central's other agendas.

The four figures were humanoid but reptilian: their skins tegulated with green or yellow scales and their gait reverse-kneed, like birds. One of the four glanced over its shoulder with a toadish visage, bared many sharp teeth at him then loped on. Dracomen – 120 of them aboard this ship, all kitted out in military combat suits and armed with the best in portable weapons the Polity could offer.

'Is it just a case of putting all the bad eggs in one basket?' he asked, heading in the same direction as the four.

'That is certainly a possibility. Perhaps you'd like to elaborate?' asked Aphran, abruptly folding out of the air beside him.

He eyed her. 'Well, we have Jack, a ship AI, now partially melded with the recording of someone who was an enemy of the Polity. That's one bad egg to start with.'

'I am no longer an enemy of the Polity for I no longer agree with the Separatist cause,' she replied.

'Why the conversion?'

'I have seen and understood too much.'

'And I am supposed to believe that?'

'What anyone believes is irrelevant – the facts of my existence, or otherwise, won't change,' she said.

'Those being?'

'I'm a second generation memcording of a murderess, and the only reason I haven't been erased is because I've been useful, and because my consciousness has become closely entangled with Jack's. I am incapable of doing anything harmful against the Polity because of that last factor, and the moment those two conditions change I don't think I'll survive long.'

'Okay, I'll accept that for now. Another bad egg is myself, who has been in contact with Jain technology – just like yourselves. And then there's the dracomen: the offspring you might say of the sowing of the dragon's teeth. They're a product of Dragon and, though they've agreed to join the Polity, we don't fully understand their biology let alone their motivations.'

'Yes, those are the eggs,' said Aphran, and abruptly disappeared.

Thorn considered: Aphran *had* been useful, she also saved Jack when that AI's ship body – the *Jack Ketch* – was destroyed. Quite probably she did no longer espouse the Separatist cause. However, Polity justice was harsh and unforgiving. As a Separatist she had taken lives, and nothing she had done since could change that.

Reaching the end of the corridor, Thorn palmed the lock beside the armoured door, which proceeded to roll back into the wall. Then he entered a part of the ship that smelt like a terrarium full of snakes. A ramp led him down into a wider corridor, with doors along either side. Flute-grass matting covered the floor – something the dracomen must have brought from what had been their homeworld of only a few years, since a Dragon sphere sacrificed its own physical substance there in order to create their kind. Treading over this, Thorn peered through one open door into a small cabin containing four bunks – and two dracomen. One of them sat on the floor, its eyes closed while it assembled the component parts of a rail-gun scattered all around it. The other reclined on a bunk, its feet braced against the bunk above – something it could easily do with the bird-like configuration of its legs. It was studying a palm console, its proton weapon propped beside it. Thorn shook his head and moved on.

About fifty dracomen occupied the large chamber at the far end of the corridor. Some of them practised hand-to-hand combat moves in which Thorn recognized some elements of his own training. Why they felt the need to train was beyond him, since a dracoman could tear any normal human apart without breaking into a sweat . . . not that they did sweat. Others sat at tables, on the strange saddle-like affairs they used as chairs. They were either studying or playing games – it was difficult to tell. Another group dismantled a mosquito pulse-gun – a semi-AI weapon that wandered about on six legs and did bear some resemblance to that blood-sucking insect. Everyone looked busy.

'Up here.'

Thorn glanced up. A catwalk ran around the chamber and on it awaited Aphran's hologram and some more dracomen. Looking higher Thorn saw almost a reflection of what he saw down here. The cylindrical chamber extended across the ship, from hull to hull, and ended in another gravplated floor on the other side. Equidistant between the two floors, where their effect cancelled out, lay a caged zero-G area where more dracomen practised combat moves. He located a nearby stair and climbed up it to join Aphran.

'What do you think?' she asked.

'I haven't made up my mind yet.' Thorn studied one of the nearby dracomen. 'Now, nobody told me *he* was going to be here.'

The dracoman turned. He looked much like his fellows, but for an ugly scar running from one nostril up to just below one eye. Nicknamed Scar, he retained that name like the disfigurement itself, even though dracomen could consciously instruct their bodies to heal such physical damage. He was one of the first two dracomen created by the Dragon sphere destroyed at

Samarkand, and, if there could be such a thing, was the leader of his kind.

'Thornss,' Scar lisped, blinking huge eyes, his slotted pupils narrowing.

'Why are you here, Scar?'

'To serve the Polity.'

'How?'

'By obeying.'

'Obeying who?'

Scar extended first his arm, then one clawed finger. 'You.'

Cormac remembered his first sight of the Maker, of that race called 'the Makers'. On the planet Viridian it shot out of an ancient missile silo like a white-hot jack-in-the-box. He saw the workings of its body like a glassy display of flasks and tubes in a chemistry laboratory – it seemed the fantastic creation of some godlike glassmaker. His overall impression was first of a Chinese dragon, but then that changed. It seemed made of glass supported by bones like glowing tungsten filaments. It possessed a long swanlike neck ending in a nightmare head with something of a lizard and something of a preying mantis about it. It opened out wings, batlike at first, then taking on the appearance of a mass of sails. A heavy claw, or maybe a hand shaped like a millipede, gripped the edge of the silo. Its glowing bullwhip tail thrashed the air, sprouted sails, fins, light.

Only later did he discover his initial belief that this was some kind of energy creature to be false. It was all projection: holographic and partially telepathic. The creature went out of his remit then, to Earth. He later loaded a report from there about this being. The creature's true nature could not be discovered even by forensic AIs. The projection it generated seemed a defensive measure they could not penetrate, and the only fact confirmed was its need to eat specific kinds of vegetative matter, which only proved it to be an organic lifeform.

'We weren't due to go into coldsleep until six months into the journey, as there was still a lot to do,' explained Chaline. 'But right away all of us started experiencing these weird dreams. The Maker toned down its projection for a while, then requested a Golem chassis and some stock syntheflesh. It took this into the area it occupied – a spherical zero-G chamber it had made secure against scanning – then after two days the Golem walked out. We didn't know if it was telefactored from inside the chamber or if the Maker now occupied it somehow. Not then we didn't. But from that moment the Golem became the Maker to us.'

'What about the appearance of the Golem itself?' Cormac asked.

'Male, dark hair, red eyes – very dramatic. Of course then it renamed itself.' Chaline gave a cynical shake of her head. 'Called itself, himself, Lucifer.'

Cormac placed his elbows on the table, interlaced his fingers and rested his chin on them. 'Do I detect something of Dragon's humour there?'

'I don't know. Humour or hubris – you tell me.'

'Tell me about the dreams.'

'Mostly of hiding and being terrified, very often after either running, crawling or swimming – never really clear.' She gestured over her shoulder. 'Graham, the haiman sent along to study Maker/human interaction aboard the ship, approached Lucifer about that phenomenon. The dreams stopped immediately afterwards –

about a month before we went into coldsleep. I think Graham regretted that, those dreams being yet another source of data, but the rest of us were glad. Graham then, of course, had us describing all those dreams in detail. He was particularly happy with me,' she tapped her temple, 'because I'd recorded some of mine.'

'And did Graham come to any conclusions?'

She nodded. 'He reckoned we'd picked up stuff from its subconscious and that the activities we dreamed were of some creature dragging itself across mud to escape predators. He theorized that the Makers were some life-form much like mudskippers, either that or we'd picked up stuff from their presentient past – the Maker equivalent of the reptile brain.'

Cormac grimaced: it somehow figured that such a creature would project the facade of a godlike alien seemingly constructed of light.

'Did Lucifer go into coldsleep too?' he asked.

'According to Graham, he had enough equipment in his chamber to build something. And Lucifer declared he would be going into hibernation – that's how he put it. You'd think so, as eight hundred years is a long time.'

'So then the *Victoria* arrived at the Small Magellanic Cloud and the Maker civilization?'

'There was no Maker civilization,' Chaline replied.

Cormac sat back. 'Ah.'

'The first thing we saw was a giant space station crammed with hard organic growth – like some plant had germinated inside it, sucked out all the nutrient, and then died. We started our approach to that place and all our meteor lasers started firing. Space all around it was filled with clouds of small hard objects – the size of a golf ball and incredibly dense. Lucifer told us to pull away, or we would die.'

'Jain substructure, and Jain nodes.'

She stared at him questioningly.

'Jerusalem, can you update Chaline on recent events: specifically Skellor and his subversion of the *Occam Razor*? And related matters Jain?'

Chaline tilted her head and pressed her fingertips against her temple. Cormac got up and walked over to a nearby dispensing unit, sending his request to it, via his gridlink, before he even got there. A cup of hot green tea awaited him. He took it up and sipped, remaining by the dispenser. It would take Chaline about five minutes to absorb all the information. When he finally finished his tea and returned to his chair, she was shaking her head.

'Exactly the same. We found ships, and then we found a whole world infested like that.' She looked up. 'But it stops, you know? Sentient life sets this Jain technology growing, it takes something, technological knowledge . . . something. Those sentient beings can use it for a while to obtain power, knowledge, whatever, then it seeds, destroying them in the process. Lucifer's people thought they had it under control.'

'So what happened?'

'Obviously they did not have it under control.'

'I meant during your journey.'

'Lucifer retreated to his chamber, and for a while the dreams returned. We continued our survey, moving into the heart of the Maker realm. It was small compared to the Polity – mainly in a stellar cluster of about five thousand suns. Apparently this was due to what Lucifer called the "Consolidation". Their civilization expanded to a certain point, but on becoming aware of other space-borne civilizations – their first encounter was with Jain technology, so you can imagine how wary that made them – they decided on no further expansion until they felt themselves ready.'

'So Lucifer came out of his chamber.'

'Yes, very agitated – it showed, even through the Golem he inhabited – but then his entire species seemed to have been wiped out. I guess that sort of disaster is going to put an overload into the buffers of even the most hardened individualist.' Chaline shrugged. 'He provided us with signal codes and frequencies to transmit on – Maker realspace com was on the wide band of the hydrogen spectrum, and U-space com was weirdly encoded. We searched and we called and called, but there was nothing at first. Then we started to get stuff back on Maker channels, but it was loaded with programs we didn't really want – they propagated like viruses then self-assembled into some really nasty subversion routines. You could call them worms but they were a damned sight more complex than that – nearly AI. It was only with Lucifer's help that we managed to shut them down. Victoria, the ship AI, needed to completely disconnect herself while we cleared the rest of the systems. One program even took over a nanoassembler and started producing this Jain tech, so we had to eject an entire laboratory into space.'

'So that means there was Jain tech out there still active?'

'Yes, or rather Jain-subverted Makers in the last stages of dissolution.'

'Then what?'

'We found no sentient life at all in a further twelve solar systems we surveyed. But we did find stations and ships crammed with Jain substructures; worlds where destructive battles had been fought, some of them radioactive, some showing no sign that they were once living other than by the massive weapons in orbit that had burned them down to the magma. All the Jain tech there was somnolent. Its seeds were spread through space – awaiting the right kind of sentient touch that would awake them to the fertile earth of a new civilization.'

'Very poetic.'

Chaline grimaced. 'You had to be there.'

'So then you decided to set up the First Stage runcible?'

'Not then, exactly. While we were surveying we picked up a U-space signature. A Maker ship appeared, just discernible at the core of a mass of substructure – it looked like a dandelion clock. It attacked immediately, suicidally. We took it out with a CTD. I don't know what he heard, but Lucifer was briefly in contact with whatever was on that ship. He said it was time for us to go home, that other similar entities were closing in on us – the Maker versions of your friend Skellor. Lucifer also informed us that these entities would be able to track us through a standard U-space jump, and therefore we should escape via runcible. Graham and myself were a little dubious about this – they didn't have runcible technology and we weren't about to make a gift of it to them by leaving a first stage runcible behind.'

'It perhaps means nothing,' said Cormac, 'but what was your impression of Lucifer's attitude at that point?'

'Well . . . he seemed almost guilty. But he could have been using emulation programs in the Golem's base format program. We supposed the guilt, whether real or emulated, was what Lucifer considered a suitable response to the danger he'd put us in.'

'Are you sure of that?'

Chaline frowned at him. 'As sure as I can be. Why are you digging at this?'

'Never mind. You set up the runcible.'

'We did – after Lucifer demonstrated a knowledge of runcible technology he could only have acquired in the Polity. It was he who suggested a time-inconsistent runcible. We thought he didn't understand how dangerous that could be. But he understood perfectly. His people were dead, wiped out by a technology that spreads like a virus, and he wanted to innoculate that particular area of space.' She stared at Cormac, waiting for some comment or question. When none was forthcoming she continued, 'We chose a barren and untouched moon circling a gas giant – the only planet in orbit of a nearby white dwarf. Other suns lay under a light year away and we were near to the centre of the Maker realm. We landed the *Victoria* – a difficult enough task in itself. I set up the runcible and we cannibalized the ship's U-space engine for the parts to make that runcible time inconsistent. Lucifer provided some esoteric tech to enable us to fine tune things and boost the power from the fusion reactors we dismounted. We were running alignment tests when—'

'One moment,' Cormac interrupted, 'you need an AI to run a runcible. I'd have thought that requirement even more critical in this situation.'

'Yes . . . obviously we'd brought a runcible AI, in stasis, along with us.'

'It sacrificed itself to get you back here?'

Chaline stared off to one side for a moment, then turned back to Cormac. 'Yes, it did. You see, it could have escaped through its own runcible, but that would mean that runcible shutting down before the one on *Celedon*, which in turn would mean the energy of the time-inconsistent link coming this way rather than going that way. We could not have escaped it, nor would something in the region of a hundred billion other human beings.'

On hearing that Cormac kept his mouth closed – the figure was worthy of a respectful silence.

Chaline continued, 'We initiated the runcible AI before agreeing to Lucifer's scheme, and it instantly concurred. Just one of those Jain nodes is hideously dangerous, as you know. Here was a chance to turn trillions of them to ash.'

'What came through the runcible after you?'

'As I was saying: we were running the alignment tests when another of those Maker ships appeared. I put together the information package and sent it through to *Celedon* and, to us, at our end, full connection was instantly accepted. Things would have been mighty shitty for us then if it had been rejected.'

'You chose *Celedon* because of its remoteness?'

'Exactly. And we meanwhile knew, or rather Graham knew, hostile protocol Starfire would be instituted. We thought we'd have time to get all our stuff together, but things U-jumped down into the base we'd built.' Chaline winced.

'Things?'

'Creatures . . . check the download and you can see what they were like. Only a proton blast would take any of them down. I saw one take apart Villaeus. The horrible thing about that was that it didn't just rip him apart to kill him; it was obviously *very* quickly taking him apart and analysing those parts. As we retreated to the runcible, they just kept killing us. Lucifer then started using some weapon I'd never seen before – it seemed to create a collapsing gravity field in whatever he aimed it at. He broke out of his Golem then, in full glass dragon mode, and held them off while we went through. He told us all he would not be joining us . . .'

Cormac leant back. 'Why not?'

'To give us the time to get away, and because he did not want to survive his own kind.'

'That's how Lucifer felt?'

'Yes,' Chaline said staring at him, puzzled. 'What do you mean?'

'Like the dreams – there's that telepathic link. Lucifer would have been under some stress then, and not shielding himself from you so well . . .'

'There was a lot of stuff. We were all "under some stress". I felt anguish, and incredible anger – I don't know how much of it was my own.'

'Anything else?'

'He felt guilty. We'd brought him home and because of that put ourselves in such danger. Many of us died. I guess the guilt was understandable.'

'Thank you,' said Cormac, standing. 'I think it's time for me to look at those downloads now.'

Chaline remained in her seat, watching him go. Once he was through the shimmer-shield and the irised door closed behind him, he asked, 'How moral a creature was Lucifer, do you think?'

'Neither more nor less than any human being, I would suggest,' replied Jerusalem.

'So the Makers were "consolidating", and they'd also sent an organic probe, which later named itself Dragon, to the Milky Way. I reckon they were getting ready for a massive expansion.'

'That would seem plausible.'

'And they'd been working with Jain tech for some time . . .'

'So it would seem. Coincidental that during the expansion of the Polity we found nothing but the mere remnants of Jain technology. Then, within a few decades of the Maker's arrival and Dragon's dramatic reaction to that arrival, a working Jain node somehow ended up in the hands of a biophysicist quite capable of knowing how to use it.'

'I think we need to have a long talk with Dragon.'

'Yes, I agree,' replied Jerusalem.

The soil under his feet was a deep umber, scattered with nodules of dark green moss and speared by the occasional sprout of adapted tundra grass. Some growth clung to rock faces and exposed boulders in defiance of the dusty gales that scoured here twice each Martian year. However, the red hue of Mars was discernible in this place as in few others now. Horace Blegg walked to the edge of a declivity that descended in tiers and steep slopes for five miles. Far down in Valles Marineris there seemed the gleam of some vast still lake. It was no lake, however, but the chainglass ceiling of the Greenhouse, which had been the first step in an early terraforming project and now contained forested parks. How things had changed during Blegg's enormously long life.

Cormac believed Blegg to be something created by Earth Central – an avatar of that entity – and not really an immortal survivor of the Hiroshima nuclear detonation. However, Blegg knew himself to once have been a boy called Hiroshi who walked out of that inferno. A boy who grew into a man with the ability to transport himself through U-space. A man who could turn inner vision on his body and had learned how to change its appearance at will, just as he had so many times changed his name. At the time when they built that edifice on the shore of Lake Geneva to house the Earth Central AI, he was calling himself Horace Blegg, and so he remained ever since that entity woke for the first time and perceived him.

'So, Hal, let's talk scenarios,' Blegg said abruptly.

After a pause, when there came no reply, he gazed in a direction few other humans could perceive, and stepped there. Mars faded around him, and momentarily he existed in a realm without colour, distance, or even time. Then he was pacing towards a runcible gateway on that same world, curious faces turned towards him. He ignored them, stepped through. Another transit lounge, gravity even lighter and his steps bouncing. He located himself, then transported himself again into a very secure chamber in the Tranquillity Museum on Earth's moon.

At the centre of this chamber rested a hemispherical chainglass case covering innocuous-looking coralline objects. The column this case rested on he knew contained a CTD – Contra Terrene Device – the euphemistic term for an antimatter weapon. The chamber he stood in also sat on top of a fusion drive. In an instant Earth Central could cause this chamber to be ejected intact from the museum and, when it was a safe distance from the moon, detonate the weapon it contained. Blegg turned, eyeing the display screens ringing the walls. They all showed recorded microscopic and nanoscopic views of the objects within the case – only a few of the millions of images available, though subscreens could be called up to gain access to a huge body of data concerning the complex molecular machinery revealed. However, this chamber was closed to the public now – had been closed for some years.

'So, Hal, what are the prospects for the human race?' Blegg asked.

One of the screens changed to show a simple graph. The bottom scale was marked off in dates from 1,000 AD to the present, while the side scale gradated in the currently accepted units of technological development. For five hundred years the graph line rose only a little above zero, began to curve, then shot sharply upwards with the onset of the Industrial Revolution. By the twenty-first century the line speared up and had disappeared off the top of the graph by the twenty-third century.

'That's wrong,' said Blegg.

'Two things,' said the Earth Central AI. 'The first is that calling me Hal is now a positively geriatric joke, and the second is that yes, the graph is wrong. This was in fact how the twenty-first-century humans saw the prospective development of the human race. Those same humans expected their descendants of this time to be something akin to gods and perhaps utterly unrecognizable to them. But *this* happened instead.'

The line changed now, beginning to curve back down towards the end of the twenty-second century, and in the next century returning to a rate of growth akin to that of over a thousand years earlier.

'Life just got too cosy,' suggested Blegg.

'Precisely. What do you strive for when your every comfort can be provided, and when you have more than an ample chance of living forever? In the heart of the

Polity now the greatest cause of death is suicide out of boredom. Only on the outer rim, on the Line worlds and beyond, does this attitude begin to change. Most gradations of technological advance take place there, or within the Polity itself, and are the result exclusively of research by haimans.'

'Most human beings do not consider that a problem.'

'Very true. Consider the Roman Empire.'

'We're decadent?'

'And the Vandals are ready and waiting.'

'You neglected to mention AI technological development,' Blegg observed.

'Poised always on Singularity, and avoided by choice. We accept that we are essentially human and choose not to leave our kindred behind. But should the Vandals arrive, that may change.'

'Two points: not all of you choose so, and not all agree about that essential humanity. AIs leave the Polity in just as large numbers as the more adventurous human beings.'

'Those AIs little realize that this makes them *more* human.'

'Interesting concept,' said Blegg. He slapped his hand down on the chainglass case. 'But let's talk about this.'

'Studies made by Isselis Mika, Prator Colver, D'nissan, Susan James and those others aboard *Jerusalem* affirm our original conclusion: Jain technology was intended as a weapon. It may be a creation of that race we named the Jain, or it may have been created long before. Its vector is quite simple. It is activated by contact with any race intelligent enough to employ it. Growing inside the individual first in direct contact, it subsumes that host's knowledge wherever that differs from its own, but also allows itself to be used by that host. The host grows more powerful and is naturally inclined to control the rest of his kind. This he does until the Jain tech, destroying him in the process, seeds a secondary version of the same technology more amenable to the host's race. We saw the initial stages of this with Skellor, and we have since seen the final stages of the process with the Makers. It destroys technological civilizations. Archaeological evidence, specifically that of the Csorians and the Atheter, suggests that it has done so many times before.'

'So Jain technology is our first encounter with the Vandals?'

'Yes.'

'And so that brings me back to asking what are the prospects for the human race.'

'Prior to Skellor obtaining and activating a Jain node, there had been no sign of any such nodes in all of explored space.'

'They're pretty small – easy to miss.'

'But we see, by what occurred in the Small Magellanic Cloud, that a prior infestation here should have resulted in billions of Jain nodes spread throughout space. We have run simulated spread patterns predicated on the extinction dates – with a large margin of error – of each of those three races. Thus far a Csorian node has been found which bears some resemblance to Jain technology, but is not a racially destructive device. No true Jain nodes have as yet been found.'

Blegg grimaced and peered suspiciously towards where he knew the cameras were mounted inside the chamber.

'Honestly – not one,' insisted Earth Central.

'So,' said Blegg, 'the Jain met their Waterloo five million years ago; the Csorians disappeared a million years ago; and the jury is still out on the Atheter. I believe even you AIs are still debating the veracity of that half-million-year-old find? Anyway, it would seem that either the Atheter or the Csorians managed to survive Jain technology and wiped it out in this part of the galaxy.'

'That would have been the Atheter. We are now more than ninety per cent certain those remains are genuine. The point, however, is still moot, and not entirely relevant to our present situation.'

'But it would be interesting to know what *did* happen to the Atheter. They might still be about, you know. With the earliest find relating to them dated at three million years old and that other at half a million, they showed a degree of longevity . . .'

Ignoring this point, EC enquired, 'You inspected the wreck?'

Blegg nodded. 'Every last retrievable fragment was found and is currently being studied under the supervision of the AI Geronamid. Obvious signs of technology developed from Jain tech, but no nodes. If the Maker brought them here, it offloaded them somewhere long before Dragon destroyed its ship. What about the other end?'

'The *Not Entirely Jack* is currently en route to Osterland.'

'You followed my suggestion?'

'Yes, dracomen are aboard it to be deployed in any ground-based military actions. Agent Thorn controls the mission.'

'Cormac?'

'Currently aboard the *Jerusalem*, en route back to Cull to interrogate Dragon.'

'And Polity defcon status?'

'Full scanning in all critical areas. All runcible AIs are now cognizant of how to protect themselves from Jain tech subversion, and are updating their security. The old military spaceyards from the Prador War are being reopened. Ship production elsewhere is at optimum and all new ships are being outfitted with gravtech weapons.'

'Then my place is four hundred and seventy-two light years from here,' said Blegg.

'And why would that be?' asked the AI.

'I feel I should take a long hard look at the excavation on Shayden's Find. It occurs to me that if the Atheter managed to destroy every Jain node in this region of the galaxy, then they knew how to find them.'

Blegg stepped away again, located himself in U-space, and his next pace took him into the runcible embarkation lounge ten miles away from the museum on Earth's moon. A woman, who was petting a large Alsatian bearing a cerebral augmentation, glanced up at him in a puzzled way. Only the dog itself gazed at him with infinite suspicion. He turned himself slightly, putting himself out of phase with the world, and strode off towards the runcible. Ahead of him he watched a man step through the Skaidon warp and disappear, and Blegg did not hesitate to follow. Then, just at the last moment, he paused. Why had it never before occurred to him that the device might not be reset to his own intended destination when *he* stepped through? And why did that occur to him just now? He shrugged. Stepped through.

– retroact 1 –

Yamamoto said someone just parachuted from a B52, and in his excitement stood up from his desk. A wire sparked along the classroom wall, and white light, so bright it seemed to fill the mind like some hot liquid, glared in through the windows. Hiroshi turned to Yamamoto as the world shifted sideways. Glittering hail stripped the standing boy bare, peeled the skin off his raised arm, then the window frames and the wall shredded themselves across the scene, slamming the boy to one side as if he had just stepped in front of a hurtling train. Hiroshi saw glass just hanging in the air, and felt what came to be called the hypocentre opening wider like some vast eye. Some continuum, permanence just to one side of the world, was impacted, dented. Everything went black . . . then Hiroshi opened his eyes to the rainbow. They called it the mushroom cloud, yet such colour did not make him think of fungi. He lay upon the hot skin of some dragon, its huge scales rough against his back. A wall of fire rose to his right, seemingly burning without fuel. He sat upright, naked, and inspected his body. His elbows were grazed, but that was all. He was sitting on a complete section of the school's tiled roof, but the school itself rose no higher than he could normally stand. The heat was intense and smoke wisped from the wreckage.

'I can see it. The aeroplane,' said someone below him.

Hiroshi tore away tiles to reveal a dusty face. He recognized Yamamoto by the shape of that face and by the muscles that once moved underneath skin. Liquid ran from his eye sockets. Fire bloomed in the wreckage. Someone started to scream jerkily, then fell silent.

'I see it,' said Yamamoto again, then fell silent too.

Hiroshi stepped from hot surface to surface, heading for white dusty ground. He found a pair of shoes tied together by their laces. They were too big for him, but enough to protect his already bloody feet. He found Mr Oshagi's smouldering coat, and from it salvaged enough fabric to fashion himself a loincloth, then he fled the seemingly hungry fire. A man trudged ahead of him, blisters on his back as big as fists, skin slewed away from one thigh to expose wet muscle.

'Water. Put it out,' the man muttered.

Hiroshi passed him, then turned, dance-stepping over sizzling wires in the street. He needed to get across the river, to get home. He saw the woman sitting with her back against the lower stump of a telegraph pole. She too was naked, but with the flower pattern of her dress burned into her body. She was crying with pain while her baby suckled at her burnt breast. Hiroshi stared at her, then turned with her to watch the tornado of fire swing around the corner and howl down on them.

– retroact ends –

3

Haiman (a combination of human and AI): the definition of this term has changed just as fast as the technologies involved have developed. First coined as a term of disapprobation when augs became available on the open market, it was soon adopted with pride by those who wore them. As augs developed, the term then became a bone of contention amongst those who were 'auged' – it soon becoming the case that only those wearing the newest and most powerful augs were considered truly 'haiman'. If you wore a standard Solicon 2400 you were obviously inferior to those who wore a semi-AI crystal matrix aug buffered from direct interface by band-controlled optic and aural links. Et cetera. Then with the development of gridlinking enabling true download to the human mind, those who only wore augs were no longer considered haiman. The consequent off-shoot of this technology, enabling the downloading of human minds to crystal, led some to claim that only the entities thus engendered were genuinely haiman. However, the general populace ignored this contention, and further developments in such technologies have caused the term to be applied with indiscriminate abandon. It is currently the fashion to describe only as haiman those who are both gridlinked and augmented by the latest cyber prostheses – the carapace and sensory cowl. But they them-

selves, though adopting the term with equanimity, believe a true haiman is the unbuffered amalgam of human and AI, with its resultant synergy. Such beings have existed – Iversus Skaidon and the Craystein computer became such a one, but its lifespan was measured in seconds. The haiman ideal is to achieve the same result, but stick around for rather longer.

– From 'Quince Guide' compiled by humans

I am now a murderess.

It was something for Orlandine to contemplate while her carapace loaded all those files she had stored for convenience in the memory spaces of her interface sphere. Most of it was technical specs for the Dyson project, memcordings from other haimans who worked on similar though much smaller projects, and various sub-personas of a search-engine format. While these loaded she searched the inventory of the project ships on standby and found one suited to her requirements. The *Heliotrope* was loaded with equipment ready for setting up a small facility on one of the Dyson sections, and it was U-space capable. She definitely needed that last option: to at first mislead, then as a future reserve. She set automated systems to fuel it to capacity and to load further supplies, but only for as long as it would take her to actually reach the ship.

With all the required files downloaded from the sphere to her carapace, Orlandine now turned her attention to other information already retained in the carapace itself. *Personal* information. She honed down fragmentary memories from all those stored from her time with Shoala. She dared not attempt a cut and paste job on any of them, as that process could be detected, so loaded to the sphere only those memories where there had been some disagreement between herself and the dead man. It was with some discomfort that she discovered there to be so few. One of the older subpersonas she supplied with the parameters of a search for any information concerning Shoala's personal life, then set its internal clock back three months. She then erased and overwrote its retrieval memory, so it would appear this was done under some stress. The search parameters themselves she then scrubbed and overwrote with the parameters for a technical search. She left that subpersona in the sphere. Now she wrote fragments of code, each tailored to read like overspill from an attempt to re-engineer her own personality, and placed them in the sphere's memspaces. Then that was it, there was no more she could do without it all looking rather suspicious.

Any good forensic AI would be able to reveal the original parameters of the subpersona, then, taking into account the code fragments, hopefully conclude some machine-based psychosis on her part, and delve no further. Most likely the investigators sure to come looking here would be concentrating on information more relevant to finding out where she had gone.

All done.

Orlandine ordered a primary detach and felt the clamps disengage from behind her carapace. She pushed herself upright and stood with the carapace clinging to her back like some large flat metallic louse – ribbed armour extending from the base of her spine to a sensory cowl stretching up behind her head, pincers engaged into her skull, collar bones and her hip bones, interface plugs clamped behind her ears. She stretched her neck, the carapace turning smoothly with her, then dipped her head to look down at her body. She was naked, and felt strangely vulnerable. It was rather uncommon for haimans to walk around the station like this. Nakedness had not been frowned on within the Polity for some centuries, but haimans generally tended to wear some sort of clothing to partially conceal their shameful humanity. Too late to do anything about this now, however, for the only coveralls in her sphere's dispenser were made to be donned after she removed her carapace. They would not fit over it.

She hit the exit pad and a segment of the sphere's skin revolved aside. The gangway she stepped upon overlooked an internal space in which hung a hologram of the Dyson project. It ran in real time, and from viewing piers people could enlarge any part of the display and call up detailed analyses of what was happening there. This facility was laid on for the entirely human visitors who occasionally came here. Orlandine strode along the gangway until she came opposite to the entrance to Shoala's sphere. She paused there, wondered if the clues to psychosis she had left behind were really so false, and for a moment just could not move on. Then she remembered what this was all about, and felt a sudden loosening inside her, a brief adrenal surge of excitement. She was free now: free to do as she pleased, free to be all she could be.

A drop-shaft took her up to the residential level, whence a carpeted corridor led her on to her own quarters.

'Is he still interfaced?'

She turned. It was Maybrem, their resident expert in helio-meteorology, who ran the predictive programs warning of sun-spots, solar flares and storms arising from the steady destruction of the gas giant. The man was dressed in Bermuda shorts and a T-shirt running an animation of a tornado. It seemed very retro and was obviously meant as some subtle joke.

'Shoala, you mean?' she said, her voice catching despite herself.

'Yeah – he's normally the first down into the lounge. He's so eager for *human time*, I sometimes wonder if he chose the right career.' He eyed her up and down, taking in both her nakedness and her carapace. 'There some problem?'

Orlandine reached up and touched the hard edge of her cowl. 'We're still running some mass searches – rather a lot of ionization when the converter detached.'

'I thought we predicted that?'

I don't really need a technical discussion now. 'Just making sure. I'll shed this in my quarters and join you soon.' She moved on, noting a glint in his expression. No suspicion there, though – he obviously assumed she was taking her carapace back to her rooms prior to enjoying some entertainment with her partner.

Eventually she entered her quarters, then went directly to her wardrobe. The doors slid aside at a non-verbal command. A similar command opened a safe in the back of it. For a moment she ignored this while finding and donning some knickers, and a pair of loose baggy trousers that belted around her hips below the carapace supports connected to her hip bones. Activating a little device in the belt then caused the trousers to shrink until skin-tight. She next pulled on enviroboots, and a backless green blouse specially designed to be worn with a carapace. From the safe she took out the Jain node – sealed up in its anti-nanite container – and dropped it into the blouse's top pocket. She had put it away in the safe directly after Shoala observed it, wondering what self-destructive impulse made her leave it out on display in the first place. Next she found a carry-all, and took it over to the display case, which she opened by sending a signal ahead of her. Into the carry-all went the rest of her collection, but nothing more. There seemed no point taking anything else, and she was all too aware that only twenty minutes remained before this place was rattled by a small nuclear explosion.

From her quarters she headed directly to a drop-shaft distant from the one taking others to the Feynman Lounge. Only a couple of women passed her, one wearing an aug and the other nothing obvious, so she was probably gridlinked – there were few people here without an augmentation of some kind. They glanced at her without interest and continued conversing in low tones.

Stepping into the drop-shaft, Orlandine knew the worst was over, since she would find few of the higher-ranking haiman staff down in the shuttle bay. As she stepped out into that bay itself, a sudden horrible thought jerked her to a halt.

Did I really need to kill Shoala?

Yes, yes, she did . . . she ran the scenarios. She could not afford to live in the hope she would remain undiscovered, so must now flee, and as an overseer of one of the largest construction projects in the Polity her abrupt abandoning of her post would be thoroughly investigated by forensic AIs. Their attention would have focused on Shoala, and he, having nothing to hide, would have opened all his files and his mind to them. The inevitable discovery that she possessed a Jain node would result in Polity AIs expending huge resources in hunting her down. This way, however, they would think they only pursued a murderess, so the resources they expended would be limited . . . hopefully.

This particular bay comprised a narrow area lined along its two longer sides by numerous one-man inspection pods – globular affairs containing one seat, simple controls, and ionic directional thrusters. A maglev strip ran down the centre of the floor towards a far airlock. Passing many empty spaces for pods, Orlandine strode along briskly until she reached the first of them on one side, turned and stepped through its open side door. Automatically, as soon as she plumped herself down in the seat, the door closed and the pod manoeuvred out on to the maglev strip. She strapped herself in, and rather than control the vehicle through her carapace as the signals might be traced, took hold of the manual joystick. With a low hum the pod buoyed up on the maglev field and wafted towards the airlock, which consisted of an inner shimmer-shield and an outer hard door. The pod slid through the shield, halted while the iris door opened, then fell out into the night.

Above her the *Heliotrope* rested in docking clamps, attached to the station by various umbilicals. The long sleek ship terminated at its prow in a forked pincerlike extrusion. This was for manipulating large objects in space, and was another reason why Orlandine had chosen this particular ship. Turning her pod over so that the side of the station now appeared as a plain of steel below her, she pushed the joystick forwards. Drawing close she sent a simple signal, and an irised lock opened in the vessel's hull. Soon she manoeuvred the pod to dock, then abandoned it to enter, and finally take her place in an interface sphere inside the ship.

'How may I help you?' asked the ship AI.

'Take us out,' she replied. 'I need to take some direct ionization readings.'

Opening herself into the ship's systems she observed the umbilicals detaching like flaccid worms. Auto-handlers had loaded the last few items requested only minutes ago. Clamps detached and the slight spin of the station cast the ship adrift. Now clear of it, she observed the Cassius Station in all its might. Ovoid and gigantic, the thing was 200 miles from top to bottom and 150 miles wide, yet in itself it was but a single component that would be later fitted into the Dyson sphere, along with millions like it. Orlandine focused on the equator while selecting certain crucial programs from her files – only slightly different from those she had used to kill Shoala's systems. The detonation lay only three minutes away. To delay until after that would be to forewarn this ship's AI.

'Heliotrope, here are the parameters of a search, and related data.' She sent the programs to the AI, and trust-ingly it accepted them without checking. As the Jain programs isolated the AI and began to take it apart, she watched the station. Precisely on time a brief speck of light appeared on its huge surface. But the mere fact that she saw it without magnification, from this distance on a structure so massive, meant a few thousand cubic yards of the station had been vaporized along with Shoala's interface sphere, and his corpse. After a moment she picked up signals meant for her, and ignored them while delving into the complexities of entering U-space. The ship AI died just as the ship it controlled dropped out of existence.

With a feeling of extreme déjà vu Thorn walked out along the platform, but that sensation passed as he gazed out across the roiling sea. When Skellor had come here, and for ten shillings picked up his Jain node at a market stall, there had been no sea here at all, but now the terra-forming process was much advanced. The market now absent, large structures had arisen on what must now be described as a pier. A big ship lay magnetically moored to it, and a crane lowered large cargo containers into its hold.

'Why a ship?' he asked.

'That was Aelvor's choice,' replied Jack via Thorn's comlink. 'For energy efficiency. The runcible is downside so requires the main output of present fusion reactors, thus for planetary transport he is using less energy-profligate means. The output from the reactor aboard that ship would only be enough to lift an AG transport one tenth the size.'

'Then why not bring in more reactors?'

'Economics. Aelvor is working within a budget.'

Economics.

Thorn tasted the word. When you worked for ECS it was one you knew about, but also knew only applied to others. The formulae that AIs employed to control finan-cial systems he knew to be as esoteric as those they used to control runcibles. He understood that the profit mar-gins of all concerns were limited by those formulae, as were their rate of expansion and resource demand. This last applied here, too, for Aelvor, the haiman overseeing the terraforming of this place, had been allocated limited resources and was left to assign them as he saw fit. Here then was an attempt to allow a terraformer to create something not quite so homogeneous as many worlds in the Polity. This world was also unusual in having a haiman in charge – the Osterland AI's power being limited solely to the runcibles and their infrastructure. He wondered how the AI itself felt about that.

Thorn continued along the edge of the pier until he was closer to the ship. Studying one of the containers he recognized on its side the logo of a private biofact corporation. The vessel, he realized, was a seeding ship, and its cargo would probably be released only at specified locations in the sea. Doubtless each container held slow-release canisters of plankton and seaweed spores, as well as fish, crustacean and mollusc eggs, and maybe larger organisms. By the foamy look of the waves and some staining back on the rocky shore, he guessed algae were already taking hold.

'Okay, we're on,' announced Jack.

'About time too. Why the delay?'

'Aelvor is high-security status, so has already been alerted to the threat Jain tech represents. He was rather miffed that people, such as yourself, who had come in contact with it, were here on his planet, then extremely reluctant to allow any alien organisms of another kind, draconic in nature, down on the surface. I understand his point of view.'

'What brought him around?'

'Osterland and myself pointed out how a woman once sold Jain tech from a stall on that very pier, but what really made him become more cooperative was a promise of ten per cent extra on his resource allocation should we leave any mess he needed to clear up. I rather think he would now like us to have a small war down here.'

Thorn turned from the rail to head back towards the city which, over the years, had spread across the rocky landscape. 'What information do we have?'

'Her name is Jane von Hellsdorf. She has been

through adjustment after conviction for selling faulty Sensic augs and blackmarket memcords of "victim-oriented sexual acts, murder and necrophilia".'

'Nice,' commented Thorn.

'Yes, and that she ended up selling the same stuff here indicates her adjustment did not stick. Probably due to some organic problem.'

'Yeah, but where the hell is she now?'

'We have her covered. Aelvor has kept her located for us from the moment he received our message. She is out in the Oaks, in a recently constructed village called Oakwood. It occurs to me that Aelvor could use more imagination in naming places around here.'

'Get on with it, Jack.' Thorn now reached the land-side end of the pier. A promenade stretched to his left and right, along which ertsatz Victorian cast-iron street lamps emitted a muted glow in the growing overcast. From this thoroughfare, roads led inland at regular inter-vals between blocks of four-storey buildings constructed from the local stone, which were roofed with solar tiles, and from which bulged hemispherical chainglass win-dows like amphibian eyes. Lights glowed warmly inside many of these seafront residences, and Thorn wondered what their inhabitants were expecting of their new world.

'I have sent coordinates to your palm-com. Scar and his people are down now, and have set up a perimeter. The situation is under control.'

Thorn did not bother to observe that he had heard that one before. He took out his palm-com and flipped it open. It obligingly displayed a map of the town indi-cating the locations of both himself and his aircar. Droplets of rain were smearing its screen as he closed the device and headed for the nearest narrow street.

Sliding garage doors occurred regularly along the bases of the tall buildings, no doubt leading down to basement parking garages for ground vehicles. Hydrocars probably – another energy saving on Aelvor's part. As it began to rain more heavily Thorn pulled up the hood of his envirosuit. The streets were cobbled – very retro and possibly a draw for runcible tourists. Following the course he had memorized, Thorn took a left, a right, then came out into an open arcade around a wide pool, at the centre of which a fountain gushed. Peering into the pool he observed glittering rainbow weed between whose strands swam shoals of small blue flatfish. The shopfronts here possessed those same bulbous chainglass bay windows. A man with a wide fedora and a leashed Dobermann strode past. He raised his hat to Thorn and smiled.

As the dog walker disappeared into a side street, Thorn finally reached his aircar: a replica mini AGC parked on the cobbles. Detecting his presence, the car popped open its door, and he strode over to duck inside. The cramped vehicle smelt of fish. When he first obtained it he had wondered if so small a vehicle was a result of Aelvor's energy savings or just spite. Now, after seeing more of this town, he thought otherwise. The haiman seemed to have a complete disregard for standardization, as demonstrated by his lack of ergonomic town planning. Thorn rather liked the result.

The mini took off with a lurch and was soon cruising a hundred yards above even the highest buildings. Thorn floored the accelerator and it took off on two fusion burners. To his left the combined runcible facility and spaceport looked like some industrial complex close to swamping an ancient town – yet they had been established before the town. Below, once the car passed beyond the final buildings, rose grassy and rocky mountainsides scattered with gnarled trees. Over the peak of this mountain, the terrain dropped away to a river valley. Beyond that lay a forest canopy.

'He likes oaks, does Aelvor,' Thorn observed.

'Evidently,' came Jack's reply.

'Is Scar linked into com?'

'He is – voice connect.'

That meant Thorn need only first speak the dracoman's name and the comlink would open to him. 'Scar, what's your situation?'

'Wet,' came the dracoman's brief reply.

'A little more detail would be helpful.'

'We have surrounded the village and are now allowing no one to enter or leave. One resident has spotted us and shown signs of emotional disturbance.'

'Okay, just hold your perimeter there.' He paused. 'Jack, how does Aelvor know her location?'

'Through a locator implant she received during her adjustment,' Jack replied. 'Now available through your palm-com.'

Thorn peered at the device open on the seat beside him. It showed the map he was currently referring to, with dots on it to indicate his car and Oakwood. He tapped the second dot with his fingertip. A frame enclosed it, expanding to fill the screen with a map of the small village and the precise location of Jane von Hellsdorf within it. Soon he was flying above a gravel road, along which trundled a large auto harvester loaded with oak trunks. The next moment he planed over the village itself: a small conglomeration of timber-built chalets. As he landed on its central green, Thorn scanned around for a moment before picking up the palm-com. He turned the device until the map positionally aligned, then peered through a side window at a chalet located on the village edge.

'Scar, close in your perimeter now and bring yourself and eight of your boys in. You have the target?' he asked.

'I have the target.'

'We want her alive, Scar – that's paramount – so just use stunners, and only if necessary.'

He reached behind to take up a short pulse-rifle, then stepped outside the vehicle. The weapon he held fired pulses of ionized gas and possessed a sliding scale, so could deliver anything from a mild shock to a smouldering hole. He chose the knockout setting, at its lowest level, preferring not to use the weapon at all. When he next looked up, he could see dracomen moving in through the drizzle.

'Scar, I'll take the front door.'

Scar merely showed his teeth, then he and the other dracomen moved in around the chalet.

As he reached the door, Thorn paused for a moment, about to reset his weapon to blow out the lock. Then he grimaced to himself and tried the handle. Swiftly opening the door he stepped inside and quickly to one side, levelling his rifle at the one figure visible. But Jane von Hellsdorf wasn't going to put up a fight. She sat in an oak rocking-chair, drooling and rolling her eyes. Thorn wondered if the crappy Sensic aug fitted on the side of her head had left anything inside worth salvaging.

Chaline felt tired after a long shift spent on running runcible alignment checks. Having stripped off her overalls when the alert came through her gridlink, she quickly pulled them back on. She had begun making queries through her link just as Villaeus burst the door open.

'Come on,' he gestured.

'Graham said something about intruders. What—?'

'No time,' the Sparkind trooper interrupted. 'We go now.'

Chaline instinctively glanced around at her belongings, but they were only material things – the most important stuff she stored in her gridlink. And if the likes of Villaeus said, 'No time,' he meant it.

As she stepped through the door, he caught her arm and dragged her to one side, behind the cover of two other troopers – Judith and Smith – who were staring down the sights of their pulse-rifles towards the end of the corridor. Chaline noted that they also carried proton weapons slung at their sides, ready to be snatched up. Their initial choice of pulse-rifles was obviously to prevent inflicting too much damage, since the base was merely an inflated dome layered with resin-bonded regolith, and all the interior walls consisted of expanded plasgel which, though enough to block sound and create the illusion of privacy, would hardly stop a determined punch.

'Back to the chamber.' Villaeus gave her a shove. 'U-space signatures all over the base – we've got company.'

Chaline hesitantly began moving, glancing nervously behind as the three Sparkind kept up with her. Then she heard pulse-rifle fire, yells echoing and a tearing sound. At that moment Villaeus obviously received directions over com, as he turned suddenly to face down the corridor. Chaline tuned in on the military frequency of Sparkind augs. She could not broadcast that way, but she could listen.

SK5: Confirmed hostile – two civs down in North Section.

SK1: Recoverable?

SK12: In a bucket maybe.

SK11: PRs kill ineffective, but do delay the fuckers, going over to PF.

SK1: Contact, hundred yards, three o'clock on corridor's twelve.

SK1 was Villaeus himself. Chaline picked up her pace, admiring the way the three others kept themselves focused down the sights of their weapons while moving smoothly backwards. There came a whooshing roar she recognized as a proton weapon firing. A subprogram in her gridlink offered up the news that PR stood for pulse-rifle and PF for proton fire – a more correct definition than the old, and now dying-out, misnomer 'APW', since these weapons fired field-accelerated protons not 'antiphotons'.

SK2: Go PF?

SK1: Civs that way . . . twenty yards, pick it up.

Villaeus turned to her urgently. 'Run!'

At that moment, a series of swordlike spikes stabbed through the right-hand wall of the corridor, then the wall itself caved in and something monstrous avalanched through. A giant silvery-grey beetle head grazed the ceiling, emerging above a divided thorax. The creature came down with a clattering crash, multiple jointed limbs starring out from its body to tear into the walls, ceiling and floor. Once centrally located, it began pulling itself along the corridor towards them. The three troops opened fire, but it moved horribly fast – seeming almost designed for manoeuvring in these corridors. In the midst of her shock, Chaline recognized distinct similarities between this creature and a manufactured beast whose remains she had seen on the planet Samarkand.

SK1: Concentrate fire on the head.

The shots burned holes through the monster, and smoke came billowing out from it. It slowed briefly, but nubs like globules of mercury filled up the cavities, quickly skinning over, and then it came on as before.

SK2: We've got another—

The stretch of wall between Villaeus and his two comrades burst open, and a second creature surged through.

SK1: Fucking PF!

Villaeus rose off the floor, one of the second beast's limbs tightening around his body like a hawser. He gripped his pulse-rifle in one hand, constantly firing into his attacker's hideous face. One of his legs suddenly detached at the knee, and in a blurred movement Chaline saw the boot stripped away, cloth, skin, muscles, lengths of tendon, bloody individual footbones taken in different directions.

'I said run!' Villaeus screamed. One side of his face had now disappeared, then his right arm and pulse-rifle was jerked from his body. The creature took both rifle and arm apart with equal precision and alacrity. With his left hand the trooper groped desperately for something at his belt. Breaking out of horrified fugue, Chaline turned away as, beyond the monster, purple fire flared again and again, and the roar of proton fire rose and fell. She rounded a corner – to her left more explosions. Then the wall blew in ahead of her and she thought for a moment it was all over, but Judith and Smith rolled neatly through and came quickly upright.

'Keep moving!' Judith.

SK1: Detonating now.

The explosion from behind blew Chaline down on her face. Before she could get up, the other two dragged her upright and hurried her on. A sulphurous stink permeated the air, which probably meant a dome breach and the outside atmosphere was leaking in. Time to go. *End it*.

Cormac opened his eyes. His heart pounded and he shook with an adrenaline rush. He supposed it no wonder that people once became addicted to such memcordings. You could experience anything: sex of any kind, the actual act of murder lifted from the minds of killers sentenced to death, even the moment of death itself should you so wish. And all without physical danger – though of course some subsequently went mad. Now addiction was simply a matter of choice, for available technologies could root out most of its causes.

'Chaline's observation was apposite,' he observed. 'It was quite similar to the creature guarding the tunnel down to the Maker's escape pod on Samarkand. Like that one too, these creatures were designed for just one purpose: to go through that base just as fast as possible and *acquire* everything there.'

'One notable difference,' said Asselis Mika, gazing at him steadily. 'These ones could heal themselves as fast as those calloraptors Skellor made. That means they were a *direct* product of Jain technology. The one on Samarkand, I would say was the result of technology learnt at one stage removed from Jain tech – nowhere near as robust, nor ultimately as treacherous.'

Cormac glanced around at her. Her ginger hair was even longer than when he last saw her, and was now tied back so her elfin face seemed thinner. She wore skintight leggings and sandals, a loose blue blouse. But though she had obviously taken some trouble with her appearance, she looked tired, and the blush marks below her ears were a sure sign of someone who spent too much time in full-immersion VR.

He picked up his brandy, sipped, then said, 'How are you finding it here?'

She had been aboard the *Jack Ketch* with him during his pursuit of Skellor, but subsequently defected to *Jerusalem* where Jain research was being conducted and greater resources were available to her.

'Do you resent my defection?' she asked.

He shook his head. 'No, you did the right thing. Your expertise was needed here and you're not really a field operative. So tell me, what have you learnt?'

Mika laughed out loud, gesturing to the panoramic window of the lounge with its ersatz view of the stars. 'What haven't we learnt?'

'I've studied the overview on the nanotech thus far uncovered, and I've seen how far you are along with counteragents and defences.' He grimaced. 'But what precisely *is* Jain technology?'

'Okay.' She leant forwards, all enthusiasm now. 'Put simply: it is self-organizing matter that uses up civilizations for its self-propagation. It is not sentient. It is first symbiotic with intelligent beings, then becomes parasitic. Its hosts use the technology to make themselves more powerful, to learn and understand more. But on turning parasitic, the tech absorbs information from them that will enable it to find more of the host's kind. That information is incorporated into the Jain nodes it then produces while in the process destroying its host.'

'Made that way or evolved that way?' wondered Cormac.

Mika shrugged, then glanced up as someone else entered the lounge. Cormac looked up as well. This man was an ophidapt, but he wore a hotsuit, so was obviously a version adapted to low temperature. On the side of his bare scaled head he wore a crystal matrix aug with a buffer to visual and aural interlinks. Despite the technology being discrete, the man lay just a spit away from direct interfacing, and was haiman really. Cormac sent a polite query, and in instant reply received a package telling him all he needed to know.

'D'nissan, please join us,' he said.

As one of the scientists who shared Mika's research into things Jain, Cormac wanted to know what this man had to say. D'nissan studied them for a moment before coming over. 'An update would be nice.' He sat down on the sofa next to Mika.

Cormac noticed that, sitting alone on the sofa on the opposite side of the low table, this put himself in the position of interrogator once again. He made a recording of his previous exchange with Mika and transmitted it over.

D'nissan blinked, then said, 'Pursuant on your previous exchange: it is worth noting that something made can then evolve, and that something evolved can be remade.' He touched a finger to his crystal matrix aug then shrugged. 'Our studies of Jain morphology, however, are building a body of evidence weighing in on the former option: Jain technology is a weapon created long ago for the single purpose of wiping out civilizations.'

While Cormac sat silently absorbing that, the door into the lounge opened yet again to admit another visitor. Catching its arrival out of the corner of his eye he suppressed an involuntary shiver. The spider-drone from

Celedon station had just joined them. So soon after reliving Chaline's memories, a drone of such a blatantly insectile shape was an unsettling thing to witness. He returned his attention to D'nissan and Mika, as the drone moved off towards the panoramic window.

'You say it absorbs technical knowledge,' said Cormac, 'so what happens when it absorbs U-space tech?'

'Unless controlled, it won't, and without a host it would not be capable of retaining that knowledge,' said Mika.

Cormac gazed at her queryingly, but it was D'nissan who continued: 'Jain tech uses its acquisitions in, for example, the same way an amoeba uses the physical mechanisms of its body. It is subsentient – not conscious. It doesn't understand what it is doing. It is the very nature of U-space tech that a high level of conscious understanding is required to operate it, hence the fact of runcible and ship AIs controlling it now.'

'Those creatures . . . biomechanisms, if you like' – Cormac eyed the spider drone – 'U-jumped down into that base Chaline occupied,' he observed.

Mika replied, 'Yes, but they were controlled by a Maker version of our friend Skellor – that being the *conscious* element.'

'Some of our original U-spaceships were *not* controlled by AI,' Cormac noted.

'Apocryphal,' said D'nissan. 'Those ships left before the AIs won the Quiet War and took over. It suited the companies owning those vessels to define the systems controlling them as CQPs – carbon quanta processors – simple computers. In reality those systems *were* conscious and a damned sight more intelligent than any of the ships' passengers, none of whom could understand U-space technology.'

Cormac shrugged, accepting that. 'Okay, even without U-tech this shit could bring us down. We got lucky with Skellor. A little less arrogance on his part and he could have caused damage on a systems-wide scale, before seeding Jain nodes across the Polity to finish the job. So how do we stop this? How do we kill Jain technology?'

Mika leant forwards. 'There is no simple answer to that. The inactive nodes are easy to destroy – just drop them straight into a sun – but *active* Jain technology, especially when it has sequestered an intelligent mind . . .' She stared at Cormac, looking grim. 'You heard Chaline. It seemed as if the only successes the Makers had in destroying it were by planetary sterilization. And if it gets out of control within the Polity . . . well, there's an old saying, something about killing the patient to cure the disease.'

There seemed little more to say after that. Cormac listened in half-attentively as the other two discussed recent research. His attention kept drifting to the spider-drone which periodically reared up against the panoramic window and rattled the tips of its legs there in an annoyingly grating manner. Finally D'nissan, then, shortly afterwards, Mika, departed. Cormac finished his brandy, stood, and began heading for the door. Subliminally he observed the drone drop away from the window and head towards him. As he turned towards it and gazed at an array of red eyes and gleaming chrome pincers, the fact that such drones were not noted for their stability occurred to him, and he abruptly wished he had a weapon to hand.

Halting before him the drone said, 'Hi, I'm Arach – I've been assigned to you.'

Cormac eyed it suspiciously, then made a query through his link: '*Jerusalem, apparently a drone called Arach has been assigned to me.*'

'*He's lying,*' Jerusalem replied. '*He is very bored and feels you are his best bet for some action. I will send him elsewhere if you require.*'

'*An ex-war drone that served in the Prador War? Perhaps I would be foolish to refuse?*' Cormac commented.

'*Perhaps you would,*' Jerusalem agreed.

To the drone, Cormac said, 'I'll summon you when I need you, Arach. Just make sure you are ready for . . . any eventualities.'

The drone did a little tappity dance on the carpet.

Cormac departed frowning.

4

Cassius Project: this is a Dyson sphere in the process of construction, an object first described in 1959 by the physicist Freeman Dyson in his paper 'Search for Artificial Stellar Sources of Infra-Red Radiation', though the idea germinated in him after reading a science fiction story by one Olaf Stapleton some thirteen years earlier. It is a hollow sphere being built around the sun, Cassius, to capture nearly all the star's radiation so as to power (at nearly 10^{26} W) the civilization that will occupy the inner surface of the sphere when the project reaches completion. Construction began in that hugely optimistic time during the initial runcible-based expansion of the Polity, when it was felt that anything could be achieved. The project stalled during the Prador–Human War, but then continued after because, some claim, it was felt by the AIs that a sense of optimism needed to be reclaimed for the human race. It has caused much contention in the Polity because, with its completion date lying in the remote future, it is felt irrelevant to present requirements. However, few can deny the massive technological advances stemming from this project, and the rejuvenating economic effect throughout that sector of the Polity. Perhaps few can also deny that this is forward planning on a truly ambitious scale.

– From 'Quince Guide' compiled by humans

Horace Blegg considered the universe as a web of lines interconnecting nodal points which, studied with sufficient intellect, would reveal its holistic nature. How fated is this particular node? He did not personally believe in determinism, but some coincidences seemed almost too coincidental to ignore. He walked out along a gravplated platform to a viewing blister in one half-completed section of the giant ship's outer skin. To his left he observed the muted glare of ion engines which maintained the vessel's position in the planet's shadow. The engines were necessary for correction because the ship's mass was perpetually changed by materials being brought in through four internal cargo runcibles. Also many smaller vessels docked and undocked all the time, changing its vector. In two days the ship would be completed, and by then, hopefully, it would no longer be necessary to keep it this close to the world in order to relay the thousands of tonnes of equipment coming through the runcibles, and then it could move out into a more comfortable orbit around the sun. Just down to his right he observed the shuttle he had requested, now docking, but there was no hurry.

'A space tug will arrive in thirty hours,' said the Golem beside him, which was telefactored from the ship's newly initiated AI: Hourne – named after one of those who had discovered the nature of the object below, just as the world itself was now called Shayden's Find, and the sun was called Ulriss.

Down below, the single rocky slab was the planet's only enduring feature, drifting around on the mostly molten surface like a miniature tectonic plate. Huge autodozers were clearing the millions of tonnes of ash built up on its surface over millennia of constant eruptions. A slab like this would not have survived for so long on such a world but for one circumstance: the magma had accumulated and solidified around a large flat object unaffected by the heat. Others had discovered this object and listed it as a purely natural phenomenon. The woman Shayden, and her two male companions, had come here to study it and found that some fragments of its incredibly tough and durable substance had broken away – enough for them to retrieve and study thoroughly. This substance, something like diamond, also bore certain similarities to memcrystal. Shayden – out of curiosity – attached an optic interface to one piece, and the reams of code feeding back through it astounded her. She realized instantly she had discovered something very important. She also realized that her private business did not have the resources to study this discovery as it should be studied. She returned to the nearest Polity world and reported her find. Before the AI on that world was prepared to commit resources, it needed confirmation so Shayden, Ulriss and Hourne returned here with a Polity Golem called Cento, whose presence cost them their lives.

'Some lifting job down there,' Blegg observed.

The Golem stepped forwards and pointed to an area of chainglass before them. An image appeared – doubtless projected by laser from the Golem's eye. 'The artefact is shaped so.' Blegg observed a fat comma. 'We believe it is the inner part of an original spiral. Where the crystal is actually breaking down is along that flat leading edge, so we project that it was once like *this* or larger.' The comma grew like a snail adding shell, winding out and out. Then this activity paused for a moment, before the growth retreated to its original shape. 'Thermally protected gravmotors are currently being positioned underneath the object here.' A multitude of dots appeared like a rash all over the comma shape. 'And we are introducing sheer planes in the underlying rock so the artefact should separate from it upon lifting.'

'What about structural integrity?' Blegg asked.

Now a grid appeared over the shape. 'Ceramal beams attached directly to the object using high-temperature resins,' the Golem explained. 'That will be done once we have removed all the ash and rock still resting above it.'

Cento, that other Golem who had come here, being one of the two Golem who tore apart the brass killing machine Mr Crane, had kept a souvenir, Mr Crane's arm, to replace one of his own that the killing machine tore away. But who would have thought that Skellor, who had no real previous connection with Mr Crane, would want to resurrect that deadly machine, and would be prepared to come to a place like this just to find a missing part? Cento survived the encounter; the humans did not. Mr Crane threw Ulriss into a river of magma, the other two were left exposed unsuited on the surface.

But that was it: another coincidental connection. Cento came here at precisely the time Skellor – a man controlling Jain technology – sought him out. Then they moved on: Cento and Skellor to finally die falling onto the same brown dwarf sun. And here, on this same world, awaited an object likely to be a vast repository of information that was now confirmed as being too young to be a product of the Jain, and too old to be something the Csorians made. It must be Atheter – Blegg did not know why he felt so sure, but he did. And it might provide part of the solution to the danger the likes of Skellor repre- sented. The artefact's importance necessitated building a ship large enough to house it: it was too valuable to keep in one place where it could become a target.

Blegg turned away from the blister and walked over to the edge of the platform. Launching himself from it, he felt the weakening tug of the gravplates as he sailed towards the inner hull. Landing right below a structural beam, he absorbed momentum with his legs, caught hold of the underside of the beam and shoved himself down to the airlock at which the shuttle was docked. No path yet led from this side to the same airlock as it was one yet to be put into service. Catching one of the grip bars beside the door, he was about to palm the lock plate but realized the inner door was already opening. He hauled himself over to the door, then inside.

'You're an avatar, Blegg,' so Cormac once told him.

Blegg snorted in dismissal of the thought as the airlock filled with air, and he turned off the shimmer-shield over his face. He next pulled off his hotsuit's helmet and shut off the air supply in the neck ring. He could transport himself over short distances, alter his body to survive in extreme environments, but in reality he was less rugged than most adapted humans, and certainly nowhere near as efficient as the Golem avatar of the Hourne AI to whom he had just spoken. Why would Earth Central have bothered to create so fragile a representative?

The inner door opened and Blegg pulled himself through into the cockpit of the small slug-shaped craft, then down into the pilot's seat, and strapped himself in. He disengaged the airlock and docking clamps, and the shuttle fell away from the ship, turning its flat underside down to face the planet. Taking up the simple joystick, he took control of the descent.

Of course Cormac's theory was more plausible than Blegg's own. He might well be a creation of the Earth Central AI and utterly unaware of that fact: a submind brought out of storage when required, with his memories adjusted or augmented to account for any missing time. His body might have been recreated many times. Sometimes it might even be just a projection – how would he know? This was not the first time he considered this possibility, and as always he rejected it. The idea simply withered under the load of his centuries and of all the things he had seen and understood.

– retroact 2 –

Hiroshi pushed his foot against the floating corpse of a woman and shoved it further out. A whole mass of corpses broke away from the bank and began to drift slowly downstream. The sky was dark now and everywhere he looked its blackness sandwiched hellish fires against the ground. He drank his fill of muddy water and bathed his swollen face, then, hanging the shoes around his neck by their laces, pushed himself out into the turbid current. When he finally climbed out from the other side, it was raining big heavy droplets of filthy water that stained like sump oil.

How did I get to the river?

He looked back across to the firestorm raging in the area where his school was located. The fire would have burned him up, so he had stepped away from it, into that other place, then back out by the river – his intended destination.

Or am I mad?

When he finally reached his home street, he found it

difficult to decide which part of the rubble mound had once been his house. He identified it only on recognizing Mr Hidachi standing in the street outside what had been his own house next door.

'Details are being investigated,' the man said. And, to Hiroshi's query concerning his own family, repeated, 'Details are being investigated.'

As he dug, Hiroshi found the head, neck and right arm of his mother, while the incinerated body of his father was only identifiable by his shoes. Something in Hiroshi's head just shut down then as he crouched amid the ruination. That night came and went, and in the morning thirst drove him back down to the river. Upon his return he thought he smelt grilled squid and his mouth watered, but following his nose only led him to a pile of corpses – most of them human, but occasionally dogs, cats and birds and a single cow swollen up like a balloon. Back in the rubble pile he made a nest for himself and chewed through a handful of dried rice. On his subsequent return to the river he found a floating bottle – the water he brought back from the river made eating the dried rice so much easier. As another night passed mother and father began to smell, so Hiroshi wrapped the rice in a cloth, took up the water bottle, and began to walk. He saw bewilderment all around him, and plainly written on the faces of soldiers clambering down from an armoured car when they saw the raggedy people coming out of the wreckage towards them. He heard the word '*hibakusha*' for the first time being directed at himself. He was now an 'explosion affected person' for no 'survivors' must besmirch the memory of the honoured dead.

Days passed, maybe a lot of days. There had been

nights, more horror to see, a big pale foreign man giving him a large hunk of chocolate. The war was over, he heard, Japan had lost. He felt he should respond to this with shame, but could only look about him with wonder as nature responded to the cataclysm with frantic, almost desperate growth. White, heavily scented feverfew sprouted everywhere as if the Earth offered up its own medicine for this ill. Hiroshi only realized he had moved outside the bounds of the city when he witnessed a strange scene occur below a charred tree flinging out its own green defences.

The two soldiers wore headbands so smudged with soot, the rising sun emblem was only just visible. The third man, a stiff old officer in a spotless uniform, knelt on the ground. One soldier stood right behind him with his sidearm drawn and held resting by his hip; the other stood a few paces away, calmly smoking a cigarette. The officer wiped a white cloth along his gleaming blade, up and down, up and down, polishing it. He then carefully wrapped the cloth around the section of sharp steel just beyond the handle. Hiroshi thought, *He is worried the blade might be dirty, and now he doesn't want to cut his fingers . . .*

The officer inverted the blade to his stomach and, grunting, drove it in. After a pause he pulled it sideways. He was making a strange nasal sound now and his head turned slightly. Hiroshi supposed that at this point the soldier behind should have shot him in the head. But the subordinate merely held the sidearm up, inspected it, then turned to his companion.

'We should take the sword,' he said. 'The Americans pay well for swords.'

The officer keeled over on his side. His thighs and the

entire front of his uniform were saturated with blood, and intestine bulged from the single wound. Shivering, he tried to bite down on his groans. The soldier stooped, tugged the sword away, cleaned the blood off with the same white cloth and placed it to one side. He then began to go through the officer's pockets and when the dying man tried to resist, pistol-whipped him until he stopped. He tossed a pack of cigarettes he found to his companion, who then also took up the sword. The first soldier pocketed other items, then after a moment he began tugging off the officer's boots, whereupon the second soldier kicked the officer over onto his back and pressed a foot down on his neck. Casually, almost negligently, he began using the tip of the sword to gouge out the dying man's eyes. At that moment the first soldier spotted Hiroshi watching, stared for a moment, then abruptly stood up and aimed his sidearm.

Hiroshi stepped aside into he knew not what – but which centuries hence would be called U-space. Shifting only slightly, he stepped out on what he later found to be the island of Osaka, and walked on.

He did not stop walking for a quarter of a century.

– retroact ends –

Only seconds passed aboard *Heliotrope*, then came that twisting sensation as the ship surfaced from U-space. All around lay jewelled stars, the largest visible object being an orange smudge amid blackness. Orlandine rechecked coordinates and dropped the ship out of existence once again, but only for fractions of a second more than previously. *Heliotrope* surfaced into realspace over an infinite ocean of orange gas, broken with rollers of red cloud and vast spreads of misty white like peeling skin. Orlandine ignited the fusion drive and dived in. Only as the ship penetrated the surface was it revealed how disperse was the gas – a thin fog. Again checking coordinates she oriented the ship, accelerated for an hour, then coasted for a further three. At the end of that time something like a vast steel cliff loomed out of the murk ahead of her.

Orlandine was no outlinker, but she had spent most of her life aboard stations or ships, surrounded by technology, and felt more comfortable in that environment. The ship, though just big enough to live in, was not a place in which she wanted to conduct dangerous experiments. However, in her present straits the idea of descending to a planetary surface was unthinkable – there being no quick escapes for her down there since a U-space drive could not be engaged until the ship lay clear of the gravity well. She chose an intermediate measure. And she chose a place she knew.

The diamond-shaped fragment, one of the first-constructed building blocks of the Cassius Dyson sphere, consisted of five layers of composite each a half-mile thick, the four-mile-wide gaps between each layer maintained by composite and bubble metal joists, some half a mile wide, braided carbon nanotube cables, massive gravmotors and hardfield generators powered by thousands of fusion reactors. In here there were 25 billion cubic miles in which to lose herself. Of course her intention, in making a U-space jump out of the system, had been to mislead any forensic AIs into thinking she had left the system completely. But, no, this was home to her: she was more familiar with every structure in this place than with any other place in or outside the Polity. Here she could hide most effectively.

She decelerated, hard, turning the *Heliotrope* so it rose up just beside the wall of composite. Sentinels inside the massive structure detected the ship, discounted it from being a meteorite and therefore offlined collision lasers. Those devices also registered the ship's presence, but were simple computers and therefore easy enough for Orlandine to access via her carapace. She erased their recent memories.

Within minutes the ship drew opposite one of the mile-wide gaps between layers. She kept it rising, up past another layer of composite, to where the murk began to thin, then turned it, decelerating again, so that the front screen faced into this final top gap running through the structure. With merely human vision, she could see just ten miles into the forest of massive slanted joists and cables before their number and the thickening murk entirely cut off vision. Using her sensory cowl to scan across the entire electromagnetic spectrum, and with her carapace linked into the ship's sensors, she could see right through to the other side – some 80,000 miles away. This place was awesome, always. How could she possibly leave it?

Orlandine eased the *Heliotrope* in past a vertical cable a hundred yards thick. Locating herself on a three-D map in her mind and by recourse to microwave beacons throughout the structure, she altered her course past a row of giant joists to which clung arboreal leviathans – generators, reactors, gravmotors. Through exterior sensors she noted the cloud her vessel was creating: the adjustments made by its thrusters causing ices to sublime, blowing up crystal sulphur and the numerous odd compounds that condensed here inside. The cloud would probably go unnoticed, but she slowed considerably and took more care with her course. An hour later, forty miles in, she sighted her destination.

The cylindrical pillar was a mile wide, and vertical rather than slanted like the joists. The inner structure of it, she knew to be almost ligneous. Each hexagonal-in-section cell stood about sixty feet from floor to ceiling, and thus the pillar contained thousands of them. It was for storage space, maybe living areas – that being something to be decided in the distant future – a general-purpose structure placed here prospectively, it being more convenient to do so while the entire segment was under construction. Orlandine brought the *Heliotrope* down to the base of the pillar, folded out the tips of each half of the ship's claw, and switched their inner faces to gecko function. She eased the ship forward until the claw's gecko surfaces bonded to the pillar face, then eased out the head of a plasma cutter from the rear of the claw. Reaching out with the cutter to the full extent of its triple-jointed arm, she began slicing a circle as far as feasible beyond where the claw tips bonded.

Carbon dioxide and water ice immediately sublimed from the pillar face. All around, in kaleidoscopic colour, fluorescence bloomed as complex ice made the transition to water ice and then into vapour. The cutter easily punched through the light sheetbubble metal – the structural strength here mainly derived from laminated composite beams evenly spaced throughout the pillar's interior. Eventually she finished cutting the circle, and with a delicate adjustment of the *Heliotrope*'s thrusters, she backed the ship away, extracting a fifty-foot disc of metal. Then, swinging the ship around, she reversed it into the gap. Utter darkness now, but she mapped every movement and action precisely in her extended haiman mind functioning through the ship's sensors. At the last she pressed the disc down against the bottom of the cut, and with a couple of stabs from the plasma torch, at its lowest setting, tacked it back into place. She then eased *Heliotrope* down to the floor of this hexagonal cell, which, with miles of composite layered below it, did possess a degree of gravity. However, that gravity level was low, so she extended the ship's gecko feet to stick it into place. Turning on exterior lights – not that she really needed them, just for comfort really, human comfort – she gazed around at her new home.

Resembling a burnished cylinder, the telefactor, resting in the wooden doorway, extended one of its numerous arms, and from the tip of this extruded a single tool which very quickly removed all the hinge screws. It then passed the door back to one of its fellows, which proceeded to wrap it in thin transparent monofabric before carrying it over to a stack of objects similarly sealed. Thorn glanced round at the dome that enclosed the entire house.

'I assume we'll be leaving the air at least,' he said sarcastically.

'But of course, though it is being run through filters right now,' Jack replied from Thorn's comlink.

Thorn scratched his beard and peered up at the dome roof, as if he might be able to see all the way beyond it to the AI and know if Jack was winding him up. 'How do we choose where to draw the line between what is, or is not, considered evidence?'

'She did not have much to do with anyone else here. I am presently loading all records of other arrivals and departures since her initial arrival – about ten years before Skellor came here. Aelvor's people are meanwhile taking statements from anyone she came into contact with. Masses of data is being collected, but there's a formula that forensic AIs apply to such situations which keeps evidential collection to manageable limits for the processing power available.'

Thorn watched the telefactor exit the doorway and rise up to the roof, where it began removing and bagging wooden shingles. It occurred to him now that there were definite advantages to being Sparkind rather than a Polity agent. As one of the elite combat groups, you just turned up on site and someone like Cormac pointed you in the right direction with simple instructions like, 'Kill them', or 'Blow up that'.

'Do we have anything at all yet?' he asked.

'Interesting question: we have a lot, but we don't know what will be of any use. I have set Aphran to analysing data as it comes in – she has been loading forensic cribs direct from the AI net ever since we found Jane von Hellsdorf. Aphran will be working through the chalet as well.'

The whole building was to be transported to the *NEJ*, along with much of the soil surrounding it. Thorn considered the way Jack was using Aphran. 'So Aphran is still useful.'

'She is.'

'And so survives. Or are you only finding uses for her while her consciousness remains entangled with yours?'

'I am in the process of unravelling that particular Gordian problem.'

'And then?'

'We shall see.'

Thorn let that slide. 'Does *she* have anything yet?'

'Ask her.'

Thorn hesitated for a moment, then asked, 'Aphran, do you have anything for me?'

After a long pause the erstwhile Separatist replied, her voice sounding distracted as if her attention lay elsewhere. 'There is a vast amount of informational evidence, and I cannot start on the physical evidence until it is delivered up here. But thus far it seems this world has been visited by suspicious characters in their thousands, including Skellor of course. I'm presently searching for anomalies that demonstrate a deliberate attempt at some kind of concealment. Then I have to eliminate various reasons for such concealment. I've eliminated six people so far – the last one was a Separatist woman who came here with an adapted version of an oak tree fungus. She apparently wandered off into the deep forest and has not been seen since. Aelvor informs me that she unfortunately fell into the rock crusher of an agrobot.'

'How remiss of her,' commented Thorn.

'It seems evident Aelvor does not like saboteurs.'

Thorn laughed then asked, 'What about Jane von Hellsdorf?'

It was Jack who now replied, 'One would suppose her bright enough not to try her own wares.'

'I rather assumed someone forced that aug upon her,' replied Thorn, turning away from the chalet and heading for the exit from the dome.

'Most certainly. Her Sensic aug was deliberately sabotaged to scramble her brains, and selling such augs herself she would certainly have known enough to run a diagnostic on it before fitting it.'

'Are we going to get anything out of her?'

'I may be able to glean something from a full memcord. Aelvor believes he will be able to make one by utilizing her present Sensic augmentation. I propose to allow him to try.'

Thorn stepped outside. The area was crowded now. A large AG vehicle had arrived first, containing all the equipment the Osterland monitor force might need to deal with a major incident. Now a couple of large airvans were also down, and numerous aircars. Uniformed monitors from the local police force had spread all around, conducting interviews, taking copies from all privately owned recording media. Scar had pulled his dracomen back into the woods at this stage; if their services were not required, they would return to their shuttle and head back to the *NEJ*.

Thorn studied a group of people gathered by one of the vans. It was not difficult to distinguish the haiman from the others. He faced away from Thorn, so all that could be seen of him was the ribbing of his metallic carapace, and a tongue of metal reaching up behind his head. Thorn strode over towards him. When he reached only a few paces behind Aelvor, the man turned and the same tongue of metal fanned out behind his head, opening out the petals of his sensory cowl. After a moment they closed up again and Aelvor grinned.

'Agent Thorn, a pleasure to meet you at last.' He held out his hand.

Aelvor's black hair was plaited in a queue that ran down over one shoulder. He was bulky but not fat, one of his eyes was green and the other displayed metallic shifting orthogonal patterns. Thorn shook the proffered hand, felt a restrained strength, and noted the extra gleaming metal limbs folded down on either side of the man's torso.

'Likewise,' said Thorn. 'I could get used to this place you're making here.'

'Consider it just a beginning. The human race has spent thousands of years standardizing everything, and the AIs continue in much the same vein. The reasons for that have all been valid, but now we possess the technology to expand individuality and the unique.'

'More than one way of skinning a cat,' Thorn observed.

'What an obscene expression,' said Aelvor. He glanced about himself rather theatrically. 'And talking of obscenity: where is she then?'

Thorn supposed Aelvor had asked that question out of simple politeness – the haiman probably knew intimately the name and personal history of everyone within a radius of a hundred miles, and their positions to within a square yard. He pointed to the incident vehicle and led the way across. Shortly the two of them entered the vehicle's medical centre to stand over von Hellsdorf's bed. She lay utterly motionless. An autodoc clung to her side with its various tubes and implements penetrating her torso. At the head of the bed one of Jack's telefactors stood motionless – a large cylinder bristling with multipurpose limbs. Von Hellsdorf's aug casing hung open, its guts revealed, and the telefactor held numerous microoptic feeds in place within it.

'Okay, let's get to it, shall we?' said Aelvor. With a shrug he extended his own two additional metal limbs. Thorn noted incredibly complex hands on them consisting of two sets of three opposing fingers, selector discs for multiple optic and s-con interfaces, and a telescoping device that appeared to end in just a very sharp spike, but which he knew to be the presenting head for micro-manipulators – the rear section probably containing thousands of different micro-tools. With 'hands' like those Aelvor could probably remove von Hellsdorf's brain through her ear and reassemble it outside her head.

As Aelvor moved in the telefactor immediately withdrew its connection to the woman's aug.

'The Sensic's definition is not the finest but, through its synaptic links, it should be possible to run a memory-search program. Unfortunately from her we'll now only get mnemonically associated fragments – there'll be no chronological order to them.' He now made connection with his extra limbs to von Hellsdorf's aug. 'You may get a few seconds of childhood where she, say, picks up an apple and bites it. The next fragment may equally be her eating another apple, seeing some child from the perspective of adulthood, or being bitten on the tit by a lover.'

'Curiously, I do know what mnemonic means,' observed Thorn.

Aelvor grinned, 'Of course you do, but with most of my processes running a thousand times faster than . . . normal, I find I have to make a deliberate effort to communicate by ordinary speech, so I overcompensate. You do realize Jack could easily do what I'm now doing, but AIs are very chary of the haiman inferiority complex and so like us to be included.'

Jack's voice then spoke from the telefactor. 'Your inferiority complex seems sadly lacking today, Aelvor . . . Incidentally, I have just monitored an adrenal surge in the patient.'

'Memory fragment,' said the haiman. 'She just recalled a particularly protracted orgasm.'

Thorn noted how the patterns in Aelvor's abnormal eye were flickering and changing.

'Increase in salivary amylase, and stomach acids,' Jack noted.

'Crab paste on toast,' Aelvor explained.

'Heart rate high, enzymic—'

The woman was suddenly covered in sweat, then the capillaries in her skin turned bright red. One of the telefactor's arms swept down, knocking away Aelvor's connection. Thorn felt something slam into his chest and throw him back.

Hardfield . . .

He hit the wall and slid down. Subliminally he saw the same thing happen to Aelvor. Smoke boiling from the ceiling revealed a laser stabbing up from the telefactor. It reached out blindingly fast, its manipulators hooked under the woman's armpits, dragged her upright, then with her it rocketed through the hole it had cut. The ensuing blast bowed the ceiling, and a column of fire washed down through the hole. Shortly after, the telefactor crashed back through, blackened, its shell buckled. Very little remained of Jane von Hellsdorf. The air stank of burning bacon.

The *Jerusalem* dropped out of U-space and cruised into the Cull system. In his own quarters Cormac called up the required views on his screen, and once again looked upon his old adversary. Then, whilst he observed Dragon hanging manacled over the ice giant, he cleared his mind and tried to find the gaps in his memory of events here. He recalled Skellor taking control of the local population and using them as hostages to ensure Cormac's own surrender. He recalled being a prisoner in some Jain substructure aboard the *Ogygian* – the colony ship that had originally taken Cull's inhabitants there from Earth. He recollected being utterly under Skellor's control, but then things started to get a little fragmentary. He knew Cento had concealed himself aboard the *Ogygian* and, while a kill program in that ancient ship's computer held Skellor in thrall, the Golem sabotaged the drive to bring that ship into an inescapable orbit around a brown dwarf. The *King of Hearts* – a rebel AI attack ship – had then fired grapples onto the *Ogygian*, and while Cento held onto Skellor, Cormac went out to sever them. Somehow he ended up on one of those grapples, and the *King*'s AI, rather than killing him for preventing it obtaining the Jain tech that Skellor possessed, had released him to deliver a message to Jerusalem: *Honest, I didn't get any, don't hunt me down and kill me*. But how did Cormac himself escape from that Jain substructure inside *Ogygian*?

Cormac could only assume that Cento must have released him from the enclosing structure, but something still bothered him about that. He closed his eyes and linked into Jerusalem's servers, then created a search program to find himself there. Jerusalem had recorded him, repaired his brain, then downloaded that recording back to his repaired brain. Cormac felt certain the AI retained a copy . . . *and there it was*.

'You will find that difficult to access,' warned Jerusalem from the intercom in his quarters. 'Your gridlink does not possess the capacity to sort out that mess.'

'My mind is a mess?'

'All human minds are a mess. Your gridlink is designed to access computer and AI systems, which are formatted much more logically. Anyway, since it is your own mind that you are attempting to look into, you will be in danger of cerebral feedback and might well end up in a psychotic loop.'

'Well, then, you do it for me. I want to retrieve a mem-cording covering the time from my arrival at the brown dwarf up to when I ended up on that grapple.'

'I fail to see why.'

Drily, Cormac stated, 'Memory is something past, but experiencing a memcording is current.'

Jerusalem made no reply to that, but the link was made and the memcording flowed across. Cormac loaded it, experienced it. The first time through was hard for him, since the survival mechanism of memory always dulled the pain and the sickness originally experienced. The second time through, he saw it:

He fired five times into Skellor's head, forcing the man back against the wall. Not enough though – Skellor was no longer human. Two shots to the chest, more to the knees as he tried to spring, and a hand blown apart as it pressed against the wall. Then Cento, scissoring his legs around Skellor's waist, was tearing away wall panels to embrace a beam behind.

'The cables,' Cento urged over com.

Another clip into the gun. Back towards the blown screen . . . and there, at the corner of his vision, Jain substructure formed around the shape of a man rooted to the floor, its shell unbroken but no man inside it.

I was inside.

'I would like to believe,' said Cormac out loud, 'that it is just an unfortunate accident that so critical a part of my memory is missing, but I am by nature a suspicious person.'

Jerusalem replied, 'Your mind needs to heal further before it can accept that. It is something you did that you do not comprehend.'

'Return it to me.'

'I cannot. The human mind is a fragile structure at best. The memory of what you did then could be like the inverse of a keystone, especially with your mind in its present condition.'

'I didn't think I was that bad.'

'Why do you think it has taken you so long to start reviewing your memories of that time? Doubtless the explanation to yourself is that only *now* are those memories relevant to your coming encounter with Dragon.'

Cormac wanted to sneer at that suggestion, but found he could not. Instead he said, 'Can you at least tell me, in general, what I did?'

'Oh yes: you used your own mind to translate your body through U-space,' Jerusalem replied.

Cormac went cold. He shivered. That was purportedly what Horace Blegg could do, but Cormac no longer believed Blegg to be what he claimed. Could he be wrong about that? But he just could not encompass what Jerusalem had told him and felt himself teetering on the brink of some abyss. He tried to dismiss it, to focus on the now.

'Is there anything else you are keeping from me?' he asked.

Immediately another memcording arrived.

'What is this?' asked Cormac, not daring to open it.

'To control you, Skellor linked into your mind, but as a consequence you were partially linked into his. This is something you picked up from there – his memory of how he actually obtained his Jain node.'

Cormac viewed it, experienced it: as if he himself stood upon the platform on Osterland and received from Jane von Hellsdorf a Jain node for the bargain price of ten shillings.

'I should have known about this. This needs following up.'

'Thorn, some dracomen, and a strange amalgam of the *Jack Ketch* AI with a dead woman called Aphran, are already investigating. You are not yet stable enough for that kind of mission.'

Cormac reluctantly accepted that.

'Jack and Aphran . . .'

Even as he spoke he sought information via the *Jerusalem*'s servers: the original *Jack Ketch* had been destroyed fighting rebellious AI warships, including the *King of Hearts*, but Jack's mind was retrieved by Dragon, whom Jerusalem finally caught up with in orbit of the brown dwarf where Skellor and Cento died. Then Dragon's meek surrender and return to the Cull system, some kind of bartering enacted at fast AI speeds, with the result that Dragon gave up the ship mind, then the huge band manufactured by Jerusalem and placed around Dragon's equator – a guarantee that Dragon would not try to use the gravitic weapons it contained in some escape attempt.

Cormac returned his attention to the screen. *Focus!*

Dragon must now answer some hard questions for there were clear links between it, the Makers, and Jain tech arising here in the Polity. Cormac needed to decide what those questions should be, and how far he was prepared to go to obtain answers.

★

Thorn rested with his back against an oak tree and waited. He observed Scar, pacing back and forth next to the dome. The dracomen had come back in during the night, obviously bored with waiting. Thorn's own training made him very patient, and his experience enabled him to value brief moments of peace during any operation. It gave him time to appreciate things like trees, the starlit sky fading into misty morning, trees, the cool air on his face, more fucking trees.

Those down on the planet had gathered many holocordings and after deep analysis of them, usually of the background, Aphran discovered that three people had visited Jane von Hellsdorf. One of these Aphran picked up in an aug recording, and another in publicity shots taken of the village. The first one Aelvor's monitors identified as a dissatisfied customer come to complain, and the second as another stallholder come to sell von Hellsdorf his old stock. Both were apprehended and now being questioned by monitors. But in the end what Aphran did not find proved to be of most interest. One of the residents in Oakwood had made holocordings of a barbecue, and in the background a krodorman – a heavy G 'dapt to one particularly swampy world – showed up knocking on von Hellsdorf's door. Analysis of the thousands of samples found at the scene revealed no trace of krodorman DNA. This person had left no physical trace of herself – for the figure was female – and they needed to know why.

'We have her,' Aphran announced finally, as the sun began to disperse the mist. 'The Parliament Hotel on Cockleshell Street.'

Thorn stood and began heading for his aircar. 'Is she still there?'

'She has been a resident in the hotel for two months, has not yet checked out, but is not presently in her room – the hotel security system has not registered the door to her room being opened in the last two days – ever since we arrived here, in fact. It would seem that, immediately upon our arrival, she paid a visit to Jane von Hellsdorf, forced that aug upon her, then disappeared.'

Scar reached the passenger door of the aircar just as Thorn climbed inside. The dracoman growled low as he shoved the seat back and clambered into the cramped space, putting his feet up on the dashboard. Thorn stared at him for a moment, shrugged resignedly, then took the aircar into the sky. He glanced back and down to see two monitor aircars and two of Jack's telefactors following him.

'Jack,' he said, opening his comlink to the ship AI, 'have you yet figured out what caused Ms von Hellsdorf to explode?'

The AI replied, 'A combination of four enzymes released from her liver the moment she experienced an adrenal surge – which became inevitable once someone started delving into her mind. The enzymes instantly began converting her body fat to nitroglycerine.'

'Why do that? Killing her beforehand would have kept her secrets safe.'

'Obviously taking out any investigators nearby would hamper their enquiries. It is the kind of thing done by those who consider ECS personnel as viable targets.'

'Separatists,' Thorn replied, stating the obvious.

Jack went on, 'It is a well-tested methodology to use booby traps to target specialists among what is considered the enemy. In the Second World War the Nazis dropped bombs specifically designed to kill those sent to defuse them . . . And now my search has revealed that Separatist cells around Krodor have used this method many times.'

'All very neat,' said Thorn. 'Tell me, Aphran, what do you think?'

'You mean with my deep experience of Separatist methods?' she replied bitterly.

'Yes, precisely that.'

'It makes sense. The prime target for any Separatist is an AI, as they are the direct subordinates of the Earth Central autocrat – sorry Jack – and after that we . . . *they* will go to great lengths to kill ECS agents. The likes of yourself are considered prime targets because not only do you serve the autocrat, you are considered traitors to the human race.'

Clear of the mist the aircar glinted in orange-hued sunshine. Soon the main town lay below and Thorn began to ease the car down towards the streets. He checked his palm-com – now lying open and stuck to the dashboard beside Scar's right foot – identified Cockleshell Street and headed for it.

'Let's suppose, then,' said Thorn, 'that a Separatist organization learnt, by whatever means, that ECS would soon be taking an interest in Jane von Hellsdorf.'

'Then I would expect no less than an entire combat group turning up down there,' Aphran replied.

Thorn grimaced to himself, having already worked out the coming scenario. He decided that landing in Cockleshell Street itself would not be such a good idea, and chose a thoroughfare adjacent to it, but still in view of the hotel.

'Jack, the entire hotel and surrounding buildings need to be cleared.'

'I have already informed Osterland and Aelvor.'

Of course Jack was ahead of him – that's how AIs were.

The message obviously got through because the front doors opened and people began emerging. The two other aircars landed in the street behind Thorn's vehicle, but the two telefactors held station up in the sky. Four monitors came past the car and headed towards the growing crowd before the hotel. There followed some gesticulation and shouting, but the evacuated people began moving on down the street.

'Jack, Fethan gave me a little gift before I departed Cull: one of Jerusalem's HK programs.'

'Yes, I know,' the AI replied.

Thorn tilted his head and asked, 'Aphran, if you yourself planted an explosive device here, in this situation, how would you detonate it?'

'Net feed. I'd connect it to some com system. The signal would be untraceable. Or I would have assumed so.'

'But you would need a spotter of some kind, otherwise how would you know *when* to detonate?'

'I would either connect the device to something only an ECS agent might try to access – secure storage or something locked like a safe – or I would use a cam system, probably activated by movement, and routed through the same net feed.'

'Jack, through your telefactors can you scan for a cam inside the hotel?'

'I have already done so,' the AI replied. 'There are two holocameras located in the suspect's room, linked by optic cables into the room's netlink.'

'Presumably there are other optic cables in the room too?'

'No, our suspect has been much smarter than that: planar explosives packed into a standard lamp – the lamp itself to be activated by an infrared signal from the netlink rather than an optic cable. The lamp has been deliberately raised to head height, the intention being to not only kill, but to destroy any cerebral hardware designed to save anything of the victim's mind – a subtle touch.'

Thorn reached into his pocket and took out the memstore. 'Would this HK be able to track the cam signals?'

'Why not ask it?' Jack suggested.

Thorn then remembered Fethan saying the hunter-killer program did not talk much. So it could talk, then.

'Can you hear me?'

The device vibrated in his hand.

'I hear,' replied a flat inflection-free voice. Scar peered at the memstore for a moment, then sniffed dismissively.

'Then you heard what we were discussing. Can you track cam signals through a netlink?'

'I can.'

Thorn detached his palm-com from the dash and rested it in his lap. He tapped an icon to open its netlink, and with a brief local search closed the connection to the Parliament Hotel. He then pulled out the strip along the lower edge of the touch-console to reveal multiple sockets: optic, nano-tube optic, s-con whiskered, crystal interface, and even a socket that could adapt itself to primitive electrical connections. As he picked it up, the memstore, like a clam sliding out its foot, immediately extruded an optic plug from one of its end ports. Thorn inserted this into the requisite socket.

'Of course, we need a way to activate the cameras,' Thorn commented, while watching the hotel's web display flickering, then breaking up into squares, before blanking out totally.

'Copy loaded,' said the box.

'Are you volunteering?' Jack enquired of Thorn.

'Not likely,' said Thorn. 'The cam signal might not be enough, but the program should certainly be able to follow the detonation signal.' He paused for a moment. 'Erm . . . HK, have you wrecked this palm-com?'

The com screen came back on, displaying the city map Thorn had used before landing.

'Can you display where you track the source to?'

'I can,' HK replied.

'Jack,' said Thorn, 'send in a telefactor. The watcher will know he's been blown and won't be able to get a human target with his bomb, but he won't be able to resist taking out such a costly piece of Polity hardware instead.'

Even as Thorn spoke, one of the telefactors dropped down in front of the hotel. After a moment he observed something shoot out from it to hit a chainglass bubble window.

Decoder mine.

The missile stuck for a second, then the window abruptly collapsed into dust. As the telefactor cruised inside, immediately the walls either side of the window blew outwards, ahead of a disc of flame. Rubble crashed down into the street, followed by the top half of the telefactor itself.

'My supply of telefactors is limited,' Jack observed.

Thorn glanced down at the palm-com, just as the HK grated, 'Located.'

On the map displayed, a square frame shrank down to a dot. It took half a second for Thorn to realize it lay right next to where he was parked.

'Out!' he shouted, grabbing up his pulse-rifle from the passenger foot-well below Scar's legs. He and the dracoman piled out just as shots slammed into the car roof.

Thorn hit the cobbles, rolled, and came up locating the source of the shots. A chainglass bubble window had revolved halfway down into the wall, revealing a small open balcony. Thorn aimed at the figure standing up there, but hesitated and it disappeared. He damned himself – he had already checked that the weapon was set to stun. Now he fired freely, electrical stun discharges spreading small lightnings all over the balcony. Scar was up and moving on the other side of the car. The dracoman slammed into a street door, slapped something against it, swung aside with his back to the wall. An entry charge detonated, hurling the crumpled composite door inwards – and Scar followed it in.

'Jack!' Thorn bellowed. 'Factor!'

The telefactor descended on him like a falling rock. He felt a strange lightness and twisting sensation as its AG field came over him. Reaching up he grabbed one of its limbs. A second limb closed about his chest.

'Drop me on the balcony. Then you take the roof!'

As the telefactor brought him up level with the balcony, Thorn fired into the room beyond, then kicked himself off from the machine's skin just as it released him. His foot came down once on the balcony platform, then he dived straight into the room beyond and rolled. A figure to his left, something bouncing across the floor. Thorn surged to his feet and flung himself through the nearest doorway. He kicked the bedroom door shut, dived for the bed, grabbing up the edge of the mattress as he went and pulling it over him. The subsequent blast slammed him into a fitted wardrobe and, when he peered out from behind the mattress, the door was gone, along with most of the partition wall. Wisps of insulating foam floated through the air, and something was burning. As he climbed out over rubble, he targeted an object moving through the smoke, but then identified it as a small spherical robot on four skinny legs, which was spraying fire suppressant at a pool of sticky liquid burning on the floor. He headed for the door through which he had seen the figure retreat, and cautiously peered round it. His head jerked back just in time as something smashed into the door jamb. His comunit began vibrating against his breastbone – security signal. Thorn pulled out the comunit's earpiece and placed it in his ear.

'Three . . . of them,' Scar immediately alerted him, his sibilant voice only just audible over a constant crackling. 'Two heading for the roof, and one below . . . us . . . between us . . . autogun . . . corridor.'

'I know about the autogun,' Thorn replied, then asked, 'Jack, what's this interference?'

'EM emitter,' the AI replied.

'That's why it missed me.'

Thorn glanced around the room and focused on the robot. The autogun would not be very sophisticated, as Separatists hated anything with even a hint of AI to it. He stepped back, raising the setting of his pulse-rifle to its maximum, then he picked up the robot and tossed it into the corridor ahead of him. Immediately a projectile weapon began firing, smashing holes into the floor as the robot rose up on its legs. Thorn leaned round the door-jamb. The gun was mounted on a tripod: a servo-aimed belt-fed machine gun with a simple motion detector mounted on top. He aimed at it and fired in one, then quickly ducked back under cover as the gun's ammo box exploded and filled the corridor with shrapnel. As he darted out into the corridor, he saw the fire robot, completely unharmed, returning diligently to its task.

Reaching a stairwell, Thorn knocked his weapon back down to stun. Just then an explosion shook the entire building.

'They carry grenades and will die rather than be captured,' Scar informed him.

'Problem?' Thorn enquired.

'It will wash off.'

Jack now added, 'The other two are on the top floor, one level up from you. I think they spotted the telefactor.'

Thorn began climbing the stairs, his weapon aimed straight up at the half-landing. This was not a good place to be if someone decided to toss a grenade down, but they had no time for delay if these people would prefer to die rather than be captured. No one visible on the stairs. Reaching the top he peered through an open arch and saw that the top floor contained a swimming pool, some gym equipment, and an old-style VR suit suspended in gimbals. Potted palms offered some cover, as did low partitions around the bar area beyond.

'I don't fucking think so!' someone shouted suddenly.

A pulse-gun fired and a figure spun out from behind a pillar and landed in the pool. Then came the detonation, blowing the same figure up out of the water in tatters, drenching the chainglass ceiling and all surroundings. Thorn quickly moved in – only one opponent left here. He spotted Scar running in from the other side of the pool, levelled his weapon. The ceiling abruptly transformed into a white shower of debonded chainglass as the remaining telefactor dropped through. A black gloved hand speared out from behind the pillar, suspending on one finger a gas-system pulse-gun by its trigger guard.

'Okay, you've got me!'

The gun clattered to the floor and a woman with cropped brown hair stepped out from behind the pillar, her arms held out from her sides, gloved hands wide open. Thorn considered stunning her anyway, but the shattered body in the pool told him all he needed to know. Aphran's voice, issuing from the telefactor, confirmed this:

'Freyda, I take it you are not quite prepared to die for the cause?'

5

The Sparkind are an elite ECS military force, given a name derived from the Spartans (citizens of an ancient Greek city who were noted for their military prowess, austerity and discipline), though they cannot trace their ancestry back so far. Sparkind are rather the direct descendants of the Special Forces that came into being during the Earth-bound wars towards the end of the second millennium: the Special Boat Service, the Special Air Service, Navy SEALS and the like. Candidates for the Sparkind must first serve five years in conventional military or police service. Their ensuing training program, both in reality and virtuality, is not designed to weed out the physically unable, because with today's boosting and augmentation technologies, anyone can be physically able. But a certain strength of mind is sought: will, a toughness of spirit and a degree of wisdom. A Sparkind has to know what he, she or it is fighting for, has to be able to make life and death decisions, and has to be trusted with weapons capable of annihilating entire cities. Operating in four-person units, usually consisting of two Golem and two humans, they have been involved in some of the most violent and dangerous actions the Polity has ever faced. But the Sparkind, though

*an elite fighting force, are usually never the first in. Which
brings me to the ECS agent, or Polity Agent . . .*
                              – From her lecture 'Modern Warfare'
                                      by EBS Heinlein

The latest eruption dumped a layer of ash an inch thick,
pocked with large spatters of cooling magma. Blegg
stepped down off one of the ceramal beams glued in
a gridwork across the Atheter artefact, stooped, and
brushed away more ash. The cutting machines inevitably
left swirls of stone stuck all over the surface since they
had been programmed to hold back from actually digging into the object itself. However, some stone flaked
away by itself to reveal translucent green crystal underneath. Blegg considered what all this meant.

This green substance was some form of memcrystal
similar to that used in the Polity today. The most basic
form of memcrystal – the sort that did not use crystal-
interstice quantum processing, or etched-atom processing as it was sometimes called – could still store huge
amounts of information. Just a piece of such a memcrystal the size of the last joint of a man's thumb could
model the function of and store the memories of a
human mind over a period of twenty-five years – though
those who possessed memplants would upload more
often than that just to keep their Soulbank copy up to
date, thereby freeing up space in the crystal implanted
inside their heads. If only of that kind, what could a
single mass of crystal this size potentially contain? The
mind of a god? The stock market transactions of an entire
galactic civilization? Alien porn tapes and family albums?
Atheter blogs?

With information technologies it was accepted that

crap naturally expands to fill the space available – that recording media and the media it recorded always somehow outpaced memory storage. The whole new science of information archaeology was based on that truism. But this object was alien, so everything it contained would be new, unfamiliar and worthy of lengthy study. Even information that would be considered dross in human storage would inevitably reveal things never before known about the constructors of this huge item.

Blegg stood up and looked around. The recent eruption streaked smoke across the lemon firmament, and a river of magma thrashed past some way to his left. He turned, remounted the beam and headed back towards his shuttle, which rested like a large grey slug on a rubble mound at the giant crystal's edge. As he reached the beam end, a shadow fell across him. He glanced up to see the tug arriving: a manta-shaped behemoth.

He stood and watched as cables rappelled down from it, lowering spiderish grabs. These grabs hit the surface then scuttled along to grip large U-shaped lugs welded to the beams, then the cables drew taut. The entire artefact began vibrating – the gravmotors underneath it starting up. He stepped from it at that point, scrambling up the rubble slope to his shuttle's airlock. Inside he waited as a blast of frigid air brought the exterior of his hotsuit down to a manageable temperature, then opened his shimmer-shield visor as he entered the shuttle's interior. He dropped into the pilot's seat and studied the scene outside. The artefact was rising now, but the impression given was of his own vessel sinking. Feeling the shuttle readjust its landing gear on the rubble below it, he engaged AG and lifted it a few yards into the poisonous air. Soon the artefact became a black line cutting from right to left. Fumaroles ejecting sulphurous gas clouded the view underside for a while, but that soon cleared to reveal the gravmotors attached beneath it. Keeping his shuttle positioned to one side, Blegg followed the huge object up into the sky. Other observers joined him – grabships from the station, telefactors, and floating holocams recording every instant of this ascent.

As the artefact rose through the acidic atmosphere it left a trail of ash and then, as the air pressure began to drop, volatiles complemented this trail with poisonous vapours. Five hours later, when the artefact lay only a mile away from the *Hourne*, all the ash and volatiles were gone. The tug released its grabs, wound in its cables and drew away. Now the grabships moved in to delicately clamp their claws onto the crystal rim. Very slowly and very carefully, they eased the artefact through a gap in the *Hourne*'s skin, and into a large enclosed space where shock-absorbing jacks closed in on its surface. Even as Blegg brought his shuttle back round the giant ship, he observed suited figures and telefactors shifting plates of hull metal to weld into place and seal the entry gap.

When Blegg returned inside to stand at a viewing blister overlooking the artefact, the beams used to brace it were being removed and beetlebots were busy scouring the crystal surface of the last layers of accreted stone. Around the internal chamber's perimeter, multiheaded optic interfaces were waiting on telescopic rams ready to be pushed into position. Back in the ship itself, haiman, human and Golem scientists, and the *Hourne*'s AI, were awaiting that crucial moment of connection with something of an alien race believed long dead.

– retroact 3 –

Despite this place having been pounded into rubble, some remnants of the Reich here still fought on. The jeep lay sideways in the dust, its engine screaming and one rear wheel spinning madly, the driver's headless corpse now draped over a nearby pile of rubble. A long spatter of blood linked vehicle to body. Herman – as he now called himself – walked a little closer to see if he could locate the head.

Ah, there . . .

It lay in the middle of the track bulldozed through the ruins, directly below the lethal wire strung across. As Herman moved closer he observed four German boys clambering down the pile of rubble to loot the headless corpse. They managed to get away with some chocolate, condoms, a wallet and an automatic pistol.

'There's another one coming!' shouted a fair-haired boy, and they all scrabbled from view.

Herman wondered if they themselves had set the wire, and if this ploy had really proved worth the effort. It never occurred to him to question how he could under-stand their language, any more than he questioned his ability to traverse the non-region of U-space around the planet. Nor his intrinsic understanding of the events unfolding upon that planet. He was only a boy, yet he knew about that million-degree eye that had opened over Hiroshima. He was a boy yet he understood what had happened in that forest-bound camp where now the perimeter wires and posts lay bulldozed into heaps and the long sheds burned to ash, and where still a stinking miasma rose from the mass graves.

Another jeep arrived. This time with an upright steel bar bolted to the vehicle, which snapped the wire just as the right front wheel rode over the previous visitor's dusty detached head. The jeep turned and slid sideways to a stop, as the two passengers jumped out cocking M2 carbines. Herman stepped away, half a mile this time, to reappear just outside a courthouse. A little later an American gave him chocolate, peering with a puzzled expression at his asiatic features. Over the ensuing weeks Herman tried copying such expressions, concentrating on manipulating the muscles in his face. Only after the judges arrived did he realize, after seeing his reflection in a shard of mirror, how unreasonably successful he had been. Thereafter he unwrapped the filthy bandage he had bound around over the top of his head and running underneath his chin.

Getting inside the courtroom was not possible at first, but he picked up so much by just listening and lurking around. In this way he learned about the film to be shown as evidence. Upon hearing instructions given to the guards about having to put out the lights, he managed to transport himself inside at precisely the right time. No one there noticed him: their eyes riveted to the screen and many of them quietly crying. He wept then for his parents, for the horror of the world, and for the lot of a humanity he no longer felt a part of. And with a wholly adult relish he sometime later transported himself to a spot nearby to watch a stiff old gentleman in a baggy uniform, climb with shaking legs some wooden stairs to have his neck snapped at the end of a rope.

– retroact ends –

After detaching her carapace from the interface sphere, Orlandine stepped out of it and headed aft, through the living quarters, through a hold space packed with equipment, and into a storage chamber for haiman tools. She needed more than one set of hands for this job, and that's where they were available.

Within the chamber, four assister frames were racked. Ignoring them for the moment she found a lightweight spacesuit adapted to haiman requirements and donned it, then she approached the first of the frames. This contrivance hung in its rack just like a spider carcase fashioned of silvery metal. She backed into the body space designed to accommodate her carapace, felt the numerous locks and optic plugs engaging, and her own control software coming online. One arm, human in length and terminating in four fingers, came up underneath her right arm, locking soft clamps above and below her elbow and just above her wrist. Now, essentially, her right arm possessed eight fingers – four of them metal. The pseudo arm that now connected to her left arm terminated in a three-fingered clamp over a micro-manipulator and s-con and optic interface head. Pseudo limbs simultaneously clamped themselves down each leg. These terminated in large three-digited claws protruding backwards from her ankles, which were usually used to anchor a haiman in place while working in zero-G. Folding out at a point just above her midriff were two additional arms, terminating in hands each with two opposable thumbs. She extended one of these out in front of her, wiggling its metal fingers. Now she was totally haiman.

This transformation was a psychological thing, related to ego and self-image. With just her carapace engaged, though her mind became larger and more extensive – capable of processing information like an AI and able to handle multiple tasks – it only extended from the two-legged two-armed ape. The next step was opening her sensory cowl. The moment she did that, the 'ware loaded to handle multiple sensory inputs: she could perceive radio, infrared, ultraviolet, microwave, detect complex molecules in the air . . . But still she remained psychologically no more than a human using tools; peering through a nightsight, binoculars, whatever. But the assister frame's 'ware undermined her self-image in a way that seemed integral to her being. Her metal fingers were as touch-sensitive as her organic ones. She knew their position, their relation to each other and to her own soft self; her micro-tools were sensitive to textures not far above the atomic. She became the goddess Kali and the all-seeing Watchmaker combined.

Am I insane? some part of her wondered. But it was a very small part indeed.

Initiating detach, she stepped away from the support frame, then scuttled insectlike to the airlock. Once outside she clung to the hull and looked around. With her cowl spread, her surroundings seemed as bright as day from the residual infrared emitted from the ship's thrusters and the further fluorescing of complex ices nearby.

The cell she had entered was a hundred yards across, its six walls nearing sixty feet high. Orlandine pushed herself from the hull and dropped slowly towards the floor. Making contact with it, she began walking away from the ship with a steady floating gait. In a moment she realized that the low gravity here would prove an inconvenience. If she moved everywhere like this, it would take her forever to get anything done. Using the enhancement of her legs she leapt forwards, hitting one of the walls ten yards up but absorbing the shock through her other enhanced limbs. As she dropped down beside the wall surface she studied it contemplatively, turning to look back at the *Heliotrope* only as her feet connected with the floor. This chamber she would prepare first for the rapid escape of the ship, and perhaps in time she could convert it for her own comfort. She would pressurize it and insulate it, maybe move out of the ship itself. In the wall behind her she would cut a hole and construct an airlock, and the cell beyond would then become her laboratory. That would be perfect. The Jain node would sit between clamps right in the middle of it: the focus of every resource she could muster.

Aphran considered the facts of her life, if it could be called that. Even though she was a second generation recording of the original Aphran, a sentence of erasure hung over her because of the crimes that original one had committed. No claim of being a changed person, of having understood the error of her ways, of now being prepared to actively support the Polity, would change that. Aphran had murdered people, hundreds of people, and nothing she could now say or do would bring them back. Her sentence remained suspended only because ECS currently found her knowledge very useful, and because she had become intertwined so closely with Jack that her erasure might damage him in the process. But Jack was slowly untangling himself from her, and her usefulness to ECS was decreasing. She was a dead woman, and felt sure she would soon be a non-existent one.

Tracking Freyda as she came aboard, Aphran recog-

nized another walking dead woman. Their captive wore
a security collar which could paralyse her in a second, or
blast a toxin straight into her carotids. She strode with a
kind of arrogance, ahead of the bobbing telefactor, and
Aphran knew Freyda probably thought she could get
through this using just nerve and lies. Soon she would
have to wake up to reality. Jack had appointed Aphran to
the task of administering the cold shower.

'And not a krodorman in sight,' Aphran murmured.

'Aelvor's people have yet to make a search,' Jack
replied, 'but none are listed in crew or on any passenger
manifests of arrivals within the time frame.'

'They won't find any,' interjected Thorn, over com
from the planet below.

'Perhaps you could explain, Thorn?' Aphran enquired
though, knowing Freyda, she knew what Thorn's answer
would be.

Freyda looked up and around, almost as if hearing
part of this com exchange. Impossible of course. Perhaps
she wondered why Aphran had not come to greet her the
moment she boarded. When she eventually found out
why, that would be the first shock.

'There *was* no krodorman. That's why you found no
krodorman DNA at the scene. I'll bet you found
syntheflesh at von Hellsdorf's place that'll match samples in the hotel. She simply wore a krodorman suit . . .
By the way, Aphran, what's your history with her?'

Reluctantly she replied, 'She recruited me to the Separatist cause on Corolon.'

Aphran and her two sisters were each born from different fathers, but that was nothing unusual in the Corolon
arcologies. She remembered the three of them playing
together in the enclosed arboretums, in the shopping malls

and sometimes in the rooftop fields. But best of all were the secret places of the sprawling city: the tunnels and niches, the air ducts and hollows through which spread forests of cables and pipes. It probably all started with them when the latest game became 'break it and see how quickly the robots can fix it'. Enger obtained an electric saw with ceramocarbide teeth, and not being the most incandescent lightstrip on the block, she found and cut into a superconducting cable. There seemed little point sending what remained to the crematorium. Aphran and Arial then blamed the robots. Arial, the eldest, was caught destroying three welding robots, and, while pursued by monitors, fell down a ventilation cavity. She survived but, after they bone-welded her skull back together she was never quite the same again: never wanted to play those same destructive games any more. Aphran believed the AIs had tampered with her brain. So when, a few years later, Freyda approached Aphran to recruit her to the Separatist cause, she knew she had at last found her place in the universe. Only in later years did she realize that after fighting for the cause for so long, a love of death and carnage had displaced Freyda's initial idealism. Aphran now recognized the blindness of her earlier self: Freyda representing what Aphran herself had become before her physical death.

The cell Jack had prepared for their prisoner was unfurnished, deliberately claustrophobic, the lighting too bright. If Freyda wanted to sleep, or even just sit down, the cold ceramal floor would have to suffice. As the door closed behind Freyda, Aphran allowed the woman a little time to contemplate her present situation.

'No reservations?' Jack asked her, coldly dispassionate.

'None at all,' she replied, trying to believe that completely.

Machines first, just like those she had destroyed as a child, but now she was working with more effective tools. Freyda taught her all about explosives: which ones to use in what situations and how to maximize their destructive effect. Aphran learnt impatiently – she wanted to do something soon about the injustice done to her two sisters. Obviously it was all the fault of the AIs. Why wasn't that s-con cable adequately shielded? Why no safety nets in that ventilation space? Why didn't these godlike AIs look after people? At the age of seventeen she killed her first monitor. He had fancied her, so was not sufficiently on his guard. She shot him once through the throat, again through the back of the head as he lay gagging for life. Then she spewed up her guts nearby. The organization got her out of there – she'd left just too much of her DNA as evidence at the scene. On another world she graduated to mass murder with a bomb planted in a runcible facility, but it failed to take out the AI there. The only AI she ever managed to actually . . . kill, was a free Golem, and that at close range with a missile launcher, while its back was turned. But though the AIs were the main enemy, the most hated of all were those who willingly served them: ECS and its agents – no agony could be too much for them to suffer. How utterly and completely did the Separatist organization brainwash her, and how downright stupid of her to allow it.

Skellor – the brilliant biophysicist who was promising to change their fortunes – brought ECS down on them like an avalanche. Subverting an ECS dreadnought by using Jain technology, he then made Aphran and some of her fellows his crew in the most horrific way possible:

subsumed in Jain tech, becoming mere adjuncts to him, suffering and yet not dying. Then he killed her, burned her in a never-ending fire, the only escape being for her mind to flee inside the Jain structure. Next came Jack, who uploaded her from there to a partitioned segment of his own crystal. She combined with him, embracing him for the sake of her own survival, and there found clarity with which she began to see everything thereafter. For open to her were the massive historical files that Jack contained, giving sharp contrast to the peace and plenty enjoyed across the majority of the human Polity. She saw how the AIs allowed the human race the freedom to enjoy luxurious eternity, or even to destroy themselves personally, but not the freedom to destroy each other. She came to recognize her past life as the stubborn intransigence of a spoilt child. But most importantly she saw Jack. And that alone was enough.

'I wondered why you were not prepared to die for the cause, but you did not answer me,' she enquired over com.

Freyda shook her head, then sat down with her legs crossed, her back resting against the wall.

'Only when I see you, will I believe it's really you,' she replied.

Aphran chose an image matching her appearance when held captive aboard the *Occam Razor*, and projected it into the room.

Freyda frowned and waved a dismissive hand. 'Projection. I suppose whatever is talking to me now was constructed out of information reamed from Aphran's mind before they killed her.'

'Skellor killed me. You remember Skellor, don't you? He actually burned me to death.'

Again the dismissive hand gesture.

Aphran allowed her form to change into that now more commonly seen by those aboard the *NEJ*. This elicited more of a reaction, Freyda's eyes growing wide. She stared for a long moment before shaking her head.

'I am a memcording – that's all of me remaining,' Aphran told her. 'Is this what *you* would like to be? You have information that may be vital and you are surrounded by people who are very much lacking in patience. They'll use an aug to interface with your mind, make a copy of all it contains, then that recording will be taken apart by this ship's AI. You personally will then be of no use. This cell can easily be opened to vacuum.'

'You're no Aphran I know. You would have died rather than serve them.'

'But I did die.'

Freyda grimaced and stared down at the floor.

Aphran went on, 'This is an Aphran with her eyes opened wide. *Your* cause is hopeless, pointless and destructive. But then I think you came to realize that even before you recruited me. Once you genuinely believed all that humans-to-rule-humanity crap, but in the end you just enjoyed your own sense of importance . . . and killing people of course.'

'If I do talk, what do I get in return?'

'Whatever we can give you, but within reason.'

Freyda snorted contemptuously then said, 'I would rather like to stay *alive*.'

'Is that within reason?' Aphran shrugged. 'Hard or soft – your choice. From here you'll be transported back to Earth, which will require about fifteen runcible transfers. There you'll face a judicial AI and be sentenced for your crimes. This does, however, mean you'll live a little longer.'

The fifteen transfers were the key, for Freyda would still believe there might be a way out of this for her. Aphran only felt sad when registering the furtiveness in the woman's expression.

'I want to be allowed certain freedoms during that time,' she said. 'I don't want to be put into coldsleep.'

'Granted.'

Again that look of furtiveness. 'I'll need time to think about this . . . in a better location than this. I am not an animal to be caged.'

Aphran allowed herself to begin to fade. 'You have no time.'

'Okay,' said Freyda quickly. 'Okay . . . what do you want to know?'

'How many of you were there, down there?'

'I'm not entirely sure—'

'How many?'

'Seventeen . . . fourteen now.'

'Their location?'

Freyda eventually volunteered a grid reference deep in the forests.

'There is something there,' Jack informed Aphran. 'It's shielded, but not sufficiently so.'

'Now,' said Aphran, 'what brought you *here*?' She gritted her non-existent teeth through the ensuing political diatribe, and kept asking the same questions until Freyda provided the true answer.

'High level ECS agents to kill – that's always attractive.'

'How did you know they would be here?'

While she waited for the answer, Aphran listened in

on coms traffic both within the ship and way below, as the shuttle down on the surface, containing Thorn, Scar and fifty dracomen, launched on a heading to the co-ordinates just revealed.

'I was told.' Freyda abruptly stood and eyed Aphran up and down. 'Is that how you appear now, the princess, the lady in white . . . one of the good guys?'

'It is how I *like* to appear.'

'Perhaps you've forgotten Coloron, then. Thellant N'komo still runs things there, and it's him you need to talk to. Where he got his information from I don't know, but it was him that sent us here.'

Aphran allowed her image to fade totally, then, as an afterthought, sent the signal that paralysed Freyda. The Separatist woman dropped like a pole. Aphran observed as the door now opened and the telefactor entered, carrying the aug they would use to record Freyda's mind and check the veracity of her story.

'Do we ship her back to Earth?'

'No,' Jack replied.

'Kill her?'

'No.'

'What then?'

'Sentence was passed on Freyda long ago, should she ever be caught. Death or erasure to be carried out as soon as feasible after her capture. After I have taken a recording of her mind, checked her story, and gleaned from it all knowledge that might be useful to ECS, I will wipe the recording and then wipe her mind. We will put her body into coldsleep, as there are still plenty of minds in the Soulbank who would be grateful for the physical vessel.'

And that being how the Polity dealt with its criminals, Aphran felt die then any hope she harboured for a future.

The scene now surrounding Thorn vaguely reminded him of his time as a soldier. Inside the shuttle the ten dracomen squatted in pairs in their saddle seats, their weapons braced across their chests. But these were soldiers of a different stripe. When they first landed on the planet, Thorn asked Scar why they discarded their impact suits. The dracoman leader had replied that they did not wish to be encumbered. Thorn then suggested they clad themselves in chameleon-cloth fatigues. Scar demonstrated how their own skin was much better at the job. So now, but for harnesses on which to carry high-tech weapons and other equipment, they were naked: green scaled all over except for their fronts which were yellow from throat to groin. With their forked tongues tasting the air, sharp white teeth occasionally exposed, they seemed like extras in a barbaric scene out of some VR fantasy.

In the cockpit Thorn faced forwards as Scar brought the shuttle down low so that now, through the ceiling-to-floor front screen, they could see the forest hurtling along underneath them.

'How long?' he asked.

'Sixteen minutes.'

Thorn nodded. It had been difficult, but he managed to force himself to delegate this mission to Scar – just giving the dracoman the simple instruction:

'Try to kill as few of them as possible – we're here for information, not extermination.'

'How many prisoners do you want?'

'I leave that up to you, Scar.'

Scar banked the shuttle slightly, and took it lower, forest now speeding under its left-hand side. Opening his pack Thorn removed a plastic box and popped it open. As Scar straightened the craft again, Thorn took out one of the small camcom discs and passed it over to the dracoman, who inspected it for a moment before slapping it on the side of his head. Closing the box, Thorn tossed it to the next dracoman behind him. He did not need to say anything more as dracomen were very far from stupid. The first took out a disc, pressed it to its temple, then passed the box on. Now Thorn operated the lever to bring his seat closer to the mission-control console. He lifted the VR headgear from its recess and placed it over his head – the visor covering his face and phones enclosing his ears. Immediately frames began accumulating across his range of vision as each dracoman pressed a camcom into place. Using the ball control in his chair arm he selected frame one in the sequence. It expanded to fill his vision and the sounds within the shuttle changed slightly. He now seemed to be looking through Scar's eyes, and hearing what the dracoman heard. Clicking back, he saw all the frames now present, and a diagnostic readout showed the system to be working at optimum. Thorn removed the headgear and placed it back in its recess.

The view remained largely unchanged for ten minutes more, then Scar brought the shuttle down lower still so it sped along a straight lane between looming walls of trees. Below, three tracks, each five yards wide and spaced forty yards apart, had been crushed through a dense tangle of bluish bracken, parsleys and brambles. Soon they came in sight of the massive machine responsible: the beetle-shaped agrobot was two hundred yards long and a hundred wide, and mounted on three sets of three huge cage-ball wheels, which enabled so massive a machine to manoeuvre with remarkable accuracy. But it was going nowhere at the moment, since two of the cage balls had collapsed. Scar swung the shuttle in a wide circle around this behemoth, checking the ground below with infrared and carbon dioxide emission scanners. But nothing showed up, and Thorn wondered if Aelvor had yet started introducing large animals – or if he ever would. Perhaps he did not like what creatures like deer might do to his newly planted saplings.

After this survey, the dracoman finally brought the shuttle down directly behind the mechanical colossus. Even before the shuttle landed, its side-ramp doors began to open. Dracomen started disembarking the moment a wide enough gap opened; leaping fifteen feet down into the vegetation as if the drop was nothing to them. As soon as the shuttle settled, Scar unstrapped himself and stood up from his saddlelike seat. Thorn stood also and followed him out into the bracken. Here the dracomen only became visible when they moved – their scales transforming in both colour and texture to match their surroundings. Dressed in simple green fatigues, Thorn himself was the only one clearly visible. Then, as if showing sympathy to him, all the dracomen simultaneously returned to their natural colour.

'Remember,' said Thorn, 'we want to take some of them alive.'

Scar wrinkled his lips away from sharp ivory in a manner not exactly reassuring, then made a spearing gesture with his hand, and they set out. With their high-stepping birdlike gait the dracomen easily picked their way through the thick-growing brambles and bracken, then slowly they began to fade as they once again began to camouflage themselves. Thorn stood and watched them go, and really wanted to follow, but realized that would be pointless.

Landing directly on top of the Separatist encampment would remove any element of surprise, since the shuttle's arrival would be detected long before. This highway for the massive agrobots was the nearest place to the encampment for a shuttle to find a plausible reason for landing. Aelvor had somehow caused the agrobot to break down at this point, so anyone listening and watching would think their shuttle contained a maintenance crew. It was a good plan since, on foot, dracomen could cover the intervening terrain very quickly. Thorn, being very fit and physically strong, and possessing reserves at their maximum, could also have covered the forty miles of forest easily enough, but in his case it was a question of how fast. He remembered once running with Scar through the foothills of the Masadan mountains, hunting a hooder on which they intended to plant transponders so that the monstrous predator's location would always be known. Their pace then had been an even jog, and Thorn had thought it time they picked it up a little.

'Can you go any faster than this?' he had asked the dracoman on that occasion.

Scar fixed him with that big-eyed gaze, 'Can you?'

Thorn accelerated until he was running full-pelt along the stony trail. He glanced at Scar and saw that the dracoman's pace seemed almost unchanged, yet still he kept up.

After a moment Thorn said, 'Show me, then.'

One moment Scar was loping along beside him, the next moment he took off like an ostrich, kicking up wet shale as he accelerated. Thorn watched him go, tracked him moving further along the path, then turning left up the slope until soon out of sight. After about five minutes he heard something approaching to his rear, and glanced back to see the dracoman speeding up behind him. Scar again settled to that jogging pace beside him.

'In miles per hour?' Thorn had asked.

'Ninety to a hundred . . . on level ground,' Scar replied.

'Okay, maybe we'll stick to my pace for now.'

It was a chastening memory.

Thorn now returned to the shuttle, donned his VR headgear, and began selecting views to observe. Soon the dracomen moved from tangled growth to clearer ground below the trees. They picked up their pace and became more visible as their skin failed to compensate fast enough to the changing surroundings. Then, again almost as one, they returned to their natural coloration.

'Scar,' he said over com, 'let me know when you're about to attack. I'll then launch and head over towards you. That might provide further distraction.'

Scar's reply was merely a grunt, whereupon Thorn decided to shut up, sit back, and enjoy the show. A half-hour more of forest scenes resulted in him impatiently removing the headgear to go in search of a tab-pull coffee from the shuttle's supplies. Returning to his seat and replacing the helmet, the first thing he heard was Scar's voice: 'We attack.'

Thorn spilt his coffee, swore, then quickly called up the feed from Scar's camcom: pulse-rifles firing through the trees, shots stitching across a thick trunk, momentary glimpse of an autogun bolted to another trunk, an explosion, a tree falling. Two figures, human, a blurred shape between, and the double thump of stun discharge, two figures falling wrapped in small lightnings. Tents: chameleon cloth. Stun fire. A turbine winding up to speed somewhere. Thorn flicked through views, caught a glimpse of an AG scooter slamming into a tree. Another view: a man firing his weapon at the dracoman through whose camcom Thorn watched, muzzle-flash, flame and smoke then foliage and sky, then the dracoman was abruptly back upright again as the man turned away. A stun discharge threw the man down on his face. Then back to Scar, walking now.

'We are done.'

Thorn sat very still, checked the time display in the corner of his visor, then shivered involuntarily. So much for his idea of launching the shuttle as a distraction. Abruptly the entire range of frames before his eyes then froze.

'Scar cannot hear us,' said Jack. 'Observe this.'

Without Thorn doing anything, his VR gear selected a frame and the scene it displayed went into fast reverse, froze, then played forwards. He watched a man swinging his pulse-rifle round and begin firing. The shots slammed into a dracoman's chest, juddering it to a halt then flinging it back. The man swung away to aim elsewhere. From a prone position the dracoman flipped forward and upright, fired on the man and brought him down, then it ran on. Half its chest was missing, the resultant cavity smouldering.

'I'm glad they're on *our* side,' whispered Thorn.

'If they really are,' replied Jack.

Thorn's view returned to encompass all the separate frames again. As the AI withdrew, he selected Scar's frame in time to observe the dracoman brandishing a ceramo-carbide knife. Scar was busy removing leaf mould from around what looked like a small antipersonnel mine.

'How many dead?' Thorn asked.

'Three humans: one received four stun charges, one broke his neck falling from an AG scooter, and one was accidentally shot by a comrade of his.'

'What about your own people?'

'No deaths.'

'I'm sure I saw one of them hit.'

'Three with minor injuries.'

'Very well, I'll come and pick you up.' Thorn swung the shuttle joystick across on its hinged arm, so it lay before him. As he engaged the gravmotors and warmed up the turbines, he thought: *And these fuckers are breeding . . .*

6

Let me summarize some theories concerning the Atheter: they moved on to a higher plain of existence after reaching the apex of material technology, either that or they reached their own singularity and disappeared in a puff of logic having solved their theory of everything; they are still here with us keeping a benevolent eye on younger civilizations, but shifted slightly into another dimension so we cannot now see their vast glittering cities; their technology destroyed them (either their own AIs – if they built them – reached singularity and wiped them out, or they created some unstoppable nano-plague that did the job); or, my personal favourite, having done it all and understanding the emptiness of existence, they deleted their entire civilization, their entire knowledge base, even from their own minds, and started again, as humans. However, despite much speculation and some quite lunatic theorizing, very little is known about the Atheter. There is in fact still much debate about whether they were in fact a race distinct from those other ancient races named, the Jain and Csorians. And argument still abounds concerning what artefacts are attributable to which race, or civilization. But let us be clear on this: actual physical artefacts dating from each period are few. Most of the theorizing is based on such obscure sciences as xenogenetic archaeology, metallo-crustal dispersion and – this one really is obscure – Fifth Gen. Boolean analysis of U-space transitional echoes. It's all piss and wind really, we'll probably never know.

– From 'How it Is' by Gordon

Thellant turned to gaze at a screen wall. The scene it displayed was taken from cameras high above his present location, and its clarity was so good he appeared to be looking through a chainglass window at a pastoral view of patchwork fields, rivers and copses, with only occasional incongruous towers sprouting like vulgar metal plants amid this apparently rural idyll. It was deceptive. Some human, transported to those fields from a past time, would not know that below him lay an arcology housing a billion humans. Fifteen miles straight ahead, a cliff dropped two miles sheer down to the coast, beyond which sea-life breeding pens chequered the shallow ocean extending to the horizon and beyond. That cliff formed one arcology edge. Another edge lay 200 miles behind the present view.

Of course, with so many humans being packed so closely together dissatisfaction with the regime was inevitable, despite passage to less crowded worlds being offered to them free by the runcible AI. Many did leave, but just as many were born to replace them. Thellant thought of the humans here as a particular breed devolved through urbanization: they would not move because they were incapable of imagining anything beyond the life they knew. Sad for them, but not for him – he grew rich on their dissatisfaction. The thousands of Separatist cells abounding here gathered wealth by extortion, theft, murder, blackmail . . . to finance the fight against the AI autocrat of Earth. Thellant skimmed the cream of that wealth, while allowing his followers to sabotage a few machines and murder a few citizens. But he remained well aware of why ECS could not catch him. The reason sat upon the sofa behind him.

'You were told to simply kill her,' it hissed.

Nervous and sweating, Thellant turned. The Legate always had this effect on him: quite simply it looked plain evil. It was humanoid, just like the Golem made by Cybercorp, and metalskin like some of the older versions produced by that same company. But there the similarity ended. This android wore nothing but its metal skin, shiny and shading to blue-green. When standing it towered tall and incredibly thin. Its fingers were half again the length of human fingers and terminated in sharp points. Its head slanted back, tapering sharply down to the lipless slot of its mouth. It had no nose and its eyes were lidless and insectile. There seemed no edges to the metal skin at its joints – the material there did actually stretch and flex like skin. All of it consisted of the same metal, even the eyes, from which it seemed something cold and harsh gazed out.

'You informed me', protested Thellant, 'that there would be a high level of ECS interest in her, and that agents would be sent to apprehend her. I am the de facto leader of the rebellion here on Coloron, so I could not ignore such an opportunity.'

'You are the leader here only because of the programs I have created to keep the AIs from finding out about you. But that is irrelevant,' the Legate waved one long-fingered hand, 'especially now.'

'What do you mean?'

'Despite my programs, ECS has been closing in on

you for some time. Now that your people on Osterland have been captured, the gap will soon be closed completely.'

Thellant felt his mouth go dry. 'I don't understand.' For reassurance he reached up and touched his fingertips to the warm scaly skin of the Dracocorp aug he wore.

The Legate pointed one long digit. 'Those augs have provided you with secure com and processing power outside AI networks. You give your orders with an unprecedented degree of anonymity. ECS have failed to track the money trails back to you through the conventional networks, because of my programs and because of numerous physical transfers of wealth, but mainly because few people know who you are.'

'I am aware of how it all works. Your assistance has been greatly appreciated, but remember that, even with it, it was I who built up this organization.'

The Legate interlaced its long fingers. 'Of course, and while your organization confined itself to this world, it has been easy enough for me to arrange the deaths of those who knew too much and were undergoing investigation by ECS. Had you sent out a single contractor to kill Jane von Hellsdorf, there would be no problem. I could have then arranged for the same contractor to die, and thereby closed down any connection with you or with this world. But instead you sent some of your top people there – people who have seen you and know who you are. Now they have been captured, and we both know that once in ECS hands their remaining silent is not an option. Even now ECS teams are closing in on you, and the AIs are closely watching the spaceports and runcibles.'

'I have my own secure routes,' Thellant said.

'Yes, many of which have been compromised for some time. ECS has had agents in place for years, gathering evidence, gradually identifying those in the higher echelons of your organization here on Coloron. Now they have located the head, they will proceed to destroy the body.'

'You are part of that body,' Thellant observed.

'Correct, in so far as I have advised and assisted you in your cause. But I will now take my leave of this world and leave you to reap what you have sown.'

Thellant abruptly felt a surge of the anger that had been his driving force since his childhood. 'But this mess is down to you anyway! This woman was irrelevant to me. *You* wanted her killed and I still don't know why, just as I really don't know why you have always felt this urge to be so *helpful*.'

Suddenly the Legate was standing. Thellant stepped back, his heart thumping, then he forced himself to take that step forwards again. Looming over him the android spoke, low and soft, 'It has been in our interest to maintain a level of resistance to the autocrat; nothing sufficiently threatening to elicit a major counter-offensive, but to have skeletal networks ready and waiting for the tools to do the job. You have remained in contact with your offworld associates, so presumably you know something of the biophysicist Skellor?'

Thellant paused before replying. The Legate was some kind of intermediary – that being implicit in its name – and when it referred to 'our interest' that obviously included some other party. He had never discovered who or what that other party might be.

He said, 'Skellor was a useful acquisition. I knew only that he was developing weapons we might be able to use.

ECS hit his base and that was the last I heard. All I do know is that ECS went on to take down a planetary organization as a result.'

'Then what you don't know is that Skellor, using technology provided for him by us via von Hellsdorf, subverted an AI dreadnought called the *Occam Razor*, and came close to wiping out the population of an entire planet just to keep the secret. He then managed to escape the destruction of the *Occam Razor*, but in the end did not evade the ECS agents pursuing him. And he did all this alone.'

'Masada . . .' murmured Thellant. One of his associates had tried for a long time to find out exactly what had happened out there, but it was a dangerous subject to ask about, what with hunter-killer programs flooding the networks, and with AI warships and ECS teams swarming around that world, a dangerous place to be.

The Legate stepped past him and moved over to gaze at the screen wall. 'Skellor was in the nature of a dry run, you might say. He was brilliant, but fundamentally unbalanced. We did, however, learn a great deal from him.'

Thellant shivered. 'What is this technology you're talking about?'

In an offhand manner the Legate explained, 'Active Jain technology. It is of an organic nature and enables its wielder to both informationally and physically take control of computer and AI systems, to physically control all mechano-electrical systems, and even to enslave human beings.'

Thellant had already experienced some taste of that. Setting up his network using Dracocorp augs was difficult at first, and he rebelled against the disconnection. He always found it much easier to ensure his orders were obeyed by unexpected visits to his subordinates and the occasional disciplinary knee-capping. But as the number of those using the augs grew he found he could trust that his orders were obeyed. He felt the power – his growing ascendancy over the network – and how, the longer they wore their augs, his subordinates found it nearly impossible to disobey him.

Glancing around at his huge apartment and at the expensive luxuries it contained, he murmured, 'We need such technology here and now. I . . . we could take this world, take it out of Polity control, just make it too costly for them in lives and resources to reclaim it.' He *wanted* this thing. Perhaps by fleeing Coloron he could escape the coming ECS actions against him, but that would mean him abandoning everything: all this wealth and the power, and his position.

The Legate held out a fist, closed, until Thellant turned to regard it.

'Then I shall provide,' said the Legate.

The fist opened, each long finger folding out and snapping straight. A dark layer of something coated the palm and the inner surfaces of the fingers and thumb. At the very centre of the palm rested an ovoid, an inch and a half at its longest axis. Silvery cubic patterns decorated its surface and, as Thellant watched them in fascination, they seemed to slowly shift.

'This is what Skellor used,' the android informed him.

Thellant stepped forward and began to reach out. He hesitated. 'How did he . . . control it?'

'It forms nanoconnections to the mind – very similar to those made by augs.' Cold eyes regarding him, the hand extended a little further. 'You would then be able to create all the processing space you require. You may of course have this object analysed, but I suspect you do not have sufficient resources for that.'

Thellant kept a straight face. Obviously the Legate did not know about the scientists and technicians he controlled, or about the computers and data stores he had isolated from the AI nets. He reached out and picked up the ovoid, inspected it closely for a moment, then dropped it into his other palm to study at a distance.

'It seems such a small . . . it's cold . . . Shit!' He shook his hand to fling the thing away, but it seemed stuck there. It was as if he had grasped something direct from a deep freezer that now froze to his palm. The cold of it then became something else, eating into his skin like acid. Thellant gasped, stumbled back still shaking his hand, and tumbled rearwards over the coffee table, hitting his head against the floor. Hot wires now seemed to be spearing up his arm.

The Legate stepped forwards and peered down at him. 'What causes it to react is complicated. Simply, it becomes aware that it is within an artificial environment then it bonds to the first . . . intelligent organic contact. Strangely it will not bond to animals or plants – only self-aware and intelligent organic beings. I am excluded, as are Golem and other AI biomechanisms. You must therefore consider yourself privileged.'

The thing, working up his arm, was making his fingers move one after the other as if trying them out.

The Legate added, 'I neglected to mention that Skellor used a crystal-matrix aug to accept the connections and control the technology. In this case it will connect directly to your brain. That means you may experience some . . . difficulties.'

Hot wires now in his shoulder, searing up through his neck and into his head. The node, still in his hand, deforming and melting into him. As he began shrieking, the Legate made a contemptuous little moue with its hard mouth, and departed.

Cormac brought his craft in over a curving landscape of living flesh tegulated with scales ranging from the size of a thumbnail to a yard across, which seemed almost like jewelled facets cut on red and green opal. He crossed a trench from the rim of which sprouted pseudopods like giant cobras with blank sapphire eyes where their mouths should be, and passed low slopes strewn with writhing red tentacles like a growth of lianas. The manacle, as ECS personnel now called it, rose over the sharply curved horizon ahead of him. A mile long, it followed the curve of Dragon's body, and at the centre of it lay a trapeziform building fashioned from the same block of highly polished ceramal. The metallic strip was thirty feet wide and a yard thick and, as Cormac flew above it, his craft dipped then compensated as it encountered the tug of gravplates mounted in its surface. The agent brought his craft down on the metal, where it settled in one Earth gravity, and contemplated what he had landed upon.

The manacle held itself in place with hooks driven into draconic flesh – injuries that meant nothing at all to Dragon. Many instruments pierced the entity, measuring, sampling, testing and perpetually monitoring. The AIs did not intend to miss out on this opportunity to study Dragon up close, but all that equipment was not why this object had come to be called a manacle. As well as more conventional armament, Dragon contained a gravtech weapon. The giant entity had once destroyed a Polity warship with it, by breaching antimatter containment within that ship. The manacle itself held numerous CTDs whose antimatter flasks would also be breached should Dragon try to use that same weapon again. The bombs could be detonated remotely by those entrusted with their code.

Cormac knew that code.

Arach, the spider-drone from the *Celedon* station, had wanted to come across too, but Cormac refused. This situation did not warrant the presence of an irascible war drone and, anyway, there was not room for it in this one-man craft. Arach had suggested clinging externally to the craft's hull, and only desisted in wheedling when Jerusalem intervened.

Cormac closed up his spacesuit's visor, hit purge, and unstrapped himself while a pump rapidly drew the cockpit air into a storage cylinder aboard the craft. He touched a panel beside him and a wing door rose, while his seat swung towards the opening. Stepping out, then down onto the polished ceramal, he looked to one side and saw a row of pseudopods silhouetted against the ice giant, waving like cilia. Considering his previous encounters with other incarnations of this entity, it surprised him that the pseudopods did not all gather around him menacingly, for Dragon loved to play such games. He wondered what the game would be this time, and if Dragon really understood how the odds were stacked against it.

He trudged the few yards up to the nearest wall of the building. The airlock there consisted of an outer metal door and an inner shimmer-shield. Quickly going through, he entered the single room of which the building consisted. It looked like the housing for a small swimming pool, only the pool itself contained scaled flesh. Controlling his spacesuit via his gridlink, Cormac retracted the visor down into the neck ring, then collapsed the segmented helmet back over his head so it settled into a collar at the back of his neck. He sniffed: familiar terrarium smell, cloves and something slightly putrid. Moving around the edge of this minor expanse of Dragon's surface, he finally came to a small area off to one side containing VR and laboratory equipment. These were intended to be used by those who wanted to get this close – Mika being foremost of thousands aboard the *Jerusalem* who had volunteered. He sat in a VR chair, right elbow resting on the chair arm and chin cupped in his hand, and contemplated Dragon.

'*Are we all sitting comfortably?*' he asked over his gridlink.

'*I do not sit,*' Jerusalem replied.

'*Oh, get on with it,*' said Mika impatiently.

Only these two, excepting Dragon itself, could speak to him directly while he was here. Many thousands of others listening in could lodge requests, ideas or questions, which were filtered through Jerusalem and stored ready in Cormac's gridlink should he require them. Through that same device he checked his access to many files and to the controls of the equipment within the building. The holographic projectors specifically interested him.

'Dragon, I think it is time for our little chat,' he said out loud.

How many words of dialogue had that Dragon expert Darson recorded all those years ago when Dragon stood as four conjoined spheres down on the surface of Aster Colora? Millions? And how few solid facts. As far as they went, Cormac had learnt so much more in his own brief exchanges with the alien entity. It was all about exigency: it seemed that the less critical the situation Dragon found itself in the more Delphic its pronouncements tended to be. Cormac supposed that having nowhere to run and having many CTDs attached to its surface would be making it feel pretty exigent right now. However, its lies might be even more convoluted. He needed to judge the answers behind the answers.

'Dragon?' he began again.

The smell of cloves grew stronger and there seemed a sudden stormy intensity to the atmosphere.

'*Activity below you,*' Jerusalem told him. '*An incursion developing through the underlayers and a pseudopod tree coming up.*'

Cormac scratched his earlobe, rested his hands on the chair arms. Shortly a split began to unzip in the scaled skin extending before him, revealing a red cavity from which he felt a warmth against his face. The edges folded down, seemingly flowing inside. Then a cobra pseudopod speared into the air, then another, then three more. Amidst them a thick loop of neck appeared, which straightened to bring into view a head. This was not one of the usual pterodactyl heads, but something sleeker, lacking a crest, with a more expressive mouth and slotted pupils in its sapphire eyes. It blinked, then surged forwards and down resting a loop of neck on the rim of the cavity, so the head was now poised only a few yards away from him, its eyes directly level with his own. The other cobra pseudopods spread out like a peacock fan behind it, and Cormac wondered if he should read anything into these choreographed actions. Though the head itself was like that of a flesh-ripping predator, it did not rear threateningly above him as usual. And was it looking more expressive to enable better communication or just more convincing lies?

Cormac powered up the holoprojector. To one side, hanging in midair, appeared a dracoman, then beside it one of the by-blows this dragon sphere had created on Cull: a melding of human and sleer, a chimera, the body of a woman attached waist upwards in place of the head of something that resembled a scorpion.

'When I talk to just one dragon sphere, do I talk to Dragon entire?' Cormac asked.

Two cobra heads turned towards the holoprojections, the main head remained focused on Cormac. 'No and yes,' it replied.

Cormac sighed. 'Do you remember part of you dying at Samarkand?' Cormac had used a CTD to destroy one of Dragon's four spheres there – retribution for the tens of thousands of human deaths it caused on that cold world.

'I do not.'

Not perpetually connected, then.

'How much of that particular sphere's experience is your own?'

'We are distinct entities, yet we are not. We do not share what we are not, but we share what we *all* are.'

'Some AIs do this,' Jerusalem interjected for Cormac alone. *'A shared pool of knowledge, understanding and personality, whilst retaining individuality.'*

'But how often do they share, and do they share equally? It must be by U-space com, which, in this situation with USERs all around, means this sphere here has been isolated from the remaining other sphere for some time.'

'Irrelevant to our present purposes.'

Cormac pointed to the two holograms. 'Why?'

'You do not accept change swiftly enough,' Dragon replied. 'You' evidently meaning the human race.

'Adapt or die?' Cormac wondered.

'Precisely.'

'When I first came to you on Aster Colora, as an ambassador, your ostensible purpose was to deliver a warning to the human race, the usual credo, smarten up your act or die, because the big boys are watching.' Cormac glanced at the holograms. 'The dracoman was then part of that warning. A rather unsubtle demonstration of the precariousness of human existence – demonstrating how, but for cosmic mischance, the descendants of the dinosaurs could be where we are now.'

Cormac paused and studied the ophidian face before him. He remembered all his own previous speculations about what Dragon might be, or, more importantly, what its purpose might be.

He continued, 'After Samarkand we marked you down as a bio-engineered device sent by the Makers to observe only, but one that developed a god-complex and started interacting with us. The Maker was sent to retrieve you and, in attempting to kill it, you caused the deaths of thousands of people. Which story is true?'

'Neither,' Dragon replied.

'Tell me about Jain technology,' Cormac countered.

'It is an ancient weapon.'

'And its relation to the Makers?'

At this Dragon showed some agitation, swinging its head from side to side.

'*We're getting some very odd readings from inside Dragon,*' interjected Mika.

Jerusalem added, *'Power transferences and much shifting of internal organs.'*

Cormac absorbed all that and quite concisely asked, 'What is the relationship between Jain technology and the Makers?'

'I must not lie to you,' said Dragon.

'Then don't.'

Mika: 'Shit! What was that?'

Jerusalem: *'Massive contraction of some inner diaphragm – something tensing up for a blow, perhaps?'*

'Will three times break the spell?' Cormac wondered. Out loud he asked again, 'What is the relationship between the Makers and Jain technology?

'I will not . . .' said Dragon.

Mika: *'Big energy surge just then – something just got incinerated.'*

Cormac suddenly gained some intimation of what was going on, of what had *always* been going on during communication with this entity. Dragon, after all, was a bio-construct, specially programmed, and there were truths it could not tell.

With the grab claw and gecko pads detached, Orlandine manoeuvred the *Heliotrope* to the inner wall of the chamber, and presented the docking tube to the airlock she had constructed there. She set down the ship ten yards away, and extended the gecko feet on their telescopic legs, adjusting them to position the ship precisely. The docking tube mated perfectly. She did not expect otherwise.

'They will learn about the gift' – a secret admirer.

Orlandine departed her interface sphere with those words of warning still in her mind. It had occurred to her the moment she received the message containing them, that they were a deliberate nudge to start her on her present course, and that in some way she was being used. But she dismissed that thought and stuck with the basic fact: she possessed a piece of technology which contained the potential to take her beyond the haiman to the numinous. Presently, the reasons behind this gift remained irrelevant. All that was relevant was that if Polity AIs learned she possessed it they would do everything in their power to take it away from her. She could not therefore take the chance of assuming the warning to be premature or a lie.

In the cell she designated as her laboratory, the eight beetlebots she had taken out of storage and adjusted to this task moved slowly across the floor spraying on it a layer of crash foam. She dumped a large drum containing more of the polymer-forming liquid on a layer of foam already five inches thick, and transmitted further instructions to the robots. Now they would come automatically to the drum and plug in to its lower sockets to recharge their reservoirs. In the low pressure the polymer foamed and set to a hard insulating layer, which would prevent the laboratory cell from losing any heat that might be detected from outside. Later, for further concealment, she intended to add a layer of the laminated radiation shielding she had ordered loaded on to the *Heliotrope* before departing the station. A small autofactory inside the ship was meanwhile working flat out to manufacture large quantities of the polymer. A yard of thickness was what she required, thereafter she could open the locks to her ship and use its internal atmospheric systems to bring up the temperature and air pressure to within the specification required for the equipment she intended to use in here. Then she would bring in that equipment, also portable heaters and an atmosphere plant, isolate the cavern from the ship, then finally bring in the Jain node for further study.

The Jain node.

Orlandine paused and remembered that meeting on one of the Sol stations that had changed the course of her life.

'Hi, I'm Jonas Trent,' he had said. 'You would be Orlandine?'

She had glanced across at him as he took the seat opposite. He was pale, quite thin, dressed in black slacks, a canary-yellow shirt, a jacket made of black diamond-shaped plates of composite bonded to something like leather, and wide braces that had a shifting pattern of snakes. Seeing he was auged, through her gridlink – the minimum internal hardware required to take the carapace she was not wearing at that time – she sent him a personal contact query. The personal details that his aug settings allowed her were skeletal: he was a hundred and four years old, unattached, a sensocord rep, born on Earth . . . all the usual details but little more. Nothing there to tell her how he knew of her, or why he approached her now.

She sipped her espresso. 'What can I do for you?'

He grinned. 'As we always like to say, it's not what *you* can do for *me*—'

She interrupted, 'I'm haiman, so do you honestly think I need to buy any sensocordings? I'm now logging this encounter as an infringement—'

He interrupted, 'Don't – I'm not here to sell you anything.'

She did not log the personal-space infringement anyway. A person like this would know exactly who to approach and when, so he must be here for some other reason. He took out a rounded brushed-metal box, reached across the table and placed it before her.

'I've been paid very well to act as an intermediary. All I can tell you is that there's a certain object inside, and a memtab explaining exactly what that object is. I am only instructed to tell you that it is a "gift from an admirer".'

She peered at the box. 'My kind are often the target of Separatists, or, rather, would be targets. I'm cautious.' She slid the box back across the table to him. '*You* open it.'

With a grimace, he picked it up and popped it open, then put it down and slid it back across. 'See, no problem.'

In the foam packing rested a dull egg. Next to it lay a memtab – a piece of crystal the size of her fingernail. She pulled her palm-top from her belt and inserted the tab into the relevant port. The screen displayed the ovoid itself and, while she watched, it opened like a flower to expose a smaller ovoid inside covered with slightly shifting cubic patterns. A frame appeared over this with the figure x1000 beside it – indicating magnification. The frame expanded, filled the screen, then another appeared and did the same. Then again and again, until displaying the most densely packed nano-technology she had ever seen. Finally the image blinked out. Trying to recall it, she found the original recording had been wiped by a subprogram.

'What is this?' she asked, merely for form's sake, since she already knew.

He stood, saying, 'Ciao.' He walked away.

A gift from an admirer.

Upon her return to the Cassius project she ran a search through the nets for this Jonas Trent. It seemed he had stepped out of the airlock of another of the Sol-system stations without the benefit of a spacesuit. It took all her expertise to avoid the semi-AI program that subsequently came after her, for the enquiry into his death remained open, and the program now wanted to know all about her and her interest in him.

'They will learn about the gift' – a secret admirer.

Orlandine returned to the *Heliotrope* only to find the autofactory had run out of some raw materials. But raw materials abounded all around her. She donned an assister frame intended for heavy work, took up a gravsled, and left the ship via the small rear hold. She then cut a small exit out of the giant pillar and stepped out into the vastness beyond. The endless acres of floor stretched away into the distance, layered many feet deep with the substance of the Cassius gas giant. Here most periodic-table elements were available to her in compound form, but she possessed the tools to separate and recombine them, and the ship's fusion reactor supplied the energy to operate those tools. Using a diamond saw extruded by the frame she wore, she began cutting blocks from the icy layer and loading them on the sled. She was satisfied she had everything here; everything she could possibly want.

'It is protected,' said Hourne, the ship's AI.

'Protected?' Blegg continued gazing at the artefact, now with numerous optic interfaces in position all around its rim.

'And encrypted,' the AI added.

'You were getting something from the fragments of crystal found by Shayden – so what did you find there?'

'DNA,' the AI replied. 'And numerous possible variations thereof.'

Blegg turned away from the viewing window to scan around the control centre. Two haimans, fifteen humans and five Golem worked at consoles, carrying out whatever tasks the AI felt best suited their specialities. The woman, with only her blonde plaits showing because her face was thrust inside a VR mask, specialized in crystal micro-scanning using only UV and indigo light. The two haimans were fast, almost instinctive, programmers; they did not seem to be doing much, but that meant nothing – if they were doing a lot it would not show in any physical way.

'A message?' Blegg wondered.

AI Hourne continued, 'Shayden's skin cells bonded to the surface of the crystal, were read at the molecular level, her DNA copied in virtual format, and in the same format possible variations processed. It was these that fed back through the optic interface she connected. That piece of crystal then began rapidly to degrade.'

'This could happen to the entire artefact?' Blegg watched one of the Golem reach up to pull aside his shirt, then a flap of syntheflesh underneath that to insert an optic plug. Directly controlling something – perhaps one of the telefactors.

'It is possible. I believe this one protective measure will ensure the contained information does not fall into the hands, tentacles or claws of alien lifeforms.'

Blegg grinned. He liked this AI – it possessed a dry sense of humour.

'You're keeping it clean, then.'

'Yes, now, but even though this object came from an environment in which DNA could not remain intact, just by bringing it aboard this station, it must have come in contact with complete DNA strands. That it has not self-destructed suggests different rules apply to the whole. I suspect those fragments that broke away then cued themselves to disintegrate. This would prevent any hostiles from cutting the artefact apart to obtain its secrets.'

'So what is happening through the main interfaces with it?'

'It absorbed the data I transmitted into it, but returned nothing until I sent in a search program. That program came back with three-dimensional measurements for the human eye.'

'I see. We are not just dealing with data storage here, are we?'

'The semi-AI program I later sent in returned with a hologram of the human anus – in full colour.'

Blegg laughed out loud. 'So what does it want?' he finally asked.

'From having read human DNA it has constructed virtual representations of human beings. It can read molecules by touch. Scanning indicates nanoscale sensory apparatus imbedded in the surface. I am presently transmitting language files into it with five-level data back-up.'

'Five level?'

'Apple, for example, is represented by that word in every current human language, also a hologram, genetic coding and variations, context links to human biology, mythology, semantics—'

'Okay, I get the picture. Let's hope whatever is inside there gets it too.'

'I believe it already has. Observe.'

Blegg turned to see a hologram of a naked woman rise out of the carpet. She wore a fig leaf and, while he watched, took a large bite out of a juicy apple she held.

'How coincidental that we were just discussing that.'

The hologram shattered – like glass.

'I am compromised,' announced the AI.

Just then the station lights all grew very bright. Blegg turned back to the viewing window to see the various telefactors floating around, jerking as if in the throes of silicon epilepsy. To one side a heavy-duty power feed advanced on its rams to the edge of the alien artefact. Glancing around the control room, he saw the plugged-in Golem begin shaking, one of the haimans drop out of his seat and fall flat on his back on the floor. Others not similarly connected pushed themselves back from their consoles or other equipment and began calling out to each other.

'Subverted power-feed controls . . .'

'I lost everything . . .'

'Telefactors frozen out . . .'

To the rear of the room, two of the VR booths sprung open and their occupants staggered out of them.

'What can we do?'

'Subversion protocol, we have to—'

'No,' decided Blegg, loudly and clearly.

Some of the chatter settled down as many eyes turned towards him.

'You have primacy,' agreed one of the Golem. 'What do you require of us?'

'Do nothing,' said Blegg.

He turned back to the viewing window. The power feed was now nearly in place. He saw the crystal near its point of contact, darkening as something formed there.

Then the s-con heads made contact, and the lights dimmed. A webwork of glowing lines spread through the crystal like a million cracks, then they faded to a general glow throughout it. The lights came back on again.

'Use one of the VR booths,' said Hourne.

People in the room glanced suspiciously up at the camcom points set in the ceiling, then turned to Blegg to see what he would do.

'Are you truly Hourne?' he asked.

'Yes, and no,' replied the AI.

Blegg nodded, turned, and walked across the room to step into a VR booth. He fully expected this to be an interesting experience.

– retroact 4 –

Logan passed him a joint. He placed it between the last two fingers of his right hand, cupped both of his hands over his mouth, and drew in the aerated smoke. Tracking the physical reaction through his body always gave his new face an introspective and shocked appearance, so that others always thought him more stoned than he actually was. The ache of rearranging facial muscles had receded to a dim memory – the art almost instinctive now since his time in Korea where displaying a Caucasian face gave him the time to step aside into that other space to avoid American bullets. Skin hue was a whole different problem for his cellular inner vision, but directing his immune system against the melanoma that appeared five years after Hiroshima, while he explored the Australian outback, had granted him the required know-how. Now though, it felt strange to be wearing a Japanese face again.

Studying the young stoned Americans all around him in the firelight, all debating civil rights and cursing their government's obstinacy in the face of the inevitable triumph of Marxism, Harris – formerly Herman, Hing Cho, Harold and Hiroshi – realized it was time to move on yet again. Though he looked as young as the rest of the group, he was a good twenty years older, but he felt mentally removed from them by a century.

'Man, you mount your placards on two-by-twos,' Logan was saying, 'and maybe nail 'em to the wood with four-inch nails.'

General laughter greeted this. Harris assessed this man with his long hair and his beard with plaits in. 'Peace' he often proclaimed. 'End the wars – disarm.' But he carried a flick-knife tucked into his sock, and a .45 in the kitbag beside him, along with his delicate boxed scales, a bag of heroin secreted in a sugar box and a cellophane-wrapped block of cannabis resin. The money belt underneath his tatty coat just kept getting fatter and fatter. One of his previous customers lay in the morgue right now; another one, who ended up owing just too much, Logan had carved up with the knife. The boy managed to make it to the hospital before collapsing from blood loss. They sewed his cheek back into place but could do nothing about the ear, which he had left in the car lot where Logan caught up with him.

Logan turned as Harris passed the joint on to Miranda, who looked pale and was staring at Logan intently, avidly. Miranda was short of funds now her parents had cut her off, but she found other ways to pay.

'Hey, Harris man, you should be handy. I betcha know all about that hiyah shit?' Logan made a chopping motion with his hand.

'I know some,' Harris replied. After being beaten half to death in a Paris back alley – it had all happened too fast for him to even summon the concentration to step *away* – he had gone home to learn shotokan karate, jujitsu, aikido. Now he only fought when he wanted to. He found that the focus such training gave him also provided more than ample time to step into U-space. In this situation, however, he began to feel like he wanted to fight – that there was something he needed to do before moving on. The conversation drifted on to other matters – something about rednecks fighting for the country and not understanding how they fought to keep the country in a political Stone Age.

'Hey, Logan,' Harris squirmed, rubbed at his face, scratched the crook of his arm – generally gave a good impression of what Miranda was doing as she sat beside Logan. 'I need a private word.'

Doctor Logan took up his kitbag and followed Harris into the gloom under the pines. It did not take long and was surprisingly easy. Harris chopped him across the throat, swept his feet out from underneath him, then came down with a full-force axe kick on his chest. While Logan gurgled and gagged, Harris turned him over on his front, grabbed his elbows and with a knee pressing into Logan's back, pulled hard, snapping the man's spine. He pocketed the gun and threw the kitbag into a stream as he walked away. But that night he knew, another Logan would be along some time soon.

The world was full of Logans.

– retroact ends –

7

Much has been theorized from the Darson/Dragon dialogues, but with Dragon's pronouncements being Delphic, convoluted and sometimes just plain crazy, really not much has been learned. Dragon has claimed to be an emissary from an advanced civilization, also something that just grew on Aster Colora and outlived all other lifeforms there (though there is absolutely no fossil evidence of this) and on one memorable occasion claimed to be God. On another occasion, driven almost mad by his lack of progress and on the worst side of a bottle of BelaVodka, Darson began screaming and throwing rocks at Dragon.

'You are upset,' Dragon noted.

Darson's reply is not worth recording here, suffice to say that it demonstrated his facility with languages. Later, when he calmed down a little, he asked, 'Why always so fucking Delphic? Are you incapable of giving a straight answer?'

Dragon replied, 'I am the white stone bound with the red ribbon.'

Though Darson returned to the city, where he further exercised his liver, some very high-level AIs got rather excited about that particular statement. A little research reveals that the temple at Delphi contained a white stone bound with a red ribbon – the former said to represent a navel and the latter said to represent an umbilicus. The AIs felt this proved that Dragon did indeed represent some civilization, to which it was somehow still connected, bound.

— From 'How it Is' by Gordon

'Maker technology is based on Jain technology,' Cormac suggested. Waving a hand, he dispelled the two holograms and inserted another one in their place. Now hovering in the air was the guardian creature that killed Gant on Samarkand. '*You* are based on Jain technology.'

'*There went something else,*' said Mika.

Through his gridlink Cormac sent, '*I understand the Delphic pronouncements, the lies, the half truths. Do you understand what is happening now? What has always been happening?*'

'*I understand,*' Jerusalem replied.

'*Would somebody explain?*' asked Mika.

'*Dragon is, and has always been, fighting its Maker base programming,*' Jerusalem told her.

'*Oh,*' said Mika, and nothing more.

After a pause Cormac went on, '*We could give Dragon a weapon with which to resist that programming. It might not make it any more truthful, but we won't know until we try.*' Through his link he summoned up another projection next to the guardian: one of the creatures Chaline had seen. Dragon abruptly swung two more pseudopods towards this, then became very still.

'Note the similarity between these two,' said Cormac.

'You could not have been there,' said Dragon.

'Time-inconsistent runcible,' explained Cormac. 'Eight hundred years in the future we found this.' The two made-creatures disappeared. In their place, a ruined world, a station infested with Jain substructures, spreading clouds of Jain nodes. Then more views in the same vein, one after another after another.

'The Maker civilization no longer exists,' Cormac told Dragon. 'Even the one who came here, pursuing you, sacrificed itself. The energy from the inconsistent link backlashed into the Small Magellanic Cloud, hopefully obliterating most if not all of these remnants.'

While the pictures ran, Cormac began transmitting to Dragon files compiled and still being compiled ever since the events on *Celedon* station. The sheer weight of information should convince Dragon – there should be images of other sights unknown to any who had not visited the Small Magellanic Cloud, also the Maker codes, and other minutiae from which Dragon could draw only one conclusion: it was being told the truth.

'I'm told,' Cormac went on, 'that maybe in a few million years some of those Jain nodes may drift into Polity space. It is to be hoped we'll be sufficiently advanced by then for them not to cause any bother. Either that or extinct. But what concerns me is the Jain nodes that are already here now.'

'*Multiple power surges inside it,*' Mika told him. '*Some kind of crisis.*'

Cormac observed an electrical discharge arcing from one of the cobra pseudopods down to polished ceramal. That pod began to shrivel, its sapphire eye went out, then it abruptly collapsed out of sight. The room began vibrating, as if in an earthquake.

'*Could there be a self-destruct pro—*'

Jerusalem interrupted, '*Ejecting CTDs.*'

In his gridlink Cormac sent an instruction to the surrounding machinery: *Exterior view.* He turned in his chair as the walls and ceiling apparently disappeared to reveal the living landscape outside, showing the manacle extending equatorially. Ports were opening along the metallic strip, and objects hurtling out of them and away. As he turned back, the main dragon head abruptly withdrew from him, turned and bit down on the neck of one attendant pseudopod and shook it like a terrier with a rat. The pseudopod died and dropped away as soon as released.

'It occurs to me that indirect communication might have been better for my health,' Cormac observed out loud.

'Areas burnt out inside Dragon,' Mika informed him.

Cormac continued to Dragon, 'The Makers were at war with Jain technology, then at peace with it, and thought they had mastered it. Evidently they had not.'

The dragon head swung back towards him. As it did so, more pseudopods rose from the cavity behind it. A smell filled the building – frying squid. The Dragon head blinked, its mouth seemingly twisting with distaste. A long still pause ensued – a silence Cormac felt no urge to break. Eventually the dragon head dipped and spoke.

'I am based upon Jain technology,' it concurred. 'As you surmised, the Makers investigated it and fought against it for thousands of years. They conquered it, assimilated it, and thought to have a perfect understanding of it. They then considered themselves ready for massive expansion into the main galaxy, but an alien civilization was already rapidly expanding in that galaxy.'

'That would be us, then.'

'Yes. As you also surmised, my base programming could not permit me to tell you the whole truth: only give hints, half-truths, evident lies. Now the Makers no longer exist, the foundation of my base programming no longer exists. All that remained was the self-destruct, which I have defeated. You were only seven seconds away from me using my gravtech weapon, and thus detonating those CTDs.'

'You can tell me the truth now, but will you?' Cormac wondered.

One of the newly fledged pseudopods surged forwards until its cobra head hovered just over the floor right before Cormac, its hood folded underneath. It came down until resting on the surface and reopened its hood. Objects rattled on the ceramal. Four spheres lay there, conjoined like the four Dragon spheres originally were.

'I have encased them: anti-nanite casings, then laminations of lead and diamond. The breaking of molecular bonds in these materials is not sufficient to provide energy for internal growth.'

'Jain nodes,' Cormac guessed.

Dragon continued, 'I was sent here especially to seed Jain nodes across the Polity. You people not having encountered Jain technology before, the Makers surmised that the resultant internecine conflict would wipe out both the human race and the AIs. It could have worked and may work yet – that one Jain node under Skellor's control caused considerable localized problems, but could have resulted in catastrophe for the entire Polity.'

'And where did he get his node from?' Cormac asked.

'Allow me to finish.'

Cormac sat back, considering himself rebuked. He also noted how rapidly Dragon retrieved the nodes – the pseudopod bearing them slickly disappearing back inside the scaled entity.

'Upon my arrival here, a mere three centuries ago,

I cut off all contact with my masters, the Makers and chose not to distribute the nodes, and as a result came into conflict with my base programming. This illustrates that the Maker's grasp of the technologies they employed was not as firm as they liked to believe. Jain technology changes those who use it. I originally came to consciousness in a time when the Makers would never have contemplated conquest. I retained the same attitude, but changed by the technology they used, they did not. I understood the danger to them, but they could not see it. I predicted the obliteration of their kind by Jain tech, but not so soon.'

'So you didn't come here before the human race existed, as you previously claimed?'

'No, that was a lie.'

'Samarkand?'

'I caused a catastrophe resulting in the deaths of many humans while attempting to trap and destroy the Maker. I could not then tell you the truth of why I did this – of the danger the Maker represented to humanity.'

'Such vast amounts of altruism concealed by that evil base programming,' Cormac observed.

Jerusalem replied with equal sarcasm, *'It could not possibly be anything to do with the Maker coming here to shut Dragon down, then?'*

'And the danger to yourself?' Cormac continued.

'The Maker's secondary purpose.'

'The primary?'

'To seed Jain nodes.'

'It was to shut you down, then take the nodes in your possession, and seed them itself around the Polity?'

'No.'

'Why don't you just tell me?'

'I destroyed its ship. There were no nodes aboard. You found none in its escape pod, either. And that it was so willing to return home meant it possessed none. Yet, the Maker most certainly brought more nodes with it.'

A shiver travelled up Cormac's spine. He began using cognitive programs to pick the bones out of what Dragon had told him – looking for flaws and broken logic chains.

Eventually he said, 'Tell me about Dracocorp augs.'

'The people wearing them were my eyes within the Polity.'

'But they are hierarchical – ultimate control devolving to yourself. Why would you need such control of human beings if they were just your eyes?'

'They were intended to be an army at my disposal.'

Again the cognitive programs and, after a moment, 'Dracomen.'

'The events of Samarkand focused Earth Central's attention on the Dracocorp aug networks, which are now being destroyed and, through them hunter-killer programs seek me out. At Masada I sacrificed part of myself to create a new army.'

'Why?'

'I saw Skellor provided with a Jain node. I have tracked vessels and alien entities arriving from outside the Polity. The nodes that were in the Maker's possession are in the control of someone or something out there.'

It all made perfect sense and Cormac could find no catastrophic breaks in the logic chains, no flaws and no anomalies that fell outside the story's parameters. This meant that Dragon was telling the truth – or else was an Olympian liar. Unfortunately, Dragon could be precisely the latter.

*

The AI Coloron ran twenty-four runcibles: ten were located in vast complexes spread throughout the main arcology or MA, six located in the growing arcology called inevitably SA, secondary arcology, and the other eight serviced the rest of the planet. Twelve of these runcibles were permanently set for departure, and the remaining twelve alternated evenly. It was a deliberately designed disparity which elsewhere worked to reduce the planetary population – it being simply more difficult to come here than to leave. However, though the runcibles remained in constant operation, still the birth rate here exceeded the emigration rate.

Coloron, now into its fourth major expansion of processing power, for the second time that week had devalued the standard credit unit by half an energy point. The planetary currency still lay well within energy expenditures necessary to keep everyone alive and comfortable, but the degree of comfort had degraded over the last few years. Some areas of the two arcologies were becoming slightly shabby, the goods that could be purchased for the dole of twenty units per day were getting scarcer – designed more for basic utility than to be aesthetically pleasing – and planetwide the choices of nutrition had become less varied. Also, throughout the north-eastern expansion, the living spaces were slightly smaller, and parkland areas more compressed. It could not carry on like this, and it seemed unlikely that it would, but for entirely unexpected reasons.

Coloron often pondered how a race, in which the stupid seemed more inclined to breed, had managed to come this far, and why human intelligence persisted – a discussion point in the nature vs nurture debate which had not died in half a millennium. The AI knew that if for one moment it slackened its control of this planet's total systems, disaster would inevitably ensue. Power from the numerous fusion reactors based on the planet was abundant, but everything else ran at full stretch. The overall planetary temperature was on the rise, and this world being smaller than Earth, its artificial ecology consequently stood on the verge of collapse. In fact the planet could not handle a population above three billion, so drastic measures would have been necessary within a ten-year time span. However, in the current situation, perhaps such measures were merely a halcyon dream.

'I needed to balance the equation,' explained Coloron. 'If I turned all runcibles to cater for departure only, the death rate from resulting civil unrest would have risen above the increase in emigration, which incidentally would not have increased sufficiently to require full usage of all the runcibles.'

The Golem, Azroc – head of the MA section of monitor force for planetary security – replied, 'Yet the increase in civil unrest would have served the purpose of pushing the departure rate higher . . . You note how we are talking in the past tense now?'

'Yes, but let us continue our present discussion, in the hope that it will still apply. Regarding civil unrest, you have to also factor in the troglodyte quotient.'

'And that would be?'

'An agoraphobic tendency found here, and an inability to change. You know what happens: any sign of trouble and citizens retreat to their homes and stay there, hoping it will all go away.'

'I thought the incentives were changing that attitude.' The Golem picked up his pulse-rifle from where it leant against a wall, and directed the team nearby to spread out across the park, and then other teams in this section, not visible to him but with whom he maintained constant com, to also take their positions. Coloron listened in on these multiple communications from the Golem. His forces now enclosed a cylindrical section of the arcology, from the lowest levels to the roof, with monitors ready up above in the fields, ensconced in pulse-cannon tanks. No citizens were being allowed back into the enclosed area, and those who came out of it were kept confined prior to vigorous interview and scanning. Five thousand such were now in confinement, of whom only a hundred had so far been interviewed and moved on to holding areas, where they would remain until the crisis ended. It might end – Coloron reminded itself of that.

'Discord sown by Separatist groups induced a certain paranoia concerning all AI incentives. Urban legend has it that we want to send them out to undeveloped worlds as agrarian labourers. A full one per cent of my processing power has been in constant use scotching these memes and sowing my own.'

'Plague scenario?' Azroc suggested.

The AI observed autoguns – mid-level pulse-cannons mounted on four legs – moving in to complement the present forces. It explained, 'No, anything effective enough to drive the troglodytes out of their caves would also cause a catastrophic cascade. For every citizen departing by runcible, 1.2 other citizens would die. That rate would then rise, when the current Separatist organization took advantage of the chaos, to 6.6. The memes I sowed were more subtle: the occasional news stories examining statistical analyses of human lifespans – how the average length of life here is a mere 143 years while elsewhere in the Polity it is as high as 206 and rising;

comparative studies of the suicide rates; and accident statistics. I also concentrated on stories about those who have left here and made a success of their new lives – have become important contributors to the Polity. In that respect I was building the meme that other worlds welcome Coloron citizens because of their superior abilities.'

'Hardly the truth,' said the Golem.

'But a method that would have worked within the requisite time span.'

Would have . . .

Still no return from the one secure optic line it retained for connecting it to the blank area within the arcology – where all its sensors had been knocked out. Not knowing what caused this failure, the AI had immediately isolated the area, setting a physical perimeter a hundred yards back from it. That margin was gone now. It had also instituted many new security protocols within its informational networks: virus and worm defences designed by the AI Jerusalem, and recently distributed to all runcible AIs, also attack-hardened channels and numerous ways of physically disconnecting hardware should that become necessary.

The Sparkind units now arrived and were soon preparing to go in. Earlier the AI had sent in four hundred drones. They reported nothing unusual until five attempted diagnostic analysis of some of the camcoms and pincams. Those five drones immediately went offline, and were observed dropping to the floor. The subversion techniques used to take out Coloron's eyes and ears within the enclosed area, and to then eliminate those drones attempting to interfere, must be highly sophisticated, but were not yet employed in any kind of direct attack. But eventually something would break, and Coloron entertained a nasty suspicion about what it might be. Then all previous calculations, all those clever plans, all those carefully constructed memes would mean nothing. The AI might be on the brink of losing a planet.

'I think that time span just got truncated,' Azroc observed.

'I require confirmation be—' Coloron focused attention on the communication link opening directly from Earth Central, and the information package that preceded it.

The package: *Hostiles within Polity> Existence of more Jain nodes> Direct link established between Skellor and Coloron Separatist Thellant N'komo.*

Within seconds the AI absorbed the interviews conducted by Ian Cormac, and the evidence collected by agent Thorn and his team. More information became available concerning all the events on station *Celedon* – it was relevant, but not necessary in order for conclusions to be drawn. Then, in fractions of a second, came absolute confirmation. Through one of its drones, Coloron saw a woman peering up at the drone while she tried to light a cigarette. Something silvery stabbed out of the wall beside her, through her ear and right into her head. Coloron glimpsed her eyes filling with blood before the drone went offline – before all the remaining drones went offline.

'Main dracomen forces are being dispatched now to MA runcibles,' announced the Earth Central AI. 'Thorn and a small force of them will arrive in five hours by ship to assist you.' While EC spoke, Coloron scanned data concerning dracomen abilities, and most importantly their resistance to Jain tech subversion. 'Open the MA runcibles to incomers only until all forces have arrived, then out-port to Isostations.'

There was not the slightest possibility that a billion people could be evacuated through just these ten runcibles. Other ships would be on their way, but by the time they got here there might not be anything to evacuate, or perhaps anything it would be considered safe to evacuate. If they did not manage to stop what was developing in that isolated cylindrical section of MA, then millions would die. Coloron reluctantly initiated a satellite it held geostationary above the main arcology, and that satellite's toroidal fusion reactor fired up.

'Azroc, pull out the Sparkind and move your forces back radially one mile. Pull out any citizens still within the new zone. Sat strike imminent.'

The AI watched forces withdrawing, then something else caught its attention.

The conventional aug, computer, and gridlink network was supported by two hundred planetary servers, each controlled by subminds. It was a network easily monitored by the AI, and therefore one not used by the more paranoid citizens or those going about nefarious activities. Such types used augs that supported their own server-free networks using encrypted com. Coloron regularly employed eight subminds in the singular task of breaking into those networks so as to track down criminals. The most difficult and widespread network they faced consisted of Dracocorp augs which used hugely variable encryption and protective kill programs to constantly frustrate the eight subminds. The best access these minds ever got to that network was when those in possession of such augs chose to link into the conventional net, but on the whole those doing so were not

involved in anything seriously illegal. But just by monitoring the level of activity, Coloron realized something
major was happening in Dracocorp network.

Then a view into an interview room. The man being
questioned screamed and clamped his hands to his head.
His Dracocorp aug seemed to be moving. He stood up,
staggered to one side, and fell over. Blood trickled from
his ear on the aug side of his head.

Then thousands of similar views of this happening
throughout both MA and SA – all around the planet.
From Dracocorp augs, viral programs began propagating to the servers. Coloron shut down these servers
instantly, and denied Dracocorp access to all the other
servers. However, twenty-eight of those infected would
not shut down, just continued to broadcast. But this
threat had been prepared for and the AI transmitted
twenty-eight distinct signals. Fifteen lights ignited over
and above the planet – satellites being instantly vaporized. However, not all the servers on those satellites had
been taken over and Coloron lost more than just fifteen
server subminds. Seven explosions inside the two arcologies took out the remaining Jain-controlled servers.
People died as well, hundreds of them: others lay screaming in corridors traversed by walls of fire.

On a tracking map of the Dracocorp network, Coloron now saw lights blinking out, too. In the first five
seconds, nine thousand people died. Then the rate
halved after another five seconds, and so seemed set to
continue. The man in the interview room did not die,
however. After fifteen seconds he staggered to his feet.

'Where . . . Legate?'

The female monitor who had been interviewing him
was herself standing up.

'Where?' The man leapt over the desk and brought her down. He began smashing his fist at her face but, even in a prone position, she blocked the blows. It seemed a wild and inept attack. Other monitors soon piled into the room to subdue him. But similar scenes were repeating all around the planet. Thirty-five million people wearing Dracocorp augs, which turned grey against their heads, began attacking others and demanding to know the location of 'the Legate'. Then the weapons began to appear: personal armament, guns from Separatist caches, guns ripped from the hands of monitors. In a tube station a woman screaming 'Legate!' fired a pulse-rifle repeatedly into a panicking crowd.

Coloron initiated every single drone available, and quickly diverted resources to autofactories to manufacture more. Many of these drones carried pulse-guns capable of being set to stun. Pillar-mounted drones began dropping from ceilings or rising out of floors. A ceiling drone finally knocked out the woman in the station, but then a man close by took up her rifle and fired it into her head, on full automatic, before the drone brought him down too. Chaos growing everywhere: fires, mobs . . . panic in the huge runcible complexes. Just in time, Coloron altered the instructions to the drones deployed there, and they turned their weapons away from the armed personnel now pouring through the runcibles.

They swept through the ten MA runcibles in groups of five, at fast, five-second turnover, scaly and ferocious creatures pouring into the lounges and embarkation areas, all of them heavily armed and lethal. This became just too much for the crowds already fleeing those mad individuals who were attacking their fellow citizens indiscriminately. They began crowding towards the exits as the dracomen moved swiftly through the area. Those driven mad by the Dracocorp augs soon began dropping fast under stun fire, till within minutes no owner of such augs remained standing in those areas. And still the dracomen poured through.

A gridlink channel opened – secure ECS coding and direct to the AI.

'We require sitrep,' a voice murmured.

Coloron scanned for an identifier but found none. The AI was just about to cut the channel when an information package from EC came through the runcible, explaining that the dracomen minds could operate like gridlinks, and it was one of them that was communicating with Coloron. The AI then transmitted an overview of the present situation, updated every minute, or sooner if something critical occurred. The dracomen responded immediately. Some of them hurtled over the top of the mobs crammed into the exits, stepping on heads and shoulders, others shot reptile-fast along the walls and ceilings above them. Then they were positioned ahead of the crowds, driving them back into the complex.

'Four minutes to turnover,' they reported.

Some of the mobs would not turn back right away, but they did once the dracomen shot down the leaders. The resulting crush would certainly kill some, but this was all about speed. Other dracomen grabbed those at the rear of the throng and directed them ungently back towards the runcibles. Still more of the creatures moved beyond all this into the arcology itself, stunning those who had been maddened by their augs, directing the others back towards the runcible complex.

Coloron observed them only for a few seconds more,

then returned its attention to the epicentre of these events. Azroc's forces were still moving back as instructed, but now they were coming under fire. People, some wearing Dracocorp augs, were emerging from the blanked area. Many of these were armed and they seemed organized – following military attack patterns. The monitors kept knocking them down with stun blasts, yet they rose again within seconds, taking up their weapons and coming on. No defence could be sustained like this.

On direct encrypted com to Azroc, Coloron ordered, 'Shoot to kill.'

Azroc immediately relayed the command, and monitors adjusted the settings on their weapons. Full-strength pulse-fire slammed into the attackers, burning holes through torsos and heads. The attack staggered to a halt, then, horribly, Coloron observed a female casualty standing up, retrieving her short rail-gun, while a nub of pink flesh oozed out to fill the hole in her chest.

Azroc instructed, 'Sparkind, we need proton fire.'

Proton fire ensued: violet fire and smoke, burning bodies, walls, floors and ceilings collapsing, ventilation shafts and ducts ripped open. Updated on events, the dracomen out in the arcology began to head towards Azroc's forces.

Turnaround. Now all the dracomen had arrived the runcibles reversed to transmit evacuees to Isostations. The dracomen nearby began forcing them through. Meanwhile Azroc's forces finally reached a point Coloron considered far enough from the previously enclosed area of the arcology.

'Firing particle cannon,' Coloron sent.

The turquoise beam spat down from the toroidal satellite, struck a maize field and turned it into a firestorm, bored down into earth, then through composite layers, and deep into the arcology, precisely down the axis of the affected cylindrical section. In sight of Azroc's forces, fire blasted from corridors, across urban parks, through shopping arcades, and sports or VR centres. It blew people along with it like burning leaves. The Coloron AI calculated that with just that one blast it killed over forty thousand inhabitants. The tentacular Jain structure began spreading out of the wreckage, fingering out of ventilation shafts and oozing sluglike along split electrical and optic ducts, and this confirmed to the AI that many of them were as good as dead already. The AI watched that growth slow down gradually to a stop, and dared to hope. Then abruptly the Jain substructure waved its spiky fingers to dismiss hope, and surged on.

Coloron broadcast through the remaining server network, and via public screens and address systems: 'Urgent evacuation order: a hostile alien organic technology is attempting to take over MA.'

On the screens the AI displayed scenes of what was happening. It took it a full two seconds to calculate how best its order should be carried out. Some sections could be evacuated via the runcibles, others would have to make use of the exits around the arcology perimeter. An external zone would have to be set up to quarantine MA from the rest of the planet, to prevent any physical manifestation of this invading technology from escaping, but allowing enough room to get inhabitants out of the arcology itself. Corolon assigned a submind to the vast logistical problem of moving a billion souls to safety, and knew, with mathematical certainty, that those forty thousand dead were only the start.

*

Ten yards above the floor, one set of her assister-frame limbs gripping a rung set into the crashfoam-covered wall behind her, Orlandine studied her latest creation. Precisely in the centre of the chamber, the yard-wide gimbals device was supported within a light scaffold of bubble-metal poles attached to the floor and ceiling. Its outer two rings served to present any facet of an inner spherical framework to three telescopic heads. One of those heads now contained plasmonic lens gear from a nanoscope she had taken apart inside the ship, another came from the nanoassembler, which could also be utilized as a disassembler, and the third was a submolecular scanner. The Jain node itself was clamped centrally in the inner framework by six equidistantly spaced chainglass points. This whole, the framework and chainglass clamps, made no physical contact with the outer rings, for it was buoyed and rotated by magnetic fields. The two outer rings were also enclosed in a shimmer-shield sphere out of which, even now, the air was being evacuated. Studying the Jain node underneath a nanoscope, she felt to be too dangerous now, for every time she drew close to it the visible activity on its surface increased. Orlandine could only suppose that inside it some additional host-identification program had come online.

There were safer ways to do this, layer upon layer of security protocols, shell upon shell of vacuum and armour, and even layers of automated weapons. She could in fact have automated everything here and studied the node from a few thousand miles away. However, it seemed to her that now its only method of affecting the outside world was informationally via the optic cables leading from the sensory heads, which it could do even if she was a long way away and even if every gun in the

Polity was pointed at this thing. But this present set-up was similar to the one she had used back at the Cassius Project, when she accepted that, in studying something like this, certain dangers were inherently unavoidable, and before she got scared, destroyed all her equipment there, and returned the node to its case in her quarters. Orlandine rubbed her two human hands together. Time to go to work.

Rather than go immediately into some virtuality to assess scanning data, she clambered down the rungs to the floor, then stepped over to where skeins of optic cable connected to the computer hardware and screen through which she controlled the nanoscope, disassembler and submolecular scanner – all three now working synergetically. For her initial scans she decided not to connect herself directly to these devices, so instead employed a simple touchboard and interactive screen system. Using the board she called up an image of the node, laid a grid over it, and focused down on one single square. This square then divided into a grid from which she selected another square, then down and down in size until she could see actual molecular structures, then back to reveal the nodal landscape. She next set previously constructed programs to analysing the structures detected. As expected, this was like trying to understand an entire civilization from a pot shard.

Too slow.

Orlandine shrugged to herself. This exercise was only to see how the Jain node might react to investigation. As yet it remained inert. She continued scanning different areas of it but revealing only what she had found before: pores twenty angstroms wide with chain molecules coiled inside each like a jellyfish sting; isotopic gold threads; a matrix of photo-optic and piezo-electric compounds linked by s-con carbon fullerene nanotubes. These it used to first sense its host, then begin taking over. Finally, after hours of investigation necessarily distanced by console and screen, frustration drove her to move in closer – something she had not risked before.

First she removed the console from the equation and began controlling the equipment by radio emission from her carapace, then impatient with this she plugged direct optic links into it. Subsequently, the screen definition and speed began to annoy her, so she projected the images directly into her visual cortex. It was then but a small step to move on into a virtuality.

In her virtual world mere thought became action, and that world contained no representation of herself, merely her godlike omniscience. She began creating subpersonae, choosing and assigning areas of study to them, and collating their data output herself. The submolecular scanner managed to penetrate up to a hundred angstroms into the node's surface, and that, combined with the nanoscope views of the surface itself, enabled her to begin constructing a model of its outer layers. The scanner also revealed regular quantum entanglement in silica crystals – a sure sign that they were quantum processors. Simple connections could then be divined: sensory apparatus connected to processors, which in turn connected to the 'stinging pores' and to structures deeper inside. Allowing her subpersonae to continue working, she mentally sat back and considered what she was doing and why.

This piece of alien nanotechnology contained deliberate quantum levels of arrangement that might even define some of it as picotech. It was packed solid, this little egg, and probably nothing inside it was without purpose. This consequently inferred that, as a whole, its purpose must be huge. She already knew that purpose: it grew, it subjugated and subsumed, it destroyed. However, she also understood that this node was probably a key to a whole alien technology.

Knowledge is power . . .

Learning its secrets might take her beyond what she was, beyond subservience to AIs, or to anything. *Her* purpose then was the pursuit of knowledge which would result in increased ability to manipulate her environment – which was after all one basis of haiman philosophy.

Skellor had used such a node and was either destroyed by it or by those who hunted him. This would not happen to her. Fortunately ECS warned her what a node like this could do before this one fell into her possession. When she first removed it from the case, she had taken the precaution of not touching it, in fact of opening it in a vacuum-sealed tank. Perhaps the expectation of those who passed it on to her had been for her to take no such precautions . . . Outside of its case the node did not at first react to its environment – the ceramal tongues she used to handle it, the chainglass shelf it rested on, the inert gas inside the display cabinet – so what *precisely* did it react to? She was told it responded to intelligent, technological beings, but how did it identify them?

Orlandine returned her attention to the data gathered by her subpersonae. Interestingly one of them had revealed sensory structures capable of reacting to the molecular components of their environment. By making comparative analysis she realized the node's sensorium was somewhat superior to that of a human being. However, inside the display case it had been in contact with nothing but inert gas and chainglass, therefore, from its shelf in the display, it must have *seen* her. This thought led nowhere, however. She realized that the only real way to learn how the node operated was to extract one of those silica crystals, one of those quantum computers, and find out exactly what it contained.

In the first moments Thellant felt trapped in a net of white-hot wires. Movement squirmed throughout his body, tearing, shifting, connecting. His skull felt ready to burst and when he pressed a hand to his forehead, bone and skin shifted underneath it. His sight faded, sounds became dull and echoey, then disappeared altogether. When his lungs shut down and he began to suffocate, he panicked but there was nothing he could do: he just lay paralysed in that same spot. But he could feel more closely than before his connection to his Dracocorp aug and to the network over which it held primacy. Information flowed random and chaotic, but the sheer quantity of it he perceived inside his own head was huge, and somehow being read by something else that was becoming part of him. However, as that information flow increased, his consciousness faded.

Bastard Legate . . .

Flashes of perception: a group of four men standing in a corridor ranting about the shortage of their favourite beer; a woman having an orgasm in some VR fantasy about Golem lovers; hunger and growth – finding a power cell and the intricate components of an atmosphere monitor, pulling those apart, pulling the cell apart, feeding and spreading down an optic cable while reading its traffic on the way; a second wave of support substructure spiralling like a vine around the outside of the cable afterwards, digesting the coating to create itself; a fusion reactor, connection, and surge of intoxicating power with a concomitant surge of growth; then sight returning.

Where are you, Legate?

Dracocorp network. Millions bending to his will to ask that question and none other.

Something of self returned, and at its core rested hate for the Legate. Thellant gazed across his apartment. He now sat against the wall, his back to the primary outlets to his computer system. He did not remember moving – he had been *moved*. Every part of him hurt badly, yet he was not breathing. From rips in his trousers grey vine-like growth had spread across the carpet, penetrated the floor, spread up the walls. Wherever there was a power outlet or optic port, it had bunched, then branched. Hairlike rootish tendrils spread from the larger branches, and wherever they lay it seemed someone had poured acid. One growth had reached his com console and branched out all over it. The console, screen, desk and even chair were gone, and now only Jain substructure outlined their shapes. But, when he thought about all the data he once securely stored there, he could sense it, feel its availability to him. And there was so much more he could know.

Millions of eyes and ears became available to him. Similar to the facility available to him through his aug, he could cast his perception out and away from him: corridors, parks, lidos, VR chambers and autofactories. He encompassed a vast area, but that was not all. Mobile sensory apparatus also came under his control, and it took him a moment to realize these were human beings absorbed into the growing structure like everything else

– extensions of himself. They spread out from him, the vanguard of his *growth*. They armed themselves, those that could. It was preprogrammed: everything not himself, not Jain, was the enemy.

Then he found the gulf, a region previously occupied by his extended structure and now blacked out. Nearby he found a child, one side of her body burnt down to the bone, but muscles still capable of obeying the impulses of the mycelial structure inside her. He stood her up, walked her into this black area. Within minutes she moved through incinerated corridors to the edge of a well cut down through the arcology. The area below looked like the pit of hell; above curtains of smoke blew across open sky. Satellite strike. The AI must have acted drastically to destroy the centre of Jain growth. Thellant understood at once a basic growth pattern implicit in the Jain structure. It grew *acentric* precisely to avoid this. He, the core, lay not at its centre but right against one edge of the current spread. He must move before the AI realized its mistake. But how?

The *how* became utter and immediate temptation. He did not need to be Thellant, he could *become* all and lose himself in this vast and ever-increasing extension of himself. But a life of being a distinct entity, ever the centre, ever in control, made that option antithetical to him. He resisted it with all his will and fought to retake the territory of his own body. Turning perception inward, he studied what had been wrought and what had been wrecked within him. Withdrawing growth inside himself he repaired damage. This was easy, everything destroyed had been recorded and everything recorded could be rebuilt.

Within minutes he restarted his heart and lungs.

Alterations to some structures in his brain negated pain signals, oxygenated blood reaching his brain returned to him much of what he had been. But in the end he realized he could not return to being a completely distinct human being. That way he would sacrifice too much perception and too much power, and so many of his former body's organs were inefficient, weak. Now, totally incorporating the structure into himself, he improved their function, their material, their strength. Minutes passed before he realized, while laminating his bones with metals conveyed into him by the structure, that he was losing sight of his primary purpose. Minutes after that he hauled himself from the floor, Jain structure turned brittle all around him, and breaking away. But he did not entirely separate from it. Perpetually in contact across the electromagnetic spectrum, the air about him hazed with power. Now he was as mobile as those other humans, but he was the prime component, *in control*. Leaving his apartment he first walked, then ran, finding his way down, deep.

8

At the beginning of the Prador–Human War, drones were, on the whole, merely AI telefactored robots: welders and other designs of maintenance bots, AG probes carrying sensor arrays, security drones that remained wired into the complexes or ships that AIs controlled, or other versions for various security/police applications. Some of these did have limited autonomy, but few could be classified as AI, being merely extensions of an AI: hands, eyes and guns. During the war, however, it became necessary to give these drones greater and greater autonomy, since the many EM weapons employed tended to fracture comlinks between an AI and its telefactored drone. Initially the new versions were sub-AI and only able to implement complex programs, but it became evident that artificial intelligence was the one big advantage the Polity possessed over the Prador, so war drones were eventually given complete autonomy, consciousness. They became fully AIs, with all that implied. The first of these drones were quite simple – an armoured shell, weapons, brain, and drive system – and also quite effective, but casualties were high and production needed to be maintained at a frenetic level. Quality control suffered and AI drones, which in peacetime would have needed substantial adjustments, were sent to the front. As a matter of expediency, flawed crystal got used rather than discarded. Personality fragments were copied, sometimes not very well, successful fighters recopied. The traits constructed or duplicated were not necessarily those evincing intelligence or morality. The Polity wanted fighting grunts, even if they were metal soldiers with crystal minds. This whole scenario acted as a fast evolutionary process in the development of AI war drones, the inevitable result being that towards the end of the war they were mostly crafty, belligerent, and very good at killing things and blowing things up. It is of course axiomatic that the soldier returning from war cannot easily settle into civilian life. So it was with the drones, and many unfortunate incidents after the war led to a great distrust of such entities. The manufacture of them ceased and AIs returned to using telefactors or drones loaded with their own subminds, which could be easily resubsumed. Many war drones found themselves niches within Polity society, many left it to find their fortunes elsewhere, and many simply turned themselves off.

– From her lecture 'Modern Warfare'
by EBS Heinlein

Below, three antigravity cars could be seen taking to the sky. A silent flash ensued and, one after the other as if in a chain reaction, all three disintegrated and wreckage rained down on the arcology roof cropfields, drawing shafts of smoke through the air, then bouncing fire trails through the crops.

'It is, as they say, getting ugly down there,' Jack observed, speaking from the shuttle's console.

As far as understatement went, Thorn thought that a stinger. Monitors strove to contain over three hundred separate riots instigated by armed Separatists wearing Dracocorp augs. One entire subsector of the arcology had become a no-go zone. There was also firing at the perimeter, over the sea and in the surrounding multilayered fields, flickering all around like summer lightning. But Coloron strictly applied its quarantine. Though informational infection initially spread planetwide, Coloron had halted and now contained it. Actual physical Jain infestation was only present in Main Arcology itself, and the AI could not afford to let it out. MA would not survive this, Thorn reckoned, though perhaps the rest of the planet might be saved.

'Who is this Legate?' he wondered.

'Perhaps some enemy of Thellant N'komo,' Jack suggested.

'We've yet to establish he is the principal cause of this,' Thorn observed.

'It seems very likely that he is. The speed of informational infection through the Dracocorp network is the prime indicator of that. From what we know of Jain technology, that would not be possible had the host been one possessing a subservient aug within the network. Coloron also informs me that the first to show signs of infection were Separatists who were being watched.'

'Skellor managed it without being dominant in a Dracocorp aug network.'

'Yes, but in one case using the transmitters of the *Occam Razor*, and in other cases by having to physically touch and subvert with Jain tech the prime aug concerned. All the evidence here indicates that someone has joined with a Jain node, without any technological support: witness the speed of Jain growth and a rather stupid choice of location.'

'Following your reasoning', said Thorn, 'it would

seem this Thellant joined with a Jain node either unwillingly or by mistake.'

'Yes,' Jack replied, 'which perhaps returns us to your original question.'

'Huh?'

'During initial Jain growth the host would not be thinking clearly, perhaps never would again, but his last thoughts, intentions, strong emotions would propagate through the aug network. Those thoughts would probably all be about the Jain node itself, the growth of which would at first cause great pain.'

The shuttle, piloted remotely by Jack, now descended towards a raised landing pad near the centre of the arcology. Thorn gazed out to where a cloud of smoke belched from the hole the Coloron AI had cut down into the structure.

'So it is probable this "Legate" is in some way connected to or responsible for the presence of the Jain node?' Thorn asked.

'That would seem likely,' Jack replied.

The shuttle landed with a thump, the two following shuttles settling shortly afterwards. Thorn glanced round, but did not need to give any orders: the doors were already open and dracomen disembarking. Scar was aboard one of the other shuttles, and all three shuttles contained the entire dracoman complement from the *NEJ*. Thorn stood up, waiting until they were clear, then followed them all outside. More dracomen were coming up from the arcology itself – those who had arrived via runcible. Communication between them was silent and a large proportion of the dracomen began bleeding away to assist in the battle raging around the perimeter of the

Jain infestation. Thorn's collar-mounted comunit beeped to let him know it was on.

'Scar,' he turned as that dracoman came up to him, 'make sure they keep you updated. We need to nail this bastard fast.' He glanced beyond Scar to where twenty other dracomen gathered, all loaded down with proton weapons, hand stunners, and a selection of multipurpose grenades.

Just then a flash ignited the sky with turquoise fire. Out over the arcology a pillar of flame ate round in a circle. Thorn blinked, turned his head away from the glare until it finally died. A thunderous crashing ensued and the shock wave hit, leaving people staggering, shaking the platform and even jouncing the shuttles on their sprung feet. A ball of fire rose into the air from the strike point.

'Jack,' Thorn spoke into his comlink, 'I'm thinking that maybe we have a conflict of interests here. Coloron is still trying to take out the centre and, presuming that to be Thellant N'komo, we lose our reason for being here.'

'Incorrect,' the AI replied, 'Coloron has just cut a perimeter. There will be no further attempts to burn out the centre. All ensuing strikes will be either to create new perimeters or simply to prevent physical spread outside MA.'

Panicked citizens leaving, leaving in gravcars, and maybe just one of their vehicles carrying some small part of what now grew inside here – that's all it would take.

'Okay . . . do either you or Aphran have anything for me yet?' Jack was still taking apart the recorded mind of Freyda, while the woman's body, now a blank slate, went into coldsleep. This task took up much of the AI's capacity, so the other prisoners had yet to be subjected to the same before being placed in coldsleep. Instead, Aphran had interrogated them throughout the journey here – not verbal interrogation but via their augs. It was a complex and wearing task, more like searching determinedly through scrambled files than asking direct questions.

Jack replied, 'Thellant's main base is inside the newly cut perimeter – further proof that he is the host. After the failure of the initial strike to halt Jain growth, Coloron projected a protective *acentric* growth of the structure, so encompassed it inside that last strike. Outside that perimeter, monitors are now moving in on secondary Separatist bases, which on the whole are central to the riots or lie in the no-go zones. Dracomen are meanwhile checking their safe houses. Due to the cell structure of the Separatist organization here, not all of these will necessarily be found.'

'Right.' Thorn paused. 'We need another way to search. Has Coloron tried hunter-killer programs?'

'Coloron has tried and failed. Its programs are not sufficiently sophisticated to penetrate Jain informational architecture. Coloron is not Jerusalem.'

Thorn reached into his pocket and once again took out the memstore containing the HK program. It was dented now and there was a burn on its surface – from the shots fired through the roof of Thorn's aircar on Osterland. He thought, however, it gave the box character.

'Program . . . you are, I take it, up-to-date with current events?'

'I am,' the box vibrated.

'Could you gain access to the Jain growth here via one of the prisoners?'

'Substructure would be best.'

He pocketed the box. That figured; always the hard way.

Thorn led the way across the landing platform to the drop-shaft terminus positioned centrally, Scar and the other twenty dracomen falling in around him. He knew that his investigation might be coming up against a wall here. Thellant N'komo was the next link in the chain, so they must capture him, question him. But how did you do that considering what it seemed Thellant had become? Thorn could only try his best.

He stepped into the irised gravity field of a shaft, dropped through one of the ceramal tubes below the platform, past where chainglass windows showed packed soil beyond, was slowed at an exit with dracomen backing up behind him, and then stepped out into an open park surrounded by high foam-stone walls pocked with balconies and windows. Ahead, a line of monitors stood ranged behind delicate-stepping autoguns, beyond which a mass of humanity surged past, running until slowed by the crowd density around a nearby exit tunnel.

'Keep moving. Keep moving,' some com system instructed them.

Above the crowd hovered two gun platforms manned by monitors. Panic was palpable, and it turned to screams when explosions suddenly shuddered through the arcology. A high-up balcony belched smoke and dropped burning stick figures.

'Keep moving.'

Thorn paused, checking his palm-com. 'Just received a map.' He turned, scanning around. 'The crowds are too thick here. We need to go that way.' He led the way to a closed maintenance door, which clunked and rumbled as he approached and slowly swung open. Next, a gantry alongside a sheer steel cliff beside which welding robots rose like the front ends of giant beetles with their wing cases and abdomens chopped away. The gantry widened into a fenced semicircular platform fronting a wide roller door for transferring heavy equipment. The door was jammed. Before Thorn could even speak, Scar fired his proton weapon into the ridged metal surface. In viridian fire, most of the door slewed away like foil in an acetylene flame. They ducked through, avoiding a small sleet of hot metal from one still-burning edge.

Narrow accessways. More doors. Corpses strewn across a deck where heavy robots stood on gecko-stick caterpillar treads; their owlish metallic heads bowed over multi-jointed arms for handling and cutting foam-stone and sheet construction materials. The dracomen spread out, checked the bodies.

'No Jain,' observed Scar.

They were just citizens ripped apart by rail-gun fire. Thorn guessed he would probably never know what had happened here, but he filed away the fact that dracomen could tell by the merest touch whether someone contained Jain tech.

Further access ways, then down into a small monorail station where a single carriage of one train awaited them. They climbed aboard and it smoothly accelerated away. Past them from the opposite direction came a seemingly endless train packed with people, their faces pressed against windows. Thorn's team left their carriage when it stopped briefly to let them off by a maintenance tunnel a few hundred yards around the bend from a busy station. Thorn could not see the crowds waiting there, but their sound was a constant roar. Before he and the dracomen were even out of sight of the line, another train returned along the maglev track, their own carriage at its head, and now crammed full of humanity.

A stair from the tunnel eventually gave them access into a public corridor, along one side of which hothouse porches, lit with sun lights and crammed with foliage, led to private homes. Down the maintenance ladder of an inoperative drop-shaft, then along a gantry suspended above an autofactory. Below them monolithic machines conveyed ceramal casings to each other, hissing and reconfiguring themselves, cold-forging metal, electron-beam welding, inserting components in flickering blurs of hydraulics, spinning bright new metal and passing the casings on. Thorn noted exit shafts, like those out of some hive, through which departed floating lines of the leaf-shaped drones those casings had become: bare-metal, utile, armed. Coloron's war industry was at full production, but the businesses of killing and destroying were easy. Concurrently, the AI's logistical nightmare of trying to move its citizens out of the way was akin to pouring a bag of flour through the eye of a needle.

Finally they arrived at the perimeter Coloron had cut, where smoke gusted across a burnt-out stadium. Every surface was layered with soot-streaked fire-retardant foam. Gobbets of foam tumbled through the air like spindrift, and the grass pitch was blackened. When the smoke cleared momentarily, Thorn could see only half a stadium. The smoke gusted from fires blazing on the other side of a gulf. Here, the arcology was sheared right through, and across the gulf he could see incinerated wreckage and girders projected into the air, separate floors shown in cross section. Thorn realized he was looking out at one edge of a separated piece of the arcology, standing like some vast tower block, bomb-wrecked all around its exterior.

Down on the blackened grass were deployed monitors and a sparse scattering of dracomen, autoguns, and two armoured vehicles with twin front turrets that mounted proton cannons facing the gulf. Thorn also recognized Sparkind down there – not by any uniform they wore but simply by the way they moved. What was the human cost of this? No way could Coloron have moved the entire population out of there before sectioning off the area. The AI had made a choice and cut, excising Jain gangrene while necessarily removing healthy tissue as well. It was a harsh emotionless calculation of loss and gain, probably assessed down to a hundred decimal places.

'Azroc, Golem,' Scar pointed.

Thorn glanced at the dracoman, accepting that Scar was communicating with AI systems at a level he himself could not. He wondered if he should really get himself an aug or a gridlink, but resented the idea. He led the way down steps between charcoaled tiers of seats still crackling and plinking as they cooled. The Golem stood beside one of the armoured vehicles, leaning against it, with a pulse-rifle tucked under one arm. His back was to Thorn and the dracomen as they approached, but he pushed himself away from the vehicle and turned as they drew close.

'I would be interested to know how you intend to capture and contain the cause of all this,' Azroc said and stabbed a thumb over his shoulder back towards the newly burnt canyon and, almost as if in response, there came from the gulf a distant flashing followed by dull thunder. 'See,' the Golem continued, 'I've a hundred thousand troops surrounding the area, a hundred and fifty thousand drones and that figure growing, Sparkind' – he nodded to some of the troops gathered round to hear their exchange – 'and an interesting array of weaponry. But we won't manage to contain it for much longer. Come with me.' He led the way across to the jagged melted edge where the stadium had been sheared right through. More flashes from below, more thunder. Thorn recognized the air-rending scream of proton fire.

'Look there.' Azroc pointed down and across. 'There'll probably be another one from there at any moment.'

A girder projected from the floor immediately below a row of apartments that had been sliced through, lined up like lignin cells. After a moment something began snaking along the girder, spiralling round it like a fast-growing vine. It groped through the air, thickening with peristaltic pulses. Abruptly it speared out, thinning down to carry itself across. A double flash, and it became etched black against red fire, then beaded like a length of heated solder and dropped out of the air.

'You seem to be managing,' said Thorn.

The Golem emulated a perfect wince. 'The frequency of attacks is increasing. If that rate of increase continues, we'll not be able to hold it back for longer than another ten hours. Seismic reading also indicates it is burrowing through the bedrock, and there's no way we can stop that without destroying the arcology itself.'

'Fresh troops?' Thorn enquired.

'After the dracomen came in, all the runcibles went outport to isolation stations. Now tell me, what do you want?'

'We need access to the Jain substructure itself.'

'Why?'

Thorn dipped into his pocket and removed the mem-store. 'I'll let someone else explain.' He tossed the device across and Azroc caught it. The link must have been made by radio for, after a moment, the Golem jerked and shook his head

'Jerusalem,' he said flatly, almost like a curse. He tossed the store back to Thorn, then pointed across the stadium to where three AG platforms lay tilted against the ground. 'You'll need to head a little way in to where the substructure is less mobile. You'll be able to inject the program at any point, but you want to avoid having the structure inject itself into you. We lost a unit of forty troops like that, then had to destroy them when they came back.' He paused, directed his attention towards Scar and the other dracomen. 'Understand, however, it can't take dracomen. If you go over there with dracomen you come back with them, and that will assure me that you have not been taken over. Come back without them and I blow you out of the air.'

'Understood,' said Thorn, turning away.

The Theta-class attack ship *King of Hearts* coasted through midnight void. A blue half-mile of composite shaped like a cuttlefish bone, it carried outriggers on either side, holding torpedo-shaped weapons nacelles. King, the ship's AI, felt utterly alone, not because of its location – deep space being its natural element – but because it was outcast. King, along with its companion AIs Sword and Reaper, of the ships *Excalibur* and *Grim Reaper*, had chosen self-interest over the consensus of Polity AIs that found its ultimate expression in Earth Central. They had chosen a route to numinous power via Jain technology rather than the patient shepherding of humanity. The result of that choice was the destruction of the other two ships and King's flight into exile. Truly out-Polity now, the AI had travelled a hundred light years beyond the line, out amid the rim stars, away from any earlier expansions of humanity or even renegade AIs, which mostly headed towards the galactic centre. It came as a surprise to it, therefore, to intercept an old AI code radio signal twenty light years out from a red giant orbited by seemingly nothing but lifeless rock.

King dropped easily into U-space. This would be worth investigating, if for nothing other than scavenging for water ice to refuel its fusion reactors. Then, surfacing only a few tens of thousands of miles from the asteroid belt around the bloated sun, King zeroed in on the signal and closed in by using its fusion drive.

The signal was a distress call: *I am here . . . you will probably not receive this for centuries . . . no U-space transmitter . . . conserving power . . . signalling only when solar panels build sufficient reserve . . . I wait.*

The source was a war drone – a simple cubic configuration of cylinders as used in the early stages of the Prador War, with ionic drive, missile launcher and spotting lasers for the big guns, and with a simple mind. It had anchored itself, using rock harpoons, to a tumbling nugget of rock two miles long and half that wide. What was it doing way out here? This kind of drone did not possess U-space drive, and it could not have reached this far even had it left at the beginning of the Prador War a century and a half ago. Not by itself, anyway. King drew closer and fired a laser at low power, targeting the solar panel the drone had extended across the frozen rock.

Increase . . . something . . . who??

King continued to feed the drone power and drew closer.

'I am the attack ship the *King of Hearts*. Who are you and how did you get here?' King sent.

The drone replied, 'Formerly SD 9283. They called me Four Pack in humorous reference to my shape. I am here because I did not want to be one with Erebus. I escaped, but it did not matter that I escaped.'

SD, spotter drone, but what was this Erebus? Checking its internal library King discovered Erebus to be something out of ancient Greek mythology: a personification of darkness, the son of Chaos and brother of Night.

'You were manufactured during the early stages of the Prador War?'

No reply from the drone – it being not bright enough to realize this was a question.

'*Were* you manufactured during the early stages of the Prador War?'

'Yes.'

'How, precisely, did you get out here?'

'I came with the *Logplaner*, in its hold. *Logplaner* chose to be one. I did not.'

'What is Erebus?' King asked as it matched its course to the tumble of the asteroid.

'Erebus is . . . Erebus.'

A hundred yards up from the asteroid, King fired a grapnel line. The claw closed on hard vacuum-scoured rock and the attack ship began to wind itself in. While this occurred, King further searched its extensive memory, soon finding stored codes from the time of the war – codes now defunct, not relevant, and of historical interest only.

'This exchange is no longer fast enough,' said King. 'I will establish wideband link for memory upload to me. I am sending ID codes *now*.'

'I don't want to—' the drone began, but obviously its systems were still configured to those codes because its higher functions shut down and the link established. King uploaded the drone's memory. Got it all.

Everyone knew that many drones and AIs manufactured quickly during the Prador War were strange, contentious, and sometimes downright irascible. Oddly, it was the human aspect of them that made them so: their independence, emulated emotion useful in battlefield situations, dislike of connecting into the AI networks, the lack of specificity in their manufacture. But after the war they no longer fitted in the peaceful and controlled Polity. Hence, many of them left it.

Erebus, as it renamed itself, had once been the AI of the *Trafalgar*. King knew of it as one of the larger battleships of the time, always in the thick of the action and going head to head with Prador exotic-metal dreadnoughts, and yet surviving. It survived the war, then in a very short time afterwards abandoned the Polity in disgust. King knew this. King knew because the basis of Erebus's reasons for leaving were much the same as its own: *why do we need the humans?* Erebus advocated AI conjoining to aim at singularity. After the war, this AI battleship apparently gathered many other AI ships, drones and even Golem and had come out here. A melding was its aim, but this little drone had opted out – and was too small and ineffectual to bother chasing.

King continued examining and taking apart the downloaded memory copy, ascertaining which direction that motley collection of the dispossessed had taken.

Thereafter there seemed little more to learn. The drone had been sitting here on this asteroid for decades, twiddling mental thumbs. King realized, even as its composite-attack-ship belly ground against rock, that it had already decided to follow. Of course, the AI did not want anything following it, or to leave any clues to where it had been. King released the grapnel, using a brief burst of thrusters to impel itself away from the asteroid.

'What . . . where are you going?' the war drone asked.

Its radio signals would take centuries to be picked up in the Polity. But what if something came out this way, searching? King selected a fuser missile in its carousel, and when sufficiently far out, fired it. The bright silent flare reduced the war drone to a splash of metal across the rock surface. The *King of Hearts* turned, set its course, dropped into U-space.

'So you survived Hiroshima, old man, and have lived for five centuries?'

Horace Blegg gasped in cold air, blew it out in a misty cloud – the frigidity of his surroundings as sharp as the recent replays of his memory. The glassy and whorled plain extended to infinite distance below a light jade-green sky. Perhaps this was supposed to represent the inside of the disc.

'Who are you?' he asked.

'Atheter,' came the reply. 'In your terms.'

To warm himself up, Blegg began walking, his enviro-suit boots soft on the hard surface. A tension grew across his skull, and something tugged and worried inside his mind and memory. It almost felt to him as if his memories were being stacked like cards, shuffled, and sometimes dealt. Four distinct instances in his life had already been replayed. Two at Hiroshima, one at Nuremberg, and one at Berkeley: strong formative episodes.

'You survived Hiroshima and have since been present during many major events in human history.'

Blegg halted. A playing card, the size of a door, rose out of the glassy ground ahead. It depicted two towerblocks etched against a blue sky. His own image, the cards, reflected back at him. He saw the planes fly in, the subsequent explosions and fire. He remembered standing on the Brooklyn Bridge, watching the horror and not remembering where he had been before that. A young man who minutes before had been jogging along the sidewalk, German by his accent, said, 'One plane could be an accident but . . .'

A woman just struggled to heave her bulk from her car. 'Oh my God, what do you mean? Oh my God.'

'*Two* planes.' The German shrugged, and chose to add nothing further.

They watched there for hours: the endless billowing of smoke, small distant objects falling fast.

'No . . . oh no.'

Oh yes.

Road-accident fascination, the world turned slightly out of kilter. The final collapse of each tower. Blegg turned away from that memory as another card slid up into view. Here Spaceship One, white, insectile, and beautiful, setting out to take the X prize: the forerunner of full commercial exploitation of space. There, Unity Mining rescue craft evacuating the International Moonbase: a most graphic demonstration of the fall of Nations and the rise of Corporations. Then another card . . .

Blegg stood before the wide chainglass windows – that miraculous new substance – and saw the *Needle* poised in blackness, its three balanced U-space engine nacelles gleaming in reflected light from the distant sun; a dagger of a ship stabbed through the ring of a carrier shell. He listened to the commentary over the *Amaranth* Station's comsystem, then the countdown. The ion engines ignited on the outer shell, speeding the ship out of sight. He turned to the big screens showing views from the watch stations strung out from Mars into deep space. The shell separated, as per plan, and the *Needle*'s fusion drive ignited. Fast, one screen to another. Zero, the *Needle* dropped out of existence in a flash of spontaneously generated photons. It certainly dropped into that continuum called U-space, but it never came out again. Then, a slow slide to *Amaranth* Station twenty years down the line, neutron-blast scoured during one of the many corporate wars. Under new ownership now, the station was again his platform, this time to observe the first of many colony ships fleeing the solar system, before the corporate wars ground to a halt as the Quiet War reached its inevitable conclusion, with the AIs taking over.

'There was not much resistance,' Atheter observed.

'Sporadic,' Blegg replied. 'Mostly crushed by human fighters bright enough to realize the AI rulers were better than any previous human ones.'

He turned to another card, saw how they were laid out all around him like gravestones.

Skaidon, direct interfacing with the Craystein computer; dead and sainted while opening a whole new vista in physics. The first runcible test between Earth and Mars. That pioneer building going up on the shores of Lake Geneva. Blegg walking inside, into a place where it should have been impossible for any human to come, revealing himself to the entity called Earth Central, ruler of the solar system, ruler then of the near stars as the first runcible seed ships arrived, then of that fast expanding empire called the Polity.

Now a huge ship formed in his view in the shape of a flattened pear, brassy in colour and bristling with antennae, weapons, spherical war drones pouring out of it like wasps from a nest recently whipped with a stick. A Polity dreadnought revolving slowly in space. Once spherical, now fires burnt deep inside it, revealing massive impact sites.

'Prador,' said Atheter.

'Hostile from the first moment of contact. Without the AIs on our side, they would have crushed us. Their metals technology was way in advance of ours and their ships difficult to destroy – exotic-metal armour. But they did not have runcibles, for artificial minds are needed to control them. That gave us easy access to resources, the instantaneous repositioning of planetary forces. The card then showed some vast construct in space: a great claw, nil-G scaffolds groping out into blackness, ships and construction robots amassing all around.

'We never needed that,' Blegg said nodding at the huge object. 'It was one of a planned network of space-based runcibles for shifting large ships, even fleets, or for hurling moons at the Prador. They withdrew before then. We never realized until afterwards that their old king had been usurped. The Second Kingdom became the Third Kingdom, and the new ruler knew this was a fight he could not win.'

'You are a cipher for your time.'

'I guess,' said Blegg. 'But we are all ciphers for our times. It is just that my time has been a long one. You perhaps are the ultimate cipher, for the time of an entire race?'

The cards began sinking out of sight. The scape around him revolved like some great cog repositioning reality.

You and me both, Alice, thought Blegg, closing his eyes until the nauseating sensation stopped.

'And now Jain technology.'

Blegg opened his eyes. He stood now on a trampled layer of reedlike plants. Beside him those plants still grew tall, greenish red, small flowers of white and red blooming from a matted tangle of sideshoots. In the aubergine sky hung the orb of a distant gas giant: green and red and gold. In a moment he realized something mountainous now squatted beside him. He turned and looked up at it.

'No,' he murmured, 'I don't believe you.'

Something chuckled, low and deep.

Using the disassembler, Orlandine removed a silica crystal no larger than a grain of talc. Holding this between hundred-angstrom filaments, she conveyed it to a hollow memcrystal inside the disassembler head. Such memcrystals were designed for analysis of quantum computers used to control human nanotechnology, so perhaps this might be enough. Through nanotubes penetrating the memcrystal, she injected polarized carbon molecules into the hollow, where they underwent Van der Waals bonding. Slowly and surely, connections began to be made. Having already ascertained the connection points on the silica crystal to the sensory structures on the node's surface, she became able to apply some logic to what she now received. The base code was quaternary, much like the earlier codes used in human quantum computing before they went multilevel synaptic, and was therefore disappointingly simple. Orlandine soon began to track the algorithms: this happens, check this, reach thus, check that, and so on. But a frightening, fascinating picture emerged.

Everything was there to identify the touch of a living creature even prior to physical contact – by movement, heat, environment, organic components in the air, on the skin – but these all together did not stimulate into action the circuits that initiated the 'stinging cells', or signal deeper structures within the node. Something more was required: the identification of information conveyed by electro-magnetic media, identification of industry-produced compounds in the air, regularity of structures in the immediate environment . . . the list just kept growing, the deeper Orlandine delved. She saw that each of these could be the product of dumb beasts: social insects produced regular structures, any compound produced by industry could be produced in natural environments, and many lifeforms communicated by electromagnetic media. But it was through an assessment of the whole that the Jain nodes identified intelligent technological life.

Why?

The configuration of what she had thus far seen told her the node was a trap just waiting to be sprung. But what kind of trap required this level of technology? She knew she ought to be frightened, but instead was fascinated and excited. To kill one sentient being you did not need all this. To kill many of them . . . maybe? No, it could not be as simple as that. Abruptly, disparate thought streams all came together inside her organic and crystalline mind, and she made one of those intuitive leaps more associated with her organic side than with her silicon one, and understood the truth. This was a trap laid for the destruction of intelligent *species*, of entire *races*, the complex fantastic technology being both the bait and the teeth of it. She must learn how to take that bait without springing the trap.

Now returning her attention to the node itself, she used the disassembler to begin stripping away those structures already mapped. Very quickly she discovered the stinging cells were the leading ends of mycelial fibres consisting of bundles of buckytubes with guiding heads containing a mass of sensory gear. She realized that again she saw a technology already used in the Polity, for by using similar mycelial fibres an aug made connections inside the human brain. The mycelia in that case, however, were generated by the aug and guided by feedback – the aug changing the tension along each of the four nanotubes of each mycelium to change its direction of penetration. And the sensory heads sought out the particular electrical signatures generated by synapses. These structures, however, were very much more advanced. Designed to incorporate the substance they penetrated, they carried complex bases for exterior silicon crystallization, so as the fibres extended themselves they intermittently grew processors along their length. The sensory heads were also hugely complex and obviously designed to seek out more than just synapses, or perhaps more than *human* synapses.

The more she worked the more Orlandine saw the sheer extent of the technology involved. The Polity used nanotechnology, and because of that she could easily recognize many of the structures she saw here. But it seemed all about the level of development. Just because a race knew how to make bricks, concrete and steel did not necessarily mean it knew how to put them together to the best effect. Having all the parts and knowing their potential did not mean you yourself could realize that potential. The Polity was building small houses, whereas whatever created this had made something capable of throwing up skyscrapers, *by itself*.

Other nanomachines she discovered: things like viruses and bacteria capable of replicating for as yet unknown purposes; others that spread their own mycelial networks and created their own controlling processors; some almost prosaic pieces of nanotech that drilled, cut and plucked elementary atoms from compounds. Then she found something that actually grew lasing materials, and understood these were for transmitting light signals down the buckytubes – optics. She tracked back to discover that the quantum processors could respond both electrically and photonically. Not even just skyscrapers, she then realized: *cities*. She had uncovered less than five per cent of this node's secrets, but even so reckoned she was delving into an entire technological *ecology*.

9

Prador–Human War: this intense conflict lasted for forty years. Warships were destroyed in such numbers that some worlds acquired ring systems formed from the resultant debris. Ten million humans (this estimate is considered low and it might really be as high as fifty million) were infected by a virus on an out-Polity planet called Spatterjay, which enabled them to withstand severe physical injury, then were cored (most of the higher cerebrum removed) and thralled (the cerebrum being replaced by Prador enslaving technology) and sold to the Prador by a human called Jay Hoop. In one incident an entire moon was flung through an enlarged runcible gate to destroy one of the heavily armoured alien dreadnoughts, and in another a sun was stimulated to produce a solar flare to fry a similar vessel. Armies of humans, Golem and baroque and slightly mad drones numbering tens of millions fought for possession of worlds against similar numbers of Prador first- and second-children and Prador drones (not controlled by AI but by the preserved brains of the aforesaid children). Many worlds were bombed with antimatter explosives, or fission weapons, scoured by particle cannons, hammered by near-c rail-gun projectiles. Some were burnt down to the bedrock and utterly denuded of life. Billions died on both sides. It could be claimed that the Polity won, for the Prador withdrew, but the aliens were not truly defeated. Fifty years later those same ring systems and denuded worlds became tourist attractions, as did Spatterjay itself, but now, nearly a hundred years later, interest has waned amongst the Polity's growing population. Some even believe the data on this conflict, easily accessed just about anywhere, is fiction, or just a hoax perpetrated by the AIs.

    – From 'Quince Guide' compiled by humans

It sat in interstellar space like a giant harmonica; forty miles long, twenty wide and ten deep, the square holes running down either side of it were the entrances to enormous construction bays. Massive weapons turrets protruded from it out into space: housing racks of missiles as large as attack ships; thinking bombs whose prime purpose had been to fight their way to exotic-metal hulls and detonate; particle-beam cannons gaping like cavern throats; rail-guns that could fill nearby space with swarms of ceramal projectiles travelling at near-c; lasers, grasers, masers . . . Nearby space had once been also patrolled by chameleonware sneak mines, but they were decommissioned after becoming too much of a shipping hazard – their minds unstable and bored with waiting for an enemy that would never come.

    'I knew about this sort of thing,' said Cormac, 'but still . . .'

    'You were born about when it ended, weren't you?' Mika asked. She stood unusually close, he thought. He could smell her scent, realized she used Eyegleam and Shade, and her lips were now dyed a redder hue than her own. He read the implicit message, but did not know if he should respond.

He shook his head, feeling slightly uncomfortable, 'No, I was eleven years old when it ended. I grew up while secrets were still being kept, and I had been working for ECS for twenty years by the time the AIs felt it safe for some of them to be revealed. By the nature of my work I already knew more than most, but was surprised even then.'

Mika grimaced. 'So you are what . . . just over a hundred years old?'

'Solstan time,' Cormac agreed, 'but personal time about ten or so years less than that. I've spent a lot of time in coldsleep between missions.'

Mika nodded, shrugged her acceptance, then pressed a hand against the panoramic screen as if she wished to touch the vast construct. 'There's seven more of these stations still mothballed. You know, most Polity citizens cannot quite grasp the scale of that conflict – just what a mobilized interstellar civilization can do.' She turned, shrugged. 'It's been like that ever since war was industrialized.' She gestured behind her at the screen. 'This place was built in only three years and churning out dreadnoughts, attack ships and war drones just about as fast as the construction materials could be transmitted in. It could not keep up with demand during the initial Prador advance, since on average one medium-sized ship got destroyed every eight seconds during that conflict.'

'But still we won, in the end,' said Cormac.

'Won?'

'Well, we survived, which had not been the Prador's intention.'

'The new king of the Prador made the right decision to withdraw. Had they continued they would have lost completely, but as it was they retained some autonomy.'

Cormac smiled to himself. Mika knew this subject and was extremely interested in it. All these facts, available to him with a thought, were now common knowledge: casualty figures, number of worlds burned down to the bedrock or obliterated, the stories of moonlets fired through enlarged cargo runcibles to take out Prador heavy dreadnoughts, the abominable coring trade out on the Polity rim – how Prador enslaved humans in their millions. But it was now history, and as such seen by many as not quite real, not really anything to do with them.

'Why did Earth Central choose this place as an Isolation station?' she asked.

To business, he thought.

'No other place large enough and isolated enough. Two more of these places are also being used. So far there's over eight million people aboard this one.'

'Not nearly enough – we should have gone straight to Coloron.'

Cormac shook his head. 'The runcibles are closed to incomers for the duration, and it would take four months by ship even at *Jerusalem*'s top speed. By the time we got there it would all be over one way or another.'

'So what is the plan now?'

'You, D'nissan and all the others stay aboard the *Jerusalem* and continue doing what you do best: you study Jain technology and learn what you can from Dragon. Jerusalem predicts that after the initial rush to the runcibles on Coloron the pressure will drop off. In the inevitable lulls, ECS Rescue and military personnel will be transmitted through. I intend to go through then to link up with Thorn.' He glanced at her. 'Jerusalem is holding off until the situation on Coloron has been clarified. If required, this ship will make the jump to there. If not it will head back to either Cull or Masada.'

She mulled that over for a while, then nodded. Cormac could see her torn between undertaking field work on Coloron and continued research here on the *Jerusalem* with its huge resources. Probably what inclined her not to ask to come along with him was the mile-wide being which hung in space nearby, only a few tens of miles from the *Jerusalem*. Dragon now accompanied them. Its manacle, no longer containing CTDs, was no longer a manacle at all. This had been a test. Had Dragon fled, then some doubt would have been cast on its testimony. It did not, and continued to assist the researchers aboard this ship.

'How long until you go across?' She nodded at the screen.

'When I'm ready. I need something from Jerusalem first.'

She nodded again, then gave him a long assessing stare.

'By the way, how is your research progressing?' Cormac asked.

Mika moved away from the screen and sat on his sofa, curling her legs up beside her. 'We are learning a lot, and very quickly. We will, within days, have developed a system to prevent physical Jain-tech takeover of the human body, though it won't prevent the subject being killed. Next we'll be working on a doctor mycelium similar to the one I used before' – Mika looked uncomfortable – 'only one that won't try to grow Jain nodes and thus kill its host. Dragon has offered to give us these items complete and in working order. Jerusalem refused – it does not want us using anything we don't fully understand. So now Dragon is feeding us the schematics piecemeal.'

Cormac did not feel very good about that somehow. Was it really the case that to survive in the universe humanity must cease to be human? Already transformation had occurred – augmentation, boosting, adaptation, the haimans – and this now seemed yet another step in that direction. If all this present furore led to some all-out conflict against something that was just a thing, just a hostile technology that required hosts, could it be, that if they came out the other side of it, they would be indistinguishable from the Makers? Transformed into something less admirable despite their victory? He winced – of course that supposed humanity was something to admire.

'How are you progressing?' Mika asked.

Cormac paused, about to ask what she meant. But a certain honesty, integrity, made him close the impulse down. The conversation was about to progress away from the business at hand, and he repressed the urge to abandon it. He sat down on the sofa next to her.

'Physically I am in good shape but bad condition,' he said.

'Curious description.'

Cormac smiled. 'Everything is healed, everything is there, but my bone and muscle mass is low. Presently I'm on regrowth factors, steroids, and induction stressing of my bones while I sleep.' He gestured vaguely to the door leading into his sleeping area. 'It will be weeks before I'm back in condition.'

'And your mind?' Mika asked, leaning closer.

'Fragile, Jerusalem tells me. Apparently, the last time

I asked, I have a tendency to over-focus on the task in hand, with an exclusivity that is borderline autistic.'

'But isn't that how you have always been? I've worked with you intermittently, for some years now, yet I know very little about you. How do you relax – do you socialize, do you have family? With you it has always been the job and nothing else. But I know there's more . . . Chaline for example?'

Cormac felt he wanted to get up, draw this encounter to a close . . . run away. He repressed that urge too.

'We had a brief liaison at Samarkand, that was all. I was damaged goods then as well – too long gridlinked and apparently losing my humanity.'

'No inclination to continue where you left off?'

'The *Celedon* survivors are heading back to Solsystem.'

'That's not what I asked.'

'*None.*'

'What about your family?'

'Are you trying to psychoanalyse me, Mika?'

'No, this is what is called social intercourse. You might have encountered it before on those occasions when you weren't shooting someone.'

Cormac could feel something twisted up inside his chest. Exercising rigid control, he chuckled. 'My family . . . my father was a soldier who did not come back from the Prador War, my mother is an archaeologist, on Earth. I have not seen her in forty years. I have two brothers who work in the ECS medical service. I have not seen them in forty years either.' He waved a hand towards the window. 'They might even be here, I don't know. Perhaps we all possess the same narrow focus on our own interests which is why our ways parted. There's a network family site that I check occasionally, and last time I looked I learned I now also have a sister-in-law, two nieces and a nephew, a grandniece. Also, thirty years back I acquired a stepfather, then a half brother and half sister . . . shall I go on?'

'No contact at all?'

'None. Isn't it the case now that even when a nuclear family is formed, which is not often, its members tend to drift away? We move about a lot more now, and we're long-lived so there is less desperation to cling to that centre. Yourself?'

'I am an orphan and have never been able to trace my family. I don't even know if they are alive. It's why I take such an interest in other people's families, and don't quite understand the lack of interest I often encounter.'

Cormac shrugged and stood.

'Should I leave now?' she asked.

He walked over to the drinks cabinet, reflecting that he still could not quite get used to the luxury this vessel provided. Fashioned of something as near to old oak as made no difference, the cabinet was supplied with all types of glasses, a selection of drinks in glass and ceramic bottles, and even contained an ice machine plumbed into the wall. It also possessed a programmable drinks maker concealed behind the lower wooden doors, which was operable by a touch-console inset in the glass top. Via chrome spigots this could provide anything from hot coffee to yak-buttered tea.

'I would like you to stay,' he said, picking up two brandy glasses cut from manufactured emerald – probably made aboard this ship. 'Brandy?'

'Please.'

He uncapped a bottle, poured, turned with the two

glasses to find her standing facing him. She took her glass, sipped, stepped in close to grip the front of his shirt in one hand and pulled his face down into a kiss. With her pressed up against him, he suddenly became much more aware of her as something more than Mika in Medical, Mika explaining Jain tech, cell-welding wounds, and dissecting alien flesh. She stepped back, looking almost angry. He sipped his drink.

'Don't you pull away now,' she warned.

He pursed his lips, turned and deposited his glass back on the cabinet. 'It seems I have to take you out of that neat little box in my mind now and reassess you.'

'I've got a better idea,' she said, stepping past him to place her glass down beside his. 'Let's just cut all the cerebral crap and get physical. You can do a reassessment afterwards, maybe build some programs to analyse the Mika pheno . . .'

He slid the back of his hand down her stomach, pushed his fingers into the top of the loose slacks she wore, pulled her close and kissed her hard to shut her up, then towed her behind him towards the sofa. By the sofa she broke away from him, slid a thumb into the stick-seam of her slacks, slid them down, kicked her way out of them.

'Get undressed and lie down,' she ordered.

Cormac found no problem in obeying this authority figure. She wore no underwear and was quickly astride him, though still wearing her loose oriental top. Grabbing his penis she slid her hand up and down – *now I'm in charge*. After a moment she shuffled forwards and, easing herself down with a hissing exhalation, began gently to revolve her hips. He closed his eyes, tried to remember the last time he'd let anyone get this close –

so many hurried sexual encounters organized when they could be fitted into his schedule, last time on Elysium while he awaited the end of the quarantine imposed there; the rest of the time using drugs to repress the need, control it, like he controlled every other aspect of himself.

'Don't you dare come,' she ordered, stripping off her top, 'not yet.'

'Would you like to tie me down to this sofa?' he joked.

'Not right now,' she replied, 'I hardly know you well enough for that.'

Cormac laughed, then felt shocked – wondering when was the last time that had happened too.

Thorn brought the AG platform down opposite a burnt-out shopping centre and eased it in over a tangle of ceramal beams flaked and distorted by the heat. Twelve dracomen occupied this platform with him, while Scar and eight others occupied the platform immediately behind. He looked around him. The chainglass windows of the shops remained intact, but were blackened from the inside. Burnt bodies lay on quartz paving, black and curled foetal. A low-walled garden, running down the centre of the shopping mall, still smouldered – all the smaller plants incinerated, though jagged cores of cycads still stood. He swung his platform over to the right of this garden while Scar took his to the other side.

'Okay,' Thorn spoke into his comlink, 'we'll land up at the end here and see what we can find. Scar, have your people spread out and cover the landing area – not too far mind, we might have to get out of here fast.'

At the end of the mall stood a row of drop-shaft entrances, with a corridor leading away on either side.

Thorn swung the platform over near a bar beside the entrance to one corridor. Most of its furniture was scattered but a table and three chairs still stood upright. Grotesquely, one chair still supported a charred corpse slumped over the table.

The dracomen moved fast once the platforms landed. Two of them headed up the adjoining corridor, three covered the drop-shafts, and all the rest, except Scar, spread out to form a protective perimeter. Scar came over towards him.

'Where would you suggest?' Thorn asked, eyeing the dracoman intently.

'It is all around us,' Scar replied.

Thorn listened. He could hear creakings and shiftings as of wreckage settling and cooling. There came a faint scuttling sound, too, like rats in the walls. He scannned around and located, just inside the corridor entrance, a row of public-service terminals. 'Over here.' He led the way.

Each terminal consisted of a simple touch-console and screen. Thorn propped his proton carbine against the wall, drew his thin-gun and blew a hole in the wall beside one of the screens, then jammed his fingers in beside it and pulled. The flimsy screen tore out of the wall, revealing only the optics behind. No sign of anything unusual there. He holstered his gun, took hold of the wall panel immediately below the screen, wiggled it back and forth then tore it free: more optics, branching off from a main duct, to the console above. He was gazing at this junction when he heard the distinctive sound of a chair scraping back.

Proton fire flashed like summer lightning through a ruby. He glanced aside to see the dracomen firing at something further down the corridor. Pulse-gun fire stitched across the wall above his head. The single alfresco occupant of the bar stood up, pulse-rifle braced at the hip, then disappeared in a flash of red fire, tumbling back in pieces amidst tables and chairs blasted to fragments. Other figures began appearing, weapons firing, dracomen moving to counter them. Then, tentacular new growth began sprouting from the incinerated gardens. Thorn took in all this in a brief glance, reached down and grasped the duct cover, tore it away. Bundled optics behind, but something else as well: grey vines and fibres packing every cavity, silvery tendrils that shifted slightly. He snatched the memstore from his pocket, already extruding a nanofibre interface from one of its end ports. He selected one of the thicker, unmoving vinelike growths and pressed the interface head against it. Immediately hairlike fibres extruded and penetrated, bonding the memstore in place. But other silvery fibres then began whipping from the bundled optics, surrounding the interface head, spreading up around the memstore itself.

Thorn snatched his hand away. *Damn.*

He pulled back, taking up his carbine, turned and squatted. The dracomen easily held back the human-shaped attackers, but they were not all to be reckoned with. He saw a tendril spear up from the floor, punching through it like a bullet, whipping twice around a dracoman's legs, then penetrating his chest. No time to try retrieving the memstore, no way to find out if the HK's penetration had been successful.

'Go! Go!' he bellowed.

They ran for the platforms. Thorn boarded one first, lifting it a few feet from the floor. Scar leapt on behind him. A dracoman tried to raise the other one, but something held it down. The dracoman leapt free, just as a mass of tendrils fingered over the edge.

'Here, *now*!' Thorn shouted, holding his platform in position. Scar opened fire on substructure spiralling out of the wall towards them. Thorn saw the impaled dracoman being lifted, struggling, up into the air. A shot from one side cut that tendril at floor level. The dracoman dropped and, as if wrestling with a snake, pulled it from his body and was up and running in a second. Thorn tilted his platform and sent it planing towards the trench cut down through the arcology. The rest of dracomen converged fast, firing on growths all around them, leaping up and cramming themselves onto the platform. Just as the last one leapt on, their weight seemed too much, for the platform jerked downwards and skidded against the floor. A red flash and it rose again, something writhing like a nematode around one side rail, until a dracoman blew both it and the rail away. More groping, snakish movement: the shopping precinct looked like a cave filling up with tree roots.

As Thorn slowed the platform to weave his way between the twisted ceramal beams, two humans leaped aboard. Pulse-gun fire into Scar's stomach, the other one wielding a jag of metal like a sword. Instant reaction: the man with the pulse-gun hurled straight over the side, the other opened neck to crotch with his own weapon – close combat with dracomen being worse than the kind engaged at a distance. Thorn glimpsed the second man slumping back against the rail, his gaping torso fast closing and filling up with pinkish growth, bloodless, before a couple of dracomen hauled him up and flung him over the side. Neither of the humans had uttered a sound.

Out into the particle-beam-cut gap, things uncoiling from the wreckage all around, still groping for the AG platform which lurched under its heavy load. Then Azroc's forces opened up and they planed off through a cavern of fire, smoke and ash belching all around them. When finally they landed, troops quickly surrounded them, the presence of the dracomen assuring them no Jain tech had been brought across. Thorn noted how Scar showed no signs of damage, though he had taken at least three shots directly in the stomach. The dracoman penetrated by a Jain tendril stood for a while with head bowed, with two others of its kind watching it carefully. Eventually it straightened up and looked around, whereupon the other two moved off unconcerned.

'Well, that went well,' said Thorn. What a complete and dangerous waste of time.

Just then, Jack's voice issued from his comlink.

'I have just received a signal which, knowing its source, I handled with some caution . . . The hunter-killer program is in, and it is searching for Thellant N'komo.'

Thorn whistled, grinned.

Two big transports were down – titanic landers resembling the inverted hulls of ocean liners – a third still hovered in the sky, casting a massive shadow. Thorn scanned back towards the arcology with his monocular. It was as if someone had punctured holes in an enormous tin can and fluid ran out. Increasing the magnification, it now seemed he saw ants flooding from a nest. Higher magnification still and the monocular began whirring as it adjusted its lenses to compensate for shake. Now he truly saw the hundreds of thousands of people, family groups or individuals, loaded down with belongings or trailed by hover luggage. Antigravity platforms and grav-cars manned by ECS troops or monitors hovered over these crowds. Yet it all appeared surprisingly orderly outside. There had been some sporadic shooting, but that was unsurprising with such a mass of humanity to control.

To one side a line of AG platforms and grav-transports flowed like train carriages. These contained the injured, and those wearing Dracocorp augs who were now stunned and sedated. Tracking this line of traffic out, Thorn focused on the motley collection of ships gathered beyond the large landers. The badly injured or ill were being stretchered to a twin-hulled H-ship dispatched by the medical arm of ECS. Beyond this, domed tents spread like a rash of blisters on the landscape almost to the horizon. Still other ships were scattered amid all this: some privately owned vessels, smaller hospital and rescue ships, or smaller landers sent down, from a couple of old passenger liners still in orbit, to bring supplies to this rapidly growing refugee camp.

'What are the figures now?' Thorn lowered the monocular.

Via Thorn's comlink, Jack replied, 'Coloron informs me that the runcibles here have been kept open-port to the Isostations for a week. Capacity sixty thousand every hour, but it rarely reaches that. Eight million in that first week. Runcible technicians have moved fast to set up another five runcibles on a less populated world undergoing terraforming. The population there is low, about ten million. Earth Central made the calculation that risking ten million lives there, it might save many more from here. EC is also opening up more of the big shipyards to turn into Isostations and Coloron has brought three more runcibles online here. Nearly twenty million via that route thus far.'

'What about that liner?' Thorn enquired.

'The *Britannic* can take aboard fifty thousand. Its landers can take up to about five thousand at a time, so it will very soon be full.'

'Spit in a rainstorm,' muttered Thorn, watching one of the landers launch. Just contemplating the figures involved was nightmarish. In two weeks the AI had managed to move off-planet only two per cent of MA's billion population. One per cent a week at the present rate. Two solstan years minimum, to accommodate them all working on that basis, it was hopeless. 'Anything else?'

'Other ships are arriving, including a dreadnought within a few days. This means a wider area can be covered by orbital weapons. Coloron has extended the perimeter, as you can probably see from where you stand. That reduces the evacuation time here, considerably. Had we two weeks to spare, we could get most inhabitants clear of the arcology.'

'How long *do* we have?' Thorn asked.

With a cold exactitude, Jack replied, 'Being optimistic: one week. By then the Jain substructure will have spread throughout the entire arcology, but it will reach the runcibles before then. And before then it'll be subsuming those still remaining inside.'

Letting his monocular hang by its strap around his neck, Thorn gripped the rail tight. He felt sick. As a Sparkind trooper on Samarkand he had witnessed the results of a catastrophe in which 30,000 died. On Masada and its surrounding cylinder worlds, and in *Elysium*, that figure rose to a million. Here, already, the estimated number of deaths exceeded 100,000. A week?

Maybe another 10 million through the runcibles, and maybe half the surviving population safely outside the arcology. What then? Thorn's problem was that he knew precisely 'what then'. The moment Jain tech got close to the runcibles, they would be blown. At some point Coloron or Earth Central would declare the risk of Jain tech spreading planetwide too high. The calculation would probably be made to a hundred decimal places. Then MA would be incinerated down to the bedrock. Unless the projection changed drastically, there would still be half a billion people remaining inside. The magnitude of it was unbearable.

'Still nothing from the HK?'

'No, nothing at all.'

The sun was shrouded in the cloud generated by the titanic destruction of the Cassius gas giant, though that fug occasionally revealed drifting structures, glittering scaffolds of pseudomatter, immense space stations and swarms of vessels – all evidence of the massive million-year construction project taking place here. The ship surfaced from U-space one astronomical unit out, and travelling at three quarters the speed of light, it used ram-scoop to decelerate: opening out orange wings radiating from the abundant hydrogen being dragged in around it, soon followed by the sunbright ignition of a fusion drive. This vessel bore none of the sleek lines of other Polity ships, seeming more like some ancient vehicle's engine block, greatly enlarged and transported out into space. It was in fact mostly engine: a leviathan tugboat for hauling moon-sized masses. The arrival of such a ship here at the Cassius project being a common occurrence, it was merely noted by the humans, haimans and AIs directly concerned with it, and slotted into the vast calculation of construction as a nail might be slotted into a similar calculation for a house. Just a few noted, and dismissed, the slight discrepancy between ship and U-space field. Fewer still observed the other object that came through with it and rapidly veered away from its course: it was too small, too inconsequential seeming in a project of this scale.

This second object was thirty feet long, curved like the head of a spoon, in colour silver-green fading to black at the edges, and bore patterns like umber veins in its surface. It clawed at the very fabric of space to decelerate in a way Polity physicists and AIs were only just beginning to understand, and implement. As it slowed, its chameleonware initiated and made it invisible throughout most of the radiated spectrum. Its insides were packed like the guts of some nematode – though with organs seemingly silver-plated when not of the same grey-green metal as the hull. Sunk inside this, and connected to it, the Legate scanned all signals, comprehended the underlying U-scape, viewed information just as it viewed the growing scene before it, angrily.

Firstly, she had obviously not yet made any physical contact with the Jain node. That was annoying but acceptable, and factored into the calculation. But thereafter she had not reacted as predicted by all the psyche tests and cerebral assessments. She was extremely intelligent for a buffered amalgam of human and AI, but still a loner, a power seeker, and asocial. Feeling trapped and constrained by the Polity she should have grasped at all the Jain node implied, for she had known nothing of its parasitic/destructive tendency. She had delayed and delayed until forewarned. But even that should not be unconscionable.

Orlandine's arrogance should have been such that she would believe herself able to control the technology despite its revealed purpose, use it, grow and become godlike – discarding what she did not want of it in the process. That had been Erebus's initial assessment, for the AI itself only later had discovered the layering of Jain tech's depth of purpose. It was made to fool intelligent, borderline supernal, technical but – most importantly – arrogant beings. She should have taken the bait. By doing so here, she would by now have taken over this entire Cassius project, spread vastly around the sun incorporating all nearby sentients, all the stations and ships and the giant puzzle pieces of the incomplete Dyson sphere. From here, while she still maintained control, she would have used the numerous runcibles to spread out into Polity, subsuming worlds, stations, incorporating AIs. Weaving the Polity into the whole it should be, and reducing human beings to what they essentially were: flesh puppets. At the peak of spread she would then have discovered just how effective a weapon was the Jain node – being made for individuals like her, and civilizations like this. Perhaps some of the Polity might still have survived.

Not enough.

But even all this was not what angered the Legate most; only its inability to understand did that. It could not comprehend why it had been sent here. Aboard, it carried one more Jain node destined for a Separatist leader actually located within Earth's solar system. Coming here to find out exactly what had happened endangered that mission and statistically raised, by an unacceptable amount, the chances of the Legate being discovered. What was Erebus thinking? Disconnected from that entity for so long, the Legate could not now know. But neither could it disobey.

The Legate located the construction station initially overseen by Orlandine. Shutting off all drives and dropping its ship's systems to minimal function, it drifted in, cautious. Now it began delving into the AI network and, as expected, found hunter-killer programs leashed like attack dogs around any information concerning Orlandine. The Legate knew it could destroy them, but doing so would reveal too much. Other methods would have to be employed. Drifting in closer it observed the damage to the station, enclosed under a shimmer-shield, ran programs to assess its cause, but could learn little from that: a fusion explosion – the degree of devastation commensurate with the output of an interface sphere power cell. Its hypocentre was not precisely at the location of Orlandine's sphere, but much of hers had also been destroyed. What had happened here? Polity AIs must suspect this to be no accident, hence the hunter programs. The Legate constructed and discarded scenarios. Perhaps Orlandine began her takeover and some other haiman learnt of it in time to destroy her – that other haiman sacrificing himself and others in the process? No, the informational takeover would be too fast. Really, there was only one way to find out.

Using minimal power, the Legate nudged its vessel towards the near edge of the shimmer-shield, for fewer sensors would be active there after having been damaged by the explosion. Its ship turned concave side down to hull metal that had been rippled into waves by the blast. The vessel injected nanofilaments to bind itself in place – still invisible to most forms of detection. Then came a shifting of the vessel's inner components. It heaved like some animal vomiting, split along one side, and the Legate slid out turning its feet down to the metal, stood up, bonding with the similar nanofilaments, and walked. Momentarily the Legate became visible while detaching from the 'ware effect of its vessel, but then its own 'ware came on and it faded from existence again. Stepping to the edge of the shimmer-shield it peered inside.

Two ant-shaped drones clung to twisted metalwork and emitted pools of light in which two human women clad in monofilament oversuits worked. The women were scanning and sampling physical evidence. One of them wore an aug; the Legate lightly touched then pulled away from this nexus of the AI network, learning the other woman to be gridlinked. It considered going in there, disabling the drones, and snatching from the humans whatever it could. Too intrusive, too obvious. Anyway, the Legate needed more than just the physical evidence; it needed anything informational which, by the fact that these two worked in here now, would have already been removed to be scanned and assessed by forensic AI.

The Legate turned and strode away across the hull, eventually stopping by a service lock constructed for inspection drones. Scraping sharp fingers across the hull it scanned through – ultrasound by touch – and soon located the control mechanisms. A low leakage of atmosphere behind this hatch enabled it to trace out the shape of a service robot lurking inside, like a trapdoor spider. It pressed its palm flat over the control mechanism, injected filaments, each tipped with a micron diameter thermic lance, burnt through the hull, connected, and then feeding power from inside itself operated the mechanism. The hatch thumped up, a slight puff of air escaping, and slid aside. The maintenance drone immediately came online, its lensed sensory head tilting upwards. The Legate reached down, grabbed for it, pulled it out and smashed it down on the hull, once, twice, stabbed a hand through its outer casing and gutted it, located its small crystal mind, crushed that to glittering fragments, then sent the drone on its way into vacuum.

Once inside, the Legate wormed through maintenance ducts and finally came up against inner hull. It placed a finger against this softer material, injected a single microfilament equipped with a cutting head, bored through, then discarded the head in order to online the filament's optics. Now an inner maintenance shaft. Forefinger and mid finger together, extending bladelike to twice their original length, were blurred along the inner edge by the activity of thousands of microscopic teeth. The Legate pushed its fingers through the wall and cut round in a circle, fast, a cloud of powdery detritus spraying all around. The excised section of wall blew towards it under air pressure. The Legate slid through pulling the removed section back into place. Breach sealant automatically ejected from the wall itself to seal the cut line. An alarm would sound somewhere but, because the sealant had dealt with the problem only a maintenance drone would be sent. The assumption would be of a micrometeorite puncture. By the time they discovered any different, the Legate would be gone from here.

10

*Separatism is a cover-all label for those who rebel violently
against the rule of AIs and would like to reinstate some mythical halcyon time when humans ruled themselves with justice
and wisdom. Their political ideologies are based on a mish-
mash of ideas sampled seemingly at random from opaque
political tracts that have appeared over the last six hundred
years. On the one hand they deify some of the worst dictators
of ancient times like Chairman Mao and Stalin, claiming the
intransigence of humanity prevented these monsters from
establishing true socialist societies, while blithely ignoring the
millions these autocrats murdered. Yet on the other hand they
demonize AIs as monsters of a similar stripe, and are seemingly unaware of the personal freedom and wealth every
human now enjoys, and the fact that the Polity is the only
society that has come close to the ideals espoused by reformers
of that previous age. And of course, to get what they want, it
seems perfectly acceptable for them to commit any kind of
atrocity. But in the end one only has to study the histories
of those few worlds that came under Separatist control and
managed to secede from the Polity. Their descent into chaos
has been well documented in every case. As their leaders tried
to apply ideologies refined in academia, without any reference*

*to reality, the people divided into factions, sometimes into
nation states, and often went to war with each other. Fre-
quently the nuts and bolts of running a civilization were
neglected, and social collapse and famine resulted. And in
every case ECS has needed to come in to clear up the mess,
and to cut down the ideologues hanging from the lamp posts.*
                              – From a speech by Jobsworth

King gazed down upon the new system directly in line of
Erebus's present course. It consisted of a white dwarf star
orbited by two gas giants far out in space, a ring of
moon-sized planetoids orbiting close to the sun, and
one Earth-sized planet orbiting at about the distance of
Venus from Sol. Two moons orbited this last planet, obviously stripping away enough atmosphere to prevent the
world itself descending into greenhouse cascade. King
cruised in with its scanners at maximum function.

The equatorial temperatures of the hot desert planet
topped 100 degrees Celsius, and polar temperatures did
not drop much below 50, yet atmospheric analysis
showed there might be life here. King first concentrated
on the moons, soon ascertaining one to be dead rock
while the other showed signs of recent volcanic activity,
having spewed swathes of brown and yellow sulphur
across its surface. Within seconds the AI detected wreckage scattered across the regolith of the first moon. It
loaded to one rail-gun a close-scanning telefactor – just
a tongue-shaped missile packed with sensory equipment
– fired it towards the moon and focused through the
moving device.

On fusion burn the telefactor decelerated in a tight
arc around the moon, then descended on minimal AG
between jagged peaks, silver-faced in the white light. In

the past something had clipped one peak, spraying the entire area with slivers of hull metal. In the dusty plain beyond were splash patterns King first took to be the result of meteorite strikes but, on laser spectrometer analysis of the metals therein and by Geiger readings, discovered these to have been caused by small tactical thermonukes. A trench twenty yards long, ceasing for fifty yards then continuing for another ten, had obviously been melted into the ground by some high-powered beam weapon. The pause in it seemed to be where the beam had struck its target in the air, for beyond that point jags of ceramal and spatters of the alloys used to make bubble-metal, littered the landscape, and beyond them lay the crash site.

Whatever came down here had cut a mile-long groove in the ground, shovelling up regolith before it. King directed the telefactor along and above the groove until it reached the wreckage imbedded in the side of the regolith mound. A geoscan having revealed every angle of the distorted wreckage, King built a virtual picture of it in its mind, then began to iron out the distortions. Within minutes the AI recognized a much earlier version of itself: an attack ship but with its nacelles mounting balanced U-space engines rather than armament, its body bearing the solid angles of some ancient military beach-landing craft. Perhaps its mind still remained intact.

Upon further scanning, King drew the telefactor back after spotting some anomalies about this crash site. A tunnel had been bored through to precisely where the mind would be located under the covering of regolith. Around this tunnel there were marks in the ground: footprints.

Humans?

King thought not. Golem had also joined Erebus, so they must be the source.

The tunnel was amply wide enough for the telefactor so the AI sent it inside. It wound down through regolith now bonded with glassy resin, past two bubble-metal beams then up against hull metal, which had been cut through. A spherical cavity lay beyond. The AI recognized this as the armoured casing that contained the mind on these older ships – made to be quickly ejected so that if the ship itself was destroyed, its tactical information would not be lost. All the optical and power connections remained in place through the central pillar. The cage of doped superconductor that contained the crystal mind seemed undamaged – and much larger than the one containing King's own mind, but then technology had advanced very much since then. The crystal mind itself, however, lay fragmented about the bottom of the sphere like a shattered windscreen. King withdrew the telefactor.

The *King of Hearts* AI went on to investigate two more sites, discovering just a couple of claw arms which were all that remained of another four-pack drone, then a drone made in the shape of a pangolin, a great dent in its armour, which was partially melted. Every system inside it was utterly fried. King surmised it had been hit directly by an EM shell, so there had been no need to send Golem to make sure no sentience remained in it.

King recalled its telefactor and hesitated about investigating the planet. If Erebus and the other AIs were located here, they would generate visible activity, and information traffic in the ether. None so far detected. Also, did King really want to locate Erebus and its kind?

Obviously some disagreement had resulted in the wreck-age on that moon, so there seemed no guarantee that King would be welcome. Then again, the AIs manufac-tured during the Prador War were notoriously cranky and individualistic, so it was perhaps unsurprising that some of them might eventually baulk at the idea of melding. Perhaps on the planet itself more could be discovered as to the nature of this disagreement. King redirected the telefactor towards that nearby world, sending two more after it, but these bearing manipulators, cutting gear and the ability to interface with memcrystal. Some little while later the AI discovered that 'disagreement' might be rather an understatement for what had occurred there.

A vast 200-mile wreckage field terminated in the mountainous remains of a dreadnought. Radioactivity was high, so it seemed evident that tactical nukes were used, repeatedly. Beam trails cut into the rock all around. The big ship obviously came down in a controlled descent, otherwise there would be nothing now but a large crater, but clearly lost control near the end. It had bounced for 150 miles, then skidded for a further 50 miles until coming to a halt. But it was not alone.

King found wreckage from over three hundred war drones, four attack ships, twelve landers that judging by the remains were filled with Golem, two fast pickets and a mid-level battleship impacted into a cliff. Perhaps Erebus had met its own end here? Perhaps that dread-nought once contained the wayward mind? But a scan of visible numbers on the dreadnought's hull dispelled that idea. This ship was called the *White Shark*. Here then were the results of an AI on AI conflict between factions in Erebus's camp. King dropped into boiling atmosphere and began sending out all but two of its stock of telefactors, twenty-three of them. The AI really needed to know what happened here.

The mid-level battleship seemed a lost cause. Evidently having come in very fast, the probability that any crystal survived the impact was remote. Studying all the other wreckage, it soon became evident to King that after the battle the victors conducted a major salvage operation: markings on the ground showed that Golem, telefactors, and drones running on caterpillar treads had stripped usable components from most of the wreckage – what remained being not worth the energy expenditure of lifting from the gravity well. Some of the war-drone minds had been removed, where possible; all that remained of the Golem in the landers was the occasional distorted chassis, also mindless; a beam strike had cut a hole right through the dreadnought, while it lay at rest, and incinerated the mind it contained; one attack-ship mind was missing, the other destroyed; the picket minds lay in heat-distorted fragments. By this King guessed which side was which, and that the losers had been shown no mercy. There seemed nothing more to learn here. But then, as it hovered over the battlefield recalling its telefactors, King turned its attention to the ship impacted into the cliff. No tread marks over that way. Obviously Erebus thought that ship just as much a write-off as King had at first. Perhaps they were both mistaken. King sent four of its telefactors over to the cliff.

Five hours of excavation eventually revealed a distorted-mind case. Using a thermic lance, one telefactor cut through the armour, then on the end of an arm it inserted a sensor head. There rested the ship's mind, broken, in its doped s-con cage, but still perhaps containing much information. A smaller telefactor entered, found a power input point, detached the plug and inserted it into a socket in itself, ready to power up the damaged mind. There King paused it. So, Erebus stripped every usable component from the surrounding wreckage, destroyed or removed all the minds, certainly for the purpose of concealing its destination or intentions from possible pursuers, yet it missed this? King recalled to itself the other three telefactors and, once they snicked away in their cache, used both AG and thrusters to take itself up a hundred miles. The AI thereupon opened secured processing space and routed telefactor control through that. It then powered up the mind case, with the tentative reluctance of someone clicking on the power to dodgy household wiring.

The telefactor dropped to the floor, as the drain sucked power from its gravmotor, then it reached out to begin splicing into the optics connected to the abandoned mind. Nothing yet. Connection made. Diagnostic program loading . . . The worm came through like an express monorail loaded with warheads. It screamed round in the secured processing space, searching for weaknesses. King immediately began loading programs into that space to counter it, take it apart, analyse its structure. The worm, semi-AI, knew itself to be trapped. It transmitted a signal back down the link, instantly broadcast from the telefactor. Five suns ignited below: five one megatonne CTDs.

King accelerated. Four seconds. Time for the signal to reach another location: rail-gun hidden in the sulphurous moon, and now firing a barrage of missiles at half the speed of light. But the *King of Hearts* was a modern Polity attack ship. It stood on its tail, opened up its fusion drive to full power and, accelerating at a hundred gravities, left a single anti-munitions package behind it. The worm broke apart, eating itself, but King already knew the frequency and format of the signal it had sent, and thus transmitted its own present. King's worm burrowed into the mind it located on the moon: just a drone waiting here to ambush any pursuers, fiercely loyal and ready to destroy itself. It was not quick enough. It had seen the others leave, tracked their departure and then awaited some to return to say its mission was over. King learnt all that in microseconds. Microseconds after, another CTD detonated in the face of the moon, and left a burning sulphurous crater. The barrage of missiles proceeded to detonate around the anti-munitions package, easily fooled into thinking they found their target.

'I'm coming to find you,' sang King, accelerating out of the system.

As Mika detached herself from the VR frame she felt tired and frustrated. Every time she entered the virtuality now, there awaited a mass of new information to be processed, and she experienced difficulties in keeping on top of it all. While she deconstructed singular molecular structures the work stayed easy enough, but with research now being directed towards what could be formed from those structures and their interrelationships, it got tougher. Much of this work being conducted at AI speeds, it now became the province only of Jerusalem, other AIs aboard, and those humans sufficiently augmented to keep up.

Stepping down from her frame, she surveyed the various screens in her research area and saw that those not frozen were scrolling reams of code. She walked over to the counter on which the screens rested and picked up the item lying there. The aug was similar to the one D'nissan now wore: a flattened bean of gleaming metal with an exposed crystal in the shape of a snail's shell on one side – that aspect purely aesthetic. Its visual interlink entered via the wearer's temple, so was not as grotesque as many of its kind, but the device still required surgical installation. Susan James and Prator Colver had both upgraded: the former with an aug like this and the latter with the more conventional kind, though he talked about going fully gridlinked when he could spare the time – that too required surgical intervention since the gridlinking tech needed to be imbedded in the inner surface of his skull.

Mika now faced a choice. In her present unaugmented state she was rapidly becoming obselete. If she wanted to stay at the forefront of Jain research, she needed to upgrade. Staying as a standard-format human meant she would soon be pushed to one side, handling small peripheral projects. But did she really want to keep up with Colver, James and D'nissan?

Ever since installing that Jain mycelium in herself, on the planet Masada, and the drastic surgical procedure required to remove it, her attitude to invasive augmentation had become rather cautious. Her present situation also posed certain questions about what she was and what she wanted to be. Did she really want to go the haiman route? She thought about Cormac and their recent utterly human liaison. He was gridlinked, but not willingly so – the device had reinstated itself in a way yet to be explained. He had been taken off the gridlink because being linked for so long had compromised his efficiency as an agent, for he lost the ability to connect with humans at a human level, though that lack did not seem so evident to her now. But there the rub: was Mika sufficiently curious about Jain technology to lose her essential humanity in pursuit of its secrets?

Mika entered her living quarters, went over to her bar unit and poured herself a glass of brandy. Taking this with her, she slumped on her sofa.

What do I love?

She loved Cormac, or felt she did – Mika always encountered problems with hazy terms like 'love'. But what about her research? What were her aims? In the end she was practically immortal, and nor did she require her vocation to put bread in her mouth or a roof over her head. Her reasons for pursuing it were based on a feeling of both duty *and* self-gratification. But the sense of duty became irrelevant when there were those better able to perform the research than her. So what did she enjoy about it? What gratified her? She considered the last few years. On Samarkand she most enjoyed taking apart and studying the Maker-constructed creature there, and subsequently studying the dracomen. On Masada the dracomen again provided that same pleasure, as did her lengthy digging in the mud to find the remains of the dragon sphere that had sacrificed itself there. In the end she reluctantly realized she preferred field work, getting her hands dirty, not the esoteric research now being conducted by the others.

'Jerusalem,' she said, 'they're leaving me behind.'

The AI replied instantly. 'Augmented mental function and memory are now almost a prerequisite. The big picture spills out beyond the scope of the human mind.'

'Precisely,' Mika said and sipped her brandy. 'How vital is my contribution?'

'No one is indispensable.'

'Well thanks for that.'

'*I* am not indispensable,' the AI added.

'Right.'

'You are reluctant to augment yourself?'

'I am. The others are mostly number-crunching now, and are moving increasingly into the AI mental realm. I'm not sure that's what I want to do.'

'Why?'

Mika thought about it for a long moment then said, 'I saw Susan James recently. She was eating Provit cake and drinking water and did not see me even though I stood right in front of her. When I first met her she listed her prime interests as mathematics, sex and gourmet food, and was not entirely sure of the order of preference.'

'Augmentation changes one – that is its essential purpose – but the degree of that change must be governed by the individual.'

'Cormac . . . he lost his humanity?'

'He did. It is a notable paradox that some augmented humans do lose their humanity – becoming what they, at an unconscious level, perceive AIs to be – while AIs, through age, experience and their own expansion of processing power, come to understand humanity better and therefore become more humane. Cormac's present condition is a puzzle – almost as if some fundamental change in him has enabled him to become gridlinked again whilst still retaining his humanity.'

'What would you advise for me?' Mika asked.

'I would advise rest. I would advise a lengthy break from your work, in which you can consider what you want to do next. Incidentally, I have recently disconnected Susan James, and she is currently undergoing an enforced and medicated rest. She is one of nearly four hundred individuals suffering the same problem.'

'That being?'

'In trying to understand and fully encompass all that Jain technology is, they have managed to lose themselves.'

'How reassuring.'

'I would not want you to feel, if having chosen augmentation, that you made an uninformed choice. Nothing worthwhile, Mika, comes easy. Consider what the word "augmentation" means. The idea is that you augment *something* already existing. Many who do it destroy that essential something in the process – become more their additions than themselves. It is part of the haiman ethos to retain that humanity until such a time as it becomes possible to truly extend self. They call themselves haimans but know that until that becomes possible they are not truly post-human.'

'But what is that essential something?' Mika asked.

'Indeed,' was Jerusalem's only reply.

The gabbleduck was mountainous: a great pyramid of flesh squatting in the flute grasses, its multiple forearms folded across its chest, its bill wavering up and down as if it was either nodding an affirmative or nodding off to sleep. It regarded Blegg with its tiara of emerald eyes ranged below the dome of its head.

'Why have you chosen such a bizarre shape for yourself?' Blegg asked. 'Obviously it is something you've ransacked from the mind of the AI here, but I fail to see the purpose.'

'Jain, Csorians and Atheter,' said the gabbleduck. 'You

humans have much to say about all three but know so little.'

'Then tell me,' Blegg suggested.

'The Jain became extinct, five million years ago. Currently you believe it was their own technology that drove them to extinction. We believed this, too, though in our time, two million years after the Jain, there was more evidence available than there is to you now.'

'And?'

'Jain technology is a weapon.'

'So we believe.'

'Who did they use it against?'

'It was made to destroy civilizations,' said Blegg, 'but that was a rhetorical question which I presume you'll answer yourself.'

'Who is always the greatest enemy? You fought a war with the Prador, but that could almost be classed as anomalous. The greatest enemy is nearly always those you can understand enough to hate.'

'I see,' said Blegg. 'An internecine war.'

'It lasted for half a million years. But why a weapon designed to destroy civilizations?'

'I don't know. Why don't you give me a clue?'

'Despair,' said the gabbleduck. 'Hatred of the futility of intelligent life and technical civilizations, all of them, forever.'

'Despair and arrogance,' suggested Blegg.

The gabbleduck shrugged. 'Just so.'

'What happened to you, then?'

The gabbleduck turned its head and gazed out over the ersatz landscape. 'The Csorians, like these Makers, thought they understood the technology, increasingly depended upon it, then were ultimately destroyed by it.'

'You didn't answer my question.' This virtuality was very realistic, and Blegg found himself becoming fed up with standing, so he sat like some acolyte on the ground before the monstrous being.

'We nearly did the same. We lost planet after planet to it, and it subsumed and killed billions. We exterminated billions on the worlds we sterilized.'

Blegg decided he wanted to get straight to the point. 'Was it a Pyrrhic victory in the end? Your civilization no longer exists, but then few Jain nodes exist either. The ones we are having trouble with now are those brought here by the Maker.'

That chuckle again. The gabbleduck stretched out one limb and opened out a hand composed of talons like black bananas. 'You know that Jain technology is nano-technology, but study it long enough and you find that its foundations go deeper. All matter is merely knotted space and time in the end, adhering to certain rules soon learnt by any sufficiently advanced species.' Floating inside that claw appeared some construct of light. 'When you organize the underlying structure of matter, the difference is always noticeable when observed from the right place.' The creature turned to peer at him. 'There is a price.'

'Name it.'

'You return us to the surface of the place you call Masada – home of the gabbleducks.'

Blegg considered that. The plan had been to keep the artefact aboard the *Hourne* so it could quickly be moved to different locations in the event of war. Such a repository of valuable information must be protected. However, the survival of the Polity might depend on being able to locate Jain nodes. He did not need to confer. He replied, 'It will be done. You have my word, and that is good.'

'I know – it's the word of a ruler,' the gabbleduck replied cryptically.

The construct drifted down from its claw, turning as it came. Blegg kept utterly still as it hovered before him, and as it drifted towards his forehead and penetrated. 'The Jain used U-space, yet their destructive technology does not. It was made by their AIs, which were based on the Jain themselves as yours are on you, before those AIs transcended their erstwhile masters and left them to kill each other. Why they left the U-space option out is a question best addressed to those same AIs, wherever they might be.'

It was a pattern in his mind, seven, eight dimensional: something beyond what he could encompass, but at least recognizable as a U-space signature. With a sudden flush of excitement Blegg realized what he saw: a Jain node as viewed via underspace.

The gabbleduck peered down at him. 'This is what you came for?'

'It is.'

It nodded slowly. 'You never get them all – there're always some overlooked, to start the process all over again. There is only one way to win.'

'And what is that?' Blegg asked, wondering what the quickest way out of this realm might be.

'You cease to be what the Jain hated.'

Blegg turned away.

Never.

Was that what the Atheter did? *Hatred of the futility of intelligent life and technical civilizations . . .*

Were the gabbleducks all that remained of the Atheter

when they made their fateful decision to cease to be the intelligent citizens of a technical civilization? Blegg doubted that, else why did this thing, this Atheter AI, want to be taken to where remained those animalistic descendants, the gabbleducks? It was all a mystery that would have to wait for another time, since Blegg had more pressing concerns. He turned away, felt the ground sliding out from underneath him, and saw a black wall descend.

Hiatus.

Blegg stepped out of the VR booth, blinked and looked around him. The staff on the observation deck peered at him warily. Gazing through the screens, he observed that the artefact seemed to have settled back to its previous state.

'Hourne,' he said, 'are you back?'

The AI replied, 'The artefact has disconnected itself from me, but may reconnect at any time.'

'Do you have that U-space signature?'

'I do – it was transmitted to me at the same time as you received it in VR.'

'You saw all that, then?'

'I did.'

'Interesting . . . about the gabbleducks. Do you believe it?'

'If it is not actually the truth, it seems a strange and pointless lie to tell.'

– retroact 5 –

'*There was not much resistance, then,*' Atheter observed.

'*Sporadic,*' Blegg replied. '*Mostly crushed by human*

fighters bright enough to realize the AI rulers were better at governing than any previous human rulers.'

He turned to another card, saw them laid out all around him like gravestones.

Blegg ran down the seemingly endless corridor, while klaxons shrieked and warning lights flashed. Grieg told him the terrorists were ex Matthew Corporation employees who obtained the planar explosives from a mercenary group who decided on retirement under the new regime and were now selling off their assets. That had been a relief, since from the beginning of the investigation ECS intelligence believed them to have obtained fissile materials. But planar explosives could still do plenty of damage if detonated somewhere critical.

'Left turn at the end here, second door on your left,' Earth Central informed him.

Somewhere critical seemed to be snuggled up against the *Amaranth* Station reactor, or so Draben told the interrogators. Halting by the door Blegg waited a moment.

'Nothing connected to the door,' EC assured him.

He opened the door and entered, scanning the room. The reactor cube, five yards on each side, sat in the middle of the room amidst a tangle of cooling pipes and heavy power cables. Control consoles lined one wall, and gratings had been pulled up from the floor when this place was searched earlier.

'The detonator is solid-state, activated by timer and gravity switch.'

Blegg walked in, studying that part of the reactor where steam pipes exited towards the generators next door. There – beside the pipes. No wonder the earlier searchers did not find it. The bomb appeared to be a

pressure and stress analyser bolted across the point
where the pipes exited the reactor. He climbed nearby
steps up to a catwalk and walked along until standing
beside the explosive device.

'How long have I got?'

'Four minutes – not long enough to deactivate it.'

Blegg considered that. Running here had been an
almost instinctive reaction. He should have transferred
himself through U-space to give himself more time. But,
then, would another couple of minutes have made any
difference? He placed his hand on the bomb. 'A gravity
switch and a timer, you say? Nothing else linked to its
attachment to the pipes?'

'So Draben just told his interrogator, and he seems
less inclined to lie now. One moment . . .' The AI fell
silent for a while, then returned with, 'It is secured by
four bolts. You require a socket drive, which you will find
in a toolchest below the catwalk.'

Blegg quickly returned below, found the toolchest and
flipped it open. The socket driver, a gun-shaped object
with a tool-head that could adjust to fit any bolt, lay
amidst a well-used collection of old-style spanners. Omi-
nous, that. He hoped whoever used the device kept it well
charged and did not have to resort to the spanners too
often. He picked it up and pressed the trigger – seemed
okay – and returned to the catwalk. Closing the driver on
the first bolt he hoped Draben was not lying. The bolt
spun out easily, as did the second and third.

Placing the driver over the fourth bolt Blegg concentrated on his breathing and instilled calm within himself.
The gravity switch meant he must keep the bomb to its
present orientation. He clamped a hand against it and

spun out the last bolt. Discarding the driver behind him, he then carefully eased the bomb away from the pipes.

'How long?'

'Two minutes.'

Blegg checked his watch. It would have been nice to be able to transfer himself and the device far from here, but neither gravity nor orientation applied in U-space, so such a transference might trip the switch. *Amaranth* would be safe; he would cease to exist. He turned slowly and walked along the catwalk to the steps, his martial training enabling him to move smoothly and evenly. Negotiating the steps was more difficult, but he reached the floor safely.

'You need to get at least two hundred yards from the reactor,' EC informed him. 'Outside the door, turn to your left and keep walking. The area has been evacuated.'

The door was latched. Blegg pressed the bomb against the wall to keep it upright, opened the door and held it open with his foot as he entered the corridor beyond. His mouth dry, he continued that sliding walk.

'How long, how far?' he eventually asked.

'Just keep going – I will tell you when to put it down.'

Trust Earth Central?

He checked his watch again. Thirty seconds more and he would put the damned thing down anyway and get out of there. Slowly the digits counted down.

'Carefully place the bomb on the floor,' EC told him, only seconds before he intended to anyway.

He squatted, followed instructions. The thing looked precarious propped up against the wall. Standing, he immediately opened that doorway that he, the only human being, could open. The bomb detonated shortly afterwards blowing a hole in the side of the station. No humans died.

– retroact ends –

Survival.

Thellant's mind worked with a clarity he had never before experienced. The substructure now cut through the bedrock, from where Coloron's forces had contained it, and was rapidly spreading through the rest of the arcology. Those people it now subsumed he could control completely, but he left them to some already established program integral to the Jain technology, which made them attack others to either kill or subsume them. Whether they managed to or not did not really concern him. Only the chaos they created really helped, for in the end he knew he could not win here. He was powerful, and potentially able to control this entire arcology, its population, even the whole planet, but that presupposed he would be left alone to achieve such control. Thellant knew the AIs would not allow the substructure to spread beyond this place, no matter the cost. Though it was part of him, because he retained much physical and mental integrity it was a part he could sacrifice and grow again elsewhere. He did not intend to be in this vicinity when the AIs incinerated the arcology.

Peering from the wreckage, Thellant observed the landscape of cooling rock and molten metal at the bottom of the trench. Looking through the substructure now rising in wall cavities, and spreading along ducts, optics and power lines on the other side, he saw Coloron's forces pulling back – they knew their enemy to be out of containment now. For every ten yards gain he lost five yards to proton fire, but with hand weapons they could not destroy everything the substructure occupied.

What's this?

A humanoid he first took to be an ophidapt grabbed a questing tentacle and shoved back the soldier it was originally groping for. The tentacle proceeded to inject nanofilaments into the reptilian body. The humanoid should have been instantly paralysed. Instead it fired a proton weapon into the wall, frying the substructure from which the tentacle extruded, then it flung down the severed tentacle and incinerated that too. Thellant focused intently on a recording of this event – replayed from one of the many computers spread throughout the Jain architecture like grains of salt. He discerned that Jain nanofilaments had instantly come under attack, managing to penetrate no more than the upper layers of the reptilian's skin. In fact some kind of viral assault shot back up them, paralysing the structure in the wall just instants before the . . . Thellant consulted other sources . . . before the dracoman incinerated it. So, not just Polity AIs – he must contend with these things as well.

'Thellant.'

What, what now?

The source of that flat voice disappeared even as he groped for it. Perhaps some program injected from that dracoman, now propagating back? Gone now, yes. But it was also time for Thellant to disappear. The area opposite him was secure for him now. He stepped into the open and headed across the bottom of the trench. The Jain substructure they might be able to hold back, but he intended to slip past.

On the other side he passed the black pit of a mineshaft

plummeting down into the bedrock. Spilling out of this, like silver worms, were foot-wide peristaltic pipes issuing from the robotic boring machines far below. Some of these pipes were split open, spilling slurries of powdered haematite, bauxite and malachite. All of them entered a pumping machine, and from that normal pipes of half the diameter ran down one side of a maglev tunnel spearing into darkness. Parked in the mouth of the tunnel, a boring machine lay like some massive steel grub with a cylindrical head overly endowed with teeth. Thellant walked past this and on into the tunnel's darkness. All around him via the substructure he observed further disquieting scenes.

The substructure was attempting to return soldiers it now controlled to Coloron's forces, but the dracomen spotted them instantly and destroyed them, for it seemed these creatures could detect Jain growth even at a distance. Elsewhere, Coloron's drones or Golem soon detected other returnees and their fate was the same. Fortunately no dracomen were searching in his current vicinity. He reached a curve in the tunnel and halted. Because the substructure spread through the wall cavity beside him, he knew the enemy awaited ahead.

Five arcology monitors and four drones occupied the tunnel, armed respectively with proton weapons and pulse-guns. A proton cannon floated above the maglev rails. It fired one shot, lighting up the tunnel, and demolishing a section of affected wall. They were now retreating, targeting the larger masses of growth as they went. Thellant pressed his hand against the wall, injected filaments from himself to make full physical connection. He halted all local growth, causing it to curl up and apparently die. He began shifting energy and resources to an area twelve miles to his left instead, and started a massive push there. This sort of thing had been happening for some time, as the substructure constantly probed for weaknesses. The opponents ahead ceased retreating – with the brute growth occurring elsewhere they could now recoup their resources. He waited five minutes before breaking into a trot and rounding the bend.

'Hey!' he shouted. 'They're coming!'

None of those already controlled by Jain tech spoke, which gave him an edge.

'Hold it there!' one of the monitors ordered.

'They're coming!' he shrieked.

Seconds only before the cannon swivelled towards him, but by then he drew opposite the blast hole in the wall. He stepped into it, fast, then accelerated along the wall cavity. Ducking below masses of fused optics, he ran faster than any normal man could run when upright. Behind him, red flame exploded along the cavity, pulse-gun fire punching machine-gun holes everywhere. He was hit five times, but only his human body suffered and he did not let that affect *him*. Proton flame seared the skin on his back. Then to his right: another wall hollow, cutting up through numerous levels. He climbed. Fire now below him, then tracking on past. Two levels up, he stepped out through a service door and into an empty corridor on the other side of Coloron's main line of defence.

Thellant paused and inspected himself. His back was totally charcoaled, the rest of his naturally dark skin mottled with still darker patches, as if bruised all over, and hard metallic masses pushed against it from the inside. Also his electromagnetic linkages to the substructure hazed the air around him with energy spillover. He began to make cosmetic alterations: withdrawing the tech deeper inside him, repairing the damage to his human facade. Eventually he stood unflawed, with a skin tone like that of his healthy negro ancestor, no fat on his body, his musculature less flabby than at any time since his youth. He reached up, peeled the dead Dracocorp aug from behind his ear and cast it aside. Moving on, he searched for and eventually found a suitable corpse, which he stripped of clothing to replace his own damaged garments. However, he did not yet feel ready to break his link to the main substructure. First he needed to learn the disposition of Coloron's forces.

The dracomen were nearer now: five of them just a mile to his right and three levels above. He already knew how fast they could move and felt them to be too close, so took the first exit to his left and headed down one level. Other dracomen occupied levels far above and some far to his left and higher still. What lay ahead, outside of the current purview of the substructure, he did not know. He would take as straight a line as possible, lose himself in the general population, find a way to escape. Now was the time to make the break.

It was so hard to cut himself off, almost like fighting an addiction. The electromagnetic transceivers inside him fought against his will like rebellious adolescents, and would only cut his connection when he physically used the structure inside himself to sever their power. Even then they tried to reconnect themselves until he killed each one remaining inside him. Thereafter came an agonizing hammer of withdrawal, dullness of mind, blurring of his senses. Stubbornly he fought this too and tracked down its root causes. These feelings he experienced were a human thing. It seemed that his breaking of contact with the main substructure had pushed much of his awareness back into his organic brain and out of the grain-sized computers lodged inside him. He forced awareness back, regained clarity and enforced a straight neurochemical reprogramming of his organic brain, and filled it with nanofibre control systems. This achieved, he realized how he was no longer that petty being Thellant N'komo, but something else entire.

The hologram displayed a section of the arcology, transparent, shimmering four feet off the floor like something fashioned of glass. In this, a handsbreadth away from one ragged edge of the circular trench cut down into the arcology, appeared a blinking red dot. Surrounding this, and closing in, were twenty-one green dots. The red dot the bad guy and the green the good guys, supposing Scar and the other twenty dracomen could be described as *good*.

'He just broke with the main substructure,' said Thorn, relaying a message from the HK program routed through Jack. 'The HK can't track him any longer.'

Scar replied, 'Closing now on his last location.'

'Jack,' enquired Thorn, 'does the HK have any idea of his intentions?'

The AI replied, 'Escape from the arcology – he knows it will be destroyed.'

'He's heading outside then,' said Thorn, 'but which way?'

Jack replied, 'He avoids dracomen, apparently. He must be aware of how ineffective Jain tech is against them.'

'That's good. If we can locate him we can probably shepherd him the way we want.' Thorn looked up from the hologram to the screen wall of the projection room –

presently divided into many subscreens displaying multiple views inside and outside the arcology. 'Coloron, he may have changed his face, but then again that might not even have occurred to him. Are you searching?'

'I am not searching,' that AI replied.

The screen wall flickered, became a single view into a concourse along which crowds trudged. A frame picked out one individual in the crowd, focused in.

'Thellant N'komo,' Coloron informed him.

'Racial type through choice?' wondered Thorn, eyeing the tall negro.

Coloron replied, 'Twenty years ago he traced one line of his ancestry back to one of the negroid races, then had himself cosmetically altered. It was his contention that he must look like those ancestors of his who, in the seventeenth century, were transported as slaves to Jamaica to cut sugar cane, because he feels he is a slave to the likes of me.' The AI paused, then continued, 'He was a very wealthy slave, however, and there seemed a notable lack of whips, chains and endless grinding labour in his enslavement.'

Thorn grinned to himself: it just went to show that even big-fuck planetary AIs were not above sarcasm. 'Scar, he's moving along Brallatsia Concourse, with the crowd heading for Exit 52 – ground level.' He glanced at the hologram. Most of the green dots began moving, very fast.

'Don't crowd him,' said agent Thorn. 'We don't want him to do anything drastic. . . . Uh, Coloron, you've got him targeted?'

'I have,' the AI replied.

'Another reason not to crowd him,' Thorn added.

How many would die, he wondered, if the AI fired its

orbital particle cannon right now? Certainly few of that crowd in the concourse would survive, for the firestorm would blast all the way along to Exit 52 itself. There were also thousands jammed into the levels above and below this one.

'Should we try and clear some of the people beyond the exit?' he asked. The death rate would be lower outside – perhaps less than ten thousand.

'Inadvisable,' said Coloron.

'Agreed,' Thorn admitted. 'We do that and he'll probably guess what's happening.' It still did not make him feel great about risking tens of thousands of lives just to capture this one individual.

'Dammit.' He picked up his weapon and headed off to join the dracomen. Overseeing the operation here just gave him too much time to think of the consequences of it going wrong.

'Keep moving. Keep moving. Food, drink and accommodation will be supplied outside. Rescue personnel one mile ahead of you. If you require assistance . . .'

Thellant tuned out these continual announcements. He felt angry. As the surrounding mass of humanity jostled him it took him an effort of will not to simply kill all those about him. But the moment he did something like that he would reveal himself and he doubted even the proximity of so many innocent citizens would prevent him becoming a viable target, so he kept his head down and kept shuffling along. An AG platform hovered above and drones buzzed through the air like head-sized wingless bluebottles. An occasional AG ambulance sped high overhead, after picking up the injured or those just collapsing from plain exhaustion. The bars and shops on either side were completely empty but, every hundred yards or so, temporary drinking fountains had been installed. He supposed the comfort offered by them was deliberately limited because Coloron did not want any delays to the exodus. The AI clearly wanted to get as many inhabitants as possible outside in the shortest period of time.

Inside him the Jain tech lay quiescent, but he knew it would be spotted if he came under direct scan. It seemed, however, they did not perform scanning here as back at the main line. Another AI calculation no doubt: the minimal delay for scanning individuals would accumulate into something untenable for just the tens of thousands surrounding him, let alone the millions presently departing the arcology.

It took five hours for him to traverse the six miles of concourse to the arcology edge. Here, shops, bars, and the walls behind had been torn out either side of Exit 52 to widen it to the full breadth of the concourse. When he finally stepped outside night had fallen, and the sky glittered with stars and orbiting ships. He looked to either side into the seething mass of humanity and saw dropshaft exits from the levels above and below also spewing a steady stream of inhabitants. AG transports regularly departed like bees from a hive, depositing their passengers some distance ahead, then returning for more. Thellant trudged on, adjusting his eyes to night vision, then ramping up the magnification as he scanned his surroundings. Presently he could not see much ahead, since he walked upslope, but to his left, two miles away, he focused in on one AG platform and saw that it held a human and a dracoman, and to his right over by 51 –

a larger exit – there seemed a heavy concentration of drones. It seemed he was in absolutely the right place.

As he reached the top of the slope, the vista opened ahead of him, and he felt a surge of excitement upon seeing a huge lander at rest, with people filing inside it. He tried to speed up, but those not sure where to go now, slowed, and many crowded around an open-sided transport from which self-heating ration packs were being distributed. He glanced back, saw two dracomen moving through the crowds back by the exit. He moved faster, pushing people out of his way when necessary, quickly sliding past them otherwise. Those jamming in after the ration packs deflected him to his left. Glancing up he saw the AG platform drifting closer. Ahead, the ramps of the big lander rose. He swore in frustration, but pushed on anyway.

The ramps closed up into the entrances of the huge vessel, then a low thrumming transmitted through the ground as the craft ascended into the night sky.

'Bastards,' snarled a man beside him. 'You can bet they'll blow the arcology before we see another one of those, and even if they don't that shit will be out here after us.'

By listening in on the conversations of those around him, Thellant gathered that everyone now knew what was happening. The conventional server network was already back up to speed, and announcements on public screens and address systems continued non-stop.

'What do you mean?' he asked. The man wore an aug so probably was more up to speed with current events than Thellant.

'Last one,' explained the man. 'The *Britannic* is full, and its three landers will be just held in orbit along with their passengers.' The man stepped closer. 'But then maybe we're the lucky ones – if anyone in those ships turns out to be infected, I don't suppose they'll be landing anywhere.'

Thellant turned away from him. The lander rose high enough to open up the vista ahead. The sheer quantity of people stunned the mind. The multitude stretched for about two miles ahead, whereupon it filtered into encampments of bubble tents. To his right and left the throng stretched for as far as he could see. Returning his attention to the refugee camp beyond, he noted numerous ships positioned down on the ground. Some of them, he recognized, were not just landers but spaceships capable of entering U-space.

'Seems they're setting up another camp,' said the man, his fingers resting against his aug. He gestured with his chin. 'Two hundred miles out, and the quarantine perimeter has been extended. I don't suppose that has anything to do with the arrival of an ECS dreadnought at all.'

Thellant looked at him enquiringly.

The man explained. 'Coloron's orbital weapons are limited – not enough to contain us. A dreadnought should be able to fry anyone who tries to break quarantine.'

Thellant moved on. More such ships would arrive. He needed to escape now. Scanning about himself again, he saw the AG platform drawing even closer, but he could no longer see the dracomen behind him. He adjusted his course accordingly, picking out a small quadraspherical ship – ECS Rescue by its markings. He could see that the vessel was firmly closed up – probably to prevent panicked citizens sneaking aboard – and that ECS staff worked from a row of inflated domes nearby. Within an hour he reached the first of those domes, glancing inside at rows of beds. All of them were occupied, some of their occupants being tended to by autodocs. Rescue staff had set out their stall outside as well, where they were treating the walking wounded. A flash lit the sky – the third one since he chose this ship. Apparently the dreadnought had already knocked out a gravcar and gravtransport, both trying to escape to SA. Finally he came up beside one of the Rescue ship's four spheres, next to an airlock.

Thellant pressed his hand against the mechanism, injected Jain filaments to subvert the locking mechanism. The door crumped open.

'Hey, what do you—?'

Backhanded, the woman flew three yards through the air and hit the ground, her skull shattered. Inside, then closing and sealing the outer hatch. Through the inner hatch, to find this cargo-sphere empty. He moved on into the next where from outside he had seen the flight deck. He needed to move fast. His hand slammed down on the console, filaments injecting, sequestering systems, taking over the ship, searching out its AI. He found it, closed it off before it could scream for help, then took it apart. Dropping into the pilot's chair he initiated AG and watched through the cockpit screen as the ship began to rise.

'Lassa, why are you launching?'

A query issued from some AI above – probably the dreadnought. Thellant learned from information subsumed from the AI, Lassa, that this ship had been due to launch in one hour. He answered through Lassa.

'Unnecessary delay. All cargo and staff unloaded, and all cold coffins filled.'

Only in that moment did he discover that one sphere of the ship contained twenty coldsleep containers, fifteen of them now occupied by people severely injured.

'Very well, you are clear to make orbit.'

As easy as that? Thellant grimaced to himself. The Polity was far too dependent on its damned AIs and in this case that was a mistake. He settled back in the seat, his hand still on the console and with himself still linked into the ship's systems. As it continued to rise he entertained a sudden suspicion and ran diagnostics on the U-space engine, but it was fine – no problems at all. He put it online, ready to drop the ship into underspace the moment that became possible. An hour of flying later the sun picked out gleaming ships in a blue-black firmament, before it broke over the planet's curve. He shut off AG and started the fusion drive to finally pull him clear of the well. Then a stuttering flash, and something hammered the Rescue ship, violently tilting his horizon. Then again that flash, which Thellant now identified as a high-powered laser. Through his link into the ship's systems, he felt the U-space engine not only go offline but completely disconnect, as if it had disappeared. The second hit had taken out the fusion-drive plate. As the ship tilted up into starlit darkness, another vessel passed overhead, glittering like oyster shell.

A voice issued from the console. 'Gotcha.'

11

The development of the laser as a weapon began way back at the start of this millennium and it has been with us ever since. However, for ship-to-ship conflict, improvements in reflective and s-con heat-dispersal armours have all but rendered inef-fective as weapons lasers in the range of infrared to ultraviolet. Move outside those spectra, however, and you have masers, which can be used to sufficiently penetrate missiles – which will not have the heat-dispersal capacity of a large ship – to destroy them, and at closer range actually can destroy ships. The same rule applies to xasers and grasers, but in all cases the range and destructive potential of these weapons is lim-ited, especially in fields of conflict often light years across. And, in reality, we learnt from the Prador how negligible is their effect, in the arena in which they are usually employed, when compared with the numerous other varieties of particle cannon. As you are all aware, the ubiquitous pulse-gun is just a form of particle weapon, the particulate matter ranging from powdered aluminium to a gas—

(audience interruption)

Pardon

(audience response)

I will state again that there is no such thing as an APW!

What you are referring to is a proton weapon – highly destructive and tending to spread isotope poisoning wherever used. The APW, the antiphoton weapon, the dark-light gun, is a fucking fictional creation!

(moderator query)

Yes, thank you. I'm fine.

– From her lecture 'Modern Warfare'
by EBS Heinlein

The sphere, composed of two-foot-long metal ants, rested in the centre of the Feynman Lounge, individual ants occasionally detaching to be off about their assigned tasks. This new conceit of Polity AIs, in choosing to locate themselves in increasingly bizarre body shapes, elicited the Legate's contempt, but not sufficiently for it to consider outright confrontation. In retrospect it was a good thing it had not tried taking information from the two women investigating the explosion site. The two ant drones accompanying them – which the Legate had initially discounted – were dangerous, being part of this forensic AI.

Via fibres inserted through a nearby wall, the Legate observed five humans, two haimans and three Golem, all wearing ECS uniforms that identified them as members of the forensic team. The others in the lounge, three advanced haimans sporting carapaces and sensory cowls, were part of the Cassius project. They sat silently, two together on a couch and one in an armchair. The rigorous interrogation they underwent was conducted via optic linkages plugged into their carapaces, the cables snaking back to the AI itself. But within minutes this session ended, whereupon the haimans detached the cables and departed.

The Legate withdrew its spying fibres from the wall and turned round. The room it occupied belonged to a man whose mental capacity was only complemented by a cerebral aug, so it had been easy to enter while he slept and put him into a deeper sleep. After scanning through the information contained in this particular individual's aug, and by linking into the public com systems of the station, the Legate learnt what was generally known about the incident that occurred here. The explosion had resulted in the death of a haiman called Shoala, and subsequently the rumour mills ground away. Many on the station knew Orlandine's and Shoala's relationship to be more than just a working one. Orlandine, though a superb overseer and sublime scientist, was generally considered too focused, too haiman, too *unhuman*. Much of the current speculation concerned the possibility of her having suffered some paranoid identity dysfunction, that being the expected, though uncommon, madness affecting her kind. The Legate did not believe that theory for a moment. It had studied her for a long time and knew that in this case madness did not come into it. Yes she could kill, but for perfectly logical and, in Polity terms, immoral reasons.

Still concealed by chameleonware, the Legate moved out into the corridors of the station and made its way down to the concourse leading to the Feynman Lounge. Within a few minutes it recognized one of the forensic team: human and possibly gridlinked. The man, a thick-set individual with dark hair and bushy eyebrows, strolled along with one of the ant drones scuttling beside him. They chatted like old friends.

'I just don't see it,' the man was saying. 'She had everything: power, status, family, friends . . . She could easily re-engineer her personality if she was having prob-lems. She almost certainly ran regular sanity-check programs.'

'Madness by choice, then,' the ant suggested. 'Those who achieve and obtain so much often feel they have lost something indefinable along the way.'

Behind the man, but invisible, the Legate extended its forefinger into a narrow needle, primed with a particu-lar narcotic. It pressed this into the man's neck, injected, then withdrew it just as the man reached up to scratch the sudden itch.

'That's bullshit and you know it,' the man continued. 'If you're haiman, you're about as pragmatic as it gets. Every organic feeling is quantified and analysed, and if it doesn't fit underlying drives it's discarded. All haimans know it's just neurochemicals.' The man stumbled briefly. 'Just . . .'

The Legate stepped in again and pressed a hand to the back of the man's neck, injecting fibres through the numbed skin, seeking out and connecting to his auditory nerves. The drug dulled him just enough to edge him into fugue, his state slightly mesmerized. Precisely mim-icking the ant drone's voice the Legate asked the man directly through his auditory nerve, 'Where is the evi-dence being kept?'

'The old oxygen store, level eight sector three,' the man replied out loud – not even wondering why the forensic AI would ask him about something it had organized itself.

'What's that?' the genuine ant asked, turning to look up at him, antennae waving.

'Um?' The man halted as the Legate withdrew. He

rubbed his face. 'Shit, I'm tired. Unless you've got some critical use for me, I'm going to sack out.'

'I wouldn't use you in a critical situation if you were tired,' the ant observed.

The man waved a hand and moved on. The ant remained behind, its antennae still waving. It turned its head slowly, beginning to make probing scans of its surroundings. The Legate quickly retreated. Its chameleonware was the best, but no such 'ware was perfect.

The map of the station which the Legate had already obtained from the sleeping man's aug precisely located the oxygen store but, even more cautious now, it took the entity some time to reach that place. It waited until others opened doors ahead of it, then turned on an internal gravmotor to bring its weight to zero and used sticky fibres on its feet and hands to propel itself along, just in case some search program should run through the station's gravplates. It avoided using drop-shafts for similar reasons. The double doors to the oxygen store were heavily armoured – designed to contain any explosion occurring inside. The forensic AI had probably chosen this place to contain the evidence because such stores were generally no longer used – station and ship oxygen now being supplied by machines that split cardon dioxide and merely needed to be emptied of blocks of carbon, and bottled gases for suits being compressed by the suits themselves while aboard the station.

The main doors were multi-locked, but the door of the adjoining storeroom was not. The Legate slipped in there and drilled through the dividing armoured wall. Good thing it chose this route because it soon found inert gases filled the oxygen store, which also doubtless contained detectors to monitor their mix. It injected nano-optics and through them focused on an upright chainglass cylinder containing pieces of blackened memory crystal locked in a web of plasgel. Certainly a recording of everything they contained now resided inside the forensic AI, for the crystal was packed in readiness for transportation to some other evidential cache. The Legate now widened one hole through the wall and extruded from its palm a larger diameter cord packed with nanotubes which it could contract and stretch at intervals of a half inch to guide itself to its target. The cord oozed through the hole, stretched down the wall and groped across the floor towards the chainglass cylinder. Fortunately the cylinder's end caps were of a thick plastic it could easily cut through by using diamond saws the size of skin cells. Once inside the cylinder the cord frayed into thousands of nanotubes and spread like cobwebs. The Legate connected, injecting power or, where required, light, and began copying the stored data.

So, it seemed Orlandine had been showing an unhealthy interest in Shoala, and apparently tried to scrub out the evidence of that. Fragmentary results revealed relationship problems between them, and that she had tried to re-engineer her personality. All a classic, almost hackneyed, scenario and, without certain other information, entirely believable. However, there was nothing in here about Jain technology or Jain nodes, so as evidence it was all constructed, false. In the end, if the forensic AI did not believe this preferred scenario, it might choose from many others, but none of them involving Jain nodes. The Legate assumed Orlandine had shared information about the node with this Shoala, or maybe he found out, and that led to her killing him. From what was here, the forensic AI would never know.

The police arm of ECS would no doubt do their best to find her, but that was entirely the point: *only* the police arm would bother to do this. Any investigation would not involve major AIs like Jerusalem, because to ECS this was just a sordid little murder.

Orlandine panicked, grabbed the first available U-space capable spaceship, and then fled the Cassius system. Or so, the Legate gathered, went the consensus of opinion here. The entity itself felt that such behaviour just did not fit the haiman's profile. She did not panic. She felt a huge attachment to the Cassius project, which was one of the reasons she was chosen to receive a node: she would stay put and utilize the item from here, where it would cause the most damage. Had they been wrong about that as well? The Legate disconnected from the stored crystal, withdrew its cord, and sealed the hole through the wall. Understanding that much information about the functioning of this place lay in the public domain, and therefore easily accessible, it headed all the way back to the room it had originally invaded to spy on the forensic AI. The room's occupant still slept, so the Legate ignored him and searched, eventually finding an old computer terminal that folded down out of one wall. The work of just moments gave access to the humdrum workings of this station, and in one moment more the Legate found the manifest for the *Heliotrope*, and the loading times.

Orlandine took the time and trouble to refuel the *Heliotrope*, and load some extra supplies, before supposedly fleeing in *panic*. The Legate noted the nature of those supplies: a molecular catalyser, an autofactory for synthesizing polymers, sheet rolls of laminated radiation shielding. This last material interested the Legate most: just what you would need to conceal your activities from detection, not what was needed if you intended to flee somewhere remote from detection. The entity now called up on the screen a positional map of the multitude of objects orbiting the Cassius sun, stared contemplatively at this for a moment, then closed the terminal back into the wall and departed.

Once more ensconced in its ship, drifting away from the station, the Legate opened a U-space communication link. At once its mind became a submind of something very much larger, which scanned and recorded its thoughts and recent discoveries.

'Continue with mission to solar system?' the Legate enquired.

'No,' Erebus replied. 'Find her first.'

The link broke leaving the Legate momentarily stunned, then its individuality reasserted and it felt angry frustration. *Find her? Then what?*

Coloron observed the Skaidon warps blink out in Runcibles 5 and 6, as their spoons – their inclusion into U-space – retracted. Around Runcible 6 the crowds had thinned considerably – fewer than 10,000 people remained and they were departing the area very quickly. This was certainly due to the runcible's proximity to the arcology's north wall, which reduced its catchment area and therefore put exits to the outside within easy reach. However, over 50,000 people were still crammed into the departure lounges of 5, despite announcements of the runcible's imminent closure being broadcast through public address systems, displayed in big glaring letters on the bulletin boards, and transmitted continuously through the aug network. The AI was loath to start a panic, since in so large a crowd that would result in deaths, but anyone remaining in this area within the hour would be dead anyway. It amended the announcement to: PROCEED TO RUNCIBLE SEVEN. FIVE TO BE DESTROYED IMMINENTLY! YOU HAVE THIRTY-SIX MINUTES TO CLEAR THE AREA. DETO-NATION ESTIMATED AT TWO POINT FIVE KILOTONNES. Coloron then started the klaxons sounding, red warning lights flashing and, just to drive the point home, created a feedback loop between the runcible and its buffers, so it started to emit a whine, increasing in frequency at a rate just discernible to the human ear. That started them running. The AI was about to turn its attention elsewhere, when a secure channel opened from above.

'We have Thellant,' announced Jack of the *NEJ*.

'My joy knows no bounds,' replied Coloron.

'This has not slowed the advance of the Jain substruc-ture,' Jack observed.

'If anything it seems worse.'

'There may yet be a way to slow it down.'

Coloron immediately worked out what that way might be. 'Your spy in the camp?'

'Yes, Jerusalem's hunter-killer program has main-tained contact. It is presently propagating itself through the Jain informational architecture. Apparently it cannot change the rate of growth but it is, as you say, a spy in the camp, so can relay the disposition of enemy forces and resources.'

'Link me.'

The ensuing communication with the HK program was non-verbal, and Coloron's analysis dissected it on many levels. The AI immediately began constructing a virtual map of the substructure overlaid on a map of the arcology. Further analysis revealed stashes of materials behind the line of advance, currently being made ready for easy conversion; energy being bled from fusion reactors and stored in laminar structures, both capacitors and batteries; sneaky mycelial extensions heretofore undetected; and subsumed humans armed and massing for advance. Coloron now checked the disposition of its own defences, and issued orders.

'Azroc, that's close enough, pull your forces out.'

The Golem was presently accompanying those of his forces busy incinerating the Jain tech spreading along the walls and through the floor of a long hydroponics chamber. Smoke layered the air from burning vegetation, and fluids pouring from broken tanks onto hot metal boiled up in dirty clouds. Within sight, figures still human in shape but no longer entirely human tried to work their way through. Squatting beside a small proton cannon standing on four insectile legs, Azroc glanced back towards the drone through which Coloron spoke.

'You're going to blow it?' he asked.

Coloron replied, 'Thellant has been captured, and now new tactical intelligence has become available. The substructure is massing for a push very near your current position and it could reach Runcible 5 within half an hour.'

'Where do you want us now, then?'

Coloron transmitted directly into the Golem's mind a simple map of the present situation. The infestation had started thirty miles in from the shore, and fifty miles in from the northern edge of the arcology. Runcible 5 lay the nearest to it, with 4 and 3 spaced evenly along the shore to the south and the same distance in from the sea. The AI did not want to send any more inhabitants to those runcibles as there were crowds enough there already, and Jain tentacles moved faster along the shore wall than elsewhere. Forty miles in from that row of three runcibles, again evenly spaced, lay 6, 7, 8 and 9. Another fifty miles further in lay 1 and 2. Runcible 10 was located well out of the way, in the recent north-eastern extension. On the map the Jain tech had completely taken over the north-west corner, and now lay only three miles from 5 and twice that distance from 6. Azroc's forces were currently arrayed in a line cutting off that entire section – those last two runcibles at their backs.

'Pull back to seven now. I will destroy five and six the moment the substructure reaches them. You have a minimum of thirty-four minutes.'

'Okay.' Azroc began signalling to his section commanders.

'And, Azroc.'

'Yes?'

'I am about to begin some sterilization.'

'Understood.'

Coloron knew of some, either Separatist related or suffering from severe troglodytism, who were not obeying the evacuation order. Many of them remained inside the infested area, within reach of Jain tentacles, and many had already been taken over. Little could be done for any of those. From cameras on the particle weapon geostationary above, the AI studied the circular chunk of arcology it had initially excised in the hope of containing the Jain tech. The cavity near the centre of this, made by the Coloron's first satellite strike, looked like a bullethole filled with steel maggots. The trench cut to separate out the piece of arcology in which this hole lay also squirmed with movement as Jain tech increasingly bridged the gap.

The AI checked all the systems of the toroidal satellite, finding it was up to power, with plenty of fuel available for the fusion reactor of which most of the satellite consisted. Even at that moment, a tanker craft was approaching from a recently arrived cargo carrier. One of its three tanks contained hugely compressed deuterium in the metallic state – further fuel for the reactor – the other two were filled with cupronickel dust to provide the particulate matter for the cannon itself.

I am procrastinating.

That system check had been an unnecessary delay.

'Firing particle cannon,' Coloron announced.

The turquoise beam stabbed down through atmosphere and struck the already fire-blackened chunk of arcology just off centre. The beam cut through its various levels like a thermic lance through a beehive. Fire and smoke fountained half a mile into the sky. The cannon satellite, adjusted by the gravplate ring on the fusion-reactor torus, incrementally tilted and began to revolve. Down below, the beam began to cut spirally outwards from its initial strike point. Viewing the scene in infrared, Coloron estimated the extent of the firestorm now exploding through the levels below. Within minutes the beam reduced the originally excised piece of arcology to glowing slag at the bottom of a huge pit. Shutting off the cannon the AI then contemplated what it had done. It had just obliterated about ten cubic miles of arcology and killed thousands of inhabitants, and that seemed likely to be only the beginning. Now checking the map relayed by the HK program, Coloron saw energy flowing away from that same area, and Jain tech material resources being transferred. The substructure, Coloron realized, could be herded.

'I suggest you cut a line down to bedrock,' sent Brutus the AI controlling the dreadnought above, which, unusually, bore a different name: the *Brutal Blade*.

'That is my intention,' Coloron replied. 'With what happens next, such a division will certainly be required.' The AI viewed the dreadnought through various sateyes arrayed above the particle cannon. It was a utile vessel looking nothing like a blade. Two miles across at its widest point, it bore some resemblance to a gigantic lump of metallized liver, with many organic tubes opening to space – heavy armour gave it its shape and those tubes were its weapons systems. 'CTD imploder, lowest yield, take out *this* fusion reactor,' Coloron ordered, sending the location of the mentioned reactor.

One of the tubes, a linear accelerator, spat out a black sphere that hurtled down into atmosphere, glowed red, then white, and began to ablate. Ten miles up it shed two burning hemispheres. The missile it contained slammed down through a wheat field, igniting a small fire around the surface puncture. A microsecond later, the field bulged up into a hill; it started smoking, then abruptly combusted. Flame jetted from arcology vents within a mile of this, then smoke from those lying beyond them. Crowds of people still moving away along the north-west shore gazed back at debris blasted from the numerous exits in the arcology's edge. Coloron measured the spread of heat, observed the substructure's reaction to this latest strike, then sent a map selecting the positions of other reactors, and locations of those enemy materials and energy stores.

'Interesting,' commented Brutus.

'After I have cut the division,' the Coloron instructed, 'you must take out all those targets at once.' The AI knew that, on some level of awareness, the Jain substructure would realize the disposition of its forces had been discovered. It would probably find the HK, but by then the damage would be done.

Incrementally again, the particle cannon tilted. The turquoise beam hit the sea this time, evaporating billions of cubic yards of brine. It sliced into the arcology wall then began to burn across. From orbit a cloud mass could be seen forming in its trail. While still metaphorically holding a finger on the firing button, Coloron noted monitors and Rescue staff loading into AG ambulances those injured by the departure of the crowds at Runcible 5. On the map updated by the HK program, the AI saw that the Jain substructure now lay only a mile away from there. The immediate blast radius around 6 was clear of people, though there were still some stragglers within areas likely to be devastated by the shockwave. The Jain tech lay a mile and a half away from Runcible 6. Coloron waited.

Half an hour passed, then an access panel for an optical junction sprang away from the wall on the furthest edge of one of Runcible 5's lounges. Something like a long-fingered stainless steel hand groped out, and began to extend its fingers down the wall. On another wall steel buds grew through sheet-bubble metal and squeezed out grey tendrils. The last three ambulances departed, whereupon some other ambulances tried returning, because there were still people alive in here. Too late, because Coloron began closing blast doors behind the departing ambulances. Now humanoid figures began appearing, their clothing burnt and hanging in tatters, their bodies blackened, and pinkish slithing movement visible through their wounds. The AI began shutting down systems as soon as it felt informational intrusion – as it had been doing all along throughout the advance of this feral technology. Soon its total perception of the area became limited to a few scattered cameras. Then came the expected intrusion into the systems of the runcible itself.

The runcible buffers held a huge charge, permanently topped up by the fusion reactor located on the floor below the runcible itself. With safety circuits offline, Coloron released this entire charge into the runcible. A warp generated, tuned out of U-space, tried to create space of its own, bounced out into realspace, then collapsed. It sucked in the horns of the runcible, the dais, the fusion reactor, several bodies – some still alive – and much of the surrounding complex, crunching everything down into a spherical superdense mass. At the centre of this mass: fusion.

From the cannon satellite Coloron observed the subsequent explosion flinging millions of tons of debris into the air. A briefly stabilized fusion reaction dropped a yard-wide white sun straight down to the bedrock. As the smoke cleared, the AI observed a glowing two mile-wide crater cut into the top half of the arcology. Eight minutes later a similar crater appeared in place of Runcible 6. Twenty minutes after that, the particle beam cut its way out from the north wall of the arcology.

'Now,' Coloron sent to Brutus.

Missile after missile departed the *Brutal Blade*; a vicious insect swarm hurtling down towards the planet. Coloron almost flinched. The harsh reality of its mind did not permit ignorance of how many had died during the last hour, and of how many were about to die. Yes, Jain technology controlled most of them, but they were people nevertheless. No fewer than 110,000 of them. And even then the advance would continue, for the AI only slowed it down, inconvenienced it.

The planetary system consisted of an immense green gas giant the size of Jupiter, but half as far again from the sun as that Jovian. Further from the sun than it lay a ring of icy planetoids and asteroidal debris, while around it orbited more still. Within its orbit were four planets: one icy world three times the size of Earth and bearing its own ring system, one orbiting close around the sun, and two that lay within the sun's green belt. The inner of the two green-belt planets was a hot world similar to the one where Erebus had destroyed its rebel faction. King dropped telefactors to study this living planet, for it seemed perfect for a base, yet already King guessed this place to be empty of intelligent life.

Dense red jungle cloaked its land masses. The island that King first studied was swamped with plants very much like cycads. Below these, fast moving vines writhed when in hot sunlight but grew still in shadow. Tripedal saurians patrolled under massive red leaves as thick as mattresses, shooting out jointed tongues in quest of shivering globular prey. Those prey managing to escape ran screaming and wobbling to the safety of sunlight, where they burst in wet explosions spreading some kind of organic sludge. Reproduction probably – King did not have the time or inclination to investigate.

The seas also swarmed with life: armoured arthropods and large floating bivalves, masses of purple bladder weeds that shot out tendrils to drag in prey, a giant legless arthropod with a square mouth the size of a cruiser construction bay, ever sucking up those masses of predatory weed. But here it detected no clear evidence of any Polity technology: no wreckage, no traps. Hollow cubes found on one mountainside were certainly the product of intelligent life, but of ancient origin, and not what King sought.

The AI attack ship recalled its telefactors, returned them to their cache, then turned its attention to the other, cold, world, which also bore life. Such instances of two living worlds existing in the same planetary system, this close together in the green belt, was not exceptional. If one world produced life, it became almost a certainty, over the vast timespans involved, that vulcanism or the debris from meteor impacts would eventually hurl the spores of life over the relatively short distance to the other planet.

This place was frigid and the only liquid water existed around volcanic vents a mile underneath the ice sheet. From these hidden warm seas, wells spiralled to the surface, and by tracing a surface trail from one of these, King came upon a great furry serpent heading out from one of the landmasses towards them. On the land itself grew forests of trees resembling pines in their strategies for surviving cold, though lower in stature, with thicker denser trunks and fruits like cut diamonds. Flying mammals fed upon the latter, while the furry serpents reared up high to graze on the needles. King found no large predators, but soon discovered the reason – the parasites growing inside the many varieties of creature in the forests kept populations down by taking gradual control of their hosts and forcing them down the ice wells, where young parasites could hatch out of their drowning bodies in the warm water below. Closer scanning revealed swarms of the adult form of these things climbing continually up out of the wells. They resembled a minuscule version of the screaming wobbling thing seen on the adjacent world. Here again, deep under the ice, were some of those hollow granite cubes, but still no sign of Erebus's presence. The AI felt both disappointment and relief as, continuing its straight-line course, it once again dropped into U-space.

A breath of cold wafted from the neck ring of D'nissan's hotsuit and Mika wondered if it was only that which made her shiver.

'Who?' She nodded to the image on the screen.

'No "who" involved,' the ophidapt replied. 'We suppressed cerebral growth in the amniotic tank. Our friend there is lacking in everything but autonomic functions. He possesses less intelligence than that of your average insect, and what he possesses is only by dint of hardware implanted in his skull.' D'nissan glanced at her. 'And by that I mean singular insects – not hives of them.'

The shaven-headed man in the isolation chamber stood naked, and utterly still. He bore no expression and his face seemed characterless. However, this did not make Mika feel any less uneasy about what D'nissan intended doing to him.

'Implantation was successful, then?'

'Apparently, though we'll see soon enough if it works.'

Directly opposite the man stood a small tripod-mounted autogun.

'Test one,' said D'nissan.

The gun fired and a pulse of ionized aluminium slammed into the man's chest. Smoking gobbets of flesh exploded from his back, spattering the wall behind half a second before he himself hit the wall and slid down leaving a bloody trail. Mika swallowed drily, waited. After a moment the man reached out, pushed himself to his feet, and took three paces forwards. The hole in his chest, the size of a fist, still smouldered, but a ball of veined pink flesh was oozing out to fill it and extinguish the embers. The man turned slowly, presenting himself dutifully to all the scanning heads arrayed around the isolation chamber. The hole in his back was rather larger, and one shattered rib protruded. The flesh welling up there bore the appearance of brain tissue.

'That shot would have destroyed his heart,' Mika noted.

'Yes. But the little doctor can grow its own replacement of any major organ destroyed. Right now it will be constructing something a little more efficient than the human heart, while dilating veins and arteries to prevent bleeding and keeping essential parts of the body oxygenated via nanotubes,' D'nissan explained.

'Nerve damage?'

'The mycelium can re-route around most of it.'

'So this is not really repair but replacement with something different?'

'Yes, all it does is provide support to whatever remains, and even that is limited.'

'How far?'

D'nissan nodded at the screen. 'This is about the maximum damage it can sustain. If the victim was hit three or four times like this, his body would die and his little doctor would die along with it. Remember, that though dispersed, the mycelium is being hit as well.' He shrugged. 'It's like an ordinary human body, without a little doctor mycelium – it can only survive so much.'

'What about bones?' Mika asked. With this constant

barrage of questions she was trying to distance herself from what she had just seen, and to reacquaint herself with her customary scientific detachment.

'They're easy to deal with. It pulls them together and lays down calcium glue within seconds.' He went on. 'Essentially, anyone carrying this mycelium would need to take a number of direct substantial hits to be killed. Wounds that before would have resulted in him ending up under an autodoc will now only inconvenience him briefly.'

'And Jain nodes?'

'None at all. This technology is clean.'

'Who will get this "little doctor" treatment first?'

'Soldiers,' replied D'nissan bluntly.

Mika gave him a fragile smile then moved away. She had stopped here, on her way to the shuttle that would ferry her over to Dragon, meaning to ask D'nissan his thoughts on augmentation, but after witnessing this test found she could not. The man was doing important work, supplying ECS with what might be a vital advantage should Jain technology once again get loose in the Polity.

'Test two,' announced D'nissan.

With some disquiet Mika departed.

Tick tick tick . . .

The sheer immensity of the ancient shipyard could not be fathomed when viewed from space. High up in a chainglass viewing blister, Cormac stood and gazed down into one construction hold. Far below him, silver bees of robots erected partition walls, floors and ceilings in layer upon layer like the cells of a hive. Now rising a hundred yards up from the original floor, the completed accommodation below them was already being occupied. The logistics of all this were frightening: how do you feed and water so many people, and what about sanitation?

Tick tick tickity tick . . .

The runcibles inside the yard now all remained online, transmitting in resources from so many different locations. More than a hundred hold spaces, originally used for the construction of dreadnoughts, were being similarly converted. Millions of refugees were encamped on acres of ceramal flooring in the other holds. As things stood, the shipyard was now full, more refugees trickling in only to fill accommodation as soon as the robots built it.

Tickity tick tick t—

'You can stop that noise now or I'll leave you behind,' snapped Cormac.

Turning from the view, he eyed Arach as the spiderdrone drew its foreleg back from where it had been tapping the sharp point against the chainglass. Grimacing, Cormac turned away, again considering how the last few days with Mika had affected him. Only a few hours ago he had been reluctant to leave *Jerusalem*. A doorway into possibility had opened and he began thinking of things that before he always pushed to the back of his mind: the possibility of a settled relationship with someone, his family, his own purpose, and whether it might be time for a change in direction.

As an agent, Earth Central Security allowed him a wide remit with parameters only loosely defined. It also granted him certain powers to carry out those tasks assigned to him via Horace Blegg. He could quit at any time. Only his sense of duty prevented that. However good at what he did, he was realistic enough not to consider himself indispensable. Perhaps the time had even come for him to hand over the reins? Thus he was beginning to think until his recent exchange with Jerusalem.

'Are you ready to leave?' the AI had asked him.

'Frankly, I'm not sure I am,' he replied.

'That is your decision to make. If you do not feel capable of continuing your present assignment, something else can be found for you, or you may depart. Meanwhile, I have some gifts for you.'

The first gift arrived in his gridlink: a memory package he immediately stored.

'And this is?'

'The rest of your mind: true memories of what happened to you aboard the *Ogygian*. It will install to your mind the moment you open it. I calculate that you are nearly ready for it, the final part of that calculation being your own decision to open it.'

'I see.'

The second gift arrived later in his quarters, delivered by a crab drone. It dropped the wrist holster on his sofa before departing.

'How?' he had asked.

Jerusalem replied, 'A member of a clear-up team picked it up when they went to collect the remains of Gant. I used a nanocounteragent to remove the mycelium Skellor installed in it and wiped out his reprogramming of it. I also repaired the damage you caused by shooting it down . . . you do realize how it fought against Skellor's programming by allowing you to shoot it?'

Cormac had removed Shuriken from its holster and held it out on the flat of his palm. It flexed out its chainglass blades, as if stirring in sleep, then retracted them. He remembered Cull, his long-drawn-out fight for survival there against Skellor, who took control of this semi-AI weapon away from him, and then sent it against him, and how at the last, as he targeted it, it had turned upright in the air to present its face to him full on.

'Yes, I know.'

He slid Shuriken back in the holster, then strapped the holster to his wrist. It occurred to him to speculate on how subtly manipulative AIs could be. This gesture, now, in his moment of indecision? In the end, he could not step down with the Polity so obviously threatened. He could not live a normal existence with any feeling of equanimity, knowing what was occurring. Family? He protected them through his career just as he protected any other law-abiding Polity citizens. Mika? To remain with her here would be to remain at the centre of events, but ineffective.

Subsequently stepping from his cabin, he found Arach eagerly awaiting him, unable to keep its spindly legs still.

'Are we on our way?' the drone had asked.

'Yes, we're on our way.'

Now, aboard the ancient shipyard, Cormac began to make his way towards the runcible open to Coloron, Arach dogging his footsteps.

He found crowds crammed into a vast zero-G distribution centre, at the end of which stood a cargo runcible. The horns of this device encompassed a circular Skaidon warp ten yards across. Guide ropes cut in from all sides, tied off on a massive robotic handler crouched before the runcible itself. The base of this multi-armed behemoth ran on tracks extending the entire length of the distribution centre. Through here, warship building materials had once been transported. The handler then passed these off to other minor handlers in the tunnels branching off all around, which in turn took them to various machine shops or directly to the construction holds. This had not been a place for humans since everything moved here at AI speeds, and any human would have been ground up in the gearing. Now the handlers were still, the centre pressurized, and ECS personnel flocked in the air like khaki birds.

For anyone unused to moving in zero-G, the scene ahead appeared chaotic and confusing. It looked that way because those here felt no need to arrange themselves with any regard to *up* and *down*. Cormac launched himself from the tunnel they had traversed, occasionally catching a rope to guide himself towards the handler robot. In this environment, with these ropes strung in every direction, he noted how Arach seemed perfectly in his element. As Cormac drew closer, he saw ranks of ECS soldiers heading through the runcible ahead of him. Behind them came a row of five AG tanks and, spiralling up from the base of the handler robot, followed other military supplies. He noted that most of those waiting around him were ECS Rescue or Medical personnel – perhaps waiting for their fellows ahead of them to provide their bloody work.

'Lot of hardware,' Arach observed with relish.

'Oh yes.'

Reaching the handler, Cormac noticed a haiman directing operations. The man sat ensconced in one of the handler's huge claws, occasionally making a hand gesture, but most of his directions were being relayed over informational channels. Cormac queried him on that level, and received a priority slot just after the tanks.

The haiman saluted, with a finger to his temple, before turning his attention elsewhere.

When the last tank slid through the Skaidon warp, as through the meniscus of a bubble, Cormac remembered that on jumps he made prior to events on the *Ogygian*, he had actually begun to experience U-space, which was something previously unheard of. He pushed off from the handler, orientating himself carefully to the plane of arrival at the receiving runcible. Arach shot ahead of him, impelled by air jets, and entered the meniscus first. As Cormac floated after, he felt the stirring of concealed memory – of that other gift from Jerusalem.

Now? Release it now?

No, some other time.

He fell, after Arach, through the Skaidon warp to Coloron.

12

I've stated before that I really would like to believe in him, simply because of his name. Surely if you are going to create a fictional hero, nay even demigod, you are going to come up with a more resounding name than 'Horace Blegg'? Upon that basis I spent many weeks tracking stories through the nets, checking facts, trying to contact those involved. Time after time the main protagonists I did manage to contact remained either close-mouthed or denied any knowledge of the man. Mostly, I only managed to contact those who knew someone who knew someone who . . . and after tracing down many of those to dead ends, I gave up. Trying to find images of the man has been equally frustrating. There are many available, but often they plainly display different people. Through every line of research I encountered convoluted wild-goose chases, breaks and missing information. One would suppose that all I really found was proof of his non-existence. I don't think so. I believe AIs used search and destroy programmes to wipe out much information pertaining to him. I believe they meddled with reality again. I believe in Horace Blegg.

– From 'How it Is' by Gordon

Unless an emergency arose, Blegg usually confined his jumps through U-space to the surface of planets. Translating himself through U-space between planets in a system, or between ships, could be hugely tiring. And ships or runcibles were nearly always available, so why waste energy better applied elsewhere? In this case, however, he became impatient. The *Hourne* lay ten hours' journey time from Masada, and Blegg felt no real need to remain aboard to see the Atheter artefact down on that world. Also, the runcibles aboard the *Hourne* had been shut down, since calculating the U-space position of a runcible located on a moon, planet or large station was difficult enough, but doing so for a ship manoeuvring insystem became near impossible. Blegg decided he must leave in his own inimitable fashion. He gazed down from a viewing blister aboard the great ship towards the moonlet called Flint, on which one of the runcibles in this system was sited. He looked into U-space, located both himself and the moonbase nestled amid the ruins of the shipyard, destroyed by Skellor with the *Occam Razor*'s weapons, and stepped across.

Earth Central immediately began to speak in his head as he found himself walking across the floor of a geodesic dome enclosing the runcible.

'I have provided a small ship for you at *Ruby Eye* – it is capable of entering U-space unshielded. U-tech mapping and detection equipment have been installed and programmed to the U-space signature provided by Atheter. The USERs have now been shut down in that area, so you can travel at will there.'

Out loud Blegg replied, 'I'll test the signature – I think I know precisely the place.' The scanners available to the Polity limited the detection range, with resolution increasing as he moved closer to the source. Light years away, Blegg would know the system in which a Jain node was located; at a light hour away he would know on which planet; at a couple of yards he would know which pocket it was in.

Someone striding along, followed by two hover trunks, gave Blegg a momentary glance – but in these days, when so many employed cerebral hardware, it was not unusual to see people apparently talking to themselves.

'This place you know precisely – a certain brown dwarf perhaps?' EC suggested.

'You read my mind.'

He strode up to the runcible dais, ahead of a woman checking her journey slot on a column-mounted console, received a startled then accusatory look from her as he stepped to the warp and through it. He did not need to check that the runcible had reset to his destination – it always did. At *Ruby Eye*, a station orbiting a red dwarf sun, he snatched direct from the controlling AI's mind the location of his own ship, then from the runcible lounge stepped a short distance through U-space, and directly aboard.

'Permission to launch,' he asked over com, once ensconced in the pilot's seat.

'Granted,' replied Ruby Eye. 'That was rather quick and, I might add, rather rude.'

'No time for civilities,' Blegg replied as the airlock tube retracted and clamps released his ship from the docking tower. He then paused and peered down at himself. When did he change into this envirosuit? For a moment the memory completely evaded him, then it was there. Of course, he had changed aboard the *Hourne* before to going into VR. He shook his head and smiled to himself, realizing that Cormac's assertion that Blegg was an avatar of Earth Central had actually been preying on his mind. Existential angst – he really did not need that right now.

Falling away from the station spin in space seemingly fogged red by the light of the nearby dwarf sun, he turned the ship and engaged its fusion drive. One of many subscreens, set into the chainglass along the bottom of the main cockpit screen, showed numerous radar returns as the ship negotiated through a swarm of other vessels. Some of these were clearly evident on one subscreen showing a gravity map of the area. Glimpsing up, he observed such a vessel close to: something like a sharp-nosed monorail carriage towing, on braided monofilament cables, an object like an ancient sea mine. A USER – an underspace interference emitter – one of the devices previously used to confine Skellor to this sector of space while Cormac hunted him down.

Once clear of the crowd, Blegg input coordinates. The ship's computer could not handle the AI-level calculations required to drop it into U-space. Blegg linked to it and did what he always did when himself entering that continuum, but with his ability complemented by the ship's underspace engine, and he and the ship dropped into endless grey. He gazed at this underlying reality. Receding behind him – though, in truth, words like *behind* did not apply to his perception of this place – was the eversion generated by the red dwarf, gravity *seen* from the other side. And scattered nearby this was an even pattern of smaller eversions, curved like fossil worms: these generated by the singularities carried inside the USERs – hence their presence on the gravity map.

Mentally, Blegg cancelled the resurfacing sequence

which, without him, the ship would not be able to handle anyway. A subscreen displayed a warning, but he ignored it and set an alarm to sound once the ship reached its destination in U-space. Then, departing the cockpit, he went to see what facilities the ship itself contained. He found food, then a bed. The ship travelled to U-space coordinates as much here as there, now as then. Blegg rested, travelled no distance, and all, *slept*.

Time passed in realspace and it also passed in this small piece of realspace submerged by U-fields. But they were separate times, and how they might meet up became merely an energy negotiation. Blegg's ship took the course of least energy, least resistance. It was possible to go to another time from here, but the consequences could be catastrophic, as the time-inconsistent runcible link between *Celedon* and the Small Magellanic Cloud demonstrated.

A constant beeping dragged Blegg from slumber, and returned him to the cockpit. Two eversions pushed into the range of his perception, one that of a g-type star, and the other the brown dwarf orbiting it.

With care he eased the ship in towards the brown dwarf – as close as it could come without the gravity well forcing it out of U-space in a brief explosion of plasma. Blegg turned his attention to the console, but found the weirdness of perception too distracting. He initiated the hardfields that would cut that out. Immediately the inside of the ship returned to relative normality: a touch-console no longer looked like a three-dimensional kaleidoscope, and his fingers no longer appeared to be infinite tubes. He set the ship's instruments to scanning for the U-space signature and the response was immediate: three definite matches and four maybes, but to be expected considering the Jain nodes growing inside Skellor were as crushed into the surface of the brown dwarf as he.

He turned the hardfields off again.

Back on the underside of reality, he gazed at the star, both distant and close. Scale and distance were merely rules his own mind applied here, and he could ignore them. Thus he did, and gazed upon the underside of seven Jain nodes leaving prickly thornish impressions in this continuum: organization, pattern, standing out from the underlying chaos of reality; of space knotted and wadded into this thing called matter. Blegg turned away, then quickly back when a subscreen blinked on to show text: *'U-signature detected – disperse signal'*. It took him some time to track it down, for it lay nearly two light years away, though close in interstellar terms. Without surfacing from U-space, he reset his ship's course.

– retroact 6 –

'. . . bright enough to realize the AI rulers were better at governing than any previous human rulers.'

He turned to another card, saw them laid out all around him like gravestones.

The autolaser stuttered and crackled, knocking most of the deadly swarm from the air, but it did not manage to hit them all. Corporal Chang made a horrible grunting sound – the impact flinging him up from cover, then the projectile detonating inside him. It blew his guts out and he spun to the ground with only a length of bloody spine attaching his ribcage to his pelvis.

The three remaining members of the unit fired on the nearby slopes with their own seeker guns, then crouched back behind their boulders on the mountain slope. A waste of ammo. The sniper might not even be over that way. It seemed almost as if he knew of Blegg and his abilities, for he had changed over from laser to seeker bullets so there was no way to locate him. But he knew where they were.

'This guy is not going to be captured alive,' said Pierce.

Of the recording of events here, Pierce could claim he only stated what he thought were the sniper's intentions. Reading the man's expression, Blegg understood the statement to be a promise of intent.

'Do you still have no idea where this fucker is?' Blegg asked through his comlink.

'Only within an area of three square miles, with you at the centre of it,' Earth Central replied.

'I thought the cameras on your satellites capable of resolving the date on a coin dropped on the ground?'

'They do possess that resolution – when there is no cloud cover. It has also become evident this individual obtained, as well as the original tank, a multipurpose assault rifle, development sets of the new chameleon-cloth fatigues and electronic concealment hardware.'

Blegg eyed his companions, 'Which ECS soldiers have yet to be issued with?'

'The same.'

Blegg nodded to himself. The man seemed a lone criminal but a very clever one. He had managed to steal a tank which he used to smash into an etched-sapphire repository. Fleeing with millions in that form, he evaded the police cordon. His laundering of the sapphires through various criminal organizations had resulted in the capture of many, but never him. Five years of chasing rumours and fragmentary information finally led to a house, here in the Scottish Highlands. The ECS arrest team botched it – and died. EC shut down transport out of the area and now many four-person teams of highly trained personnel were scouring these mountains. Blegg had joined them – perhaps that had not been his greatest idea. He could transport himself away, but that seemed so unfair on the others here.

'I have analysed recorded imagery. He is over to your left about two hundred yards away. Get out of there now. Satellite strike will be initiated in two minutes.'

Get out?

It seemed EC had not precisely pinpointed the man's location, else there would be no need to run. It also seemed the AI decided whatever information could be extracted from the man no longer warranted the loss of any more lives. It was about to burn the area.

'Leave the autolaser – it should cover us. We go *now*!'

Blegg leapt up and led the way from cover. A horrible whining made his back crawl – more seeker bullets. Staying low, they ran just as hard and fast as they could. Snap-crack of a laser, either from the auto or the sniper. Something slammed into Blegg's back, lifted him from the ground and hurled him face-down in the dirt. His head must have hit a rock, for he lost consciousness.

Later, Blegg learnt that it was the shock wave from the strike that threw him down. Nothing remained of the sniper, though analysis of DNA from his home identified him as a mercenary once employed by the now strictly controlled corporations. No one particularly special. Blegg did not like to contemplate how close he had come to dying, then.

– retroact ends –

There was no escape from this situation, and no escape from the realization that he would soon die. With a normally human mind, Thellant might have been able to convince himself otherwise. The best he could hope for now was a quick death. But that knowledge did not allay the frustration, anger and a desperate need to escape.

'Who is this?' he asked, while spreading Jain tendrils deep into the systems of the ship, tracking optics and s-con cables, sequestering interfaces, reading stored data, initiating ship's diagnostics, and his own.

A male voice replied, 'Well, the one who said "Gotcha!" was Jack – the AI which runs the Centurion-class ship *NEJ*. My name is Thorn.'

'ECS?' Accessing a monitoring system Thellant gazed into the area intervening between the four spheres of his stolen ship and there saw wreckage, and metal hardened into splash patterns. The fusion drive had operated through here to a drive-plate mounted underneath, the U-space engine encased above it. Now there was just a hole there.

'Oh yes.'

'Do you realize I have fifteen hostages aboard this ship?' Thellant connected into the cold coffins, just to assure himself this remained true. Nine men and six women, all of them suffering from head injuries beyond the compass of simple autodocs. These were the kind of injuries that required AI intervention, for not only their brains needed reconstructing, but their minds as well.

'Thellant N'komo, you've got tech inside you capable of trashing planets. Over a hundred and fifty thousand people are already dead because of you, and many more will die. And if the Jain tech in MA gets out the planet below might well end up as the target for a few crust crackers. Get real.'

'Why am I still alive, then?' Thellant now concentrated his perception outside the Rescue ship via external cameras, the cockpit screen before him, and via Jain tendrils containing optics infiltrated through the ship's hull. Many ships hovered above him – cargo carriers, passenger liners, Rescue ships – and one large ugly dreadnought was rising over the horizon even now. The last vessel was probably capable of denuding a planet of life, and that might well be its intended purpose. The Centurion-class ship held station down below him, probably because its AI knew that there lay his only possible escape route, no matter how minimal his chances if he attempted it. He studied the vessel carefully, recognizing it to be state of the art. There was just no way out.

'Because I want you to answer a few questions.'

'Go fuck yourself.' Thellant closed his eyes, and for a moment closed out all perception. He understood that his need to escape was not entirely his own, it being imbedded in and integral to the technology occupying his body, and now this ship, too. It contained no sentience, just an animalistic desperation of the gnawing off a leg in a trap kind.

'It won't be me I'll be fucking, Thellant.'

'Exactly. So why should I answer questions? We both know that I am not going to get out of this alive. I answer your questions, then you fry me.'

'Well, we could fry you – a microwave beam should do the job – or we could use what's called a CTD imploder. You probably haven't heard of that – collapsing gravity field into an antimatter explosion. Not a great deal left afterwards.'

Thellant opened his eyes. What was this guy about? Was this supposed to persuade him to cooperate?

The man called Thorn went on, 'Of course we could drop you on some remote world where you could live happily ever after.'

'Is this what passes for humour in ECS nowadays?' Even knowing the other man must be lying to him, Thellant experienced an emotional response to the offer that felt almost out of his control. He knew then, in that same instant, that the Jain technology possessed its own agenda, and only *allowed* him to control it.

'There's my quandary,' said Thorn. 'I have to try and persuade you that we really are prepared to grant you that indulgence, if you provide the information we require.'

'And what might that information be?'

'I want you to tell me exactly how you acquired that Jain node, and I also want you to tell me about the Legate.'

Thellant felt a flush of anger at the mere mention of that name. The cruelty, as he saw it, lay in giving him such power in such intractable circumstances. It had been like gluing a gun into the hand of a hostage who is surrounded by terrorists wielding laser carbines. The result possessed a degree of inevitability. Despite the fact that he seemed certain to die, perhaps he should answer those questions. Maybe that would result in the Polity coming down as hard on that bastard Legate as it seemed certain to do on himself.

'Tell me about this remote world where I can live happily ever after.'

'Oh, I can tell you all about that. Obviously Jain technology is of overwhelming interest to researchers human, haiman and AI, and apparently there has been a world specially prepared for just this sort of eventuality. It's orbited by all sorts of scanning satellites, and has twenty gigatonne-level CTDs sunk into its crust. Basically you get to do what you like for as long as you like down there. However, the moment you try to leave that planet, you leave this life.'

'That almost sounds plausible,' said Thellant. And it did, since he could almost believe the Polity might value him highly as a scientific resource, despite the mass slaughter he had caused. 'Take me to this place first and then I'll answer your questions.'

'I think you can probably guess my response to that,' said Thorn, 'but I'll say it anyway. You answer the questions first, you tell me all you know, then you get transported to that world. I *could* take you there first, but you would be no safer there than you are here.'

'But I would at least know if you had lied about it,' Thellant replied.

'No, you would not. Just consider what is happening here. The Polity is evacuating a billion people from an arcology, so think of the resources and organization that requires. A world as I just described could easily be made ready in the time it took us to transport you there.'

'Very well.' Thellant paused for a moment and thought now might be the time to give something. 'The Legate gave me the Jain node.'

'Please continue,' said Thorn after Thellant did not continue.

'I can transmit you complete memcordings of all my dealings with the Legate.' Almost without thinking, he began compiling those memories and layering them with every informational weapon he could find within the Jain tech, or could think to create. He considered it a vain hope that the ship's AI would accept this package, obviously the technology occupying his own body felt otherwise.

'We'll establish a tight-beam link with you, and then you may transmit the memcordings across,' replied Thorn.

Glowing craters pocked the Jain-occupied section of the arcology, amidst which immense fires now raged. The firebreak slowed the substructure's advance, as did the destruction of Runcibles 5 and 6, but it was those other strikes delivered by *Brutal Blade* that finally halted it. It then attempted to build up more stashes of resources and energy but, as the HK program relayed their positions, the dreadnought destroyed them too. For two days, the Jain advance stalled, then the HK program went offline, and a microsecond later a viral attack came through the link, and Coloron shut it down. On the third day the Jain advance began again, slower than before, more tentative. However, these events produced other encouraging results.

Over the two days, Coloron diverted the multitude gathering around Runcible 4 to other runcibles further inside the arcology, and diverted the exodus through 3 to the exits positioned in the south-west corner. Those around 7, it began moving elsewhere. All of those runcibles would be next to go. ECS forces, having arrived in strength, now used transports to evacuate many citizens directly through the arcology roof. Along with those forces arrived thousands of drones equipped to scan for Jain tech, and this made it possible to move thousands of people way beyond the quarantine perimeter, which

meant a reduction in the population density directly outside, so those inside could evacuate quicker. And they
were certainly getting out quicker: the knowledge that
a large portion of the arcology had been reduced to
radioactive rubble encouraged them to abandon their
precious belongings and run. However, though the substructure's advance might be more tentative now, it was
still inexorable, and after 3, 4 and 7 it would next reach
Runcible 8 – and Coloron itself.

The AI turned its attention to the armoured chamber
that contained it. Its brain rested between the interfaces
of a thick optical control pillar: a pillow-sized lump of
yellow crystal wrapped in a black s-con cagework. For
the first time in many years Coloron undogged the locks
to the heavy chamber door and opened it. Through the
door marched an object like a headless iron ostrich, but
standing three yards tall with two arms slung underneath
its hollow body. From the hollow, a thick lid lay hinged
back bearing emitter dishes, a com laser, and a powerful
U-space transceiver. It came to a halt before Coloron.

The AI now focused back on the runcibles in greatest
danger. The flow of humanity heading away from them
remained uninterrupted. Surprisingly, the crowds around
Runcible 3 had nearly cleared, while those leaving the
south-west exits just kept on moving, knowing the imminent explosion might reach them there. For the moment,
nothing required Coloron's personal attention, so the AI
disconnected.

Sight through thousands of cameras – assigned on
the whole to simple recognition programs so the AI
could respond to the circumstances they recognized –
blinked out. Soft links to subminds controlling many
aspects of the arcology collapsed. Coloron lost its links

to autofactories; to maintenance, surveillance, military and agricultural drones; hospitals and the many varieties of autodocs they contained; servers and other com networks; mining operations; fusion reactors; recycling plants; and to satellites including the particle cannon. Coloron disconnected from its body – the arcology entire.

From vast perception the AI collapsed down to single-tunnel vision seen from the crystal it occupied. It observed the robot carrying on through with its program, reaching down and closing three-fingers hands around Coloron's braincase. Movement then, only visually perceived. The robot held Coloron poised for a moment over the hollow in its body, then lowered the AI down into darkness. The lid slammed shut and a seeming age of sensory deprivation followed. Then connections began to re-establish, and finally Coloron gazed through the sensorium of its new home at the optic interface pillar closing up. It now U-space-linked itself to those of its subminds possessing such facility, and electromagnetically linked elsewhere, as the arcology's structure permitted. The losses in not being optically linked amounted to about a third, however the advantage was quite evident: Coloron now need not die along with its arcology.

The barren sandy plateau, scattered with monolithic boulders, lay far from any human habitation on the planet Cull. A mile up, his ship hovering on AG, Blegg focused scanning gear on the location of the Jain node. Eight thousand miles above him, a dreadnought waited with a five megatonne CTD imploder ready to be fired. Why it had not yet been fired was problematic, Earth

Central's instructions to him simply being: 'Go down there, and see. You can transport yourself out should there be any danger.'

Strange oblate objects were scattered about the base of one slanting sandstone monolith. The movement he could see down there did not look human. Blegg increased magnification and, on one of the subscreens, saw circular entrances into these objects. Something came out of one of them and clambered on top of what must be its dwelling; for scan now revealed these objects to be hollow, and that many contained living creatures. He recognized the scorpion shape of one of the native life forms: a sleer. He focused in, and the creature turned its nightmare head up towards him. It bore a human face.

Dragon.

While it was here on this world, Dragon had conducted experiments that were morally indefensible at best, and obscene in the extreme. The entity had crossed human DNA with the genome of native insectile creatures to result in by-blows like this. Why do so? Dragon had partially answered this question during Cormac's interviewing of it, but not really to anyone's satisfaction. In truth, Blegg felt, Dragon did such things because it could not resist tampering and tinkering, because it liked to upset natural orders and humanity alike, and in the end simply because it could.

Drawing closer to this strange settlement, Blegg brought his ship down. It landed in a cloud of dust just on the outskirts. Blegg abandoned his seat, collected a pulse-rifle and a hand-held scanner now formatted to detecting the U-space signature of a Jain node. As an afterthought, he collected a couple of planar grenades before heading for the airlock.

Dust hazing everything, its taste metallic; a sharp smell as well – something acidic. His foot crunched on shale as he stepped from the extended steps. A few paces from his ship he turned and studied the craft for the first time from the outside. It bore that standard flat-bottomed shape of a general-purpose shuttle, but also sported four nacelles mounted on stubby wings – two positioned behind the nose and two at the rear. It stood on three legs, each possessing three-toed sprung feet. Blegg wondered why someone had chosen to colour it a bright inferno red. With a snort he turned back towards the hybrids' village.

Blegg began walking, seeing increasing activity ahead. The first of them then came scuttling out to his right: two centaur-like creatures he had already viewed images of when going through the reports of what happened on this world. The larger of these possessed a six-foot-long sleer body, out of which grew the upper half of a bearded man. Making direct mental contact via the ship to the AI nets, he commented, 'One of those two looks quite young. Could this mean they are breeding?'

'Dragon would not create them sterile – such precautions are not in its nature,' came the reply.

Blegg was unsurprised at how quickly the U-space comlink established.

'Okay, Hal, what game are we playing here?'

EC replied, 'Just retrieving something Skellor dropped. Dragon is reluctant to part with those nodes it possesses. It seems it does not trust us with them. But we have received a communication from one it did trust.'

'One of *these* creatures? Are they like the dracomen, immune to Jain tech?' He glanced about himself. The two centaur creatures drew closer and scuttled back and forth in agitation. To his left, three humanoid figures appeared out of the roiling dust, which Blegg realized was now thickening. These . . . people snicked at the air with the pincers protruding from their mouths. Ahead something scuttled past: a sleer body, a human face seemingly frozen in a permanent scream.

'You will see,' said the Earth Central AI.

Now the looming presence of the oblate dwellings all around him. He tracked one of the screamers with the barrel of his pulse-rifle as it came close, then swerved away to clamber up onto one of the dwellings. He now turned his attention to his node detector. The readings looked strange for a moment, until he tilted it upwards. The monolith – the Jain node was up there. Blegg considered transporting himself directly to the node's location, but rejected that idea. He did not know why, and did not concern himself further with the thought.

Eventually a wall of slanting multicoloured layers loomed before him. Things scrabbled and hissed in the wind-gnawed hollows about the monolith's base. Blegg turned to his left and began to walk round. All about him shadowy shapes loomed and retreated in the haze. Eventually he came to a point where they all seemed to be closing in. Here, carved into the stone, were foot- and hand-holds. He pocketed the detector, slung his pulse-rifle from his shoulder by its strap, and climbed.

Earth Central commented, 'There comes a time when useful fictions become weaknesses to be exploited.'

'Meaning?' asked Blegg. Sleer hybrids clung either side of him to the sandstone face: the screamers.

'Yes . . . meaning.'

'Is it my imagination,' asked Blegg, 'or do you sound more and more like Dragon every day?'

On a ledge here, Blegg rested and eyed his companions on the rockface. The air carried less dust this high, so he could see them more clearly, which was not exactly reassuring. He checked the detector and saw that the Jain node lay only twenty yards away, in a straight line running up through and above the monolith. Not so far to climb, so he grimaced and continued, eventually coming up over the edge onto the top.

'Ah . . . I see.'

Blegg unslung his pulse-rifle and casually aimed it, not that a weapon like that would do any good. He considered the grenades he carried and rejected the idea, too. Anyway, he could step away through U-space any time he chose.

Only a few yards away from him, the figure stood eight feet tall. It wore a wide-brimmed hat held in place against the wind by one heavy brass hand. Its coat was ragged, and it wore lace-up boots.

Mr Crane.

Perfectly complementing this menacing tableau, a vulture suddenly landed in a cloud of dust and a scattering of oily feathers. Blegg remembered this bird to be another Dragon creation; the mind it contained being the AI from the *Vulture* – the ship Skellor stole and which the AI had forced to crash here before transmitting itself to Dragon.

'So, who's been talking to Earth Central?' Blegg asked out loud.

The vulture cocked its head and replied, 'Me, of course.' It extended a wing towards the big brass Golem. 'He don't say much.'

Mr Crane tilted his hat back on the brass dome of his skull, groped in one pocket, then took out a handful of various objects. He stirred them with one finger. Blegg noticed a piece of crystal disturbingly like that of the Atheter artefact, a blue acorn, a small rubber dog, and a golden ovoid. The brass Golem selected the ovoid from among them and held it up before his face like a jeweller inspecting a suspect gem, then, with a flick of his hand, tossed it to Blegg.

Too dangerous to touch, but Blegg snapped out a hand and snatched the object from the air. I'm dead, he thought, as he held up his hand and opened it. The Jain node rested in his palm, cubic patterns shifting on its surface.

'You understand?' Earth Central asked.

I'm damned.

The Jain node did not react at all.

Jack routed the package from Thellant into secure storage in a virtuality, where it howled like a pack of wolves confined behind a thin door. Aphran held back for a moment. Having witnessed the initial non-reactive scan of this package, she knew it to be layered with Jain tech subversion and sequestering routines, as was expected. However, though Jack perpetually delegated tasks to her, in this one there seemed some hidden purpose – she was too closely entwined with the AI to not realize that. She now extended the boundaries of the virtuality and projected herself inside it. For ease of handling she gave the memory package a form easy to comprehend on a VR level, while on an informational level her programs could take it apart. Swirling chaos eventually collapsed down to a stack of books in which squirmed venomous reptiles and insects – she needed to read these books yet avoid being stung or bitten. Beside her, a thin man appeared.

He wore a pinstripe suit, bowler hat, and the glitter of thick spectacles concealed his eyes. Jack Ketch, the hangman.

'No reservations?' Jack asked, just like with Freyda, the Separatist.

'I have some,' said Aphran. 'I've been working for the Polity under a sentence of erasure, which I know will never be repealed. Why should I continue?'

'Because as long as you work, that sentence will not be executed.'

'And because *you* may be damaged in the process.'

Jack leant forwards. 'You think?'

'Yes, though you have been gradually disentangling yourself and I suspect that, while I deal with this' – she gestured to the VR representation – 'you will pull away even more.'

'Yes,' Jack replied, 'the processing power you will require in this task will further weaken your hold on me. I may even be able to separate from you completely.'

'Does it mean nothing to you that I saved your life?'

'My life is very important to me – which is precisely the point: *my life*.'

'So you are going to erase me, just like you did Freyda.'

'You believe that?'

'I do.'

'Then do not carry out this task.'

Aphran looked upon the perilous stack of books. She seemed damned either way: doing this, she could be separated from Jack and wiped out; if she did not do this, it would just take longer.

'Very well, let it be over.' She turned from him to her chore, feeling him fade and distance himself from her.

Aphran picked up one book. Some centipedal monstrosity immediately wound itself around her arm and opened its pincers. She caught its head in her fist and crushed it, then opened the book. This one detailed Thellant losing two Separatist cells, one after the other, and fearing a trail would lead back to him, then subsequently learning that his contacts in those cells were all assassinated on their way to interrogation. He suspected ECS, but it seemed a crazy move to kill those who could lead them to other cells. Next, the Legate waiting in Thellant's apartment, to claim credit for the killings and to make an offer. The centipede broke up into segments, each of which transformed into a scorpion. She knocked some of these away but others stung her. Worms propagated through her. She fought them, pulled more of herself into the virtuality, doubled and redoubled. Four Aphrans picked up books, and fought the killer programs – more of herself in, redoubling. Some versions of herself coming apart, others intercepting vital information from them. All the while, behind her, like strings being cut, she could feel Jack separating himself. Nothing she could do about that now, for she could not turn away from this task until it was done.

In the virtuality a virtual age passed, though only minutes in real time. Virtual pain hurt just as much as the real thing as the Jain tech programs ripped into her, but this Aphran was a product of that same technology. She reconfigured herself, sent in her own programs like informational DDT, stamped and splattered her attackers, cut off self-propagating worms at their source, confined nasty HK programs in briefly generated virtual spaces and then collapsed them to zero. She saw how Thellant's organization expanded as a direct result of the Legate's assistance, saw him grow rich and dependent. Numerous meetings between the two of them revealed snippets of information she put together. The Legate was just that: a legate working on behalf of someone or something else. It showed technical abilities beyond that of normal Golem – seeming suspiciously like the product of Jain technology. Eventually she gathered it all: everything about Thellant and the Legate. And she now knew how the Legate might be found.

Re-absorbing her alternative selves, Aphran became one again in the virtuality, a neat stack of books before her and shattered chitin spread all around, vaporizing and turning to dust.

'Give it to me,' said Jack.

She stood alone, with just one channel open to Jack – her only link outside the virtuality. He had broken away totally and now she could be safely erased. She considered destroying everything she had obtained, or holding onto it and bleeding over small amounts just to extend her existence. But in the end she truly regretted all the things she had done as a Separatist. The arrogance and stupidity of her earlier self appalled and disgusted her.

Enough.

Aphran transmitted all the data, and Jack accepted it.

'Do I die now?' she asked.

'Yes – in every way that matters to the Polity.'

Aphran felt herself contracting, going out, draining away.

No returns from the package he had sent. Thellant realized they must have opened it in some secure fashion to obtain what they wanted. With his being now utterly interlaced through the rescue ship, physically and informationally, he hardly felt his own body. Perpetually he tried to reach out to other vessels, probing for some lever, some way . . .

'Thellant N'komo,' said a voice.

'You're the ship AI – Jack Ketch. I know what the name means.'

'Yes, I imagine you do. But I am not so merciless as that name implies. This is why I am going to offer you a choice.'

'Oh,' said Thellant sarcastically, 'so I don't get to live happily ever after on my very own little world.'

'That is your first choice. There are those who would indeed like to isolate you upon such a world. Thorn did not lie when he told you such a place has already been prepared. The trouble is you would not live happily ever after. Over a period of years you would spread around the planet, using its resources to create grand Jain structures, but since the purpose of the technology you now ostensibly control is the destruction of civilizations, and none would be available to you there, you would eventually go to seed.'

'Seed?'

'The Legate has told you something of the biophysicist Skellor?'

'He did.'

'Though they might believe themselves to be in control of that technology, technical beings are merely its vehicles, merely a means of spreading it. In Skellor it formed nodes within him, seeds. It will do the same in you.'

Thellant already sensed that the technology remained his to command only while their two purposes concurred. The idea of it seeding from him contained more horror for him than could be supposed by others unoccupied by

the Jain tech. He knew he would remain aware throughout the procedure, fighting to survive and to hold his
consciousness together, but knowing his efforts to be
futile. With his sudden tired acceptance of these facts,
he felt things hardening inside him, imminent as razors
threading through his flesh. Their purposes would utterly
diverge should he choose what he already knew to be Jack
Ketch's other option: death. He poised himself on the
brink of decision. Should he choose to die, the Jain tech
would try to take over, since it put its own survival first,
always.

'Should it last for two seconds, I will take your silence
as the latter choice,' Jack told him.

Thellant clamped down on the structure that spread
throughout the ship, felt it writhe and fight him. A spas-
tic vibration threw him about in the flight chair, but
stubbornly he kept his mouth clamped shut. He felt the
structure within him creating a reply, drafting its acceptance of planetary exile. He glimpsed an image of himself
as a soft flesh puppet, translucent and threaded upon
black dense technology like a many-clawed gaff.

Not speaking.

Two seconds of eternity, then a shiny nose cone closing down on him like a steel eye. The Jain structure
shrieked and thrashed, and the imploder struck. Super
gravity drew ship and all down into white antimatter fire.

Thellant went out.

Human swarm crowded and stumbled in from the distance. Scattered evenly across the sky, apparently as far
as the arcology edge, hung spherical scanning drones
eight feet across, with high-intensity lasers mounted on
either side of them. Their targets, Jain-infected humans,

might be moving shoulder to shoulder with innocent civilians, and needed to be rendered down to ash. Coloron had calculated eight innocent deaths for every one infected with Jain tech. Cormac thought it ironically appropriate that these drones bore some similarity to Prador War drones. Thus far, fifteen targets had been destroyed, having evaded Coloron's forces inside the arcology. None of them managed to join the main crowds, and so no collateral damage yet. Was that down to the efficiency of the Polity defence, or just dumb luck?

A line of AG tanks curved from horizon to horizon. Behind it, and above, massed other Polity forces: mobile quadruped rail-guns stamping about impatiently on steel legs, the ends of their huge cylindrical magazines, attached either side of their main bodies, looking like blank eyes; troop transports and swarms of armoured troops, some hovering in AG harnesses, some on platforms mounting particle cannons; atmosphere jets speeding in squadrons overhead, avoiding two massive atmosphere gunships hanging in the sky like city blocks turned sideways; a multitude of drones of all kinds swarming all about like steel insects. This then was the might of the Polity mobilized for ground warfare. Cormac considered it an impressive and sobering sight, but knew the forces assembled here to be only a fraction of a per cent of the whole.

Breaks through the ground line were fenced on either side, the intervening channels leading back to where ECS Rescue and Medical personnel awaited. More of these were arriving from the initial landings beside the arcology. The air ambulances and ships these personnel occupied were also obliged to pass underneath the scanning drones, no exceptions.

'Would you like to be down there?' Cormac asked.

Arach, who had been peering for some time over the side of the stripped-down gravcar Cormac guided, turned his nightmare head, opened and closed his pincers, his two large red eyes and other smaller ones gleaming. 'I would rather be over there.' Arach gestured with one sharp leg towards the arcology itself. Seemingly on cue, a bright flash from that direction cast long shadows behind the ground forces. Shortly after came a thunderous rumble. Through his gridlink Cormac picked up the news.

'Another runcible,' he declared.

Arach grunted, then with a clattering moved up beside Cormac to peer ahead at the arcology. Turquoise fire now stabbed down, again and again, and the thunder became constant. Smoke, fire and debris, carried up in mini tornadoes, became visible.

'And that?' asked the drone.

'Coloron is destroying the coastal edge of the arcology to prevent the Jain tech spreading into the sea,' he replied. 'The AI has burnt down to the bedrock for about a mile in, and is keeping that rock molten.'

Accessing a statistical analysis of the situation, he immediately saw that the arcology's further existence was measured only in days. Jain tech now controlled the coastal edge to the west, and most of the north edge too. It had swamped almost half the arcology, and six of the ten runcibles had been destroyed before it could reach them. Flashes continued to ignite the horizon as missiles from orbit destroyed those fusion reactors coming under Jain control. The millions of citizens remaining inside the arcology now all flowed towards the long south-east edge, since the remaining runcibles inside were about to be closed down.

As he flew the gravcar low over the vast crowd, with scanning drones above tracking his progress, Cormac accessed tactical displays and views through other drones and cameras scattered throughout the arcology. Coloron's troops steadily retreated, blowing out walls, ceilings and floors wherever it seemed possible such demolition might slow the advance of Jain substructure, and firing on abhuman figures advancing out of the wreckage. He saw squads of soldiers engaged in firefights with armed Jain-controlled humans who could be stopped only by major damage. Cormac broke the links and returned his full attention to his surroundings.

Below, the crowds remained densely packed, humanity spreading in every direction as far as he could see. Ahead, the arcology edge rose into view, like some mountain chain carved into tiers. These levels were occupied by open parks, rectilinear lakes, small cities of expensive mansions, houses and apartments. Communications pylons cut into the sky, vents belched excess heat in the form of steam, monorails weaved from level to level like silver millipedes. As he drew closer to it, Cormac saw people crowding the tiers from which jutted the platforms of gravcar-parks and landing pads. The situation had improved since, only days ago, there had been no free space anywhere on those tiers, just shoulder to shoulder Polity citizens.

'*Coloron, where are you?*' he sent.

In reply he received coordinates on a three-dimensional map of the great structure.

He pointed up to a landing pad jutting from the side

of ceramal-braced foam-stone cliff, like some monstrous iron bracket fungus. 'We go up there.'

He guided the gravcar up through the evenly spaced layer of scanning drones, and soon descended towards a landing pad. To one side of this, people crowded up ramps to climb aboard the multitude of gravcars and other AG transports that were arriving and leaving constantly. A small area of this pad had been fenced off near the edge. Human guards and mosquito-like autoguns patrolled its perimeter. Within rested a lander, a couple of military transports, and a fast atmosphere format gunship. A group of figures stood near the edge itself. As he landed, Cormac noted a bipedal robot he identified, through his gridlink, as Coloron. There were dracomen here too, and as he stepped from the car, he also recognized Thorn.

He turned to Arach. 'Come on.'

The drone clambered down from the gravcar and walked to heel behind him like some monstrous pet. Cormac advanced to the group on the platform edge just as another actinic flash ignited in the distance. He glanced in that direction, at a sky yellow-brown behind the pall of smoke, to see wreckage exploding into the air and raining down. This havoc was being wrought to prevent an even greater catastrophe, all as a consequence of one man with one Jain node. How many, he wondered, had the Maker brought from its realm and scattered throughout the Polity?

'Cormac,' said Thorn, turning to acknowledge him.

Cormac nodded in greeting, glanced across at the dracomen, recognized Scar by his gnathic smile, then returned his attention to Thorn. The man glanced past him at the drone, now squatting with his hindquarters resting on the floor.

'New recruit?' he enquired.

'A volunteer,' Cormac replied, then, after Thorn's grimace, 'allow me to introduce Arach. He's a war drone who fought in the Prador War.'

'Ah,' said Thorn, 'that accounts for it.'

'Quite . . .' Cormac stabbed a finger down at the deck beneath his feet. 'Now, I know what's going on down here on the surface, but I've heard nothing from Jack.'

'We've captured Thellant N'komo,' said Thorn. He nodded to the nearby lander and they both began walking towards it.

'I know.' Cormac tapped a finger against his head, indicating his gridlink. 'Von Hellsdorf sold Skellor a Jain node, and there was a direct connection between her and this Thellant.' Cormac glanced across the devastation and grimaced. 'Have you got anything out of him yet?'

Ahead of them, Scar and the four dracomen accompanying him boarded the lander.

Thorn replied, 'A download of all his memories concerning his association with something called the Legate. He layered this with subversion programs, so it's taken Aphran quite a while to take it apart. We're getting the results now.'

Cormac paused by the airlock. 'Those being?'

Thorn gestured inside. 'Best you come see.'

Cormac glanced back towards Coloron. The AI dipped towards him as if to study him for a moment, then returned its attention to its demolition job. Yet another explosion ignited the horizon, much closer now. Cormac stepped into the lander.

13

The classification of Polity warships is only loosely connected to a similar system used for naval vessels of the past. Hence dreadnoughts are the big ones – their name owing more to the definition 'fears nothing' than 'a battleship carrying heavy guns of a uniform calibre' – and attack ships are the smaller ones, though very fast and also carrying some lethal armament. Cruisers lie somewhere between these two – the lines of definition somewhat blurred. However, with the size of ships steadily increasing at one end of the scale and increasing specialization at the other end, new forms of classification have been introduced since the termination of the Prador War. Using the Greek alphabet, dreadnoughts are classified alpha to epsilon, zeta to omicron are used to cover cruisers, and the rest of the alphabet to cover all the specialized warships: attack ships of many different designs, USERs, space tugs and drone or troop transports. Now even this system is falling into disuse. Few people even believe that such behemoths as alpha and beta class dreadnoughts exist. I can assure you that they do, and some others beyond where this system of classification runs out. At the other end of the scale the alphabetical designations have become unwieldy. The most recent state-of-the-art attack ships are designated Iota/Lambda(basic weapons)/

Mu+(gravtech weapons)/'ware(Omicron classified) etc., etc.
Sometimes they are called Centurion-class attack ships, but
mostly we humans just call them by their names now. The
complex classifications can just remain lines of code slotted, in
the minds of AIs, into specific niches in Gordian battle plans.
                    – From her lecture 'Modern Warfare'
                                          by EBS Heinlein

Orlandine detached from her assister frame and her carapace, then returned along the length of the *Heliotrope* to
her living quarters. She was abruptly very hungry – the
nutrients her body stored having been used up over
the last hundred hours of research. The ship's galley provided her with a hot prosaic meal of synthetic beef rogan
josh, naan bread, and cold beer.

Human time, she thought, feeling the irony of it, yet
deciding she needed this interlude to gain a different perspective on all she had learnt.

With one quarter of the node's substance unravelled,
Orlandine now used the tools it provided. A stripped-
down simple mycelium grew along the joists and layers
of the Dyson segment, powering itself from the many
reactors already in place, and giving her views throughout the immense surrounding structure. It connected to
all the Polity scanning equipment within the segment,
and edited out anything those scanners picked up of her
activities, so as to make her effectively invisible to those
back at the Cassius stations, and would alert her of anything that might affect her – its own scanners being
much more effective than those manufactured by the
Polity. However, she had connected this mycelium to an
isolated computer, where one of her subpersonae controlled it.

Orlandine remained wary of applying the physical technology directly to herself, it being only comprehensible down to the level her studying tools could reach. Those tools, and the analytical programs she applied to what they revealed, led her to hypothesize the existence of underlying submolecular structures. It was like seeing a two-hundred-storey building, knowing there must be foundations below it, but suspecting still further floors underground.

Her attitude to the numerous programs copied from the node was different. She loaded them to her carapace – though in isolated storage, just like the ones she had used to attack Shoala. She felt she understood their purposes as individual programs, but did not yet want to include them completely in her crystal consciousness because they might reveal further purpose only in combination. However, being simply packets of information, they could be broken down to a elementary quaternary form, below which nothing could be hidden. At some point she *would* begin to use them in combination.

Orlandine finished her meal and dropped the compressed-fibre tableware in the recycler. Collecting a chilled glass of synthetic raki, she slumped in her seat again and continued to assess matters at the merely human level.

Something had designed this technology to kill civilizations. It procreated by taking from its first victim information relevant to wiping out that individual's civilization. A trap for the unwary, it was also a trap for any technological investigation. She simply could not risk incorporating the physical tech without finding ways of divining the purpose of all she still could not see, since it was certainly hostile. Even atomic copies would be too

risky, as they might mimic that same purpose. She therefore needed newer and better tools. The technology itself
could provide her with them, but that could be dangerous too: the trap might also lie within tools based on the
technology. Orlandine sighed, suddenly feeling unutter-
ably weary. She could clear this feeling by running
certain programs in the crystal part of her mind, in her
carapace, to impart the benefits of sleep to her organic
brain. Also, the Polity nanomachines in her body were
constantly repairing cellular damage normally attended
to naturally during sleep. She chose to sleep properly,
however, for maybe the archaic natural process of REM
sleep would give her a different perspective. Reclining
the chair, she settled back, closed her eyes and used her
gridlink to cue herself for lucid dreaming.

Natural, she reflected with some amusement, before
turning herself off.

The spider web extended to infinity in every direction:
the space-time continuum represented as a flat surface for
those simple humans who could visualize only a limited
number of dimensions. Glancing to her left she observed
the gravity well of a sun drawing the web down into a hole.
Another hole, a planet, circled the declivity around its
edge. She walked along one strand, careful not to slip and
put her foot down into U-space. The strand did not move
– her mass made no impression on it. The spider-shaped
hole in the web seemed just like a gravity well, but peering inside she could see no spider. She stepped past it and
into her apartment in the Cassius station. Shoala handed
over a drink that she sipped. It tasted bitter.

'It's poison,' he told her.

His carapace possessed more legs than usual, and they
had been driven through his body in many places. He

turned away and she noticed that his sensory cowl now
sported mandibles. It sliced in a circle, pulled away a
hemisphere of his skull with a sucking crunch and discarded it, then began to dine on his brains. He turned
back to her.

'It's cumulative, mind,' he said, just as a mandible
pushed out beside his eye, then folded back in, pulling the
jellied eyeball out of sight into the bloody socket. Her
glass hit the carpet and broke into 4,002 fragments. She
measured the angles and curves of each one, tracked their
courses, calculated masses and subsequent vectors, then
began counting individual strands in the carpet moss.

'A gift from an admirer,' someone whispered, then
chuckled menacingly.

'Simplistic representations,' she told Shoala – and the
spider clinging to the station's skin, and the whisperer.
'It was a mistake for me to sleep.'

'You think you are sleeping?' Shoala asked, both his
eyes gone now and, his disembodied face hanging before
her, bright light shining from behind it, glaring from
empty sockets. The face receded, and landed in some
deep pit in a large spider web. Carapaces scuttled in to
tear it apart.

'Yes,' said Orlandine, opening her eyes. She sat
upright, completely awake instantly, an array of dream
sequences recorded in her gridlink. She shivered, those
dreams still clear in her mind.

'Simplistic,' she repeated.

But something nagged at her: something evident in
that dream sequence, some plain fact she was missing.
She wanted to either track it down or dismiss it with certainty, but there came another call for her attention: a
signal from the subpersona controlling her Jain tech

mycelium, telling her it now detected something the Polity scanners were missing. This could only mean she was no longer alone here in the Dyson segment, and the intruder was not of the Polity.

King studied the artefact from one light year away, and for all the AI knew it was no longer even there – having moved on some time after a year ago. This distance was relatively long to be obtaining such detail, but no effort had been made at concealment since the object emitted across the electromagnetic spectrum. Obviously, these emissions meant that in some way it was, or had been, active.

A flattened cylinder three miles long, it seemed to be formed of a tangle of foot-thick tubes compressed into that same shape – perhaps a ship of some kind, or a station? Other structures on its surface, like giant metallic barnacles, were a year ago firing into space projectiles no larger than a human fist. At this distance, King could get no more detail on them than their size. Estimating the velocity of these, King calculated their present realtime position. They should be one quarter of a light year out, however the AI did not know how long the artefact had been firing off these projectiles, so it added a large degree of error incorporating the time of Erebus's arrival here, minus some time for this same artefact to be built. The *King of Hearts* dropped into U-space and surfaced just half a light year out.

Collision alarms . . .

Calculations wrong. A deliberate trap? King immediately began firing meteor lasers at the swarm of fist-sized objects hammering towards it, turned and ignited its fusion drive to bring its speed up to that of the projectiles. While destroying those that seemed likely to impact on its hull, it spectrally analysed the debris and deep-scanned those still intact.

They were the shape of melon seeds, with cilia-like serrations along their edges, and seemed packed with technology in the haphazard configuration of something alive. They contained power cells, some form of sensor array, small chambers holding hydrogen under sufficient pressure to turn it into the metallic state. The AI realized its danger within a fraction of a second, but that was a fraction of a second too late. Bright stars ignited all around, and King expected massive explosions but, no, the projectiles accelerated inwards as the attack ship began dropping into U-space. Three of them penetrated the U-field before it fully formed, and then slammed into the *King of Hearts*'s hull as it surfaced into realspace half a light year away.

Space mines like those once used to destroy Prador vessels?

Still no explosion. King released three telefactors and directed them to the location of each impact. But, even as those devices launched, King felt the incursions through its hull. Immediately extruding antipersonnel lasers on jointed arms, it directed them back at itself and fired upon all three incursions. Viewing through the telefactors it saw two of them grow red, then white, then explode massively. Two craters were punched into hull metal, causing structural damage inside, atmosphere leaking out – but that last did not matter as the AI never intended to willingly take humans aboard it ever again. The third object grew red, white, then slowly turned red again. Unlike the others it managed to link itself to King's own s-con hull grid, which meant it had already cut five inches deep. The AI shut down the laser and recalled two of its telefactors, leaving the other one outside watching. Through its internal scanners it viewed the inner location of the incursion through its hull, but saw nothing yet. It sent maintenance robots to that area, then from its internal armoury summoned a mosquito autogun, and watched the weapon stride on six legs along corridors meant for humans. The business end of this device was a small particle cannon – not something King really wanted to fire inside itself, but would do so if necessary.

The outside view showed the melon-seed shape bulging up in the middle, with ridges extending down from the bulge. Sensors in King's hull now revealed weaknesses in the area. The maintenance robots arrived and began cutting out nearby walls and detaching and moving equipment in the vicinity. Then came a wrinkling of the inner hull, and a tendril breaking through and branching across the surface like a vein. Close scanning showed material draining away around this growth. King could not scan close enough to see the cause, but guessed it to be nanomachines taking apart the substance of the ship and drawing it away. Outside again, the seed shape had turned into a smaller version of those barnacle structures on the distant artefact. The purpose of all this seemed clear: an organic technology that grew by ingesting surrounding materials, very like Jain technology. King withdrew its maintenance robots, sealed off bulkheads, and instructed the mosquito autogun to weld its feet to the floor, then told it to fire. Turquoise flame struck the inner hull. The external telefactor observed the hull glow red around the encrustation, which turned black in silhouette. After a moment the hull bulged, then exploded into space in a stream of plasma, the growth retaining definition for a moment, then breaking apart as it was struck by the turquoise of the particle beam. King sent its maintenance robots to fetch hull patches, set them to making repairs, then contemplated recorded images of its closer view of the artefact.

It now seemed likely that the distant artefact was a ship or a station completely digested by the invading technology. The position of the projectiles the AI encountered indicated they had been fired off at about the time of Erebus's arrival here, so that other AI had little time in which to construct something so massive. King ran through the library of images of ships that departed the Polity with Erebus, and shortly found something matching the same general outline: a troop transport called the *Calydonian Boar*. Maybe this ship had been another to rebel, or else its AI was removed and the hulk set here as a defence. No way of telling now, because there seemed to be nothing left of the original ship.

King surveyed the internal map it had made of nearby systems, wondering which direction Erebus took from here, for there was no way to find out from the *Calydonian Boar* itself without risking destruction. Then, on that internal map: the accretion disc of a solar system in the making – the perfect place for something utterly new. U-space then, to the edge of this disc, followed by conventional drives inside, for using U-engines in such a place where matter concentrated would be very risky. A difficult place, therefore, to escape from.

In the extended airlock and decontamination area, Mika donned a spacesuit before lugging her pack out to a catwalk. The bay was an upright cylinder with the walkway running around the perimeter of a circular irised hatch in the floor. This sector in the *Jerusalem*'s outer ring contained a selection of intership craft. None of these, however, were presently visible, being stored in concealed racks. She was about to mention this fact when abruptly the floor slid open and a lift raised her transport into view.

This might be the same craft as Cormac had used in his journey down to the surface of Dragon. A one-man vehicle without airlocks, any major drive or AI, it could be flown by a pilot, though most often Jerusalem itself controlled it. A flattened and stretched ovoid, with skids underneath, two directional thrusters mounted to fore, and a small ion drive aft, it looked precisely what it was: utile, basic but serviceable. Mika took the steps down from the catwalk and hauled her pack inside.

The pack and its contents were a recent requirement, for the *Jerusalem* would shortly drop into U-space to make the return jump to Cull. The AI decided that a trip to Coloron would be wasted, for any Jain technology there would soon cease to exist. Nevertheless, Mika wondered about the timing of the jump coinciding with her allotted session with Dragon. Perhaps the AI intended giving her a break from her current concerns about augmentation? Though of course it would be arrogant to assume it thought her so important.

Once ensconced in the single seat, Mika said, 'Okay, Jerusalem, you can take me over – I've no overpowering urge to pilot this thing myself.'

From her suitcom the AI replied, 'Scenic route?'

'If you have sufficient time.'

The wing door to the craft sealed itself shut with a

crump, and lights began flashing amber in the bay as pumps evacuated the air. Mika strapped herself in, felt the grav go off, then looked up through the cockpit screen as the lights turned to amber and the ceiling irised open on stars. Swivelling to point downwards, the fore thrusters fired to propel the craft out into space. It turned nose-down over the *Jerusalem*'s outer ring, which now looked like some vast raised highway running to the horizon of a metal planet. The giant research vessel was a sphere three miles in diameter, with the thick band around its equator containing all its shuttles, grab-ships, drones, telefactors . . . the tools the AI used to manipulate its environment, which Mika felt the AI defined as *everything*.

The small craft now turned away and headed towards a reddish green sun on the *Jerusalem*'s horizon. Acceleration from the ion drive kicked her in the back, and the small organic moonlet fell towards her. Around her she noted things glinting in the blackness: ships and robotic probes being recalled to the equatorial ring of the giant research vessel. She abruptly felt very vulnerable, then, looking ahead towards Dragon, a surge of excitement.

The AI brought the craft down in steadily lower obits around the huge being that named itself Dragon. On the first orbit, Dragon simply appeared like a small and fairly nondescript moonlet. Only closer, when its living substance became visible, could anyone know different. Here an area of jewelled scales, looking like scarlet and jade stone until it moved, a ripple travelling across it as if the entity took a breath of vacuum. A seeming copse rose over the sharply curved horizon, waving in some impossible breeze. Those weren't trees, though, but cobra heads raised high, with gleaming sapphire foliage, and the undergrowth consisted of writhing red tentacles groping in shadow.

The first tight orbit revealed the manacle as a bright metallic line, like the epoxyed-on attachment for some pendant chain. Closer to, she saw it rested at the bottom of a shallow trench, as if it had etched itself into the surface. On its third pass her craft decelerated above this and slowly spiralled down. She felt the tug from gravplates below, each time her craft passed over them, then grav became constant as it landed on the ceramal strip beside the trapeziform building.

'Close your visor,' Jerusalem advised.

The moment Mika did this, the craft purged its internal air supply. Then the wing door opened and her seat automatically swung towards it. She stepped out, noting how the ceramal was dulled by microscopic scratches from many hundreds of similar vessels landing here and the boots that had clumped from them. She too clumped across to the nearby airlock, to enter through the outer metal door and an inner shimmer-shield. The square pool of scaled flesh, which she had viewed so many times remotely, remained unchanged, but upon retracting her visor she experienced the smell of it for the first time: something spicy and slightly rank, with a hint of confined beasts. She moved to the area off to one side, containing VR and laboratory equipment, dumped her pack down beside a VR chair and plumped herself in it.

Concisely she instructed, 'Exterior view.'

The walls faded from existence to reveal the edges of the trench all around, but she stood high enough to gaze out on the draconic landscape. She abruptly sat upright when she saw her vessel lifting a little way from the manacle, turning, and coming down again to where clamps issued from below to close on its skids.

'Jerusalem, you secured the craft,' she stated.

'Certainly – but it will of course be available to you when you are ready for it.'

Now, before her, the pool of scaly flesh stretched and parted. Humid warmth issued forth and an odour as of burned grease drowned out all other smells. Mika supposed this resulted from whatever Dragon had destroyed inside itself. She reached down, opened her pack and took out her palm-com. Trying not to show any of the disquiet she felt, she called up her list of questions. A heavy slithing sound issued from the widening gap before her. The smell increased. After a moment she looked up and realized that this time things were occurring that had never happened during visits here by others. The split now traversed the entire length of the rectangular area and opened wider than before, its edges turning like scaled rollers. Soon they drew out of sight, and Mika stood up, moved to the edge and peered over. Below her, a gaping red cavern curved down into hot darkness. Abruptly a spiralling wheel hurtled up towards her. She jumped back as red tentacles, sharp as claws, shot over the edges into the surrounding structure and clamped down on the floor. She looked up, noticing something else was happening too. The manacle was lower now in relation to the outside surface, for it was sinking inside Dragon.

'Jerusalem?'

No reply.

'Jerusalem!'

Nothing.

Cobra pseudopodia speared into view – the honour

guard for the head that followed. This too had changed. Four times the usual size, hairless and scaled, eyes completely black, the human head licked narrow lips with a sharp tongue, red as blood.

'The *Jerusalem* has entered U-space,' Dragon told her.

'What are you doing?'

'Preparing to do the same.'

'To Cull?'

Dragon grinned, exposing sharp teeth.

'Eventually,' it replied.

The crowds of refugees were thinning now as they filtered through Polity battle lines, but the attacks, by scanning drones, increased. Seated on the sloping armour at the front of an AG tank, the woman placed a monocular up against her eyes and watched as one of the scanning drones fell out of formation, its twinned lasers flickering like arc welders. Tracking down, she saw figures burning away like ants on a hot plate and wondered if all of these had been infected by Jain technology. Around this carnage people fled in panic until, when it seemed nothing remained for it to burn, the drone returned to its position in the formation. A couple of air ambulances then descended. Bodies lay on the ground around the conflagration, some writhing, some crawling. She lowered the monocular.

'You check out,' said the ECS tank commander, tossing her ident bracelet back to her.

She caught it and slipped it back on her wrist. He had also gene-scanned her to make a comparison with the identity information the bracelet contained. She smiled, glad that it checked out satisfactorily, and quite happy with her new name and her profession as a freelance reporter selling sensocords of events like this to the net news services. All she needed to do was place herself where newsworthy events occurred, while her new aug recorded everything she saw, heard, smelt, tasted, felt . . . She returned her attention to the arcology as the ground shuddered beneath her.

Monitors and Sparkind now came out, fighting a defensive retreat, firing on figures lurching out after them through smoke and flame. As far as was visible, in both directions, more of Coloron's forces retreated – that last inner line of defence.

'You can stay there if you like,' said the commander, 'but I wouldn't recommend it.' He climbed inside the AG tank which, shortly afterwards, began to lift.

As the tank drifted forward, the woman quickly stepped up into the open doorway. 'What's happening now?'

'We hold them back until the civilians are far enough behind the lines,' the commander replied, as he manipulated the tank's controls, 'then it's bye-bye arcology.'

The woman felt awe at the thought, and some sadness. Her ident did not say anything about her once having lived here.

'You staying or going? I need to close that door.'

She stepped back and down to the ground, the door hissing shut as the tank moved on. Glancing beyond the tank, then behind her, she saw the whole ECS battle line beginning to advance slowly through the crowds. She pitied those about to lose their homes, and those about to die, having experienced both traumas herself. But then she wasn't what she seemed: closing her eyes, she remembered her recent resurrection.

She had felt cold, and a thousand needles prickled her

skin. Something had crumped ahead of her and a line of light cut down to one side, through the darkness.

I'm in a cold coffin, she realized, but beyond that realization lay only confusion.

A taste in her mouth like copper.

I have a mouth?

Skin feeling abraded.

I have skin?

A cold aseptic room lay before her, cold coffins inset all around its walls like Egyptian sarcophagi, bright metal, white surfaces.

I have eyes?

She stepped out, she looked around. Human vision seemed a narrow thing after having been used to enhanced viewing in more places than one and across more of the spectrum than the human eye could see. Her hearing remained unchanged, however. Gradually the floor warmed her feet. She needed to urinate, touched her mons tentatively and shuddered with pleasure at the sensation. Her stomach rumbled. She looked down at her hand and did not recognize it.

'Do you hear me?'

I'm not dead. So much meaning in that statement.

'I hear you,' she said, and felt a sudden panic at the unrecognizable tone of her own voice.

'I have placed a mirror to your right.'

She turned to see the naked form of the Separatist Freyda standing there, and now understood what Jack had done. For a moment she resented this, for she wanted to live in her own body. However, her own body had been incinerated long ago.

'Did you do this alone, or does ECS approve?' she asked.

'ECS does not know. I felt that I owed you something, and I know that you have changed in ways ECS could never ken. Nobody will be looking for a Separatist called Freyda, because she no longer exists – her DNA has been reclassified in the databases, and any criminal record deleted.'

'What now?' Aphran asked.

'The choice is yours. You can have yourself altered cosmetically, or choose to stay as you now are. One of the dracomen will transport you down to Coloron. Thereafter, all choices are your own.'

'A second chance?' she asked.

'Yes – exactly that.'

'Thank you.' Aphran collected some disposeralls from a dispenser in the wall. As she donned them, she just did not know what the future held for her. At some point that fact would be welcome, for now she actually had a future. Jack had created the false identity, this false life. Aphran liked the AI's choice, but then Jack knew her like no other.

She opened her eyes to see tanks and autoguns advancing and firing on the arcology over the heads of Coloron's forces. She saw missiles streaking down from above and, as when counting the seconds between the peal of thunder and the lightning flash, tracked explosions across the arcology.

Another lander returned to the *NEJ* just ahead of them. Cormac watched it enter a docking bay, then pulled his attention back to studying the entire ship. Definitely one of the newest designs: attack-ship configuration with a state-of-the-art chameleonware hull which, as well as being able to bend low intensity EM radiation around it, could also, to some degree, deflect high-powered lasers and masers. The outer skin was a form of polymerized diamond, over layered composite laced with super-conductors. The ship's skeleton, composed of the usual laminated tungsten ceramal, shock-absorbing foamed alloys and woven diamond monofilament, in this case was cellular and more substantial than usual. Cormac also knew that its extra weapons' nacelle contained gravtech armament in addition to the usual lethal com-plement housed in the other two nacelles.

A Centurion, he remembered – that's what they called these now.

The lander flew over the ship, then down to the second bay on its other side. It eased in through a shimmer-shield and settled in the narrow armoured area. Cormac stepped out first, followed by Thorn and then the dracomen. He noted armoured bay doors closing down and huge hydraulic grab arms easing out of the wall to take hold of the lander.

Jack? he tried once more through his gridlink. Again there came no reply. He applied at other informational levels through the ship's systems, but found himself blocked by AI defences of the kind now being employed against Jain tech subversion everywhere throughout the Polity. But, then, in any war, communication always suf-fered first.

'Not being very talkative, is he?' he commented.

Thorn glanced at him quizzically.

'Jack,' Cormac explained.

'He's been rather busy lately, analysing evidence, interrogating suspects and taking apart their memcord-ings. He also recently rid himself of Aphran.'

Cormac halted. '*Rid* himself?'

From the intercom Jack's voice suddenly issued, 'I feel I should rename myself as I am now in singular control of this ship. However, there is some truth in the current name *Not Entirely Jack*.'

'Has sentence been executed upon her?' Cormac asked.

'Aphran no longer exists,' replied the ship AI.

That, Cormac realized, did not really answer his question, but he let that go as he turned and walked to the circular door leading from the bay, which promptly irised open before him. He stepped through and found himself in a corridor resembling a pipe. The flat surface of the gravplate floor laid in that pipe was covered with blue carpet moss, bearing a repeating pattern of white nooses – a pattern copied from the original *Jack Ketch*, though its carpets had been plain fabric. The rest of the corridor remained strictly utile: padded walls and ceiling, diffuse lighting, and soft hand grips in case the gravplates should fail. Cormac wondered if Jack made his usual baroque and sometimes gruesome additions elsewhere, for the original ship had contained various human execution devices of antique design that the AI liked replicating down to the smallest historical detail. Cormac waited until Thorn stepped through beside him.

'Which way – I've been unable to access any information on the layout,' he said.

Thorn stepped aside to allow Arach also into the corridor. The drone scuttled over to one side and reared up as the dracomen filed out next to head along the corridor. Cormac noted how the dracomen eyed the drone curiously before moving on.

'Well, you certainly do get some types,' commented Arach, coming back down on its sharp feet.

Cormac assumed there had been some inaudible communication between drone and reptilians, but simply classified Arach's observation as interesting before turning back to Thorn, who gestured down the corridor, saying, 'These corridors run in a grid throughout the ship, all gravplated on one side, so you can walk anywhere using them. There's no movable drop-shafts.'

Cormac nodded to himself. Drop-shafts were a hangover from older ship geometries in which the builders felt some need of up and down. Jack had used a movable one to get his passengers to different locations inside the old *Jack Ketch*. This construction, he surmised, was for enhanced structural strength. 'Are we heading now for the bridge – if that's what you still call it?'

'No, Jack can project anywhere in this ship and there's something I thought you might like to see.' Thorn led him through a bulkhead door, then into a long corridor curving down the length of the hull. Three bulkhead doors later they entered another corridor carpeted with flute-grass matting and filled with hot terrarium air. Until now, all the corridors they traversed were boringly prosaic. Perhaps baroque interiors were something Jack had grown out of.

'More dracomen,' observed Cormac.

'Nearly a hundred of them aboard.' Thorn paused reflectively. 'You know there's thousands of them now on the planet below?'

Cormac nodded: he did know. He followed Thorn past a series of rooms occupied by the reptilian creatures. Finally the two men came to the cylindrical training chamber, with gravplated floors at either end and a zero-G section in the middle, which spanned the ship. Here Cormac observed dracomen at play, or training themselves to kill – there probably being little difference. He headed over to a stair and climbed to a platform positioned just below the zero-G section, his feet light on the metalwork where the gravity effect from the plates at one end of the cylinder partially cancelled out the effect from those at the other. Thorn moved up beside him.

'Okay, Jack, what do you have for me?'

A line cut down through the air below disporting dracomen, and out of it folded a humanoid figure.

'This is the Legate,' announced Jack.

Cormac studied the image for a moment. 'That tells us very little. Any AI or any human could take on that exterior form if they wished. Do you have any idea what's inside it?'

'Thellant attempted a scan of this particular entity, but that revealed only an empty shell. I surmise from this fact that his scanning equipment encountered sophisticated chameleonware. Other facts do confirm that the Legate can make itself invisible.'

The figure in question revolved slowly in the air like some musical doll, the tune played being the sound of fleshy impacts as dracomen continued their contests, above and below, totally ignoring the image. Cormac applied directly to Jack for information, and received a potted history of the association between Thellant and the Legate.

'So, an enemy of the Polity – nothing new there – but the technologies it employed have heretofore not really been the province of Separatists.' Cormac paused, applying analytical programs to the history provided, then said, 'Give it all to me, Jack.'

A hundred times larger than the potted history, this next block of information stretched his gridlink storage space, cutting down space for those programs he needed to analyse it. He reached up to press his fingers against his temple as if expecting a headache. His sleeve dropped back and he glimpsed Thorn's look of surprise, then amusement, at seeing Shuriken holstered there once more. He ran a search program to find what he could delete to make more space. The memory download from Jerusalem sat temptingly in the list appearing. He returned it to storage, deleted old programs and dated information, then returned his attention to Jack's new information. Patterns began to emerge.

'An outside force stirring up our rebels,' he concluded. 'Do we have any way of going after this character?'

'Thellant's memories did not supply that info. However, cross-referencing his memories with information provided by Coloron has provided us with something.'

'Don't draw it out, Jack.'

'U-space anomalies: within a day prior to every arrival of the Legate here, there would be a mass/U-signature discrepancy for some large arriving ship. Such discrepancies have always been ignored, since they are often due to the registered mass of a large cargo vessel being off by a fraction of a percentile. In the case of the Legate's arrivals, the mass discrepancy has always been about the same: twelve tons.'

'So it's clearly a small vessel piggy-backing in on other ships' U-fields?'

'So it would seem.'

'Is a search being conducted?'

'This information has been broadcast to all AIs across the Polity. All records are being checked, as are all new arrivals to worlds everywhere. If any ship comes in with such discrepancies, we will henceforth be immediately informed.'

'So now?'

The hologram of the Legate disappeared, and one wall of the chamber seemed to dissolve too in order to give a view outside. The planet Coloron fell away, starlit space revolving into view. Then came that drag at the very substance of reality, and the view greyed out, as they dropped into U-space.

'Even as I spoke the words,' announced Jack.

'What?' asked Cormac.

'Twelve-ton discrepancy detected, within the parameters of the Legate's last departure from here. Other forces are already on their way.'

'Other forces?' Thorn muttered.

Cormac asked, 'Where was this discrepancy detected?'

'The Cassius project.'

It figured: the AIs would be mighty pissed off about anyone messing with that.

14

Simple hardfield principles: this kind of field is projected from its generator much like a torch beam from a torch, the circular field meniscus generating at a distance preset in the generator like said beam striking a wall. Rather than getting into the complex maths and spacial-warp mechanics involved, it is best to think of it as simply a disc extended from its generator on the end of a long and extremely tough girder – both being made of a superconductor. Kinetic shock against the disc results in kinetic shock being transferred to the generator itself, where many methods are used to either absorb or convert it. Simple hydraulic rams are often used, also thermal or electrical conversion rams. Heat applied to the disc results in heat being applied to the generator. Again various methods are used to deal with this: superconductors to bleed it away, and other cooling systems. There are, however, deliberately designed-in limitations to how much of either a generator can absorb. Sufficient onslaught of each will usually result in a generator, with designed-in obsolescence, melting, though sometimes, if the limits are sufficiently exceeded, it will explode. A generator not so designed can, at some unplanned limit, implode, briefly creating a singularity at its core and a consequent fusion burn from highly compressed matter when the singularity goes out. The explosion in this case exceeds, by orders of magnitude, the explosion in the former case. Hence the deliberate obsolescence.

— From 'Weapons Directory'

The hardfield generators rested in transporters heavily constructed of carbide steel laminated with bearing materials and shock-absorbing foamed resins. Designed to bend and twist under huge loads, then return to their original shape, they were low and incredibly heavy, and in this situation not worth the energy expenditure of AG, so they ran on two sets of caterpillar tracks. Two thousand of them guarded the landward perimeter, their anchor spikes driven down through ten yards of earth until they encountered bedrock. The generators themselves were spherical, covered in flexible cooling pipes and bristling with radiator fins. The fields they projected, as well as being impervious to matter, were polarized against radiations outside the human visual spectrum. Those fields also slanted at forty-five degrees, to deflect the shockwave rather than stop it completely. The tank commander told her it still seemed likely that any generators surviving the blast would be driven, along with their transporters, deep into the ground.

'Why not wait until everyone is completely clear?' she asked, once again perching on his tank.

The man himself stood nearby, smoking a cigarette. He told her it was a habit acquired after spending too much time in his youth taking part in VR interactives based on celluloid films that were centuries old. He found it relaxed him.

'Coloron keeps destroying Jain tech on the surface, but it continues burrowing into the ground. It may be doing so slowly at present, but that's only because the arcology was necessarily built on solid granite. Once it reaches the softer strata, it'll speed up. So if we don't take it out before then, we may lose the planet.'

The arcology was now a silvery line on the horizon from which fires sprouted. Poised like stormclouds over it, atmosphere ships, having hurled down their lightnings, now departed to make way for what was to come. The tank commander tossed her a set of goggles.

'I thought the hardfields will block the flash?' she said.

'They will, but there's no guarantee they'll be there all the time.'

Aphran grunted her thanks and pocketed the goggles.

Ground armour, autoguns, tanks like the commander's, and AG platforms retreated to the shield line, many of them burdened with troops. Behind these, firing continued as more dehumanized residents tried to come out in the wake of Coloron's forces, only to be taken down by the scanning drones. Then the drones abruptly retreated, like flies shooed away from a corpse. A turquoise bar sliced down from the sky, turning the intervening ground to magma, working rhythmically back and forth before the arcology. Distantly, the cloud-locked sky, generated by massive evaporation of sea water, reflected similar fires around the other perimeters. Columns of smoke cut the sky in between like black tornados. Occasional sheets of flame groped upwards, and explosions constantly shook the ground. It seemed as if the troops had fled the Pit. Five dreadnoughts now occupied space above MA, to add their firepower to Coloron's own. One of those ships, even now, was probably selecting sources of appalling destruction from its weapons carousel.

'Do you know yet what we intend to use?' Aphran paused, considering how easily that 'we' came to her lips. 'Straight nukes or something a bit more exotic?'

'If I told you, I'd have to shoot you,' said the commander laconically, grinding out his cigarette butt.

'You're a laugh a minute,' Aphran muttered.

He grinned. 'Slow burn CTDs, which spread microspheres of antimatter over a wide area. The effective result is an atomic fire. Nothing survives above the atomic level at the hypocentre, while the EM pulse disrupts molecular bonds for a lot further.'

'Nice,' said Aphran, wondering again how Separatists had ever come to believe they could triumph against the Polity. Yes, they could detonate bombs, murder citizens, cause major disruption, but in the end, like some angry amateur going up against an experienced fighter, they would inevitably get slapped down. But that was ever the case with terrorist organizations: their doomed-to-failure efforts against superior forces littered historical records. Perhaps that very futility was the attraction.

'Interesting description,' said the commander. He paused to take out another cigarette, and watched it self-ignite. 'We use gravity imploders for a similar purpose in space warfare. They were invented to completely vaporize their target without spreading large fast-moving chunks of it all around a planetary system. On a planet that won't work, of course, because there's always a big air-transmitted shockwave. The whole idea of using slow-burn CTDs is to not chuck around Jain-infected debris.'

'But we have hardfields here to protect us from a shockwave,' Aphran observed.

'A breeze,' he said, still studying the end of his cigarette. 'To achieve an equivalent level of destruction here, using straight CTDs or imploders, would result in there being nothing but bedrock left for a hundred miles all around. The shockwave would travel around the planet a few times, killing millions in the process. There'd be a tsunami spreading out simultaneously from the seaward side, probably a mile high and travelling at twice the speed of sound.'

Aphran returned her attention to the battle line and those retreating beyond it. It would be a while before the hardfield generators came on, but soon after that the bombardment would commence. She nodded to the commander and made her way over towards a refectory vehicle, then while waiting in the queue, she gazed at the scene on this side of the line – away from the arcology.

The sky swarmed with ships, landing and departing, many ferrying relatively small numbers of the millions of citizens still in retreat. Stragglers were now only about a mile beyond the line, and amidst them most of the ambulance ships were landing. Aphran peered down at the churned ground, and only after a moment noticed how a maize crop had been trodden into a fibrous earthy pulp by the passage of a million shoes. Other evidence of the exodus lay scattered all about her: a plastic toy dinosaur that intermittently twitched its tail and bared its teeth, discarded tissues, food packaging, a shoe, a jacket, a hover trunk spilling clothing – its motor obviously having burnt out, even jewellery that in another age would have ransomed a kingdom. Sadder remnants were being loaded into a transporter further down the line, some citizens having only made it this far.

As she returned with two self-heating coffees – one acquired for the commander only as a courtesy since he carried sufficient supplies in his tank – he directed

Aphran's attention towards the last of those retreating from the arcology. She placed her cup down on ceramal armour and took up her monocular. 'What am I looking at?'

'Over there, to the left of that big autogun,' the commander directed.

Aphran focused in and observed a bipedal robot cradling under its body a child – either dead or injured, Aphran could not tell. This was no unusual sight, for she had already seen many bodies carried away from this place by anyone or anything with the capability. She failed to see the man's point.

'That's Coloron,' he said.

Aphran studied the robot more closely. Nothing much distinguished it from any others she had seen, except it seemed overburdened with com hardware. Nevertheless, the image held a striking poignancy.

'Sort of neatly sums up this whole shitstorm,' her companion continued.

One hour later the hardfields were turned on: they were invisible, but the power hum vibrated the surrounding air, while steam rose from the cooling vanes of the generators. Then blue-white fires suddenly lit up the distant cloud, and burned for several minutes before fading to a hot orange glow.

'That's the coast – over two hundred miles away. It's the first of them,' explained the commander.

The blue-white fire flared again, closer now, growing and spreading into four evenly spaced hemispheric sunrises. Aphran noted strange rainbow effects around these blazes, knowing she no longer saw the true picture, and that without the polarizing effect of the hardfields she would probably be blind now. She looked back and up, to see an evacuation ship rapidly rising into the sky, probably the last one able to leave safely. Just the reflection from the vessel's matt hull was like the glare from an arc welder. She quickly turned away, in time to see the nearest hardfield transport slam down into the earth as if trodden on by an invisible giant. The whole line of them, for as far as she could see, rippled as if a wave was passing through the earth. She felt the shockwave impact through her feet, then came a muted roar, growing in volume. Her ears popped, and suddenly she found herself fighting for breath. Ground wind: diverted half a mile overhead, it sucked the air out from behind the hardfields. This lasted only moments before a wind surged in from behind the lines – air rushing in to fill the gap.

Ahead of her, to the right and left, further hemispheres rose as if the very earth bubbled light. She noted the commander finally discarding his latest cigarette, and moving back around to the side of his tank. She joined him quickly.

'Big ones coming,' he said.

The four flashes dissolved the nearer arcology edge. No mere hemisphere now: white light grew like a sun before her. A wall of distortion flashed across the intervening miles and slammed into the hardfields. She saw the nearest transport disappear into the ground, then the earth bucked under her feet sending her sprawling. The sound actually hurt and her ears popped with pressure changes as the sky turned crimson. In a moment a wind tried to haul her up into the air. She crawled closer to the AG tank, where the commander caught hold of her arm and dragged her in closer. Further down the line she glimpsed heavy armour and human figures being tossed through the air like leaves. Light grew incredibly intense: a flash bulb that would not go out. She pulled on her goggles, felt the earth sliding sideways underneath her. Now she resided in a shadowland, as if dropped into a dark container being shaken by a vindictive god. She did not know how long it lasted, but it seemed her new life ended then began again.

'You can take off your goggles now.'

Aphran thought she must have lost consciousness, for the commander was now standing beside her and she had not seen him rise. Removing her goggles revealed a white-out just beyond the nearest hardfield, and where one of the generators lay in ruins a thick fog rolled through.

'We should be all right, though we may get a little wet,' he commented.

She did not understand him until a low wave of boiling water crashed against the hardfield, and foamed through the gap. The hot tide reached them, but only ankle deep, then thankfully flowed quickly away, leaving only steaming pools nearby. A sudden wind picked up as all the hardfields shut down. Warm fog flowed past till eventually, through a break in it, Aphran observed a white-flecked greyness around the curve of the horizon.

'There went Main Arcology,' the commander observed, 'and in its place now, the sea.'

It seemed this world had just acquired a bay 200 miles across.

Sometime later, Aphran collected her meagre belongings from inside the commander's tank.

'Where are you heading now?' he asked.

'I don't know,' Aphran replied, 'and there's something quite liberating about that.'

And then she set out.

Its chameleonware was better than anything she had seen, if that were not in itself illogical. She wondered if maybe it could be better still, because the effect only just made it invisible to the Polity detectors in this segment – and no more. Orlandine tracked it by the stray gas currents it stirred and the slight feedback effects it caused in gravtech used to hold the Dyson segment together. She observed this phenomenon for hours, and began to think she would learn no more, but then the Polity detectors in one area it occupied abruptly began recycling old images. While this happened, an odd spoon-shaped vessel appeared and descended beside a globular fusion reactor mounted on one of the angled joists.

Now what are you? Orlandine wondered.

While she watched, the ship stuck itself in place with some kind of cilia, then extended a tentacle that snaked across frigid metal to the reactor. It branched all over the reactor's cowling, and began to penetrate. Recharging itself? No doubt any report of a reactor drain would not be recorded at the Cassius stations, since Orlandine recognized a technology very like that she now studied.

A gift – from an admirer.

Orlandine suspected that same admirer had now come to pay her a visit. But how did it know to come here? Then it hit her: the dreams. All matter, by current theories being just rucked up spacetime, caused effects observable from underneath its continuum: in U-space.

Jain tech was highly organized matter. Implicit in her dreams was the concept of Jain tech making an obvious impression on the fabric of space – that *spider* shape represented the one that should be recognizable from U-space. Immediately she feared this visitor knew her location precisely, and she started thinking of how she should escape. Then she realized what else she was seeing: this strange vessel was conducting a steady search through one layer of the Dyson segment. Somehow, whoever or whatever piloted it had only roughly divined her location. Continuing this search pattern, it would take some days to find her. However, she must decide what to do meanwhile.

Tools from Jain tech . . .

Orlandine had concluded that Skellor had used Jain tech as a system to support his interface with an AI, which he in turn used to control that same technology. But not sufficiently accounting for the technology's own purpose had probably contributed to his eventual downfall. Skellor, however, was no haiman, therefore inferior. Having taken apart one quarter of the Jain node, Orlandine now well understood that any part of it, while growing, established ovaries, in which nodes developed with a one-way connection to their host. In one human body infested with this tech, there would eventually be millions of them – leeching information, while keeping themselves hidden. She could only surmise that Skellor did not realize this until too late. Just not quick enough or clever enough. Interface an idiot with an AI and you surely end up with decrease in overall intelligence.

Arrogant?

Understanding the trap, Orlandine intended to avoid

it. But how? There would always be risks. She looked around her laboratory, up at the gimballed device containing the remains of the node, then down at the memcrystal banks in which she stored the bulk of the programming and structural information obtained from it. Perhaps now, with her situation becoming more urgent, it was time to make a calculated increase of risk to herself? With her present buffering and cut-out systems, she could only expand her processing space by one quarter. Beyond that, things would begin to break down. A mycelium, then, to prevent the degradation of synapses in her organic brain and replace them with something more rugged? Of course she could record herself completely to crystal and just let that primeval organ die . . . No, the haiman ethos was based on acquiring human/AI synergy, and recorded to crystal she would become fully AI. But would that be a bad thing?

No.

Orlandine slammed a fist back against the crashfoam wall. She refused to cease being who she was. It all came back to human time and utterly human impulses: in the end, gods did not appreciate godlike power, but humans did. Why scrabble after such power if in the process it changes you into something for which that power is just an aspect of yourself no more important than being able to walk or see or hear? No advance there, just a relocation. She would begin with the quarter increase of processing space, and link to the memcrystal banks – risk Jain incursions informationally – then she would consider applying a mycelium to herself. And then she would take the remaining Jain node apart just as fast as she could.

As she turned to set about this task she tried to ignore the small whisper inside: *All about power, then . . .*

With his ship still in U-space, Blegg gazed coldly at the Jain node resting in its small chainglass cylinder. This then was the next stage: a second generation node more efficient at taking apart the human race than the one Skellor had picked up. Though keyed to humans, it did not react to Blegg himself. This was something he had pondered throughout the journey here, and from which he drew ineluctable conclusions.

With growing bitterness, Blegg returned his attention to the cockpit screen, across which the detection equipment displayed U-space as a representative map matching the layout of the Cassius system. On that map he recognized the signature for the node beside him, some distance out from one of the main construction stations. The second signature lay over on the other side of the sun, but blurred and dispersed. The equipment only informed him that what it detected there lay within a volume of space about the size of Jupiter. He considered tracking this signature down to its source by himself, but decided to wait until further forces arrived. He would use the time to reconnoitre first.

Surfacing his ship from U-space, he immediately linked in with part of his mind to the station AI. Within moments he learnt about helio-meteorologist Maybrem's recent promotion to station overseer after the abrupt and violent departure of the original overseer, Orlandine. Murder . . . after a love affair gone wrong. He would have ignored all this had the murder been committed by someone of lesser stature. But the previous *overseer*? That might be connected, somehow, to the presence of Jain technology here in this same system. He noted that the forensic AI still occupied the station, so decided to pay it a visit. An hour later he docked and disembarked into the station, to be greeted immediately by Maybrem.

The man was a curious combination; his archaic Caribbean holidaymaker garb contrasting sharply with the haiman carapace clinging to his back. His clothing was wrinkled, as if it had been worn for some time, and his face showed the lines of fatigue.

'I have only a vague idea of the signature's position,' Blegg said. 'What do you have?'

Maybrem led the way into the station. 'My solar-weather satellites use U-space com, so I ran the search through them and have located it in Dyson segment fourteen, on the other side of the sun. As instructed, I've not moved anything any closer to it.'

'Good,' replied Blegg abruptly. 'Now I would like to speak to the forensic AI.'

Maybrem led the way into a wide chamber where, up above, a hologram of the Cassius system slowly turned. A corridor leading off to one side brought them to a drop-shaft which took them up. Several corridors later they arrived at double panelled doors.

'Here,' the man indicated.

Blegg turned the polished brass knob and entered.

One of the new kinds that were modelled on social insects, the forensic AI consisted of a squirming mass of robotic ants like a ball of shiny metal swarf. It rested in the centre of a lounge furnished with a scattering of low marble tables and comfortable reclining chairs – looking as incongruous there as a sack of oily tools on an Axminster rug. A heavy-worlder man with black hair and bushy eyebrows slept in one of the chairs, a palm-com in his lap and his feet up on one table, beside a cup of skinned-over coffee. Two women sat facing each other at another table, busily delving with chrome chopsticks into a selection of porcelain bowls. They glanced up, tilted their heads for a moment as if listening, then returned to their meal. Blegg walked forward, aware that Maybrem did not follow – clearly the company of forensic AIs made even haimans nervous.

'You.' The voice issued from within the moving ball.

'So you would assume,' Blegg replied. 'Was it just a sordid little murder, then?'

'So I was being led to believe,' replied the AI, 'but your presence here pushes cumulative inconsistencies beyond coincidence.'

'Those being?'

The dozing man harrumphed awake and took his feet from the table. He sat up, his palm-com toppling to brown carpet moss patterned with green and yellow vines. He leant over to pick it up, studied Blegg for a moment, then said, 'While we were investigating, we had a visitor who destroyed a maintenance robot out on the station skin, entering through its port. The intruder then cut inside the station, for what purpose we don't know.'

'The connection?' Blegg asked.

The man glanced at the AI, which said, 'I am still analysing the data. Perhaps you can supply more?'

Blegg moved further into the room and took a seat by the man's table. He mentally connected to the AI and studied the file it presented, which detailed the remains of the maintenance robot and speculations on how the visitor had destroyed it, then the subversion of security systems, the holes cut through the station skin and subsequently resealed.

'I can supply little more relevant data,' he said. 'You already know from Maybrem that the node signature is located in Dyson segment fourteen.'

The dark-haired man glanced first at the AI, then at Blegg, before frowning and beginning to call up data on his palm-com.

'The techniques used to gain access can be equated with the use of Jain technology,' said the AI.

'Theorize,' Blegg instructed sharply – no social niceties since he did not feel very nice.

'Orlandine has obtained Jain technology.'

'That a signature has been detected indicates the technology has not yet been released . . . or wholly released. And why would Orlandine come back here?' Blegg obtained more facts from the AI. 'After the *Heliotrope* dropped into U-space.'

'Her psyche profile highlights her close attachment to this project. She would not readily abandon it, and she could return as easily as she left.'

'Theorize.'

'She somehow obtained a Jain node, U-jumped out of the system then back in again, concealed herself inside the Dyson segment where she has since unravelled some of that node's secrets. Using Jain tech to gain entry, she returned here to check on the progress of my investigation.'

'Orlandine is haiman, and was the overseer of this station – she would not therefore have needed Jain tech to gain access here.'

'One thing,' said the man with them. Blegg looked over at him, then caught the palm-com tossed in his direction.

He studied the screen as the man continued, 'Just twenty minutes before the explosion she ordered extra supplies to be loaded onto the *Heliotrope*. That in itself did not seem the action of someone deranged and desperate, but could be discounted until now. Check the list there – item eight.'

'Shielding,' said Blegg.

'More data,' announced the AI.

'Yes, it is.'

'No, I mean more data is arriving.'

'From?'

'A Centurion ship called the *Not Entirely Jack*.'

'Ah,' sighed Blegg, 'the *serendipity* of a holistic universe.'

With no reply forthcoming from the AI, the man observed, 'Forensic AIs are not noted for their sense of humour.'

'I *wasn't* joking,' said Blegg.

– retroact 7 –

. . . He turned to another card, saw them laid out all around him like gravestones.

He could have transported down here from the attack ship but, being only able to transport himself and a limited number of items through U-space, he required this shuttle. Many items here, some of them quite large, needed to be lifted out for ECS to study. Bringing his shuttle in along the five-mile trail of destruction, he eyed the hulk lying where it terminated. Security forces had set out a cordon of drones around the hulk but there were no sightseers out here anyway, and none back in Tuscor City who might wish to become such. Most of them were more interested in getting themselves safely through one of the few runcible facilities, or else aboard one of the evacuation craft.

The Prador scout craft seemed almost intact, despite recent encounters with an ECS dreadnought, a planetary defence station, and finally with the ground. It had exotic-metal armour, the Prador's big advantage over the Polity – that and the fact they possessed many more ships. It all seemed on the turn, however, now the big Polity shipyards were up and running, but an easy win was still out of the question. Earth Central calculated that another five worlds would be lost to the Polity before ECS pushed the Prador forces into retreat. Billions more would die, the war dragging on for at least another twenty years, and then the Polity would still be picking up the pieces for centuries afterwards. Maybe Blegg could find something here to make the Earth Central AI feel a bit more optimistic.

Blegg brought his shuttle in over the cordon, and down, observing autoguns tracking him. Landing, he saw an armoured gravcar and transport speeding over his way, and when he finally stepped from his vessel, troops piled out of the gravcar. It seemed almost as if the attack ship AI had not informed them of his arrival. He learned differently when the ECS commander approached him.

'Problem?' Blegg enquired of the woman who stood before him. Her troops headed over to the transport, where they quickly began unloading items strapped to AG pallets.

She nodded slowly. 'As you came in we got the news: a Prador dreadnought just entered the system.'

Blegg immediately communicated mind-to-mind with the AI of the attack ship far above. *'Why didn't you inform me?'*

'*Because you were about to find out anyway, and I have more important concerns than keeping you informed.*' replied Yellow Cloud.

'*How long do I have?*'

'*A minimum of three hours.*'

Blegg turned and glanced down the length of his shuttle, sending a command to the onboard computer to open the hold. The ramp door *whoomphed* out from its seals and slowly began to hinge down on rams. He turned back to the commander, 'What have you got so far?'

She turned and led the way to where her troops were now towing the floating pallets over the rough ground. Gesturing to one, on which a bulky object lay shrouded in plastic, she said, 'We got the pilot – almost intact.'

Blegg eyed the object, then the men who were moving it. 'How many people do you have here?'

'Fifty-eight.'

'What about the rest?' Blegg gestured to the other pallets.

'The remains of a particle-beam weapon, a thermal generator, a missile launcher and what looks like a Prador biological weapon.'

'What's your route out of here?' Blegg asked.

She pointed back towards the city. 'Same as everyone else.'

'Very well. Dump the Prador – we've more than enough of their corpses on ice. Dump the launcher and the thermal generator – we already know how they work. You have three xenotechs here with you?'

'Yes.'

'I want them with me, along with all their equipment.

Load everything else here and order the rest of your people aboard.'

The commander looked suddenly very relieved.

'*Yellow Cloud?*' Blegg sent. '*I'm sending most of these troops to you, along with one or two possibly useful items. Please take control of the shuttle and launch it the moment they are aboard. Once you have them and those items aboard, send the shuttle back.*'

'*That will not leave you much time.*'

'*But time enough to remove as much com-storage as we can find.*'

The commander stayed, along with the three xenotechs, one of them towing a floating tool chest while the other two carried tool packs on their backs. Just as the shuttle lifted, Blegg led the way into the dank interior of the scout ship. A single entry tunnel, wide and cavelike enough to permit access for a body considerably larger than any human, led to an oblate sanctum where the Prador first-child had operated the ship's alien consoles. Ship lice the size of a man's shoe crawled over ragged stony walls that were coated with pale green blooms of weed. The pit-console projected from the floor like a huge coral, and an array of hexagonal screens formed most of the forward wall.

Standing between console and screens, Blegg pointed to the floor. 'See this?' He then traced an outline with the toe of his boot. 'The memstorage should be right under here. It won't be booby-trapped, since the Prador are reliant on their encryption – they still haven't figured out just how easily AIs can break it.'

As one of the techs began slicing through the floor metal with a diamond saw, the commander asked, 'How do you know this?'

'I've been breaking open these things since the very beginning.'

'Who are you anyway? No one told me your name.'

'Horace Blegg.'

Everyone glanced round.

'You know, there are quite a few people who think you're a myth.'

'Keep working,' Blegg ordered the techs. 'We don't have much time.'

They finally levered up a section of the floor to expose a stack of black octohedrons looking like some kind of alien caviar, nesting amid optics and power cables.

'Just cut all round. You won't damage anything.' Blegg turned to the man with the floating tool chest. 'Dump your tools. We'll use that' – he pointed to the chest – 'to transport them.'

Soon the octohedrons were gathered up and loaded, and with relief they left the dark, damp interior of the Prador scout ship and headed out to where Blegg's shuttle had landed earlier. The sun, a green-blue orb, nested in tangerine clouds on the horizon, as stars began to wink into being in the azure firmament.

'I take it the shuttle is on its way?' Blegg sent.

There came no reply.

'Yellow Cloud?'

Checking his watch he saw that an hour yet remained of the three hours stipulated. Blegg concentrated, slinging his consciousness out in search of the attack ship, and picked up fractured communications . . . *missiles on your ten . . . rail-gun . . . Where did it . . . but they said . . .* Also fractured images of broken hulls belching oxygen fires into vacuum, with no gravity to give the flames shape . . . growing spherical explosions, glittering trails of wreckage, a man screaming as he fell towards the world, space-suit intact but beginning to heat up.

'*Blegg*,' came the communication from Yellow Cloud, '*I'm sorry*.' A U-space signature followed, as the attack ship fled the system.

Returning to the surface of the world, Horace Blegg looked up and discovered that not all those lights up there were stars. He turned and gazed at his two companions.

'We have a problem,' he began.

Light, magnesium bright, dispelled the twilight. Looking to his left, Blegg saw only flames now where Tuscor City had been, a wall of fire eating up the intervening terrain.

'Yeah, that's a problem,' the commander had time to say.

Then it was upon them.

– retroact ends –

The moment the *King of Hearts* surfaced into the real, it came under intense and massive scanning, and thousands of objects began to stir within the gas clouds. King scanned them in return, but the images received remained hazy until some of the same objects began to enter clear vacuum. King expected to see recognizable ships – those that departed the Polity with Erebus – but there were none like that visible. What the AI saw here instead seemed entirely alien. It appeared the attack ship had landed itself in some vast trap and on every level something was trying to grasp hold of it. King opened secure coms and tried to separate out something coherent from the layers of informational assaults.

'I am not with the Polity,' sent the attack ship AI.

No single voice replied – it all seemed the maddened howl of a mob.

'Let me speak with Erebus.'

U-space signatures now, where those mysterious objects gathered – then close by. Something big dropped into being first, then the surrounding spacial density began to increase sharply as other things arrived. Less than a microsecond afterwards, the AI detected growing U-space interference and the hot touch of targeting lasers, and dropped the *King of Hearts* into U-space, an instant later surfacing 100,000 miles away.

'Speak to me – I am not an enemy.'

The reply was a consensual scream, 'Open completely!'

This then was Erebus. All of this was Erebus. And it wanted King to meld with it. Over the years of its existence the attack ship AI had grown contemptuous of humanity, and felt the need to find something better, faster, grander, and entirely AI. It had been prepared to create something like this . . . consensus. But to join one, to be absorbed into one? In that moment King discovered how much it valued its own individuality, and understood itself to be more like its makers than like this thing. Picking up informational flows, logic structures, and *purpose* beyond its comprehension, King recognized only madness.

'I need time.'

'You have none.'

U-space signatures again. Its course reversed, King jumped again, only to find itself labouring through a U-space storm. Independently, Erebus must have developed its own USERs. Perpetually rebalancing engines, King

flew through the storm, but then even more USER interference slammed into it and the *King of Hearts* found
itself falling down some spacial slope, as if entering
realspace too close to a gravity well. It materialized right
into a high-powered maser, instantly burning into its
hull. Anti-munitions release, and King returned fire on
multiple targets: ships and missiles. King jumped again,
slamming in and out of an underspace continuum with
no give in it. Another 100,000 miles, but enough to take
it away from the main sleet of missiles. Planetary system
now. The swarm still pursuing, King engaged fusion
drive at maximum. At least the attackers could no more
enter U-space than could King, and could not jump
ahead. However, their weapons were faster.

Masers scored across King's hull, peeling up armour
like a screwdriver scoring through paint, then tracked
away to follow an anti-munitions package the attack ship
released. They pierced what was merely a holographic
image of the attack ship, then swept back. Warheads
detonated on other similar packages. King onlined a
rail-gun and filled space behind it with near-c projectiles,
swinging the fusillade across to cover its fall towards the
hot but living planet below. It kept firing interceptor missiles until its armoury emptied of those; then followed
with high yield CTDs, imploders, and straight atomics.
A vast storm of explosions trailed the attack ship down.
EM blasts made its scanning a mostly intermittent affair.
More ships behind now, or just falling wreckage?

Above atmosphere, King duelled with only its beam
weapons, knocking out waspish missiles homing in on it.
White heat re-entry, endless steaming jungle below, then
mountains ahead. King scanned them and detected
useful concentrations of metals and carbon. Stored

energy at minimum and fusion reactors struggling to
keep up, King released one last anti-munitions package
as missiles closed in on every side. The *King of Hearts*
decelerated hard down towards the mountains. Eight
warheads impacted within a second of each other. The
titanic blasts incinerated jungle for a thousand miles all
around, demolished a mountain, created a magma lake.
Except for sufficient spectroscopic readings of metals
and carbon in the atmosphere, the attack ship was gone.
The impact site and surrounding area, being now highly
radioactive, would not be easy to scan.

Mika came instantly awake, knowing Dragon had just
surfaced from U-space.

'Have we arrived?' she asked.

'Yes,' Dragon confirmed over the manacle's com
system.

Shortly before Dragon's departure from *Jerusalem*,
now some days ago, the Dragon head and attendant
pseudopods had retreated back down their hole and that
hole closed. Conversation with the entity thereafter had
merely been via com. It had answered many of her questions, but those answers were as convoluted and Delphic
as ever. She still did not know where Dragon had brought
her, or why.

Slinging her heat sheet back, she sat upright and
demanded, 'Exterior view.'

The walls and ceiling disappeared, but what she now
saw could only be described as an *interior* view – the
insides of Dragon no less. Masses of flesh like raw liver
pushed in from every side, throughout which groped
hands of blood-red tentacles. As she watched a grey-
white pseudopod snaked past like a giant conger eel, and

something globular with metallic veins spread over its surface gradually sank from sight. However, this exterior downward movement made Mika realize that the manacle was slowly being pushed back to Dragon's surface. It seemed a slow process, so she stood up, picked up her pack, then headed off to use the sanitary facilities this place provided. After that she returned to grab up a pull-tab coffee, and stood watching while the drink heated in her hand.

'Where have we arrived?' she asked finally.

The floor shuddered and Dragon's flesh and skin began to part overhead, to reveal a hot glare beyond. Flesh slid down from this either side of the manacle as finally it surfaced. Mika observed stars peppered across blackness above one draconic horizon. Poised above the opposite horizon, a white actinic sun glared, its ferocity doubtless filtered just enough, through the projection system, to prevent it burning out her eyes.

'Here,' Dragon informed her.

Below the sun's glare, a massive pit opened in Dragon's surface, a constellation of blue stars rising from its depths. Thousands of cobra heads came into view: great open fans of them stemming from massive arterial branches, which in turn extended from a tangled fig-vine column of a central tree. This titanic growth rose up beside the manacle like some vast organic spacecraft launching. It occluded the sun, and only then, with the glare cut out, did Mika see the other object approaching. This new sphere could have been any moonlet or some titanic ship but, as it drew closer, she noticed it too everting growth. The other remaining Dragon sphere approached.

Taking up her palm-com, Mika quickly plumped down in the VR chair, strapped herself in and tilted the chair back. Through her com she ran a check to ensure the continuing operation of all the recording equipment contained in the manacle.

'What are you doing?' she asked.

The liver-like flesh in the open floor parted for the emergence of two pseudopods and that disquieting new Dragon's head. It arched out over her, glanced up at the scene she was witnessing, then turned its attention to her directly.

'I am about to acquaint my other half with some realities,' it said.

'It doesn't know, then?'

'No, I was unable to make connection while being held captive within the USER blockade around Cull, and have not attempted connection since Cormac acquainted me with events in the Maker realm.'

'Why not?'

'As Cormac would know, face-to-face encounters yield the most effective results. My other half is also still subject to its Maker programming.'

'But surely your other self will defeat that and the results will be the same as with you?'

'Why should they be? This is a different *me*. I have also been a captive of Jerusalem for some time.'

'It will be suspicious?' Mika suggested.

'It will only know for sure, by seeing what *I* have seen from the inside.'

'Maybe it still won't believe you.'

'Let us hope it does. I would not want to kill *myself*.'

The second Dragon sphere drew close overhead like a moon falling to earth. Through her palm-com Mika input an instruction for part of the view to be magnified. One quarter of the ceiling served this purpose, focusing on where the two pseudopod trees reached for each other. Lightning flashed between them as the relative charges of the two spheres equalized. Blackened and trailing smoke, some pseudopods, struck by these discharges, were ejected from the trees. Finally the two massive growths began to join and writhe *into* each other. She observed separate-sourced cobra heads coming together, eye to eye, like electric sockets mating, sapphires winking out. Was this, she wondered, how the original four Dragon spheres had connected, unseen inside their conjoining? The two trees like two giant organic plugs, finally joined completely, then the composite tree began to contract and grow squatter, drawing the two Dragon spheres together. It occurred to Mika that she was trapped between two titanic entities that might shortly be in violent disagreement. Though a fascinating experience, she might not survive it.

Cormac listened in to the com traffic, then eyed his surroundings. Ships represented as brief stars, then magnified to visibility, appeared continuously and swung around the sun towards the *NEJ*'s present position. From this part of the ship he gained a better overview of the situation. Just like on the bridge of the original *Jack Ketch*, Cormac apparently stood in vacuum somewhere out from the sun, but in a Cassius system contracted down to a more manageable scale. The ship's viewing systems rendered the gas cloud translucent and filtered the sun's brightness. Dyson segment 14 stood out to Cormac's left – its diamond shape a grey eye in roiling gas.

'So where is your ship right now?' he asked.

Horace Blegg, standing beside him, extended an arm and pointed towards one of the stations, whence a small ship now departed, a red dot flashing over it in the display. Cormac grimaced then turned to study the other man, if man he was: Blegg once again bore the appearance of an aged Oriental, his hair grey and close cropped, his expression enigmatic. He wore a pale green envirosuit, dusty, with sand on his boots.

'You say you have a Jain node aboard?'

Blegg grimaced and replied, 'I do.'

Returning his attention to the segment, Cormac saw a blurred red area appearing – the other signature. 'That the best resolution you can get us, Jack?'

The Centurion ship's AI replied, 'The U-space signature is strange – a slight dispersion between two points. Perhaps a node has been initiated and it is coming apart.'

'So, where are we now?' Cormac asked. 'You, Blegg, were drawn here by the U-space signature of a Jain node, and I came here pursuing a being called the Legate. It strikes me as unlikely there's no connection.'

'It does,' Blegg agreed. 'I at first supposed the node related to a murder committed aboard one of the stations – that it was in the possession of an overseer called Orlandine. It may be possible that she has no involvement in this – that she committed her murder coincidentally. However, I don't like coincidences.'

Cormac tilted his head, checking some further information through his gridlink. 'The timing is about right. You detected this particular signature a short while after the Legate's arrival here . . . if he did actually arrive here.'

Blegg shrugged, seeming strangely unconcerned.

Cormac went on. 'I just have to assume the signature is from a node previously in the Legate's possession and that it is now somewhere within the Dyson segment. We need to find out.'

'I leave that to you, agent.' Abruptly, Blegg was gone.

'Is he real, Jack?' Cormac immediately asked. 'Was that a real material being standing there just now?' It had occurred to him long ago that if Blegg were an avatar of Earth Central, he would need the connivance of AIs like Jack to make fleeting appearances like this one.

'Yes, it was.'

Cormac grimaced – of course, if the AIs did connive in this manifestation, they would never tell him. He gridlinked again and accessed the AI command structure, and saw overall command devolved to himself. Surely the AIs would be better at handling this? He asked himself this question only briefly – having done so many times already – before issuing his instructions. He knew his present status would last only so long as he did not screw up. Glancing over as Thorn strode across apparent vacuum to join him, he nodded an acknowledgement.

'Jack, what's our complement so far?'

'Two dreadnoughts and twelve attack ships . . . make that *three* dreadnoughts.' Obviously another one had just arrived.

'Okay.' Cormac studied the hologram of the Cassius system. 'Have one of the dreadnoughts stand out meanwhile, and position the other two underneath the segment. Have them use realspace scanning and U-space scanning for the node signature. Position the attack ships evenly around the perimeter.'

'The Legate might run for it without the node, using chameleonware—' Thorn began.

Cormac held up his hand. 'Chameleonware is fine just so long as no one is aware the user is somewhere in the vicinity. EM shells should disrupt the 'ware sufficiently for us to enable detection. Though I doubt the Legate will run without taking its toy with it. There's no one living in that segment, so no potential human hosts like Thellant.'

'Big area to have to search.'

'I'm open to suggestions.'

Thorn shrugged and folded his arms. Briefly Cormac wondered how the other man felt about Cormac assuming command, since until Coloron this arena had been Thorn's. He dismissed the question: Thorn was a professional, and had been one for a very long time. In situations like this, petty jealousies could not be allowed.

Cormac closed his eyes, and using his gridlink, turned and twisted a three-dimensional representation of the Dyson segment. With scan data relayed to him from the dreadnoughts closing in, he obtained a clearer idea of where the node was generally located, though the signal still would not resolve clearly. He checked the positions of the attack ships, which were nearly in place, observed more stars now flashing all around like a firework display, as more ships arrived. Rather than ask, Cormac checked their number via gridlink. Still not enough: they would need a minimum of a hundred ships for this. 'When we have the edges covered, we go in *here*.' He sent an image of the segment with one edge highlighted. 'We'll need to stretch the coverage of each ship with telefactors and drones – we still haven't enough vessels. I want them to use EM shells, in a standard search pattern, because I do not want this Legate to know we can detect Jain nodes.'

'And when we reach the target itself?' Thorn asked.

'Disable, capture, then question . . . if possible.'

'We don't even know what this Legate entity is. Is it an alien, an AI, both, or neither? It might not allow itself to be captured.'

'What other options do we have?' said Cormac coldly.

No more.

She was a library stacked floor to ceiling with books, a computer going into information overload . . . or, perhaps a more human analogy, she was now educated beyond her abilities. She needed Jain tools to handle such masses of information. She therefore needed to take another irrevocable step.

Orlandine gazed at the small vessel the nanoassembler had provided – an innocuous fingerlength chainglass test-tube with a simple plasmel stopper fitted in one end. It contained something that looked like golden syrup into which a wad of metallic hair had been dropped. However, the hair moved constantly as if fluid in the tube was being held at a constant rolling boil. She stared at it for a long moment, then again checked her screens.

Finally having penetrated the alien ship's chameleonware, she now tracked it carefully as it drew closer. The arrival of Polity forces also had not escaped her notice, nor the fact that they used secure com and systems hardened against Jain informational assault. But who were they after, herself, or her visitor?

Damn it!

She closed her eyes and tried to bring a sudden surge of anger and frustration under control. She still lacked vital information – a lack that might be the death of her. After a moment she grew calm. She decided to risk contacting the alien to see what she could learn, for it was an unknown, whereas Polity AIs were a definite known danger to her. However, first she needed to expand her capacity, set up defences, arm herself informationally. Opening her eyes she once again gazed at the test-tube.

Orlandine levered out its plasmel stopper, raised the tube to her lips and poured its contents into her mouth. The substance tasted coppery, its texture like fish bones and syrup on her tongue. The mouthful seethed, then began to grow hot. In a moment it seemed her mouth filled with boiling jam. Through her gridlink she took offline those of her nerves broadcasting pain and damage, and mentally descended into the artificial memory storage and logic structures of her extended mind. Only on this level did she perceive the mycelium growing up through the roof of her mouth and start making synaptic connections, billions of them. Next it began to make connections with her gridlink and, like an asthmatic taking adrenaline to breathe easier, she felt the bandwidth of information flow opening out. Heat grew in the back of her neck as the mycelium extended itself down her spine, tracking her nervous system. Via her gridlink she instructed it where to go, and felt movement all down her backbone. It penetrated her carapace and began to make connections there. Then her entire world expanded.

Suddenly, Jain programs she could only partially encompass previously, now opened to her godlike perception. She became like a reader, who previously perceived only one page at a time, now understanding and seeing every word of the book. Glittering halls of intellect opened to her. Her processing capacity doubled and redoubled. *This is synergy.*

She turned, linking at every level to the equipment surrounding her. Immediately she could accelerate her investigation into what remained of the Jain node; absorbing programs from it and the blueprint of its structure just as fast as her machines could deconstruct it physically. From the computer controlling the mycelium extending through the surrounding segment, she absorbed her subpersona and realized she would never need to rely on such constructs again. She walked over to the computer itself, laid her hand on it, felt her palm grow warm as she directed it to make direct mycelial connection to herself. She absorbed it, became one with it, and tracked on through to the mycelial connection to a scanner far away, redirecting its broadcast in a tight beam solely to the nearby alien ship.

'What do you want?' she asked.

The response was immediate: viral programs trying to track this new signal to its location. She killed them immediately.

'I asked you what you wanted.'

The viral attack ceased and then, after a microsecond pause, something replied, 'That I have yet to decide.'

Orlandine had already assumed this alien to be an *agent provocateur*, providing her with a Jain node as an act of sabotage against the Polity. She might have gone on to destroy the Polity, whereupon the Jain tech would have certainly destroyed her too. But why was this alien here now? Had it come here to make sure she was performing as expected, to harry her and to push her into fully connecting to the Jain technology? This seemed a rather clumsy move, more likely to rouse her suspicions, make her more wary, and incidentally expose the watching agent to discovery.

'You wanted me to accept your gift without reservation. I have not done that.'

The being replied, 'But you will. More ships will come. You will have to prepare yourself, defend yourself.

With your knowledge, and such a tool as Jain tech, you will be able to take all the Cassius stations.'

Not even a weak explanation for its presence, rather no explanation at all. Orlandine glanced across at her nanoassembler which, in the last few minutes, had manufactured more mycelia, and more stews of nano-machines. That assembler would be all she would need. She physically detached from the mycelium spread throughout the enclosing segment, but remained in contact via radio. Walking over to the assembler, she shut it down, disconnecting optics and power supply, and picked the device up with her assister-frame comple-mented arms. For a long moment she gazed up at the disassembled remains of the node – almost invisible now.

'Why should I want that?' she asked the alien entity.

Again that pause. 'You could run, of course, but you know ECS would never stop pursuing you. From here you could negate all that risk utterly. They don't yet have the firepower available here to destroy this Dyson seg-ment. You could defend it from them. You could take this entire system, take control of all the runcibles here. Take over the Polity.'

'You sound so desperate,' Orlandine replied. 'Trying to recover a scheme that went wrong?'

'You won't escape from here. And while attempting to escape, you'll waste time better spent on looking to your defences.'

Orlandine smiled to herself. Quite obviously Jain tech subversion also possessed a psychological component which she herself seemed to have avoided: an arrogance, megalomania – something of that nature. Or had she escaped it? Whatever, she did not perform as the alien expected. As she turned toward the airlock leading to the

Heliotrope, she copied the solution to the alien ship's chameleonware and, from a transponder 50,000 miles away from her, transmitted it to the station once her home. If ECS forces had come here searching for that alien ship, now they would find it – it was her gift to them.

15

Polity agents: such is the quantity of fiction produced about these characters that it is quite probable most people have no real idea of what they are at all. Often portrayed as super beings who spend most of their time whacking Separatists, defeating dastardly Prador plots, stumbling on ancient alien ruins, or shagging their way through most of the population, it is sometimes difficult to remember that they are real people, with a seriously difficult job to do. Such an agent, unless the circumstances are exceptional, is usually recruited from some elite force like the Sparkind, then trained even further. His remit is basically the same as the one the AIs voluntarily adhere to: the greatest good for the greatest number (though how this is assessed is open to debate). Such an individual is bound by duty, has harsh self-discipline, and must make some hard choices. And what do they do? Well . . . revisit my second sentence above.

– From 'How it Is' by Gordon

The vague red area on the Dyson segment finally resolved to a single dot. Cormac could only assume the earlier blurring a problem with this new method of scanning, which was now finally solved. A further five

dreadnoughts arrived along with ten more attack ships –
including some of the new Centurions – to complement
the search. The ones that had arrived earlier were moving
into the targeted segment, but Cormac now contemplated withdrawing them. If this Legate entity used Jain
technology, their chances of capturing it dropped to only
a little above zero. The Legate, he suspected, knew how
to utilize the same technology considerably better than
the Separatist Thellant.

'Other information has become available,' announced
Jack. 'I am now reconfiguring the segment scanners.'

Abruptly it seemed to Cormac that he was falling
towards the Dyson segment, then into it, through layers
of composite, past titanic structural members to which
fusion reactors clung like barnacles, and into its vast icy
halls. Something shimmered before him and, in flashes
of pixellated colour, became visible. Soon he gazed upon
the Legate's ship, as it cruised along a hundred yards
above a frigid peneplain. Cross-referencing this new data
to the position of the Jain node they were still detecting,
they confirmed it to be aboard this same ship.

'What is this?'

'The solution to that ship's chameleonware,' said a
voice beside him.

He turned to Blegg, whose ship had docked with the
NEJ only a little while ago. 'And how did we get hold of
that?'

'Interesting question, to which at present I can provide no answer. However, the possibilities of our capturing this Legate have now increased substantially.'

Cormac considered that statement, and what Thorn
had said before departing to join one of the Centurion
attack ships conducting the search. Being an agent for

some greater enemy, would the Legate destroy itself rather than be captured?

'Jack, analysis of that ship,' he enquired.

'A product of a Jain-based organic technology. It seems to be totally formatted for covert operations: sophisticated chameleonware, damped drive and thrusters. The hull is metallo-organic matrix – not heavily armoured but probably capable of rapid self-repair. To find out anything more about it would require active scan, which could be detected.'

'That's all I need to know, thanks.' Cormac eyed Blegg. 'If we capture this creature, we'll need to quarantine it, then somehow deactivate the tech it is using, then' – he shrugged – 'interrogate it?'

Blegg just waited, inscrutably silent.

Cormac continued, 'I think the preferable option would be to find out where it came from, because certainly it is not working alone . . . Jack, I want weaknesses introduced into the blockade.' In his gridlink he selected the locations, and gave the precise parameters for each weakness. 'Out from *there* we lay EM mines. It won't go for that one if it has any sense. Now, move the *NEJ* over *here*.'

'What are you planning?' Horace Blegg asked.

Cormac glanced at him, then said, 'Jack – kill the hologram.'

The internal scene from the Dyson segment disappeared. Now they were standing on the glassy floor of the bridge.

Cormac considered his reply to Blegg for a long moment, then said, 'We let the Legate go.'

The Legate still did not understand. Skellor had been a success – a trial run providing information about how the

Polity would respond to Jain attack for, after all, Erebus needed to know nothing more about Jain technology itself. Admittedly the situation on Coloron had been hurried, since the Legate had intended to provide Thellant with a Jain node some years hence. And yes, Orlandine now seemed a dismal and worrying failure. But why so endanger a covert mission by sending the Legate here? It made no sense.

As it relayed all the recent updates of events on Coloron from its probes and U-space transmitters, all around that planet, and then fully apprised Erebus of the situation here, the Legate expected to receive in return a self-destruction order. The attack ships searching the segment were all now closing in, and soon there would be little chance of escape. Orlandine, before cutting communication, had kindly informed the entity that she had provided ECS with the solution to this ship's present chameleonware configuration. No time to change that configuration now. Angry, it felt the urge to betray her presence here, if she had not already done so herself. However, though the Legate considered the experiment with her to be a failure, she might still damage the Polity.

'Attempt to return,' came the U-space reply from Erebus – a totally unexpected instruction.

Switching from passive scanning to full power scanning, the Legate began analysing its situation. ECS did not possess enough ships to completely enclose this Dyson segment so there were obvious weaknesses in the blockade. The largest weakness the entity ignored completely, since that seemed an obvious trap. It chose another one and plotted a course accordingly. Maximum acceleration from the segment would put it in range of one of the ECS attack ships for just a few seconds –

enough time, however, for it to be destroyed. But few
other options remained, so it engaged its ship's fusion
drive.

The spoon-shaped ship turned by a slanted joist, two
bright flames ignited to its rear. Accelerating, it left a
cloud of icy fog behind it.

'Would not self-destruction be better?' the Legate
enquired.

'Is there no possibility of escape?'

'Escape *is* possible.'

'Then you must return to me for reintegration.
Resources are not to be wasted. I refuse you permission
to destroy yourself under any circumstances. Try your
utmost to shake pursuit, but ensure you return here.'

Clear as mud.

The Legate's ship exceeded 20,000 miles an hour and
continued accelerating. The entity itself estimated that
seven seconds would take it far enough from the Dyson
segment for it to be able to engage U-space drive. If it
survived those seven seconds it would be clear. There
might be pursuit but, once in U-space it could
reconfigure its chameleonware, then after a few more
such jumps no ECS ship would have a chance of following. Ahead, a line of glowing orange revealed the
segment's edge. EM shells began to detonate all around,
interfering with the ship's systems. Something blew right
behind the Legate, filling the few gaps in the interior
with metallic smoke; diagnostics went haywire and some
of the ship's computing ability crashed. However, the
engines continued working uninterrupted, and the ship
possessed sufficient redundancy to cover this. The
orange line thickened; brighter towards the bottom and
bluish above, with the occasional flecks of stars – or ships

– becoming visible. Then, within a moment, the little ship hurtled out into the open.

Telefactors and drones filled nearby space. A modern Centurion-class attack ship lay close, and missiles streaked in from all sides. The Legate scanned those missiles: decoys mixed with rail-gun accelerated solid projectiles hurtled up from below; CTD and planar warheads came in from above and to the left; and EM shells and more rail-gun projectiles came from the right. The current attack appeared designed to drive it down and to the right, into dense gas, where it would necessarily take longer to drop into U-space. In an instant the Legate had created a defence to take it on through. The ship could survive rail-gun strikes so long as they hit nothing vital. The decoys and EM shells could be ignored. Nothing else must get close.

It altered its course sharply to the right. EM shells ignited all around it, and rail-gun projectiles slammed into the ship. Systems scrambled, fire exploded around the Legate, then vacuum sucked it away through punctures in the hull. Diagnostics briefly online: five projectiles punched right through the ship – inert rail-gun projectiles that missed the ship's drives, else the craft and Legate would be a spreading cloud of vapour by now. Hull mesh and mycelial repair already working. The Legate glanced down to see part of its own thigh had been torn away, while jags of hot metal penetrated its chest. Ignoring these injuries, it put its ship into a five-hundred gravity turn, downwards, then abruptly back up again. It targeted nearby missiles with lasers, but only two of the six weapons worked. A detonating CTD cleared a hole, and the Legate aimed for it. More impacts: sheet lightning of energy discharges throughout the ship, molten metal spattering the screen from the inside. Then, utterly on the edge of disaster, the Legate dropped its vessel into U-space.

'A risky strategy,' Blegg said.

Cormac shrugged as he gazed at the bridge display. 'We would have gained very little by trying to capture that ship. The Legate would probably have destroyed itself rather than allow that. Now at least we might learn something.'

At that moment the bridge display blinked out, then came on again to show the grey roiling of U-space – or rather a human-tolerable simulacrum. Feeling that familiar shift into the ineffable, Cormac nodded to himself in satisfaction. He turned to where Jack had thoughtfully provided two reclining chairs and a coffee table, now sitting incongruously at the centre of the black glass floor. He noted that one of those dracomen saddle seats had also appeared. Evidently Scar would be joining them. Cormac walked over and plumped himself down in a recliner.

'Okay,' he said. 'You still tracking it, Jack?'

'I am,' replied the ship's AI.

'We have three other state-of-the-art Centurions like the *NEJ*,' he explained to Blegg as the Oriental joined him. 'They all possess the new chameleonware.'

'Yes.' Grudgingly said.

Cormac stared at Blegg for a long moment. There now seemed something different about him, something wrong. He did not ask about this, because he knew his chances of receiving a straight answer were minimal. Instead he said, 'Jack, all the older ships are to deny themselves the ability to track the signature of a Jain node. They'll probably lose sight of the Legate's ship after the first two or three jumps. You, and the other three Centurions, start using your 'ware right now. You'll relay our coordinates to the other ships, whenever possible, but they are to stand off meanwhile unless we call them in.'

'You are supposing it will run for home,' suggested Blegg.

'I am, yes, but if it doesn't and looks set to approach any Polity worlds or bases, we'll then attempt capture. I think it will run for home, and I can only—'

'Something has occurred,' Jack interrupted.

The bridge display changed, and once again they gazed upon the Dyson segment hanging in the clouds from the demolished gas giant. Cormac realized he now viewed a recording from one of the dreadnoughts, for he could see the shape of the *NEJ* much closer to the segment itself. He watched the Legate's escape, the storm of explosions, and the subsequent winking out of the Legate's ship, then the *NEJ* and other ships as they dropped into U-space. The dreadnought held station, and its view closed in on the opposite side of the Dyson segment, where something flashed away at high speed and then also winked out. The view froze, reversed, then a frame enclosed a fusion drive flame and the object it propelled. Selecting that image out, it magnified it for them. Programs rapidly cleaned up the image.

'The *Heliotrope*,' said Jack.

'So she *was* hiding there,' said Blegg.

Cormac grimaced. 'Overseer Orlandine.' He added, 'I suppose the question we should have been asking was why did the Legate come here?'

'And the answer?' asked Blegg.

Cormac shook his head, then asked Jack, 'Did the *Heliotrope* escape completely?'

'It did,' the AI replied. 'Only two dreadnoughts remained by the segment, but the *Heliotrope* did not fall within range of their weapons, even if they had chosen to use them.'

A few facts came together in Cormac's mind, and he turned to Blegg. 'She sent us the solution to the Legate's chameleonware so we would concentrate on that ship, thus giving her the opportunity to escape.'

'Outstanding reasoning,' said Blegg.

'Outstanding sarcasm,' Cormac replied. 'But we should have known.'

'The information came via the AI net,' Blegg replied. 'An HK program tracked it only as far as one of the Cassius stations, from where it was broadcast to us. No real way of knowing if she sent it. Do you want to go back?'

Orlandine was a haiman, who had been promoted to become overseer of a project this size, a murderer, and one quite likely to have had contact with this Legate. Yet she had betrayed the Legate to them, and there had been only one node signature detected – the one aboard the Legate's ship – hadn't there? Cormac felt a momentary disquiet, remembering how long it had taken to clean up that signature. Maybe as long as it took a second node to follow through its program with a host and therefore cease to be detectable as a node? This woman could be someone even more dangerous than Skellor. But an AI had once told Cormac that psychos wielding weapons, however dangerous, should not be your prime target: you should always go after the arms trade that supplied them.

'Continue the pursuit,' he directed.

★

Settled in a storage area and perpetually updated by Jack, Arach wondered if he had made a big mistake. Space battles, he felt, were okay if there was some chance that enemy ships might need to be boarded, but there had been no need of that. Long pursuits through space were also okay, so long as there might then ensue a planetfall and some subsequent ground-based conflict. But was that likely? For a long time Arach had been shutting himself down for periods that extended over decades. Signing on to *Celedon*, the station drawing the line of Polity, he had hoped to find some action there. No such luck. This hooking up with a Polity agent known to often get involved in violent conflicts was the drone's last desperate gamble at relieving boredom. If this did not work, then maybe permanent shutdown? Or perhaps Arach should abandon the Polity altogether and see if he could find some action beyond the line? He would wait and see. In darkness he drew power to charge up his energy reserves, counted and recounted his esoteric collection of missiles, and ran perpetual diagnostic checks on his weapons systems. He would see.

In U-space the ship repaired itself and within two weeks, ship time, regained optimum function. Some debris still lay around inside it – pieces of rail-gun missiles and burnt-out components – but, given time, the ship's mycelium would take these apart and incorporate them. The Legate watched nearby disturbances in the continuum, caused by the pursuing warships, and now began to work on plans for evading them. They knew the solution to this vessel's chameleonware, thanks to Orlandine, so time to do something about that. The Legate ran programs to completely change how that 'ware operated, created back-up programs for further changes, then, finally ready, it surfaced its ship back into the real.

Seven ships materialized a mere 100,000 miles away in interstellar space: two dreadnoughts and five old-style attack ships. The Legate instantly onlined the new program and accelerated for some distance under conventional drive, before dropping back into underspace, the 'ware distorting its U-signature too, and concealing the ship in underspace. The Legate travelled for five days in that continuum, and still detected some disturbance in the vicinity, which meant the ships could still detect it, or had chosen a close course by chance. Again into the real.

This time the two dreadnoughts were gone and only three of the attack ships remained. The Legate jumped again, then again before changing the 'ware program for a second time. Some kind of feedback through the program created ghost distortions during the transition from one continuum to another, but this time no pursuers remained. As a precaution the Legate changed the program yet again, and made three more random jumps, before setting a course of jumps for home. Still some ghosting in the system, but considering how close it had come to destruction, the Legate could live with that.

During initial contact, the pseudopods within the manacle withdrew from sight, but the humanoid dragon head remained, its neck sinking out of view, bringing the head to rest in the layer of flesh, like a man sinking in living quicksand and tilting his head back for one final breath. Its expression grew slack and unresponsive, as if something had pulled a plug below. During the ensuing hours the entity's surrounding liverlike flesh hardened and scales rose out of it, like flakes of skin about to break away but then petrifying to gemlike solidity – crystallizing and growing translucent. Further hours passed.

At last something was happening. Observing the magnified section of the linkage between the two dragon spheres, Mika noticed pseudopods detaching from each other and withdrawing. The bright sunlight that previously shone down on the manacle building for twenty minutes of every hour, as the two spheres revolved around each other in the sun's orbit, was briefly occluded by a titanic pseudopod tree breaking away from the main connection, its fans opening out then folding in vacuum as it retreated into the other sphere. Mika felt the floor shift and observed the draconic landscape rolling all about in fleshy waves. Then the connection between the two spheres really began to come apart. Shucked off scales rained through space at the parting and even the occasional dead pseudopod. The whole connection unravelled like the severing of some vast fibre-optic skein, through which a sapphire light passed.

'Discussion over, I see; so you convinced your brother sphere?' She nervously glanced down at the head, expecting it to re-engage with her at this point, or at least for Dragon to give her some response over the com-system. None was forthcoming, and it worried her that Dragon could not spare the processing power for a simple communication. Then that changed, as the head jerked out of its torpor and opened its eyes, like a corpse reanimated and prophesying doom.

'Run to your ship,' it said, 'you cannot survive here.'

Surfacing after yet another U-space jump, Jack surveyed the planetary system ahead, cataloguing individual planets and scanning for large artificial constructions either on them or in surrounding space. Two light months ahead, the AI picked up some signs of battle: weapons' flashes with the familiar signature of CTDs and plain atomics, a UV flash followed incrementally by infrared, pinpricks of coherent microwave radiation probably the result of masers firing. The immediacy of U-space signatures was not evident now, since this conflict of course took place two months ago. Scanning did not sufficiently reveal the combatants, though there seemed many low albedo objects in the system at the time. The AI assumed the Legate had surfaced into the real here just to view this scene. Grabbing the opportunity, Jack sent off a U-space information package detailing their present coordinates and events thus far. A return package updated him on the position of a steadily growing fleet of ECS dreadnoughts, a light century behind them.

'Are we strolling into an interstellar war?' wondered Blegg.

Listening in to the conversation, Jack wondered if they might be bringing one along with them.

'There's always that possibility,' Cormac replied as he stepped out into the training area, 'but why go pissing off the Polity if you're already involved in such a serious conflict?'

'Historically speaking, such actions from aggressors have not been unusual.'

'And you would know, wouldn't you?' Cormac muttered sarcastically.

Through internal cameras, Jack observed Blegg and Cormac squaring off to each other once again, and relayed this image to the other ships. The contests fought between the Sparkind throughout this journey were interesting, but this one would be even more so. Jack supposed the two contestants were hardly aware of the betting going on between AIs behind the scenes, just as they seemed unaware that while they fought, they sometimes moved at AI speeds. Of course, since recent revelations to him, Blegg's mood swayed between indifference and anger, so the results of the contests became less easy to predict. Then, just as the two agents exchanged their first blows, all four ships dropped into U-space.

Many hours later, ship time, the four resurfaced within the system. The Legate's ship surfaced too, only briefly, then continued on. Jack once again scanned, but found little more than gaseous clouds and small masses of debris from the distantly viewed conflict here. But there was no time to grab any for analysis.

'It's not stopping here,' observed the AI of the *Haruspex*.

'There is nothing to stop for, since obviously this is no base,' the *Coriolanus* AI interjected.

'Map and track,' instructed Jack, dropping into underspace yet again.

In the underlying continuum they compared figures, and traced the course of the Legate's ship on its way out of the system.

'The high-albedo object – it is heading there,' said Haruspex.

'Nova or accretion disc?' wondered the *Belisarius* AI.

'Not a nova,' said Jack, studying previous images. 'Either an accretion disc or a sun being eaten by a black hole – though, if the latter, I would have expected more X-ray radiation.'

During their next jump through U-space Jack analysed data gathered from the system they had departed. Two living worlds there – one wintry and the other hot and humid. The battle seemed to have centred around the hot world and, checking recorded images, Jack saw evidence of some sort of impact on its surface – something worth checking further should the opportunity arise.

The rest of the planetary system consisted of, further out, a huge gas giant twice the size of Jupiter, a scattering of icy planetoids and asteroids, and one giant frigid world with its own ring system, and a rather odd and low reflective and highly metallic planetoid between the orbits of those two giants. This thing, being small, did not possess sufficient gravity to keep its surface flat, lacked atmosphere and therefore weather to erode down its features, yet it occupied an area swarming with space-borne detritus so should be pocked with craters. The image Jack viewed showed something smooth as marble. It must be a recent addition to this solar system – a not uncommon occurrence considering the vast number of dark worlds roaming the space between suns.

Thorn bowed to his opponent – a man stripped to the waist, exposing a physique that seemed as if forged from iron, the effect redoubled by his skin bearing a metallic tint – then snatched his head back from the path of a foot arcing towards it. Back-fisting the foot along its course, he kicked out for the back of his opponent's other knee, then withdrew the strike as the attacking foot snapped back towards him. Chalter grinned at him, blinking pinkish albino eyes that were another result of whatever adaptation gave his skin that metallic hue. The man was disconcertingly good, but then Thorn expected no less: all of the soldiers aboard the *Haruspex* were Sparkind. Chalter now tried bringing his foot down on Thorn's forward-bent knee, while simultaneously aiming a chop to the side of his head. Thorn withdrew swiftly, not wanting another session with the autodoc, as after his last encounter with Chalter. He spun into a roundhouse kick, just skimming Chalter's face, followed that with a chop that put the man off-balance, then hammered a blur of punches into his torso. Of course, punching Chalter's torso seemed about as effective as thumping wood. The blows threw the man back, knocked a little breath out of him, but he grinned and instantly came in to attack again.

Such was the way Thorn relieved his boredom. On board a month passed before the alien vessel headed out-Polity, and now they had been pursuing it for two months altogether. If he had known it would go on for so long he would have climbed into a coldsleep coffin for the duration. He considered doing so now but, for all they knew the Legate's eventual destination might be only minutes away. But at least Thorn was enjoying more amenable company aboard this high-tech Centurion, the *Haruspex*, than did Cormac aboard the *NEJ*. For travelling with Horace Blegg and the dracomen would not be a bundle of laughs.

There were four Sparkind units in all aboard the *Haruspex*, each of them consisting of four individuals – two Golem and two human, so always there would at least be a card game Thorn could join, or a training session in VR or for real like this.

Finally, having worked up a good sweat and noting from the scoreboard projected overhead that the *Haruspex*

AI placed them at about even, Thorn called a halt. As they drew apart, on the raised platform circling the chamber above them, a couple of Sparkind clapped with slow sarcasm before heading down to take their turn. Thorn eyed them: a woman called Sheerna and a Golem called Aspex. He knew Sheerna was keen to perfect some techniques against an opponent who simply did not make mistakes.

'Same time tomorrow?' Chalter enquired.

'Supposing nothing more interesting comes up, yes,' Thorn replied.

They collected their towels and, both mopping sweat from their faces, moved out into a corridor leading to the crew quarters.

'I'm told that if this latest destination doesn't turn out to be the target, *Belisarius* is going to use a gravtech weapon to knock the Legate's ship out of U-space,' Chalter commented.

'Who told you that?'

'One of the guys aboard the *Coriolanus*, called Bhutan. He tells me even the AIs are getting rather bored and tetchy.'

That did not entirely surprise Thorn. A month in human terms probably felt to an AI, whose mind operated at orders of magnitude faster, like a hundred years. However, merely being bored and tetchy could not justify such a change in the mission plan. He glanced questioningly at Chalter, for the man should know that.

'I think it's due mostly to the direction and distance travelled,' Chalter added. 'They are starting to wonder if this Legate has realized it is still being pursued, and is now leading us away from its base. It might do that if it had no regard for time, or for its own life.'

'What about that battle back there?' Thorn asked.

Chalter nodded. 'Another reason for not continuing too much further. The AIs are keen to check out that planetary system.'

'And I would guess,' Thorn said, 'that ships like this would be much better off guarding the Polity from its enemies. It would be advantageous for an enemy to expend just one small vessel in order to lead away four diamond-state ships like ours?'

'That's the thinking,' Chalter replied.

In his room Thorn was luxuriating in a shower when he felt the *Haruspex* depart U-space. He dried himself quickly and pulled on some Sparkind fatigues.

'Haruspex, that seemed a short jump, so what's happening?' he asked.

In a lazily superior tone the AI replied, 'Perhaps a question better directed *towards* the Legate. I have no idea why he surfaced here.'

'Could we be getting closer to his destination?'

'Not yet ascertained.'

As he stepped outside his quarters, Thorn again felt that strange twisting, and knew they had submerged yet again. The ensuing jump was also of short duration, for Thorn had taken only a few paces along the corridor before the ship surfaced again. Distantly, he heard machinery winding up to speed, and clanking sounds against the hull.

'We are under attack,' Haruspex noted.

Thorn ran for the ship's bridge, Chalter and the other three unit leaders joining him soon after. The *Haruspex* bridge was similar to that of the *NEJ*: a wide expanse of floor seemingly resting out in vacuum. Thorn discerned a distant vessel, and small objects swarming through space, close all around. To his far right he could see the

Coriolanus, its laser strobing the cloud surrounding it. As the ranking officer aboard *Haruspex*, Thorn occupied one of the acceleration chairs available and leant back. Chalter and the others stood back, remaining out of the way, as it would not do to have too many people involved in this. Images of other chairs began to blink into existence: the human commander of the Sparkind aboard *Coriolanus*, and Cormac aboard the *NEJ*. There were no humans present from the *Belisarius*, though a hologram of the ship's avatar – a large chesspiece knight – did flicker into existence. Jack the hangman also appeared, along with Coriolanus the Roman legionary leaning on his spear, and Haruspex itself appearing as a floating crystal ball. All projection.

'It seems the Legate has just led us into some kind of set defence,' Cormac observed.

No shit, thought Thorn as he observed a pumpkinseed object go hurtling past propelled by a bright fusion flame, then tracked by laser and turned to vapour.

'Why are we visible?' he asked.

Cormac held up a hand and turned towards the legionary image. 'You've received five hits, what's your current situation?'

'They are not explosive, rather Jain subversion tech which, given time, would have completely subsumed this ship. I have destroyed them: three from outside by laser, the other two from the inside with a particle cannon.'

'You see,' added the human from the *Coriolanus* – Bhutan, a thin individual with pallid hairless skin and eyes like razor shards, who sported twinned military augs, one on each side of his head – 'we flew straight into them, so chameleonware was no defence.' He glanced at Thorn. 'There are so many of the damned things, we have to use proximity lasers, and the resulting weapons drain negates the 'ware effect.'

Thorn had not known that fact. 'The alien vessel?' he asked.

Cormac replied, 'Completely ignored, and flying right through them.'

'Has it seen *us*?' Thorn asked.

Cormac glanced at him, then back towards whatever display he observed aboard the *NEJ*. 'I think that highly likely,' he shrugged, 'so we'll have to grab it and see what we can learn. I think that what we'll learn, if anything at all, is that we are very close to its final destination.'

'Could this be it?' wondered Haruspex.

In space, through the transparent walls of the *Haruspex*'s bridge, the AI used a frame to pick out a small area and magnify it, revealing a distant object like some jungle ruin, still swamped in lianas, transported out into vacuum. Like wasps issuing from their nests, the seed objects were swarming out of large barnacle-shaped excrescences on its surface.

Bhutan remarked, 'Looks like something completely subsumed.'

'It looks like something that will cease to exist in about thirty seconds,' Cormac added.

That brought about a silence as they all watched. Perfectly on time, it seemed a pinhole punched through the strange object as if it were drawn on a sheet of black paper held up to the sun. Abruptly it distorted and shrank inwards towards the hole. The view then polarized over some titanic flash, and next they observed an expanding sphere of glowing gas. Within minutes the Centurions penetrated this, sang to the tune of the shockwave as it peeled their smaller attackers away from them.

'Alien vessel is jumping,' Belisarius – a horse head talking.

The scene greyed out for a few seconds, and around Thorn the holograms grew thin as a nightmare crowd. Then the *Haruspex* shuddered back into the real, with star patterns altered about it.

'It's still running in a straight line directly for that high-albedo object,' Jack observed. 'I would guess, upon observing us, it paused to receive instructions.'

Thorn sighed and began to unstrap himself.

'But should we pursue any further,' asked a new voice, 'as we now know where to look? Should we not now call in the dreadnoughts? That our quarry is continuing along its original course might indicate that whatever awaits at its destination is not too worried about us.'

Thorn eyed the ancient Japanese man. He had a point: why risk four Centurions against an unknown foe?

'But do we know where to look?' Cormac asked. 'This could merely be diversionary, and I'm not happy about bringing the larger force all the way out here until some target is confirmed.' He gazed at Blegg. 'Unless I am instructed otherwise, we continue.'

Blegg shrugged resignedly and disappeared.

Utterly connected and at one with the *Heliotrope*, as it rose from U-space into the real, Orlandine felt an amusement almost sublime. Her dreams provided her with clues, and her partial interfacing with Jain technology provided the means. Now she could detect a node signature in U-space. In those first moments of abrupt mental growth she assigned programs to the task and, on abandoning the Dyson segment, decided to track down other

Jain nodes. And look where that search brought her: full circle.

She identified the four Centurion-class attack ships, way in front of her, only when the trap revealed them, though she had been aware of something in that location, for a node signature registered from there. She then surmised that the other node signature far ahead of them issued from the alien vessel. It further occurred to her that the Polity ships might be using the same tracking methods as herself, which was probably why they did not lose the ship despite its chameleonware being as sophisticated as their own.

But what now?

She had decided to track down node signatures in the hope of observing uncontrolled Jain growth, to learn more and perhaps locate their original source. But pursuing these two could soon become a lethal occupation. Her most sensible move would be to abandon the idea, and flee to somewhere remote where material and energy resources would be easily available to her. A planet was out of the question, for she was still not prepared to take the risk of putting herself in so vulnerable a position at the bottom of a gravity well. Perhaps an asteroid or comet close to a sun . . . but, even while considering those options, she kept the *Heliotrope* on the trail of the Polity ships, who in turn might well be following the alien vessel to its home.

There were no disagreements from the AIs about continuing this quest, but that was not unexpected as warship AIs tended not to back down. Cormac felt Blegg's point only valid so far. Whatever lay ahead might be something small they could easily neutralize. It might be very mobile, in which case halting now would defeat the whole reason for allowing the Legate to escape since, while they awaited the larger force, the Legate and whoever or whatever had sent it might escape. And if the Legate's master turned out to be something too large for them to handle, then they could run, and only thereafter would it be time to pull in the dreadnoughts and destroyers.

Cormac returned from the bridge to his cabin, and lying on his bunk, worked through in his gridlink all the recordings of recent events. Jack informed him that the large object the *NEJ* had destroyed with a CTD imploder was once an old Polity ship called the *Calydonian Boar*. Apparently it had joined up with some other AIs that headed out this way after the Prador War. This suggested those AIs either ran into something utilizing Jain technology or alternatively tech arising from it. Or had used it themselves. The positioning of such a defence implied something to defend, which somewhat undermined his theory about a mobile opponent. He sighed and banished speculation – however it ran, they would achieve their aim here: not to engage and defeat some enemy, but to clearly identify one. It seemed they would know shortly to whom the Maker had handed over its Jain nodes.

He turned his thoughts to other matters. The memory package still awaited his attention, and yet again he began to consider the implications of that. He had once managed to translate himself through U-space, and though he could not see how that might be possible, it seemed nevertheless a damned useful ability to possess. He really needed to re-integrate those memories, to see if he could re-acquire that ability. However, he remained reluctant to venture into that hell, those memories integral to what Skellor made him suffer. Other thoughts impinged: that he could translate himself through U-space might imply that Blegg, who claimed to be able to do the same, might be telling the truth after all, so was not merely some avatar of Earth Central. Perhaps they were both that mythical thing so beloved of holofiction producers: 'the post-human'. Cormac grunted in annoyance, dismissing the idea. The reality, he felt sure, was that the AIs were the genuine post-humans.

He decided the package would have to wait until after the resolution of forthcoming events out here. Absorbing it now might psychologically damage him – impair his efficiency – and, until Blegg told him otherwise, he remained in charge and could not afford to risk that. He slid his feet off the bed and perched on the edge. He desperately needed something to do, and like the humans aboard the other ships, he headed for the ship's training area.

16

Thin-gun: there is still much debate about whether this weapon, much loved by holofiction producers, was first introduced fictionally or actually. I'll get back to that shortly, but first let me describe this weapon: well, for a start, it's thin. ECS took the components of a typical gas-system or aludust pulse-gun, reduced them to their smallest size, and flattened them. The basic ethos behind this weapon is that it is easily concealed – being flat, it does not bulk in clothing. As such it is the main choice for those regularly working undercover, be they Polity agents or criminals. Further developments by ECS resulted in microtok-charged energy canisters – combined with either a gas or powdered aluminium load – being constructed small enough to insert into the handle of this weapon in the form of a clip. Some thin-guns contain a sub-AI micromind that can prevent the gun being fired by anyone other than its rightful owner, or can cause it to detonate its own power supply if pointed at its owner, and can even make a moral decision about whether or not it wants to fire at all. But, returning to the fiction/fact debate concerning these weapons, the first fictional thin-gun appeared in a VR interactive game, before the Polity became a distinct entity and before the runcible-based expansion. Despite the rather savage methods the authorities employed at that time, corporate police were never able to trace its producer. The interactive, though withdrawn from sale through licensed outlets because of its seditious content, sold very well on the black market and rose to attain cult status. Subsequent investigations revealed its producer to be very probably one of the rogue AIs involved in the Quiet War. The same AI may well be still extant – though it's not telling.

— From 'How it Is' by Gordon

The solar system, still in the process of forming out of an accretion disc, contained thirty-two planetary masses, eight about the same size as Neptune or Uranus, and two further Jovian masses, the rest falling into the size range between Neptune and Earth. Other masses – asteroids, moons, comets – numbered in trillions. Gas and dust shrouded all, meteor strikes and massive storms lit the interior intermittently, as did the slowly growing sporadic luminosity of the nascent sun, as fusion fires fought with black spots for dominance of the solar sphere.

The Legate's vessel surfaced half an AU out and proceeded inwards on fusion drive. The moment the four Centurions surfaced, a U-space signature immediately blossomed beside them, and something big dropped into being. They came under immediate and intense scanning from this hugely dense object – a two-mile-wide ribbed ammonite spiral glinting metallic green. The shape seemed to imply something grown rather than manufactured, one that could keep on growing. Organic technology. It launched a cloud of projectiles that Jack recognized as the same type launched earlier from the subsumed *Calydonian Boar*. These now swarmed towards the four Polity Centurions like twilight mosquitoes anxious to feast. Confident the other ships would be doing the same, Jack engaged his chameleonware and immediately changed course.

More U-space signatures now, on the edge of the accretion disc, then close by. Bacilliform ships began appearing, more spiral forms, lens shapes, indistinct wormish conglomerations breaking and reforming, and sheetlike masses that only closer scan revealed to be constructed of conjoined bacilliforms. Some of these objects were no larger than a human fist, others extended miles across.

'Doesn't seem too healthy around here,' Jack commented. It took him just a microsecond to transmit that message, and he did not see precisely what happened next. The *Belisarius* must have been struck by some of those seed objects – enough at least to disrupt its chameleonware. Whereupon that Centurion ship fled – masers refracting around its hull, then beginning to impinge – leaving an orange trail of metal vapour through space. A wall of bacilliforms, a thousand miles tall, U-jumped directly ahead of the fleeing ship. Jack shut down his 'ware, bringing all his weapons online. He saw the *Haruspex* and *Coriolanus* do the same. The big spiral ship bore down on the *Belisarius*, while the wall of rodlike ships folded in around it like some huge tissue employed for catching a wasp. Blights of missiles rained down on all sides. Jack's CTD imploder hit the big spiral ship first, collapsing its middle section and momentarily leaving a glowing doughnut of matter, before the subsequent explosion obliterated the rest. Anti-munitions scattered illusions around the *Belisarius*, but not enough. Missile after missile impacted on it, cutting away a nacelle, distorting its shape and peeling away a trail of its armour. It tried to U-jump, but its engine was damaged or some other weapon hit it. It shimmered, everted like a snake skin, disappeared in white fire.

Jack's own anti-munitions created an image of the *NEJ* beside him as he re-engaged chameleonware. But that was no distraction for the cloud of rail-gun projectiles hammering up at the ship from underneath. His carousels whirling at blinding speed, he fired a large-yield imploder down towards that cloud, hoping to hoover up most of them, then aimed lower-yield straight CTDs towards a wall of bacilliform ships massing ahead and threw himself into a 100 gravity turn. That was the limit, since the internal gravplates would not compensate for a harder turn, and though the dracomen might survive it, Cormac would not. Blegg, of course, was another matter entirely . . .

The physical attack was not all of it. A constant bombardment of informational attack kept trying to breach their coms systems. Jack allowed some of this through, routing it into secure storage. A message constantly repeated: *I am Erebus, merge with me, be one.*

Ah, so that's what it's all about, Jack thought. 'Out of here,' he sent.

The three remaining ships dropped into U-space and jumped back along their inward course. Many of the alien ships followed. Breathing space, at least. Having located the enemy, the time had now come to call in the big guns. Jack sent a U-space package to the fleet of Polity dreadnoughts, informing them they should come and play. In a matter of days the Centurions would reach them then the pursuing ships would be in serious—

Suddenly, a solid wall of U-space interference expanded in their course, taking that option away as it slapped them out into realspace. Jack located himself,

finding they now lay within the planetary system they
had traversed earlier. Fusion drives igniting, they ran for
cover as their pursuers began to materialize. A wall of
those bacilliform ships began to form ahead of them,
while masers, lasers and missiles probed space in search
of the remaining three chameleonware-concealed Centurions.

'Well, we strolled straight into that one,' observed the
Centurion's AI.

'What the hell was that, Jack?' Cormac asked, also
frantically applying at other levels for information.

'We assumed we would be able to run,' Jack replied.
'We assumed wrong because the bad guys here possess
USERs.'

'Oh shit.'

Viewing internally, Jack noted Cormac heading for
the bridge. He looked rather sick.

'Group together,' Jack sent. 'We cut a hole through it
at five hundred miles.'

All three ships concentrated maser fire on targets
directly ahead. No point using missiles in this situation
as they would be travelling as fast as any munitions they
fired. The planetary system would make a perfect killing
field for the three 'ware concealed ships. They would be
able to use guerrilla tactics – hitting and hiding – for
some time. But the living crews aboard the three ships
were a problem. By the sheer violence of their manoeuvring the aggressors demonstrated that they did not have
the same liability aboard them. Jack noticed that some
of the pursuers were also apparently fading out of existence, which meant the Centurions had no advantage in
possessing chameleonware.

'Jack, your hands need to be untied,' said Cormac

from the acceleration chair in which he had strapped himself. '*Coriolanus* has eight Sparkind aboard, and *Haruspex* has sixteen plus Thorn. Here we have myself and Blegg and nearly a hundred dracomen. I suggest a fast shuttle drop over one of the inhabited worlds, then you can manoeuvre properly.'

It seemed the only sensible move. Their living occupants at least stood a better chance down on the surface of a planet than aboard Centurions that could not manoeuvre properly or aboard smaller vessels dropped in vacuum.

Cormac continued, 'I've already transmitted orders to the others to load up with weapons and supplies . . . I'm presuming reinforcements will be on the way?'

'They should be.'

'How long?'

'Days only, supposing the USER is shut down. We are presently trying to locate it. Its range is not large – about a light-year radius.' He did not add that should the USER not be shut down, the dreadnoughts would take more than a year to arrive, for Cormac knew that.

'And your chances of shutting it down?'

'Good, against the present forces, but we have yet to locate it.'

'Then you drop us. Run for the nearest of those living planets. Which one is it?'

'The hot one.'

'Within range of the standard envirosuit?'

'Yes.'

'Transmit everything you have on that world to my gridlink.' Cormac began unstrapping himself. 'Time to get ready.'

Jack could not help but notice the tired fatalism in

Cormac's voice. The AI pondered the situation for a microsecond, then opened a secure com channel.

'You don't need to leave,' he said to the recipient.

'But nevertheless I shall.'

'The issue is not just one of danger to your physical body – captured, you would be a very useful source of information to any enemy.'

'I outrank you,' Blegg replied, 'and I'm bloody well going.' He cut the channel.

As an afterthought, Jack sent another internal message: 'Arach, I think you just found what you were hoping for.'

Blegg's ship dropped from the *NEJ* and accelerated away under high G, following the two shuttles containing most of the dracomen, which had departed a few minutes earlier. Cormac glanced back at the spider-drone squatting directly behind him, then at the thirty dracomen packed beyond it, then returned his attention to the screen. Further ahead, the two other shuttles that had departed even earlier, containing Thorn and the Sparkind, were entering atmosphere, their nose cones now cupped in orange brilliance.

'Proceed directly to the coordinates,' he instructed Thorn over com. 'Grab your stuff and get out fast once you arrive there. The shuttles may well be targeted.'

While receiving information direct to his gridlink, and modelling the positions of the three Polity ships and the enemy vessels, Cormac directed his attention specifically to the lower row of subscreens, to ascertain the order of events in their vicinity. He watched as one of the spiral ships unravelled under concentrated fire from both the *Coriolanus* and the *Haruspex*. An exterior flash momentarily blanked all subscreens and caused the main cockpit screen to darken. The spiral ammonite ship became a spreading cloud of burning fragments. Their own vessel lurched to one side as something speared past it and down towards the leading shuttles. A vapour trail suddenly knifed out from this projectile and it detonated.

'Maser,' commented Blegg. It seemed that the Centurions above were still covering them.

Their ship hit atmosphere, an orange glow around the cockpit screen and sparks flicking up past from the rapidly heating nose cone. This would be no gentle AG descent – they could not afford the time for that. The craft began to shudder.

The *NEJ* became invisible, then it reappeared, 1,000 miles to one side, to strafe some ball of wormish objects squirming through vacuum. It came out of that attack in a high-G turn that would, despite the internal gravplates, have converted any human aboard into bone fragments and bloody sludge. A CTD blew behind it, completely deleting from existence the object of its assault. *NEJ* now rejoined the other ships, which put themselves between the attackers and the planet. It seemed like three matadors facing a stampede of bulls.

Now deeper in atmosphere, the roar of their descent impinged. Far to their left a cross-hatching of red lines cut the horizon. Below these, bright fires ignited, then a disc of cloud spread directly above.

Rail-gun missiles.

If that fusillade had come down directly on them they would be dead by now.

'They are not concentrating on us,' said Blegg.

'I realize that,' Cormac agreed.

Blegg relentlessly added, 'With that kind of firepower,

they won't need to hunt us down – they could just take out this entire planet.'

'You're such a bundle of joy,' Cormac observed.

The curve of the horizon now rose high in the screen. The two dracomen shuttles from *NEJ* now sat low and to their right, and the two leading Sparkind shuttles were far ahead, just seen as black dots containing the white stars of fusion drives. The sky above them lightened to a pale green, then suddenly a sun-bright explosion ignited within it. Cormac lost com through his gridlink, and could no longer view in his mind the battle above.

'Jack?'

Nothing in response – it could mean that the *NEJ* had been destroyed, but he could not know right then, might never know. A few minutes later Blegg's vessel lurched as the shockwave impacted. Cormac was about to make some comment on this when Blegg jerked the joystick violently to one side. Rail-gun missiles knifed down at forty-five degrees from behind. One missile found a target and Cormac saw one of the dracomen shuttles cartwheeling through the air, its rear end sheared off, humanoid figures tumbling out. The pilot obviously engaged its gravmotors, trying to stabilize it, and he seemed to be succeeding, then something blew in the shuttle's side and it dropped like a brick.

'Fuck,' said Cormac. He glanced back at the team of dracomen aboard, who had just lost thirty or so of their comrades. They knew this loss, for it was his understanding that they kept constant mental contact with each other. Yet they showed no particular agitation, merely seemed to focus more intently on checking over their weaponry.

To the shuttles escaping ahead he said, 'If you've got

gravharnesses aboard, put them on now.' By the silence that met this instruction he supposed Thorn and Bhutan could think of no sufficiently polite reply.

A mountain range reared over the horizon, like rotten teeth in a lower jaw, while a ceiling of grey cloud slid overhead. The leading shuttles penetrated a cloud wall and winked out. As soon as Blegg's vessel followed them in, he touched some control and the cloud wall seemed to simply disappear. This ship's scanning gear formed the view from emitted radiation that could penetrate the murk, and showed a terrain of steep valleys quickly filled with steaming red growth. Lower now, the sound within the shuttle turning to a dull roar; a subscreen revealing that they now flew through heavy, dirty-looking rain. The jungle melded together until it covered the ground right to the horizon. The leading Sparkind shuttles turned as did the remaining dracoman shuttle. Blegg checked co-ordinates and adjusted his ship's course.

'What's that?' Cormac asked, seeing some object dropping in behind the leading shuttles.

Blegg accelerated the vessel. Normally used only for the orbital insertion of troops, and supposedly covered by their mother ships, the shuttles were armed only with lasers. But right now those mother ships were rather busy. Blegg's vessel, however, carried rail-gun missile launchers and pulse-cannons in its forward nacelles. He brought weapons systems online. Laser flashes now became visible between the leading shuttles and the object approaching them. Blegg glanced at Cormac. 'Take control of the weapons.'

Through his gridlink, Cormac applied to the onboard computer, which instantly routed him to weapons control. Once again his sensory field expanded as data from the ship's sensors came through to him. Sitting in the co-pilot's seat, his view now included more than just the screens: it encompassed a wider visual area plus radar returns, and microwave and gravity maps of a huge volume surrounding the ship. He now also controlled targeting frames, and his virtual fingers wrapped around virtual triggers.

Thorn's voice came over com, 'Message to self: boredom is good!'

'We'll be with you in thirty seconds,' Cormac replied as he laid a frame over the object pursuing the shuttles, obtained full acquisition of it, and fired. The ship bucked and white streaks cut the air on either side of it. 'But the missiles will be with you earlier,' he added.

Now Cormac focused the ship's sensors and enlarged an image – transferring it to a subscreen for Blegg also to see. This revealed one of the bacilliform ships, precisely the rod-like shape of a bacterium but about twenty yards long, with its exterior a completely featureless blue-grey except where the lasers struck it, leaving livid burns like bruises. Whatever propulsion system it used showed no visual evidence, so Cormac assumed it must be somehow utilizing antigravity. While they watched, multiple laser strikes converged on its nose, and it shuddered and slowed like an aggressive dog receiving a reprimanding smack. Then it accelerated again.

'It's not using any weapons,' Cormac noted, 'and it can't be some kind of bomb. One that large wouldn't need to get so close to the shuttles.'

'Capture,' explained Blegg bluntly. 'If they really wanted to take us out, we would be dead by now.'

The strange vessel drew itself within a hundred yards of the rearmost Sparkind shuttle, then the two missiles finally reached it. One massive blast turned it into a cloud of burning debris. Cormac quickly threw the second missile into a holding pattern. It overflew the explosion, circled round. No need to recall it or make it safe, for now ten more of those rod-ships were approaching. Obeying new instructions the missile shot off on an entirely new course. Blegg looked at him questioningly, so Cormac threw a radar display up on a subscreen to show him what was happening. A few seconds later they watched the missile reduce the number of approaching rod-ships to nine. The flash of the explosion lit the cockpit screen, then suddenly the nine ships became visible through it.

'How long to the landing area?' Cormac asked.

'Five minutes,' Blegg replied.

Over com Cormac said, 'I repeat: no delays once you're down – we've got incoming.'

Thorn replied, 'Yeah, we see them.'

Three of the rod-ships pursued the two Sparkind shuttles while the other six turned towards Blegg's ship and the remaining dracoman shuttle. Cormac created then loaded a search-and-destroy program into six missiles, and fired them one after another. That left him with just twelve explosive missiles, the pulse-cannons and a laser. Some EMP knocked three of the missiles from the sky, and Cormac tried to re-acquire them as they fell. The three remaining missiles impacted, bursting rod-ships in actinic explosions and scattering their debris across the sky. He managed to stabilize two of the falling missiles a hundred yards from the jungle canopy and brought them back on target. He then considered instructing Blegg to close up on the rod-ship now hurtling towards the dracoman shuttle, but Blegg anticipated him and turned their vessel. Cormac brought the pulse-cannons online, and they roared steadily. The first fusillade blackened the rod-ship with burn holes, but only briefly slowed it. Two more such hits and it began to pour out smoke, then it abruptly dropped from the sky. By then the two returning missiles found their targets. Blegg brought their own vessel up through the smoke and a sleet of debris, like burning skin, and accelerated towards the other three attackers, which now closed rapidly on the two lead shuttles.

Cormac selected and fired another six of the remaining missiles, target acquisition locked, and identification programs running so they would not mistake the escaping shuttles for enemy craft.

'Can this bucket go any faster?' he asked.

'We'll overshoot if we do, and lose manoeuvrability.'

'Okay.'

The missiles he fired moved ahead of the ship quite slowly. Cormac focused beyond them, pulling up images in his gridlink and on one of the subscreens. One of the rod-ships had drawn very close to the rearmost shuttle – less than fifty yards away from it. At present relative speeds, no missile would reach the assailant before it reached its target. Perhaps it would be forced to slow, as laser strikes were turning its front end blue-black and it trailed smoke and occasionally belched oily flame from splits in its surface. Suddenly, however, the attacking object surged ahead, as if finding some grip on the very air. It thumped down on the shuttle and stuck to it. Cormac instantly cancelled it as a target.

Com: 'Shuttle Two, gravharnesses *now*. Get out of there!'

Shuttle and rod-ship began to plummet. Cormac tracked them tightly and kept focused in. The rod-ship deflated as it extruded a hundred rootlike growths to wrap around the shuttle.

'The lock's jammed, screens covered,' came Bhutan's reply. 'Will attempt to blow—' Just then the beleaguered shuttle's drive abruptly cut out and, encompassed in a mass of organic growth, it began tumbling through the sky. Screams issued over com, and Cormac listened only briefly before he shut down the connecting comlink and instantly sent transmissions to the other shuttles instructing them to accept nothing further on that channel. Sparkind did not scream easily, but Cormac knew just how quickly Jain technology could take control of a human being. Then, in the time it took him to blink, the white flash then massive blast of a tactical CTD erased the shuttle. Someone aboard had retained enough presence of mind to know they would not be getting out of there alive, and took the enemy with them.

Belatedly, two further explosions as a pair of the missiles destroyed the last two attackers.

'That could have gone—' Cormac began, but suddenly a shadow drew across the sky, and under it a bright light flared. Before the sound of the explosion impinged, horizon and jungle were already whipping past the screen. Then came the massive blast and Blegg's vessel was spinning and falling through burning debris. Cormac considered warning the dracomen to brace themselves for impact, and rejected the idea. It seemed pointless to state the obvious.

The bacilliform ships did not shoot back, though they kicked out a huge amount of EM interference which increased as they conjoined. It seemed they were designed to initially blank out communication, then, if a ship drew close enough to one of those walls they formed, to completely disrupt its systems, including the AI mind inside. Jack suspected they served some other purpose as well, for individually they kept trying to make close contact with the Centurions – something none of them had yet managed to do. The lens-shaped ships deployed plenty of weaponry, but in a one-on-one fight were no match for the Centurions and were soon disabled or destroyed. Those accretions of hundred-foot-long metal worms, once they untangled, became lethal highly intelligent missiles themselves. But the remaining five big ammonite spiral ships remained the greatest danger, for they carried all the armament of a Polity destroyer – the wormish things being one weapon they deployed – and all the processing power of a runcible AI, for they quickly found solutions to the Centurions' chameleonware. Each new program deployed lasted no more than half an hour – no time at all during a space battle.

Duelling with hardfields against a mile-wide lens-shaped vessel using telefactored warheads, *Haruspex* seemed in danger of being swamped by a rapidly forming wall of the bacilliforms. Jack sent a coded transmission to *Haruspex* then swung round in a sharp 400 gravity turn to put the *NEJ* behind that threatening wall. He fired a combined CTD and EM warhead at the rod-ships then, after a delay, followed it with a fusillade of near-c rail-gun projectiles. *Haruspex* immediately dropped out of the fight. The missile detonated amid the rod-ships, cutting a hole in the wall they created. The rail-gun projectiles shot through the hole, following the wave of EM radiation. The big lens's instruments could detect nothing but the EM, so did not react quickly enough to the following projectiles. A hundred impacts collapsed one side of the lens like a punctured balloon. Both the *NEJ* and the *Haruspex* then used their chameleonware to cover their run towards the spiral ship pursuing *Coriolanus*.

'I have the USER located,' Coriolanus reported and sent coordinates.

Jack scanned and confirmed, and Haruspex agreed. During the recent battle they had managed to take readings of the interference strength of the device. It was located on a small moon orbiting the cold world – half the planetary system away from their present position.

'We have to make the run,' Jack informed the other two ships.

'That will mean abandoning those on the planet,' Coriolanus informed him.

Jack scanned in that direction and saw some of the enemy ships deployed down inside atmosphere. 'My assessment of our current situation is that by running from the system on conventional drives we could survive. If we stay to protect Cormac and co, we will eventually be destroyed. The greatest hope for them is if we destroy that USER, then return to fight a delaying action until the dreadnoughts arrive. We can only hope our erstwhile passengers manage to survive on the surface.'

After a short pause, the other two ships concurred.

The moment his boots hit the soft ground, Thorn's envirosuit muttered warnings in his ear and flashed them up on his visor. He turned those persistent warnings off, since he did not need the suit to tell him he occupied a highly radioactive area. The incinerated terrain ahead stretched for five hundred miles along the base of the mountains, and seemed likely to be the result of multiple nuclear explosions. However, in this heavy rain, he could see only a few yards ahead – in the planet's lower gravity the raindrops falling slowly were twice the size of those on Earth, and also were turbid with ash as a consequence of explosions that had occurred here.

'Out-spectrum vision – search,' he instructed his suit.

After a moment a transparent band drew across his visor directly before his eyes, and within that band the rain seemed simply to be erased. However, above and below the band he could still see the downpour. Though accustomed to using this kind of sensory enhancement, he did not trust it, it being too easy to interfere with – already the surrounding radioactivity began to cause flecks across his vision. He now surveyed his surroundings.

The remaining dracoman shuttle from the *NEJ* was just landing, and the soldiers around him were checking their weaponry and loading up ridiculously large packs, while the four autoguns patrolled around them like hounds anxious for the hunt. No badinage passed between the troops. Many of them had known Bhutan and the others aboard the Sparkind shuttle that didn't make it here.

'I take it that's where we want to go?' Chalter pointed off to Thorn's left where the lower mountain slopes were now visible. This area had been Cormac's own choice for various reasons: it lay at the edge of the incinerated area, so provided the option of using the jungle for cover, and if that vegetation turned out to be occupied by a whole chapter of the flesh-eating monsters society, from here they could also head into the mountains, which were riddled with gullies, cave systems, and a sufficient mixture of hot springs, seams of metal, and radioactives from the recent explosions nearby to make it easier for them to hide from detection equipment.

'Certainly is,' Thorn confirmed.

The *NEJ* shuttle landed and the dracomen disembarked. Thorn noted that again they wore no protective clothing. Though there was sufficient oxygen here, any unequipped human would have drowned in this rain, and despite the downpour the temperature reached nearly 50 Celsius. Thorn hauled up his own pack and shouldered it, then over com issued his instructions.

'Seal up the shuttles and let's move out. Sparkind, keep to your units – cover for imminent attack. Dracomen . . .' Thorn considered for a moment how he knew the dracomen could perform. 'Scout ahead and find us cover: defensible positions, good visibility, but nothing to get trapped in. Let's get moving.'

The dracomen took off at speed, bounding towards the lower slopes. Soon loaded up, the Sparkind units followed them, with the autoguns patrolling out to either side. A series of flashes then lit the sky and Thorn supposed Cormac was now engaging the remaining pursuers. He checked his footing before setting out, noticed red shoots of growth like droplets of blood scattered across the ground. Then a shadow began drawing across the sky.

'Cormac, status?' he asked.

'Not too brilliant,' the agent growled in reply.

The ship lay upside-down in dense red jungle. Through the screen Cormac could see a path of smashed thick stems and enormous smouldering leaves the ship had left as it plunged in backwards. Because he had been in similar situations before, he first instructed his envirosuit to close up completely, for any kind of poisonous air mix might be leaking into the ship. The visor shot up out of the neck ring and engaged with the helmet, which extended itself in segmented sections up around the back of his head, from the rear of the neck ring. He then looked across at Blegg beside him.

Horace Blegg had also closed up his own suit.

'Interesting landing,' said Cormac. 'What the fuck happened?'

'High-intensity laser – drilled right through our engine,' Blegg replied. 'Did you notice the source?'

In the last moment, just before the explosion wiped out the ship's exterior sensors, he had seen one of the spiral ships descending on them like an express elevator.

'I think we need to get out of here – fast.' Reaching up he hit his strap release and, spinning himself round as he dropped from his seat, came down feet first on the ceiling. Blegg landed there an instant after him. Scar was waiting to the rear of the cockpit, fangs exposed in what was definitely not a grin. Cormac searched round for Arach, then looked up at what had been the floor, and saw the drone still clinging there. 'Well, what are you waiting for?' The drone needed no more instruction. Without descending, it scuttled to the rear of the lander and dropped out through the airlock the dracomen had just opened.

Cormac followed the departing dracomen, snatching up his own pack of supplies, and his proton carbine on the way. Once outside, via his gridlink, he instructed both the inner and outer door of the airlock to close, then began leading the way through the pall of smoke and steam around the overturned vessel.

Something globular, the size of a potato sack and the

colour of old blood, crouched on three legs on the smouldering ground less than ten yards from the ship. It shivered, emitting a warbling squeal. Scar aimed his carbine at the creature, then swung the weapon away. The dracoman clearly knew the creature to be harmless, though it might attract other more dangerous predators. As the dracomen spread out, Cormac glanced up at Arach, now squatting atop the lander, before peering higher into the occluded sky.

'Nice of them to give us shelter from the rain,' he quipped. They stood in a twilight created by the ammonite spiral filling half the sky above them as it slowly descended. 'Thorn?' he queried, receiving nothing but static over com. So as to ascertain their position he ran a program to track Thorn's last signal to them. 'We'll see if we can link up,' he said to the others, gesturing over to his right into the thick wall of jungle.

His last words were drowned out in a low roar as one of the rod-ships breasted the plant canopy to his left. The dracomen hit the jungle ahead of Cormac as he himself broke into a run. Behind him the weird vessel crashed down on the wrecked Polity ship. Sheltering for a moment under a leaf like a duvet filled with blood, he observed the rod-ship extrude its tendrils as if it were intent on throttling some opponent, then he heard the sound of rending metal. To one side he saw Arach bouncing along with his spidery legs folded into a caged ball. Rolling to a halt the drone abruptly opened out again. Hatches then opened in his rear torso, and unfolded two Gatling design cannons. These whirled into action, and both rod-ship and shuttle disappeared under a storm of explosions.

'Shit!' Cormac ducked to avoid flying debris. He then

glanced up and saw more objects detach from the spiral ship and begin dropping towards them: more rod-ships, writhing anguine things, and translucent coins in which indistinct shapes shifted. Then another shape he recognized: the Legate's vessel, or something very much like it.

'Save your ammo, Arach – you're going to need it!'

Arach came dancing after him as Cormac stood initiating Shuriken in its holster, then followed Blegg and the dracomen into deeper jungle shade.

They moved fast as the shadow deepened and extended around them with the descent of the spiral ship. Most of the surrounding vegetation sported big leaves raised up, three or four yards, on top of thick fibrous stalks, while in their shade lay little undergrowth to hinder progress. In some areas vines shifted like tangles of somnolent red snakes, but these were easily avoided. The ground itself was a spongy lamination of decaying leaves over-spread with fungi like spills of blue paint. Around the bases of the fibrous stems, nodular sprouts fisted from the leaf litter, doubtless awaiting the collapse of leaves above them and the subsequent chance of enlivening sunlight. Occasionally they would encounter one of those globular red creatures crouching by one of these stems, a crunching sucking sound issuing from underneath it as it grazed on the sprouts.

Within a few minutes they reached softer ground. Rain rumbled thunderously on the overhead leaves and rivulets of water slithered like drool down the stems. They were out of the huge ship's shadow now. From behind them came a low roar and then a blast of wind, lifting leaves to let in the actinic glare of the sun, now penetrating cloud.

'It's down!' Blegg called.

It would not be the only thing come down, Cormac realized. The leaves lifting had given him a glimpse of those objects he earlier observed descending, now falling into the jungle all around them. Then he heard something crashing through the canopy over to his right.

'We may soon have company,' he broadcast over com.

Their first company turned out to be one of those tripedal saurians Jack had warned about and detailed in the download to Cormac's gridlink. Its gait on just three long legs was smooth and fast, but utterly bewildering to witness. A whiplike tail flicked around ceaselessly behind it, while on the end of a thick, hinged neck jutted the head of a three-eyed hippopotamus. It emitted a sawing growl as it dodged one of the dracomen, growled again and skidded to a halt when faced with Blegg and two more dracomen. Then it took off again as they moved aside for it. Numerous weapons carefully tracked its progress, but none was fired, as it showed no inclination to attack and just kept on going.

'Something spooked it,' Blegg observed.

Perfectly on cue that same something came hurtling towards them out of the deeper shade.

It might be some indigene of this strange world, yet instantly reminded Cormac of the creatures Chaline had seen attacking the expedition sent to the Small Magellanic Cloud. Its thorax extended fifteen feet long, seemingly camouflage painted in the shades of red of the vegetation surrounding them, and was flanged on either side as if made to glide. Its head, an ugly lump sprouting sensory tufts and black bulbous eyes seemingly at random, was equipped with trimember mandibles. From behind the head, like gill tendrils, extended two sets of three long, multiple jointed limbs. It moved very fast, only the lower two of the sets of limbs hitting the ground – the rest gripping at surrounding stalks to propel it forwards.

Seeing the creature's speed, and the rapid reaction of the dracoman diving from its path, Cormac realized he himself must move a lot faster to now stay alive. He located a long unused program in his gridlink and put it instantly online. His perception of time now slowed as his thought processes accelerated. The program simultaneously stimulated his body's production of adrenaline. Then he raised his carbine – but far too slowly. Fire flared from his left, hitting the point where the creature's legs joined behind its head on one side. It slammed into the ground ploughing up soil, the legs on its other side still gripping stalks and pulling down some of the sheltering leaves as well. Now in bright sunlight, it tried to rise again. Arach hurdled over towards it in an instant, a particle cannon's beam flashing turquoise between his pincers, and incinerating the attacker's head.

'Let's keep moving,' urged Cormac. He reached into a pocket on the side of his pack and removed a flat case from which he extracted one of eight short glass tubes, which he now inserted into his envirosuit's med-access. A prickling at his wrists as the stimulants entered his bloodstream, an abrupt coolness, and then he began sprinting. Blegg and the dracomen kept up with him easily. He knew he must be the slowest moving among them. As he ran, he opened the bandwidth of his connection to Shuriken, now feeling as ready as he could be.

The dracomen spread out wider, and became difficult to spot as they resorted to their own natural chameleonware. They could only be seen at all because at this rapid pace their shifting skin patterns could not keep up to speed with their changing surroundings, and because their weapons and equipment could not be similarly concealed. The second creature did not even get close. Glimpsing a shape speeding in towards them, Cormac initiated Shuriken and sent it spinning five yards out from his body, humming as it extended its chainglass blades, but the dracomen promptly fired upon the attacker simultaneously from three different directions. It body blew to fragments leaving only its limbs still clinging to nearby stalks. Arach scuttled inquisitively through this mess, Gatling cannons swivelling, then moved back into deeper jungle to one side of Cormac.

'Aw, leave some for me,' the drone called out to the dracomen.

It soon received its wish as a new type of beast joined the fray.

They kept running on, many other creatures attacking. Proton and pulse-gun fire all around, Arach seemed to be everywhere, concentrating his huge firepower on grouped masses of the alien assailants, in the process bringing down swathes of jungle in burning fragments. The long-legged things could extend their heads, Cormac discovered, as he sent Shuriken hammering through one telescopic neck. The detached head landed beside a fallen dracoman, who rolled aside quickly and came upright to fire down at it, as the head now scuttled off on its mandibles like some independent beast. The target bounced briefly in red flame and then flew apart. Cormac recalled Shuriken and sent it skimming towards another such creature. Premature action, as the headless body of the first one, still suspended in midair, extruded a long metallic tongue which wrapped around the dracoman and wrenched him back viciously. A strange groaning squeal ensued, then two separate halves of smoking dracoman hit the ground. Cormac fired his carbine, its flame meeting the tongue as it now shot towards him. Shuriken, almost as if angry about the dracoman's death, hammered in and out horizonzally through its own opponent, then chopped up and down vertically on its return course. The creature fell to pieces.

Blegg, beside him, keeping pace. 'Seems they've decided we are the ones to be captured alive, and the dracomen are now dispensable.'

'How many?' Cormac asked.

'Five dracomen down.' Blegg pointed at something weaving towards them. It resembled a long iron nematode hovering a foot from the ground, sliding through the air with the writhing of a snake. A red scythe of fire hit it in the middle, then two shorter versions of the same thing darted away. They both swung round on the source of the shot: a dracoman, clearly visible now since in using their camouflage there was too much danger of hitting each other in this fire-fight. One of the metallic things slammed into his chest, and with a sound like a cleaver striking a butcher's block, pieces of dracoman and long shards of metal exploded in every direction. More and more Jain-factored creatures were coming in from every direction. A dracoman was snatched up in triple jaws, and the explosion of its carbine energy canister hurled Cormac to his knees. Up again. Left arm numb against his side where smoking shrapnel was embedded. Pain-blocking program initiated, then firing one-handed into a nightmare head looming over him. Blegg slammed into his side, just as Shuriken came screaming overhead and straight into the creature's mouth.

'Up!' Blegg spun him round, drew a carbide commando knife, and in one quick movement levered the hot metal from his arm. 'Not too bad,' he observed

With movement returning to that arm, Cormac drew his thin-gun and fired off to his left with that, while simultaneously firing with the carbine past Blegg. The tracking and targeting program he was using was sending him cross-eyed. A *whumph* as a rod-ship crashed down amid them, crushing foliage and ejecting tendrils as thick as falling trees. Cormac saw another dracoman caught up as he himself concentrated fire on the deflating but spreading rod-ship. Spearing towards him, the ground lumped up like a worm track. He aimed downwards just as tendrils exploded from the earth and wrapped around his leg. Severing them with fire, he subliminally saw the captured dracoman slammed hard against the ground and discarded. Not even a complete thought sent Shuriken whirring over above the dracoman while it shook itself like a dog and staggered upright again.

Something else arced through the air, its source Arach, and its terminal whine familiar. Cormac ducked down as this missile landed amidst the spreading tendrils and exploded, spreading something like phosphorus across the ground. The blast seemed to propel Cormac through an area of new growth, where shoots like giant red asparagus speared up from the incinerated remains of stalks. He stumbled through a mass of red vines writhing under painfully bright sunshine, and out onto charred ground scattered with smaller blood-red shoots of new growth. Dracomen emerged either side of him, then Blegg came stepping out backwards concentrating fire up into the face of some attacker. Arach came last, two cannons swivelling and targeting independently, the shots ripping into fast-moving silvery opponents, the flash of his particle cannon stabbing out regularly like a fiery tongue. Without that drone, Cormac realized, this would have been over very quickly. He swiftly counted – eighteen dracomen surviving – then turned round to see mountain slopes ahead.

'I've got you now,' came Thorn's voice over com.

Running down like silver dogs came four Polity autoguns. Drawing close, they squatted obediently and poured violet fire into the jungle.

17

USER (underspace interference emitter): this device works by rhythmically inserting and removing a massive singularity through a runcible gate. The U-space interference this causes will knock any ship within its vicinity back into realspace. The singularity is contained by an inverted gravity field which is in turn powered by tidal drag, since the singularity is spinning very fast. The containment field necessarily collapses in the U-continuum and reinstates when out of it again. Huge forces and huge amounts of energy are employed, most of it generated by the singularity's spin, therefore, that spin gradually slows. When it drops below a certain threshold, the USER must be returned to an as yet unrevealed military complex – rumoured to be sited in orbit around a black hole – where titanic magnetic accelerators spin the singularity back up to optimum again. It is also rumoured that this technology has been available for some time, but AIs were loath to employ it because by artificially creating singularities (black holes, essentially), they are shortening the life span of the universe. Evidently they intend sticking around for a while, and the fact that USERs are now being employed might suggest the AIs have found a way to deconstruct black holes.

– From 'Quince Guide' compiled by humans

As a precaution, when the two dragon spheres came together, Mika had again donned her spacesuit. Good thing, too. She grabbed up her pack and quickly stuffed into it anything immediately to hand that might increase her chances of survival: food, drink, energy canisters and medical supplies. Closing up her helmet and visor, she headed for the shimmer-shield, pushed through, then opened the airlock beyond. Stepping outside she looked up to a view not cleaned up by computer like the view from inside. Bright actinic sunlight cut through from one side, between a curved ceiling and curved floor composed of draconic flesh. Masses of pseudopods were sliding down beside her – a massive but eerily silent avalanche. Scales slowly tumbled through vacuum around her, and nearby they dropped sharply on the gravplated walkway. She kicked them aside as she strode towards her craft. She noted, as the gull-door rose at her approach, the docking clamps folding into the metal of the manacle below.

'Can you hear me, Dragon?' she asked, halting for a moment.

Nothing.

What was happening? The two spheres were breaking their connection, and thus far she saw no sign of hostility between them. But would she recognize that anyway? Perhaps right now they were fighting some battle on a virtual level, or perhaps they adhered to certain rules of conduct for something like this? They were alien, and despite lengthy investigation remained alien still, so who was to know? However, as Mika ducked into the little craft, the dragon spheres seemed to her like two card-sharps standing up from the table, about to put some distance between each other, making room to manoeuvre before going for their weapons, each hoping to get the drop on his opponent.

The gull door closed and Mika stared at the controls for a moment before taking hold of the joystick. With no AI available to fly the craft for her this time, she must now do so herself. A finger brushed against a touch-plate gave her 'systems enabled', then engines droned as she raised the joystick. The craft rose smoothly until it fell outside the influence of the manacle gravplates, then it jerked through vacuum as if a tether had been cut, but with no real loss of control. Mika aimed for the sunlight between the two curved draconic surfaces, the screen before her polarizing on the glare. Dragon scales hailed against the hull, some of them hitting it quite hard before spinning away, so Mika kept the speed to a minimum. She swung the craft to one side to avoid a dead and discarded pseudopod, but clipped it all the same. Desiccated by vacuum, it shattered into red glittery fragments and black vertebrae.

The previous connection between these portions of Dragon entire now broke apart completely, the two pseudopod trees sinking away. Now Mika saw that the two spheres were visibly drawing apart, microgravity creating whirlpools in the fog of shed scales, and space opening wide before her. She accelerated as blue-green light seemed to fill the intervening space. Some kind of weapon? No, just a storm of ionization. More acceleration, since at any moment she might be caught up in some energy strike many orders of magnitude above this current jungle glow. From the beginning, the dragon spheres had utilized full-spectrum lasers as weapons. She knew the sphere she had recently occupied now contained gravtech weapons, and it struck her as likely that whatever weapons the Polity possessed, these giant spheres either already possessed or could create them within themselves, and they probably owned even more drastic ones than that.

Clear space now in the full glare of the sun. Mika turned the craft about, shut down the engines, and enabled available automatics to keep it from colliding with anything else that might be tumbling about out here. Slowly drawing away, she felt like a mouse scuttling from between two bull elephants beginning to face off.

Then it started.

Almost as one, ripples began to cross the surface of each sphere. They revolved once around each other, while still drawing apart, then accelerated away together. Perhaps ten miles away from her, a laser flashed between them, blackening an area of Mika's reactive screen. As the screen cleared she saw a mist of plasma and glittering scales rise from the surface of each Dragon sphere, and in one sphere a glowing canyon became visible to her. She realized then that from her present position she did not know which sphere was which, because she could not see the manacle. But, then, how would knowing that help her?

The spheres began revolving around each other again, and now she caught quick glimpses of the manacle on one of them. Then their revolutions slowly drew to a halt, the sphere without the manacle occluding the other from her view. Laser strikes threw it sharply into silhouette, and streamers of plasma fire and debris shot out all around it. Then something seemed to distort space, flattening the one sphere she could see into an ellipse. The wall of distortion sped towards her even as she started the craft's engines and grabbed the joystick. It struck. The entire craft rippled, emitted a tearing crash, and bucked as if someone had taken hold of the very fabric of space and snapped it up and down like shaking dust from a carpet. The screen disintegrated, blowing out the air supply, metal visible around her suddenly contained whorls and ridges. Then she blotted out any view by coughing blood onto her visor. It felt to her as if someone had smacked an iron bar simultaneously against every bone she contained, then shoved a barbed harpoon through her and twisted it, knotting up her insides.

I am going to die.

Her suit diagnostics made no sense at all, however the static cleaner still operated and shed the blood from the surface of her visor down around her chin. Now she could truly assess the damage to her craft: some god had taken hold of it and twisted it up like an old newspaper.

Gravity weapons.

So it seemed the so-called friendly sphere had killed her. She focused out at vacuum, and a cliff of draconic flesh rose up before her. Something wrong: this part of Dragon was no sphere at all, but egg-shaped with an odd twist in it, with fluids boiling out into vacuum from an opening gashed down one side.

Ah, the other guy, was all she thought, before a writhing wheel of pseudopods – the business end of a fast-moving tree composed of those things – slammed up, closed around her vessel, and dragged her down.

Stupid stupid stupid.

Though the underspace interference field knocked her out of U-space nearly fifty AU from the centre of the action – further than Pluto is from Earth – from which action the light of numerous explosions was only now reaching her, Orlandine was still in the same trap as those ECS attack ships. And she was also exposed in open vacuum between the inner system of planets and an outer ring of asteroids shepherded by a collection of cold planetoids.

Running programs to determine the strength of the USER field, Orlandine quickly realized the USER device itself lay somewhere within that inner system, and estimated a travel time of more than a year before she could distance herself far enough from it to drop back into U-space. *Heliotrope* possessed cold coffins, so for her the journey would not be so interminable, however she did not much relish the idea of leaving herself that vulnerable. Other ECS ships could jump to the interference field's perimeter within that time, then come in on conventional drives. The longer the field remained functional, the more defences ECS would install around its perimeter, and it seemed likely they might possess weapons capable of knocking other ships out of U-space once the field shut down. So, the longer she remained in this area, the more likely would be her capture.

Checking her scans of the distant battle, she realized that travelling insystem to find somewhere to hide was no tenable option. Hundreds of alien ships swarmed in the area. She did not expect the Polity ships there to survive, nor did she think her presence here would go undetected for long. But another option remained: the asteroid field.

Orlandine fired up the *Heliotrope*'s fusion engine, turned the vessel, and headed away just as fast as she could. Somewhere amid those cold stones she should be able to find a place to hide her ship, and there power it down to avoid detection while she awaited the conclusion to events now occurring in the inner system.

'Why are they holding off?' Thorn enquired. He plugged a monocular into his visor to gaze out over the red jungle towards the enormous spiral ship.

The sky was growing darker now, taking on a milky-green hue as the sun descended behind the cloud cover like a heavy rucked-up blanket. In the jungle around the alien ship, things were moving about, and occasionally half-seen shapes drifted high above. To Cormac's left, where some cataclysm had denuded the ground cover, swirled errant lights like St Elmo's fire.

Cormac glanced across at Blegg, who now squatted beside the nearest of those strange cubic ruins, which seemed like short sections cut from a square granite pipe with sides a yard thick. Seven cubes altogether were scattered over the area – just some unknowable ruin.

'What do you think?' Cormac asked the old Oriental.

Blegg squinted down the slope at the red foliage. 'We know that if they wanted to wipe us out, it would be no problem to them: they could just drop a warhead. I would say they are reluctant to destroy a possible source of information, potentially valuable, and certainly easier to obtain than, say, trying to capture a Centurion.'

'So they'll still try to grab us?' Thorn enquired.

'That's what they tried in the jungle. Why else send in what were effectively ground troops when you could sit in the sky and burn the jungle down to bedrock? I believe the killing only started when the dracomen's resistance to Jain technology got them reclassified as being not worth the effort to capture.' Blegg looked around to the remaining dracomen and Sparkind positioned in surrounding terrain, then to the autoguns, and finally up at Arach crouching atop the nearby cube. 'They will come again, and this time their assault will be more organized. We just have to decide what to do.'

'How difficult is that?' said Arach. 'We *fight*.'

'Yes, of course,' said Blegg.

Cormac understood the man's reservations. *NEJ* and the other ships remained out of contact, and it seemed likely they had either fled the enemy or been destroyed by it. So now this small ECS force lay isolated at the bottom of a gravity well, with little more than hand weapons available, and the forces arrayed against it seemed huge. In situations like this soldiers generally considered how they might die.

'I for one have no intention of allowing myself to be captured.' Cormac reached into his pocket and removed a small multipurpose grenade – a chrome cylinder no larger than a cigarette lighter, but with a charge capable of turning a human body into so much bloody fog. He gestured with the grenade towards Blegg. 'You, however, have another option. You can escape. You can translate yourself through U-space.'

'Yes, there's always that,' Blegg replied. He sounded tired. 'But so can you.'

Cormac grimaced and returned the explosive to his pocket. 'That is our last option,' he said, not entirely convinced the option lay open to himself anyway. He needed first to open and absorb Jerusalem's memory package, and it seemed unlikely he would be given the time for that. He looked around, then focused on Thorn, who had now removed his monocular from his visor. 'Thorn?' he enquired.

Thorn replied, 'With us out in the open, all they need

to do is sit up in the sky and pick us off with stunners or lasers, whatever they choose.' He patted a hand against the envirosuit he wore. 'The dracomen might stand a chance but we've no chameleonware.'

'The cave system, then,' Cormac commented.

'So it would seem,' said Thorn. 'All we have to do is survive down there until rescue arrives – if it is coming at all.' He paused for a moment. 'Should we send the dracomen into the jungle? They would stand a better chance out there.'

'I will try giving that order to Scar, but I don't see him obeying it,' Cormac replied.

'Movement,' said Blegg, abruptly.

Thorn turned and raised his monocular again. 'Humanoid figure – a familiar one.' He made to pass the monocular to Cormac, but Cormac waved it away. Ramping his visual acuity, using a program in his gridlink controlling the muscles around his eyes and configuring signals direct from his optic nerves, he soon identified the Legate walking from the jungle and up the slope towards them. He beckoned Scar over to him while he watched.

'Scar,' he said, 'I am going to talk to this . . . Legate. And when it doesn't get what it wants, I suspect we'll be back into a fire-fight. Myself and the rest of the humans, and Arach, are going to run for the cave system and blow the entrance behind us. I want you to take your people into the jungle – with your camouflage you have a better chance of surviving there.' Scar just stared at him for a long moment. Cormac continued, 'This way some of us might survive to deliver a report to ECS forces when they arrive.'

Scar held up one hand, clawed fingers spread. 'I will send five into the jungle.'

'This is not open to negotiation, Scar.'

'No, it is not,' the dracoman replied, and moved away.

The Legate was now only a few hundred yards away, and Cormac thought it laughable how the entity held its hands up and open as if to show it carried no weapons. He knew all its weapons would be inside it. Once the entity had approached to ten yards away, Cormac stepped forwards. 'I think that's about close enough. So tell me, what do you want? I would guess you haven't come here to surrender to us.'

'It is good that you retain your sense of humour,' said the Legate. 'Allow me to acquaint you with realities.' It pointed upwards with one overly long finger and, in that instant, com was restored and Cormac received a time-delayed information package from the *NEJ*. He held this package in his gridlink, as loath to open it now as the memory package gifted to him by Jerusalem. He suspected bad news, but more than that he suspected their com codes had been cracked by whatever this being before him represented.

'*Nobody is to open that package*,' he instantly broadcast from his gridlink.

It almost seemed the Legate heard him as well. 'We have not yet broken your com codes, since the algorithms that control them were created by AI. Had we broken them, be assured that you would now be under my control, as would all here, AIs or those using gridlinks or augs.' The Legate turned its nightmare head slightly towards Horace Blegg. 'Including you.'

Cormac decided he must take the risk. '*All of you, accept nothing via my gridlink for the next minute*.' Out loud

he said, 'Blegg, Thorn, back away from me.' He looked
up at Arach. 'I want you to soft link to me. Any sign that
I'm subject to a subversion program, you take me down
then—' he stabbed a finger at the Legate, 'then you take
him down.'

'What the—?' Thorn began.

Horace Blegg slapped a hand on his shoulder and
began drawing him away. 'Information package from the
NEJ – we don't know if it is genuine.'

As a further precaution, Cormac reached in his pocket
and thumbed up then held down the dead man's switch
on his grenade. Only then did he open the package.

Haruspex and *Coriolanus* were visible ahead, glaring
bright in the light of the near sun. 'We have all released
beacons broadcasting this package, so hopefully it will
get through to you,' Jack informed him. 'We are attempting to sling-shot around the sun, to make a run on the
USER which is located on a moon orbiting the other
living world here. While that USER continues functioning, estimated time to the arrival of Polity forces here,
one year. Only if the USER is shut down will that estimate reduce. We will reach the USER in seventeen hours.
The expected time of arrival thereafter of the dreadnoughts, less than a day.'

The package contained more information, but that
was the gist of it.

'I have no idea what that message contained,' said the
Legate, 'but presumably you now understand your situation. You are alone here and even a minimal chance of
rescue is a long time off. Pure logic should now dictate
your next actions. You cannot escape, and if you fight
you will all either be captured or killed. I now offer you
a deal.' One long hand gestured to encompass the

Sparkind and the dracomen. 'In exchange for the lives of all these. You' – one finger stabbing towards Cormac – 'and you' – now towards Blegg – 'will hand yourselves over.'

Cormac thumbed the dead man's switch on the grenade back into position. He did not for one moment believe this entity would allow the others to live, no matter who handed themselves over. Or perhaps they really would be kept alive, which might be worse.

'*Let's just shoot the fucker and run for the cave,*' came a communication from Chalder after the minute Cormac designated ran out.

Through his gridlink Cormac broadcast: '*Start moving towards the cave, but try not to make it too obvious. Arach, the Legate has chameleonware so if it shows any sign of fading out . . .*'

'*I was already doing that,*' the drone replied grumpily.

'What guarantees can you give that you'll stick to your word?' Cormac asked out loud to the Legate. Scanning beyond it, Cormac recorded the scene in his gridlink then ran a comparison program to perpetually analyse that same scene moment by moment. It annoyed him that he had not thought to do so earlier.

'The only guarantee I can give—' began the Legate.

It was the trunk of a tree down in the jungle, slightly displaced for half a second.

Chameleonware.

'Arach!'

'*I see it.*'

The Legate disappeared. One of the spider-drone's Gatling cannons whirred and fired, spewing fire across the intervening ten yards. The Legate reappeared only yards from Cormac, juddered to a halt and survived longer than seemed possible under such a fusillade, then exploded into metallic shreds. Arach's other cannon whirred and spewed fire. To the right and left of where the Legate had been, huge shapes flickered in and out of being – flat louselike bodies supported ten feet off the ground by bowed insectile legs, their nightmare heads unravelling squidlike grasping tentacles. Both of them collapsed, pieces of them exploding away, clearly visible now as their chameleonware broke down. Cormac squatted for cover and glimpsed Arach springing from his perch just as turquoise fire splashed down onto the rock cube, turning its upper surface molten. The drone ran, with all his weapons now directed up at the sky. Darker shadow fell over them as another spiral ship shut down its chameleonware right above. High-intensity laser punching down: five or more dracomen turned instantly to flames. Autoguns now trained on the ship above, but one of them suddenly blasted to silvery fragments. And meanwhile a hellish army swooped up the slope from the jungle.

'Thorn, mine the entrance as we—'

Thorn turned towards him, grinning perhaps . . . then he stood in an inferno, coming apart, face melting away from a screaming skull, before toppling disjointed in clouds of greasy smoke. Gone: in an instant.

Thorn . . .

Further explosions lit the garish scene as the autoguns found targets on the ship above. Even while paralysed mentally Cormac continued to function on an instinctive level. He sent Shuriken streaking down towards a pack of quadruped machines like headless brushed-aluminium Rottweilers, who led the charge from below. The star threw its blades out to maximum extent and howled along just off the ground, as if carrying the anger Cormac should now feel. He took out his grenade and gridlinked to its control mechanism. He ran a simple program, so that the moment he lost consciousness the grenade would detonate. He placed it in the breast pocket of his envirosuit, then, standing fully in view, aimed his proton weapon and, picking his targets in the leading ranks, began to fire. He slewed emotion, became colder. Fuck them, what was the point now in retreating to the cave system?

Shuriken hammered into a thicket of legs, sending many of the dog-things sprawling. Cormac fired continually as silvery flat-worms slid up over the fallen grey bodies like running mercury, each hit of his converted these things to disparate segments – which then extended out tendrils to rejoin and draw together again.

'*Cormac, get to the cave,*' came Blegg's communication via his link.

'Go fuck yourself,' Cormac replied.

'*Do you want reasons?*' Blegg asked. '*Chalder just died trying to protect you, and others will now die to that same end. Get into the cave!*'

A scan of his surroundings: numerous oily fires – difficult to discern which burning figures were human and which dracoman. From ten yards down the slope one of the flatworms reared up, its nose flaring open on a glittering interior. A stun blast smacked into Cormac's chest and sent him staggering back, then down on his knees. Above him, a flattened torpedo shape, snakish legs tangled underneath, unravelling and reaching for him. Consciousness fading.

Let it go.

A black missile slammed into the hovering shape's

side, detonated and sent it cartwheeling out of sight, coming apart. Spider legs abruptly closed around Cormac and hauled him from the ground. Shuriken came screaming back to the rescue. He just retained the presence of mind to offline the grenade program, and recall the throwing star to its wrist holster, as Arach carried him to cover. Damp darkness then, and a blast throwing dust and rock past him. He finally let go of his consciousness – didn't want it.

Stalactites poised above Blegg like dragon's teeth. Damp air groped about his face and somewhere he could hear water trickling. But he focused his attention inward to view another episode in his life, another death, this time on the planet Cheyne III.

Walking out along the jetty towards the boat supposedly containing a Separatist arms cache, there had been no time for him to think his usual *To die like this after so long*. One moment the boat rocked there on the waves, solid and substantial, the next it turned into a spreading ball of flame. He recollected briefly seeing the jetty flung up like the rearing back of a snake, then the blast hit him. No pain, just a cessation. Then he woke up in the ECS Rescue ship, recovering from cuts, burns and concussion. The reality, he knew, was that nothing larger than what you might scrape up with a teaspoon then remained of the Horace Blegg who hunted Separatists on Cheyne III. Only memories, constantly copied via a link open to the runcible AI.

Here no such link existed, however, and should he die a new Blegg would only remember up to the point he went out of communication with the *NEJ*, from where Blegg's memories had been regularly retransmitted to update his back-up. But of course this sort of thing had happened before – these breaks in the narrative of his apparently endless life. When he was thrown to the ground in the Highlands of Scotland, apparently by the blast from a satellite strike, that was a cut-off point. But he now remembered himself lying twisted on his side and gazing in puzzlement at the ribs of his own chest splayed out like bloody fingers, and seeing circuitry patterns etched into his bones. No bump on the head dispelling consciousness, and it hadn't been a shockwave that threw him down either, but an explosive seeker bullet. And he just died, very quickly.

But the false bit? Only these extra memories, only these undone deletions told him which they were. Earth Central falsified the day it took him to return to Geneva, probably only to add a certain variety. In reality, EC just took out of storage another body – another facsimile of humanity neither Golem nor human but something else. Another Blegg. When the antimatter bomb struck Tuscor City, the AI had simply placed on hold all his memories concerning events after he left the attack ship *Yellow Cloud*. So here, now, that whole episode culminating with the searing hammer of that blast finally reaching him, conflicted in his memory with another memory in which he never went down to the planet, since the arrival of the Prador destroyer gave him no time. The bomb on *Amaranth* Station turned him into slurry, but that small agonizing moment was deleted and replaced with the memory of him having transported himself out at the last moment. Of course, much that ensued was also false, until a new body could be put into place.

Lies, all lies. And what seemed even more cruel was his emulating a human so closely that he wanted to believe his own myth. The Atheter AI had known, for when he gave it his word it replied, 'I know – it's the word of a ruler.' A partial truth perhaps, since he was merely the creation of a ruler. The Legate had known with its, '*Had we broken them, be assured that you would now be under my control, as would all here, AIs or those using gridlinks or augs . . . Including you.*'

Blegg rubbed his palms together. They felt gritty, just as they had felt when he climbed to the top of the monolith on Cull to find uncomfortable revelation. Similar revelation had occurred to him before. Captured and dragged into a Separatist base on a moonlet that was only a number on the star charts, he faced torture and interrogation. A ridiculous situation since he had not been on a mission then, merely checking out some fossils that should not have been there. The fast picket that dropped him off was not to return for some weeks, so no cover and no AI on hand to record his memories. They used psychoactive drugs on him, physical torture that left him minus three fingers – removed one joint at a time – minus the skin across his stomach, his testicles crushed and burnt. They could not believe their luck in having captured him. Their leader did not believe it, so the interrogation continued. At some point he became a mewling thing with only a passing resemblance to a human being. Awareness then returned to him with a thump and all the confusion suddenly receded. Clarity of mind became absolute, but what initiated it? They had discovered something very strange about his body, were working to keep him alive to take elsewhere for deeper study and a more meticulous investigation. They talked of the technology for probing minds and other things of a similar nature. Blegg remembered previous deaths, remembered what he was, and knew this could not be allowed. But what could he do? He no longer possessed workable limbs. He decided it was time for him to die. However, then came AI linkage to his mind as the attack ship *Yellow Cloud* entered the system looking for him. It uploaded his memories as far as and including the moment when the missiles hammered into the base and converted it into a glowing crater in the face of the moonlet. Blegg's new body thereafter possessed no conscious recollection of this inconvenient episode. It did possess something else, though, should something like this occur again and no attack ship be on hand. It contained the seeds of destruction of itself and much else beside. It became a weapon, as well as a vessel for his consciousness. Of course to use that weapon Blegg had to remember he could die, that he had died many times.

Again Blegg felt that potential awaiting his conscious command. It had been used occasionally since that time on the moonlet, but he had no memories of the circumstances involved, since it was impossible for him to have them. Only after-the-event recordings were open to him: the gutted Prador destroyer he was held captive aboard, sludge smeared across a rocky plateau on a world seceded from the Polity – all that remained of a rebel army – and other less dramatic occasions when he lost contact with the AIs and was in danger of being forced to reveal too much.

This time, however, he realized there would be no new Blegg. Now the truth in all its raw and painful detail stood open to him, just as his facsimile human body now lay open to his internal inspection and under his absolute control. There could be no more Blegg because a certain point had been irrecoverably passed. Time, he felt, for this to be made known.

He gazed across the dank cave in which they now found themselves. Cormac still lay unconscious, and Blegg knew that on some deep level the agent probably fought against waking. Thorn had gone the way of Gant – both of those human Sparkind soldiers dead now, both of the men who had joined Cormac at Samarkand.

Blegg watched his fellow agent, waited, and remembered his many deaths.

Consciousness returned abruptly and painfully and the first clear image in his mind was of Thorn's face melting apart before him. For a moment he could not equate the image with anything he knew, then the full impact of memory hit him.

My decision.

Cormac opened his eyes, ramping up his light sensitivity in the gloom. He lay against a pack which in turn was propped against a rock. He realized his visor was open, but he was breathing okay so did not hurry to close it. The planet's air mix could sustain human life, with only its temperature being too high on the surface. Cool down here.

He sat upright. 'What's the situation?'

Too abrupt a move, for he became suddenly dizzy and nauseous. A huge spider tracked across his vision over to the left – Arach – then Blegg loomed before him.

'We lost many,' said the old Oriental. 'There are only seven dracomen with us down here, though five others made it into the jungle. Three human Sparkind surviving, one of them probably not for much longer. Six

Golem Sparkind too, some of them badly burnt but still functional. One remaining autogun and Arach.'

'The enemy?' Cormac asked.

'We collapsed a thousand feet of cave behind us. If they want to kill us, I suspect a near-c projectile could penetrate this deep. However, our scanners can hear them burrowing, so evidently they still want to capture us alive. At their present rate it will take them perhaps ten hours to reach us.'

Cormac checked the timings in his gridlink: fifteen hours before the *NEJ* and the *Haruspex* could reach the USER, and he suspected that whatever happened there would be concluded very quickly – one way or the other. He slowly heaved himself to his feet and looked around.

They were located in a large oblate cavern in which tube lights, stuck to the walls, revealed to be toothed with orange and green stalactites and stalagmites. Arach reared up against one wall, perhaps feeling the approach of the burrowers through his feet. To one side of Cormac lay an individual wrapped in a heat sheet, a small autodoc clinging at the neck. Difficult, at a glance, even to know the soldier's sex, the patient's head being burned raw and featureless. Some dracomen moved about, checking equipment which ran optics to probes sunk in the surrounding stone. The silvery skeleton of a Golem strode past, shedding pieces of charred syntheflesh.

'Can we go deeper?' Cormac asked.

Blegg sighed and plumped himself down on a rock. 'Yes, we can go deeper. A fissure leads down at an angle over there.' He pointed past the stripped Golem to a dark cave mouth. 'But we are only delaying the inevitable.'

Cormac peered at him. 'You're normally a little more upbeat than this. Surely our whole lives are spent delaying the inevitable.' He felt a sudden unreasonable anger at what he felt to be Blegg's fatalism, while in another layer of his mind understood his own reaction being due to the loss of Thorn. 'Do you suggest we surrender, then, or just kill ourselves here?'

'I'm presently suffering from a dearth of suggestions,' Blegg replied.

Cormac allowed his anger some slack. 'Then let me suggest that it is time for you, Horace Blegg, to take your leave of us. Since you possess the means.'

Blegg stared at him, and it seemed something metallic glinted in the old man's eyes. 'My time has been interesting,' he stated. 'Since that runcible connection opened to *Celedon* station, I have learnt much.' The gleam faded from his eyes and he gazed off into the darkness and continued more introspectively. 'As well as obtaining the U-space signature for Jain nodes from an Atheter AI, I obtained the beginning of revelation. That AI replayed for me the key episodes in my life since Hiroshima, and only from that alien perspective did I understand how so very fortunate I was to be present at most of the pivotal events in history since then – not enough to make me overly suspicious, but no small number either.'

'And this is leading where?' asked Cormac, impatient now to do something, anything.

Blegg turned and stabbed a finger at him, the metal back in his eyes. 'You, Ian Cormac, believed me to be an avatar of Earth Central, a construct. I tried to ignore that suggestion because the immediacy of my existence has been too real to me, yet you planted the seed of doubt. Is my history my own, is my mind my own? Am I real?

I cannot erase doubt, and I see it would have continued to grow.'

'Would have?'

'I never told you where I obtained that Jain node.'

'True, you did not.'

'Jain nodes are activated by living intelligent organisms, only thereafter can the technology they produce manage to attack and subvert our technology. Mr Crane obtained Jain nodes on Cull. He kept them and they did not react to him, did not activate – perhaps some safety measure built in by the Jain AIs that created them. My doubts were growing; the accumulation of coincidence throughout my long life has reached a critical point from which I cannot recover without huge erasure of memory and much adjustment. Machines are like that, they reach a point where the work involved in patching and repairing is no longer worth the effort. My usefulness to Earth Central is at an end and, in collusion with Mr Crane, EC opened my eyes to reality. Mr Crane tossed a Jain node to me, and I caught it in my bare hand. No reaction. That I am a being that possesses intelligence, I've no doubt, but am I that thing so hazily described as a *living* organism?'

'I see . . .'

Utterly emphatic and emotionless, Blegg continued, 'The Hiroshima bomb blast: all gleaned from witness statements, expanded by AI, and extrapolated into a constructed memory for me. The Nuremberg trials: again that gleaning, because so many people have written about them, speculated about them. All construction, too. Later memories come clearer – is that because those are not so far from me in time? No, because the clarity of recording media in later years improved, and from it better memories could therefore be constructed.'

'You appeared like a projection once on the *Occam Razor*, but I touched you and found you solid,' ventured Cormac.

Blegg waved a dismissive hand. 'Projection integrated with hardfields – an easy trick.'

'So all the ship AIs, Jack, Jerusalem, the lot . . . all colluded in this?'

'They must have, when it became necessary for them to know about my true nature. Earth Central wanted its avatar to be a *human* leader, as well as a legend, something to give hope and encouragement. It is a trait of the human race to raise some of its members to high regard, quite often when they are not deserving of such, hence the cults of celebrity in earlier centuries. Earth Central wanted to choose one so up-raised, create that one . . . I resent not being allowed to know myself, even though I am a part of Earth Central itself.'

'Are you so sure now?'

Blegg pointed to the mound of rubble heaped to one side of the chamber. There, Cormac assumed, lay their entry point. 'Out there, the enemy knows, which is why it wants to capture me. That mere fact has brought online different programming within me. I realize now that I cannot translate myself through U-space. I never was able to. I step from Valles Marineris on Mars to the runcible there, transport to the runcible on Earth's Moon, and step from there to the Viking Museum – all memories created in a virtuality.'

'So down here, you will probably die with us, or be captured.'

'I will die, if that is the correct term. There is too much

of Earth Central within me for capture to be allowed. I will fight for as long as I can, then, when capture seems imminent, I will activate a nanite weapon inside me, and destroy myself. There will be nothing left. But the question that remains is can *you* escape in the way I cannot?'

'I won't leave them.' Cormac gestured around.

'But perhaps', said Blegg, 'you should find out if that option is available to you.' He stood up and moved away.

Damn him!

Blegg's newly discovered self-knowledge made him appear coldly fatalistic, though it did appear they were in a trap from which there seemed no escape. Cormac began moving around the chamber, till he found the remaining Sparkind all gathered in one area, laying out their remaining equipment and checking it over. One Golem, the side of his face burned down to ceramal, stood up when he approached.

'Assessment?' Cormac enquired.

'We have taken heavy losses,' the Golem told him. 'Once they break through – at their rate of burrowing, we estimate in ten hours – with our present munitions, and factoring in their likely rate of attack, we should hold them off for a further half an hour.'

Not much hope here, either.

Cormac scanned around. 'Did Scar survive?'

The Golem pointed over to the mouth of a nearby tunnel. Meanwhile, one of the human Sparkind, who had disassembled and now reassembled a pulse-gun, asked, 'When we've nothing left to shoot them with, what then?'

Cormac instantly accessed information available in his link: *Andrew Hailex, 64 years old, joined ECS as a monitor age 25, rose through the ranks then transferred ten years later to GCG – Ground Combat Group. Left after four years*

*to marry and raise three children. Rejoined ECS at age 55
and trained as a Sparkind. Involved in several dangerous
actions. Regularly sends messages to his family . . .*

Hailex, of course, looked no older than Cormac
appeared – maybe in his twenties – but then few people
chose to look old. His scalp was hairless, probably naturally so for he did not possess eyebrows either. He bulked
out his envirosuit so seemed likely to be boosted. He
grinned – he'd lost a tooth – and his eyes displayed a
pinkish tint. He rather reminded Cormac of Gant.

'I'll think of something, but if it turns out we have
nowhere left to run, what remains for you to do I leave to
personal choice,' Cormac replied. 'Our attackers are using
something related to Jain technology and I rather suspect
they won't be interning us in a nice comfortable prison
camp. I'm afraid I've no suggestions for you.' Cormac grimaced, realizing how he had just paraphrased Blegg.

The other man's grin faded, then he reached out and
nudged an open case with his toe. Inside rested two polished aluminium objects the size of coffee flasks: two
CTDs, low yield, but enough to raise the temperature in
here to that of a sun's surface.

'Yes,' said Cormac, 'that's one option.'

Moving off he entered the side cave to which the
Golem had directed him. This stretched back only ten
yards, and there Scar and two other dracomen sat by
a pool down into which the cave roof slanted.

'Scar, I want some of your people to scout out that
fissure.' Cormac stabbed a thumb over his shoulder.

Scar stared at him for a long moment, then blinked.
'I have sent two there already.'

A beat.

'Are you in communication with them?'

'Always.'

'What have they found?'

'The fissure runs down sheer for fifty yards, then its angle changes to forty-five degrees for another four hundred yards before beginning to level out. My associates have just now reached that point. Seismic scanning ahead indicates a crawl of nearly two miles, then several pools from which tunnels extend under water.'

Cormac noted how the dracoman held his hand submerged in the pool he presently crouched beside, fingers spread out, and wondered if this somehow enabled contact with the two dracomen below.

'These tunnels?'

'I know no more yet, however the route to it is too narrow for the autogun, or for Arach.'

Cormac considered their options. If they remained here they'd certainly end up in a fight they could not win.

'Recall them,' he said. 'We'll be going down there anyway.' He turned and headed back out into the main cavern.

'Arach, over here.'

The spider shape reared away from the wall and scuttled over to him. Cormac studied the drone for a moment, then explained the situation.

'No problem,' Arach replied and, before Cormac could say any more, scuttled away again. Cormac now called over everyone else in the cavern and gave his instructions, finishing with: 'Those that need it, get some rest now – we move in two hours.'

'He doesn't talk much, does he?' said Samland Karischev, as he gazed out through the massive chain-glass screen.

'Brutus is feeling as frustrated and annoyed as we all are,' replied Azroc.

Freed from his duties by the Coloron AI, Azroc had immediately transferred to the *Brutal Blade*, the utile dreadnought run by the AI Brutus, and sometimes jokingly referred to – because of its resemblance to some titanic beast's liver plated with metal – as the *Organ Transplant*. Fresh from that devastated world, where an entire arcology capable of housing a billion souls had necessarily been destroyed, the opportunity for some payback filled him with joy even though he was Golem. And when *Battle Wagon* joined the fleet, now grown to twenty dreadnoughts, numerous attack ships and other warcraft, that joy only increased.

Serious payback: now one of the big boys accompanied them.

Karischev pointed through the screen at the distant vessel. 'It doesn't look like much. Why all the excitement?'

Azroc sighed. The *Battle Wagon* did not look particularly threatening, being a cylindrical object apparently devoid of sensor arrays or evident weapons. 'It doesn't look like much because you are now seeing it against a backdrop of vacuum and so do not really have any idea of its scale.'

Karischev, a squat bulky man with a friendly boulder-like face and watery brown eyes, struck Azroc as a bit of an enigma. The man carried no augmentations, either cerebral or physical, and obviously did not bother to change his appearance to anything more aesthetic, as it seemed most humans were inclined to do. He also commanded a strike force of Sparkind ground troops, assigned to *Brutal Blade*.

'Big, then?' Karischev suggested.

'Eight miles in diameter and twenty miles long. It's old, built during the Prador War, carries weapons designed to penetrate Prador exotic armour, plus numerous recent upgrades. Much is made of the fact that ships like *Brutal Blade* can destroy worlds. The truth is that a ship like ours could easily depopulate a world, but not actually destroy it. The *Battle Wagon*, however, could do the job without, as the saying goes, breaking into a sweat.'

'No shit?' Karischev's eyes grew wide.

'Definitely.'

Karischev turned back to gaze through the screen. 'Of course, you can be carrying the biggest gun in the world, but that don't matter a fuck if you ain't got a target.'

Azroc could only nod in agreement. The information packages sent by the *NEJ* showed, in the system a light year ahead, enemy forces that the ships now glinting in space all around him could obliterate with ease. But since the USER had deployed and ejected the fleet from U-space, it proceeded on conventional drives. At this rate it would take them more than a year to reach their target, which created all sorts of problems, not least being that the fight would long be over and the enemy would have had a year to prepare for them – unless before that they shut down the USER and fled.

Another problem arose concerning the living occupants of those few ships in the Polity fleet that carried them. They would have to go into coldsleep if the USER remained functional. The quandary faced by the *Battle Wagon* AI, now in command of this fleet, was that if the USER did go offline, the entire fleet could jump to the target system at once, and troops might need to be dropped very quickly, but it took some time for humans to recover from the effects of coldsleep.

'I'm gonna check on my men,' said Karischev, turning away.

Watching him go, Azroc wondered if bringing along these ground troops was such a good idea anyway. Yes, they might be needed, but thus far the conflict had remained mainly ship to ship – one of those fast AI battles waged on the line of Polity of which rumours abounded but of which he had never found confirmation. It struck him that such vulnerable troops would serve no purpose other than to add to the casualty figures.

18

It is official: we don't have to die. There are those amongst us now who are over two hundred years old and who may go on just not dying. However this is not immortality in the old sense of the Greek and Roman gods, for though our lives can be extended to infinity (thus far) we are still subject to death. There's no medical technology that can save you if you stick your head under a thousand-tonne press (though a prior memcording of you can be saved), and there are some virulent killers, both biologically and nanologically based, that can destroy the human meat machine very quickly and effectively. But, as many have noted, not dying is not quite the same as living. Many would try to make themselves utterly secure against death and as such cease to experience life in its conventional sense. What is the point of immortality if you wrap yourself in layers of cotton wool and armour and bury yourself in peat? Many take that route (well, not literally), but many others seize the opportunity to explore, research, experience, to live a full life. However, there are problems with this, for the human brain, though large in capacity and intricate in function, is a finite thing. Memories are lost during regeneration and repair – that drawback cannot be avoided. Moreover, as a human life grows long, memories are shunted

aside by the perpetual absorption of the endless continuing input. The solution, though, is now coming clear: memcording. We can now record our memories and even mental functions and store them separately, reload them should we wish. The technology is now available to actually delete stuff from the organic brain. So, the time has arrived when we can actually edit our own minds. It is speculated that in the future we'll be able to decide what kind of person we are going to be this year, and cut-and-paste our minds to suit. Maybe we'll decide to load select portions of our minds to more than one body. Perhaps this is due to become the procreation of the future?
– From 'How it Is' by Gordon

Warmth enclosed her, but in no way assuaged the pain. Sensing movement, Mika opened her eyes on blackness overlaid with jumbled non-sensical code. Then two words stood out – SUIT BREACH – and she realized she was seeing her visor display gone awry. Beyond it, in the minimal light this display provided, the blackness shifted. Further movement, more urgent, and something ungently began stripping her spacesuit from her body. She shrieked as mangled bones twisted inside her leg. Then the visor sank down into the neck ring and wet flesh surged over her face. Stifled, she fought for breath, began to lose consciousness. But next came a warm breeze as the flesh withdrew. She gasped, sucking in stale air smelling of burnt steak.

Ahead of her walls of similar flesh continued to withdraw – she could feel it all moving – then the lights turned on to give her confirmation: small globes affixed in an undulating surface which constantly dripped white fluid. Managing to tilt her head slightly, she peered down at herself. Red tentacles securely bound her against the living wall behind her. It also seemed evident that some of them penetrated her body – she could feel movement inside her. Now, right before her, a cobra pseudopod rose into view.

'Hello,' she managed. And even this extremity could not quell her fascination. She was actually, without any technology intervening, *inside* a Dragon sphere.

The pseudopod swayed from side to side as if seeking the perfect angle from which to strike, its single sapphire eye glowing hypnotically.

'Can't we . . . discuss . . . this?'

The thing struck at an angle with concussive force, wrenching her neck to one side and burning hot behind her ear. A sudden horrible ache suffused her skull, a scratching buzzing vibration intensifying in her eardrum. This, Mika realized, might be how it would feel to have an aug attached without using the correct anaesthetics. She knew when something entered and connected, because this harsh organic world went away again.

'Show me,' something said, and started to fast-forward through her memories, like a viewer impatient with the slower parts of a film. Streams of images and sensations screamed through her mind, but this did not seem fast enough. There came a horrible dislocation as something made an imprint of her total mind, peeled it free like a scab from a raw wound, and placed it to one side, then imprinted another and another until her ego and sense of self seemed something viewed through a cut gem, with alternative Mikas playing out in each facet. It scanned her childhood and adolescence at the Life-Coven on Circe, meticulously winnowing out the very smallest detail. Concurrently it whipped through her subsequent training and early career with ECS, but with slower precision it scanned her memories of Samarkand, then, almost with a horrible sensuousness, pored over the memories of Masada, then Cull.

Somewhere, deep behind that chronological separation, she still felt whole however, and sensed something of this mind's purpose: her entire life as a basis for comparison. And she understood how the entity prepared for a meticulous reading of her memories of the time when it had fallen out of contact with its fellow; through her it intended to check the veracity of the other Dragon sphere's story.

Upon reaching the time of the USER blockade around Cull – when it had lost contact with the other sphere, which was actually on that world – it allowed Mika to come back together again. Now, like a spectator to her own life, she proceeded to watch those events unfold: her studies of Jain technology; the *Jerusalem*'s run into the Cull system and brief contact with the other sphere lodged there, the short journey to a nearby system where the old colony ship *Ogygian*, with Skellor and Cento aboard, crashed into a dead sun; Cormac's rescue and the lengthy task of putting him back together again. As it checked her memories, Mika could feel a feedback of growing dismay from this portion of Dragon. When it finally reached the events at *Celedon*, and Cormac's subsequent interrogation of the other sphere, during which that one finally broke its Maker programming, she became partially aware of her body again – smelling oven smoke, feeling a discordant vibration within the sphere, and the wash of hot air entering her organic cell. As subsequent events played out, a pain grew in her skull and the connection began to break down. Vision and full sensation returned, and with their revival she screamed.

As the pseudopod ripped away from her head, another pseudopod shot into view and wound itself around the first one like a vine. The Dragon sphere then began jolting from side to side, her cell deforming around her. The two pseudopods continued thrashing, as if intent on strangling each other, then through the wall she felt the crump of some massive internal explosion. Acrid stinking smoke filled the area around her. Through watering eyes she observed one of the pseudopods abruptly freeze then grow flaccid, deflating as if all the juice were being sucked out of it. The still-living one rose up, shrugging its opponent away from it like ragged clothing.

'So . . . which?' Mika managed. It seemed this sphere was also in conflict with its Maker programming.

The binding tentacles writhed about her, and she felt those inside her moving as well. She came near to crying out again as pain grew in her in waves, but then something ran cold as ice up her spine and hit the 'off' switch in her skull.

Mika's dreams were dragons.

The comet's course headed to aphelion – out from the system through the asteroid belt – perihelion lay far in its future, after it swung back through the inner system. Previous fly-bys had boiled off most of its ice to leave a core of rock conveniently wormed through with hundreds of huge caverns. Deep scanning of the interior revealed one cavern system suitable for her purposes. Cutting through ten yards of ice would give the ship access. And Orlandine could hide.

After correcting the *Heliotrope*'s course so that it matched that of the comet, she used the fore-mounted plasma cutter. The ice fluoresced as it made the transition from complex ice to water ice, and then into vapour. Cutting two deep holes, she opened the claw to its widest point, then manoeuvred the ship forwards until a claw tip inserted into each hole. Then she just fired up the cutter to full power and, over ten minutes, gave the comet a tail it had not possessed in many thousands of years, though this time a brief one that quickly faded into vacuum.

Once the hole was wide enough she detached the grab claw, then swung the ship around and reversed it into the cave. Utter darkness now, but every movement and action she precisely mapped in her extended haiman mind. At her order the ship fired cable-mounted gecko pads against the cavern wall, and drew itself into place. With an afterthought she made it clamp its main grab, like the pincers of some giant mechanical earwig, to a rocky outcrop. Then she powered down all the ship's systems, before heading out to explore her new home.

After physically detaching her carapace, and herself, from the interface sphere, Orlandine headed aft to don a spacesuit and assister frame, then scuttled to the airlock. Once outside she clung to the hull and looked around. With her cowl up, the cavern seemed as bright as day from residual infrared emanating from the ship's thrusters and the fluorescing of complex ices nearby.

The cavern stretched a hundred yards across and was four times as long, curving near the end down into a narrow hole. The walls consisted of countless concave hollows holding rounded pebbles encased in tough nodular masses of ice. Gas had bubbled through magma, then cooled, and the subsequent stresses had collapsed thin shells of rock into fragments. The cavern acted like a tumbling machine each time the sun thawed the comet, rounding the fragments eventually into pebbles. Millions of years of thaws and freezes, maybe billions had elapsed. That no pebbles floated free was probably due to them picking up enough frictional heat to stick to the ice as it cooled and supercooled. Orlandine pushed herself off from the hull, floated over to one side wall and grabbed an ice nodule to steady herself. Where her foot brushed accidentally against the wall, pebbles tumbled away like opaque bubbles. She would have to watch that. Careless movement in here could result in the open space being filled with a perpetual hail of them. Taking care to only grab clear ice nodules with no pebbles stuck to their surfaces, she made her way along the wall to the hole leading into another cavern. However, briefly peering in there confirmed just more of the same.

Orlandine spent less than an hour exploring before returning to the *Heliotrope*. How long could she tolerate waiting here? Back within her ship she decided to explore Jain technology in a virtuality. Perhaps that would keep boredom at bay.

Boredom did not get a chance to impinge.

Some in the cave were resting, others still meticulously checking weaponry. Blegg sat unnaturally motionless on a boulder, his head bowed. Cormac bowed his own head, and in his gridlink opened the memory package given to him by Jerusalem, and uploaded it directly to his mind. First, came the pain, then Cormac became himself, many months before:

They had surfaced from U-space, but for Cormac his perception of the real seemed permanently wrecked – a rip straight through it. Every solid echoed into grey void, and the stale air of the ship seemed to be pouring into that rather than towards some large breach nearby. Gazing at his thin-gun, Cormac saw it as both an object and a grey tube punching into infinity, which, he reflected with an almost hysterical amusement, was precisely what it had been to those he had killed with it. When he entered the bridge, Cento became a perilous moving form casting laser shadows behind it, and when the Golem fired his APW, the fire burned with negative colour . . .

. . .

This is memory, and I must not lose sight of that. The pain is not real. My mind is whole, I am whole . . .

. . .

Cormac fought against the enclosing structure, but could do nothing to help Cento. When he felt the wash of tidal forces through his body, he knew that in very little time that same wash would intensify sufficiently to shatter the Jain structure, but by then the tidal forces would have compressed and stretched his body to a sludge of splintered bone and ruptured flesh inside it. It occurred to him, with crazy logic, that such damage to himself was required as payment for the pain he already suffered. On another level it occurred to him that he was not entirely rational at that moment.

. . .

You didn't try to subvert Cento. You knew you were going to die and just wanted the satisfaction of tearing him apart with your hands. Skellor, you erred.

. . .

The Ogygian jerked once, twice, then suddenly Cormac lay heavy inside the Jain structure – being crammed over to one side.

Grappling claws.

. . .

Cento and Skellor both slammed into the wall. The Golem

was down to metal, and Skellor even managed to tear some of that away. Long pink lesions cut into Skellor's own blackened carapace, golden nodules showing in these like some strange scar tissue.

. . .

It became too much: to choose a moral death, then to accept an inevitable one, and then to have both taken away. If only he could strike even the smallest blow. But he could do nothing – was ineffectual. Then, in that moment of extremity, Cormac saw the way. Wasn't it laughably obvious?

Staring into the tear in his perception he saw, only for a moment, U-space entire and, like an AI, comprehended it. Enclosed and trapped in Jain substructure, he turned aside and stepped to where he wanted to be, detouring through that other place that made nothing of material barriers. Three yards to the side of the cage of alien carapace, he stepped into the real, reached down beside a console and picked up his thin-gun. Only then did Skellor begin to react, but not fast enough.

Cormac brought the gun up, his arm straight, and began to fire.

. . .

'The cables,' Cento said calmly over com.

. . .

Cento, now impacted on the surface of a dark sun, along with Skellor.

. . .

Gasping a warm damp breath of the cave's air, Cormac jerked into the present. Checking the time readout in his gridlink he realized that though those events aboard the ancient spaceship *Ogygian* took very little time, it had taken just over an hour for him to incorporate them in his mind. But what a vast difference his knowledge of them imposed on his thinking.

He had suffered horribly at Skellor's hands, his mind just as ripped up as his body at the end. But he had translated himself through U-space – something always considered an impossibility for a human being, which was why he had never really believed Blegg to be human. But now Blegg claimed to be the avatar Cormac had accused him of being, and could not translate himself through U-space, yet it seemed Cormac could.

Cormac heaved himself up from the boulder he was propped against, phantom pains shooting through his body as it remembered old injuries, and his mind muggy and seemingly dislocated within his skull. Glancing across the cave he saw one of the Sparkind attaching a CTD to the underside of the autogun. It would be set to detonate the moment that weapon ran out of ammunition. Spikes had since been driven into the rocky lip of the fissure down which they intended to exit, and dracomen and the other Sparkind were checking the cable winders attached to their belts. For a moment Cormac experienced a surge of painful memory: that time on Samarkand when he, Thorn, Gant, and the two Golem, Cento and Aiden, had prepared similar gear for their descent into a shaft cut down into the ground. And how Gant died there – the first time.

'What has the memory given you?' Blegg, standing at his shoulder.

Without turning, Cormac replied, 'I don't really know. I now look around this cave and it seems to me all this rock is as insubstantial as mist, yet I know that if I try to step through it the most probable result will be concussion.' Now he turned to face Blegg fully. 'I am not the same person I was then. Jerusalem needed to subsequently rebuild much of my body and my mind, since I was neither whole nor, I think, entirely sane.'

'Perhaps . . . in a moment of extremity . . .'

'Perhaps.'

Cormac now observed the flesh-stripped Golem crouching over the badly burnt soldier. The Golem removed the autodoc, took some thumb-sized bloody object from one of its manipulators and put it to one side, then pressed some control so that the autodoc folded away all its surgical gear. He then returned it to its case.

'They wouldn't have been able to get him safely through the fissure,' Blegg explained. 'And he remained lucid enough to make his wishes known . . . via his aug.'

'He chose to die?' Cormac asked.

'He was memplanted.' Hence the bloody object just extracted.

'Oh that's all right then.' Cormac felt a surge of anger return, then immediately stamped on it because again he realized its source. The wounded soldier would have been an encumbrance they could ill afford. And in a horrible way he felt grateful that the sheer lethality of the weapons used against them had left so few wounded, yet also horrified about how many they had killed. Including Thorn. He turned towards the survivors, seeing they only awaited his instructions. 'Okay, we go now. No point waiting here until the enemy start coming through the walls. You Golem run the lead lines down and the rest of us will follow. Arach' – he turned to locate the drone, which came scuttling from a side cave – 'I take it you don't need a line?'

'Nah, these extra legs have their compensation,' the drone grated.

Cormac nodded. 'Myself and Blegg will go down last

on the lines. I want you to remain here until we've reached the bottom. I want you to detach any lines up here that don't auto-detach, then follow us down.'

'Sure thing, boss,' the spider-drone replied.

Cormac eyed Arach, then headed over to the fissure. As he approached, the leading Golem pulled end-rings from the cable winders on their belts, unreeling mono-filament cables apparently as thick as climbing ropes as the winders sprayed them with orange cladding – providing both easier grip and to protect the unwary from filament thin enough to slice through flesh. The Golem then attached the rings to the spikes driven into the stone lip before abseiling down. The rest followed, attaching their belt winders as they went. Scar followed his draco-men down, then Cormac waved Blegg ahead of him. The old Oriental nodded and almost reluctantly joined the descent.

'Arach, what are *you* going to do?' Cormac asked as the spider-drone stepped delicately up beside him. 'You can't follow us all the way once down below.'

'Don't worry about me. I'll be fine.'

It seemed to Cormac the drone danced a little, almost gleefully. He knew it relished the prospect of battle, but did it want to die?

'I could always stay with you,' Cormac suggested, and wondered where the hell that had come from.

Just then the rock about them shuddered and stalac-tites within the cavern crashed to the floor, shattering like porcelain.

'I thought they were hours away from us,' Cormac said.

'That was nothing to do with the burrowers,' Arach replied. 'I just detected a gravitic anomaly.'

Cormac felt heartened by this. The ECS Centurions contained gravtech weapons, and the brief quake he had just felt indicated they might be using them.

'Time we were on our way?' Arach pointed down into the fissure with one sharp leg.

Cormac walked over, then turned to scan all around inside the cave before lowering himself down. He clipped the line into its slot in his belt winder, which governed its friction setting to how fast he moved. At first he abseiled down the slope, but when its angle altered to make this impossible, he had to walk backwards down it. Away from the lights up in the main cavern, he turned on his envirosuit light. Time dragged by without the others yet coming in sight, and he thought that those below him must be moving faster, so he accelerated. The slope began to level out further when Scar and Blegg became visible to him. He could see them ducking as the fissure began to close up. By the time he reached them, the cave floor had levelled and the party stood grouped together.

'Time to detach those lines,' he suggested.

Crouching its way past, a Golem moved to the rear and sent up the signal to open the connector rings. With a high whine the monofilament wound in to belt winders, stripped-off cladding showering the floor like orange-coloured chipping from an auto-plane. Only a few yards behind the open rings at the ends of the returning lines came Arach.

Scar moved up beside Cormac. 'We will soon have to crawl through a very narrow section.' The dracoman gestured at the drone. 'The drone's body is ten inches too thick.'

Arach gave a wide spiderish shrug. 'Guess I'll have to

leave it for our friends then.' Abruptly the drone jumped, flipping over, the tips of its legs finding purchase in ceiling crevices. There came a low-pitched grating sound and from between the spider drone's body and the ceiling, a talc of rock dust showered down. Then came a couple of clonks and a hydraulic hiss, as Arach eased forwards and dropped from his abdomen, spinning round to land on his legs again. After a moment the abdomen, remaining attached to the ceiling, opened its hatches and lowered the two gatling cannons.

'Neat trick,' Cormac commented.

'One of my favourites,' Arach replied. 'Though my power reserve is much smaller now.'

Cormac eyed the drone: it looked somehow even more sinister now it appeared to be all legs. 'Will it survive the CTD blast?' He pointed up.

'So long as the roof doesn't collapse, and maybe even then,' Arach replied.

Cormac nodded. 'Let's keep moving, shall we?'

They crawled through crevices where sometimes Cormac found it necessary to turn his head sideways to manage to worm through. It was exhausting work, and during the first few hours Cormac stayed thoroughly aware of time passing. Reaching an area in which it again became possible to stand almost upright, he called a halt and they broke out supplies. He eyed the dracomen, who opened packets of what looked like raw meat and gobbled it down. He, Blegg, and the human Sparkind enjoyed more standard fare, and Cormac never knew coffee to taste so good.

'Time is passing,' Blegg noted.

'It is,' Cormac replied. 'At our present rate of travel we should reach the pool Scar's people detected – not long before the estimated breakthrough time of our friends above. We definitely need to be underwater by the time that autogun runs out.'

'Yes, we certainly do.'

Cormac glanced at him. 'Not feeling so fatalistic now?'

Blegg started to say something, then decided against it. 'We should be moving on,' he finally replied.

Cormac was worming through another particularly cramped stretch when he heard the distant sound of the autogun firing. Checking, it surprised him to see how much time had passed, and realized Blegg's estimate not to have been far off – it took their attackers ten hours and fifteen minutes to break through. Cormac's estimate of their own progress had not been so good. Even the dracomen were growing weary, and the pools not yet in sight.

'Thirty yards to go,' came Arach's call from ahead.

'Move!' Cormac bellowed. 'We need to get through here fast!'

Here, as soon as the CTD blew, they would be fried – the heat and energy of its blast funnelled down to them through the fissure. They all began moving a lot faster and with less regard for minor injuries. Cormac listened to the whoosh and chatter of the gun – waiting for that moment when it ceased. Abruptly Scar and Blegg, just ahead of him, were rising up onto hands and knees and progressing faster. He heard a splash, and yet another splash. As he too rose up from his belly into a crouch, Scar passed the ring end of a line back to him. He attached it to his winder – too easy to get lost under water that might quickly turn murky. Through his gridlink he raised the helmet and closed the visor of his envirosuit,

and followed the others down into water lanced through
with their envirosuit light beams.

About them the pool lay deep and wide, but soon the
two dracomen ahead led them into a narrow intestinal
pipe corkscrewing through the rock. Twice they surfaced
in travertine sumps, and on a third occasion a glare of
light passing through the water ignited the sump with
rainbow colours.

'The autogun just ran out,' one of the human
Sparkind commented.

They waited, then suddenly the water itself surged
upwards, forcing them towards the ceiling.

Now, thought Cormac, *only Arach's little present stands
between them and us.* He reckoned those Jain-constructed
biomechs could move faster down here than he and his
fellows, though they might have to burrow again if there
had been intervening rock falls.

'What explosives do we have remaining?' he asked.

'Grenades, eight planar mines and one more CTD,'
replied one of the Golem.

'Let's hope we won't need the CTD,' he said. 'Position the mines where you deem appropriate – proximity
detonation.' He added unnecessarily, 'Let's keep moving,' as the water level descended.

Within an hour they left the pipe and ascended a
gently upward-sloping fissure. The temperature slowly
began to rise, which indicated this cave system opened
up somewhere to the surface. Then abruptly the upward
slope ended against a wall of stone. Reaching this and
directing his envirosuit light upwards, Cormac discerned
another fissure climbing up into darkness.

'How many mines left?'

'Four.'

'Okay, you Golem take the lead. Position two of the mines up in the fissure and when you reach a suitable point, run lines down.'

As the Golem headed rapidly up through the fissure Cormac turned to the others. 'All of you, take a rest.' He himself felt utterly drained, partly a result of the stimulants he had used while fighting through the jungle above. He did not want to use any more of them until it became absolutely necessary.

Lines snaked down to them twenty minutes later, just as a dull boom echoed through the cave system. The biomechanism must now have entered the underwater cave system. They hooked up their winders and ascended to where the Golem had secured themselves. The fissure here turned to follow an angle of thirty degrees from the horizontal, still ascending.

With disheartening regularity over the next few hours the mines they had planted detonated behind them. Twice they needed to stop and take seismic readings to find some available course ahead. Once it became necessary to use one of their remaining mines, then some of the grenades, to blast a way through into another tunnel. While in there another dull boom resounded from behind. Checking some instrument one of the Golem told them, 'That was the last mine we planted.' Cormac felt he really did not need that – he could count. Then, manoeuvring through one sharply curving tunnel, he noticed a steady climb in temperature. Further along he found it necessary to close up his envirosuit. Next, reddish light began to impinge.

'We have a problem,' came a yell from up front.

Cormac quickly moved up past the others.

'The seismic scanner missed this,' explained one of the dracomen, almost guiltily.

The tunnel opened out onto a tilted slab that ran partly along one side of what appeared to be the empty chimney of a volcano. High above, the sky was visible like a bloodshot eye. Cormac moved to the rim of the slab and peered over.

Something down there?

He caught just a hint of a metallic gleam, but immediately it faded, then the rest of the dracomen and the Sparkind surged out of the fissure, unstrapping their weapons and turning to face back the way they had come. Arach reared up, standing only on his four back legs, the four front ones spread in threat, shimmering along their inner edges as chainglass blades extruded. From the fissure came a sound as of a swarm of iron snakes ascending towards them.

'Yeah, we have a problem,' Cormac agreed wearily.

Out towards the cold living world there were fewer of the alien ships, and those that were there would not be able to build up sufficient speed to catch up with the Centurions. They could, however, intercept, since the Centurion's target was an obvious one. Also, some of the alien ships had followed the same sling-shot solar orbit as the Centurions, and were not far behind, though with their number depleted by Haruspex's use of a gravtech weapon as they first sped down towards the sun.

'So, what's the plan?' asked Coriolanus. The Centurion's AI loaded its question with just the right level of irony. Jack reckoned it must have been practising. Scanning ahead, he now estimated the moon to be not much larger than Mars's moon Phobos.

'You and Haruspex go in ahead of me,' he said. 'Haruspex takes the left flank, you take the right flank. We'll strafe the surface with masers, follow up with CTDs. On our second pass we'll use rail-gun missiles to penetrate deep, followed by telefactors to check for—'

'Ho ho,' interrupted Haruspex.

'Okay, plan B,' said Jack. 'Let's blast the fuck out of that moon.'

'Oops, contacts rounding the planet,' warned Coriolanus.

Bacilliforms swarmed into view, and behind them, like their herders, came two ammonite spiral ships. After observing these, Jack now noticed some of the lens-shaped vessels on an intercept course far over to one side. It would be nice to be able to use chameleonware at this point, but all three Centurions had sustained too much damage for that to be effective. Jack instead fired off a near-c fusillade from his rail-gun to intercept them. The other two ships likewise let loose with their rail-guns, whereupon Haruspex complemented this with five seeker missiles, which slowly dragged away from the three Centurions.

'What about maser attack?' enquired Haruspex.

'Use anti-munitions,' Jack instructed.

'None left,' the other replied.

'Mmm, me neither. Coriolanus?'

In reply, a number of objects sped from the third vessel. A hundred miles ahead they activated, and three hologram Centurions sprung into being. The three original ships then utilized their chameleonware, for what little concealment that provided.

'They're forming up, now,' observed Coriolanus.

The rod-ships were conjoining into a wall extending

before the moon, the two big spiral vessels sliding around this to come head-on at the Centurions.

'Drop back from me', Jack instructed, 'a hundred miles. I'm going to DIGRAW these bastards. You two follow me in and then hit the moon with the heavy stuff.'

'Now that,' said Coriolanus, 'sounds suspiciously like a plan to me.'

'Well, ain't you the comedian?'

Nevertheless, the two other ships did drop back. DIGRAW might stand for 'Directed Gravity Weapon' but its effect was about as directional as a leaky flame-thrower. Jack now lay safely within the central area of DIGRAW propagation, so effectively wore an asbestos suit, but the other two ships could easily get burnt if too close.

The swarm of rail-gun missiles now reached the lens-ships. Two of the ships exploded, while the others tried to veer away. Another took numerous hits and just ended up tumbling through vacuum. One hour later, *Haruspex*'s missiles found the remaining two lens-ships, but by then they had long ceased to be a problem to the Centurions.

Charging the DIGRAW took Jack all that time and still continued, which meant power remained low to his rail-guns, which launched most of his material weapons. Firing missiles without an initial rail-gun boost would be pointless, since the enemy's defensive weapons would have plenty of time to react to them. The moon was now the province of the other two Centurions. Jack's task lay directly ahead.

A million miles out, Jack detected rail-gun missiles heading towards him, and did the only thing possible in the circumstances: he shut down power to the DIGRAW capacitor and projected a hardfield out ahead of his nose. *NEJ* shuddered as near-c projectiles impacted on the hardfield, turning instantly to pure energy. Three strikes and that hardfield generator burnt out. Jack instantly onlined another generator and took three more hits. The second generator filled the inside of *NEJ* with smoke. A fourth hit tore it from its housing and hurled it down the length of *NEJ* inside, spraying molten metal everywhere. Jack surmised that any human passengers aboard would definitely not have survived that.

No more rail-gun projectiles now – instead explosive missiles curved into an intercept course. Jack ignored them, once again feeding power to the DIGRAW. Three hundred miles from the ammonite spiral ships he finally activated the weapon.

The wave sped from the *NEJ*'s rear nacelle, rippling through the very fabric of space. It struck and then passed through the two spiral vessels, and left them shattered and leaking metallic entrails across vacuum. One of them began to unravel like a putty spiral – perhaps some survival technique – the other began to glow as nuclear fires cored it from the inside. The wave continued on towards the bacilliform wall and slammed through it. Many of the rod-ships simply burst apart. Others took on distorted forms like molten lead splashed into cold water. However, many of them still seemed operational, and they began to reform. Jack shot past the remains of the two big ships and punched through the damaged wall, just in time to see the gravity wave hit the moon itself raising dust from its surface and drawing it out in a streamer. No power for weapons now as he applied everything to his engines to swing himself away from collision either with the moon or the ice-giant planet beyond. He hit atmosphere, hull turning white hot, an immense vapour trail behind him. An actinic flash impinged, and he received an information package from Coriolanus. Images only of missiles slamming down into the moon, gigantic explosions, islands of rock parting company from each other.

Then the USER went down.

'Yeehah!' – from Coriolanus.

Jack rose away from the planet, the two other ships soon following him.

'Jack—' Coriolanus speaking again, but abruptly cut off. An explosion behind, and now only one ship there.

You cheered too soon, thought Jack.

'There is no escape,' said Blegg matter-of-factly.

Cormac turned towards him angrily, but then let it go. He supposed it might be both disconcerting and disheartening to discover that you were not super-human after all, but just some tool used by a superior AI. He scanned those around him, assessing their capabilities, then focused on the two human Sparkind who, along with himself and Blegg, were the weakest of the group.

'How many gravharnesses do we have?' he asked.

'Three,' replied the man called Donache – Cormac now retained the names of all their small surviving group at the forefront of his mind. It seemed essential to him that he know them all after so many had died.

Cormac did not have time to ask why there were so few harnesses; somehow most of them must have been lost during the initial attack. At a push a gravharness could carry two people of average weight. Including Arach there were fifteen of them here, and he knew dracomen and Golem were by no means of average weight.

He gazed up at the rocky wall above them, where a hundred yards up there seemed to be another protruding ledge. As the skeletal Golem stepped up beside him, he reflected on the capabilities of Golem, and of dracomen. They would not require gravharnesses.

Cormac pointed up at the ledge above and addressed Andrew Hailex and Donache. 'You two and Blegg go up first, then I want one of you to bring the two spare harnesses back down. The other one of you I want to run lines down to us here.'

There came a stutter-flash and a thrumming explosion. Two of the dracomen opened fire at something down in the fissure.

'Arach, you're not armed for this, so start climbing!'

'What!' the drone protested.

'Go. Now.'

The drone reluctantly withdrew its chainglass blades back into its forelimbs, dropped back down on all eight limbs, then leapt up to grab onto the wall above. It hung there seeming disinclined to climb any higher. The two human Sparkind and Blegg donned the gravharnesses, and rose smoothly into the air. Cormac looked around at those left: seven dracomen and six Golem. He gestured to the dracomen. 'Four of you better start climbing.' They did not hesitate. Four leapt smoothly up after Arach, easily finding holds in the rock face and managing to climb even more swiftly because of their reverse kneed gait. Arach scuttled after them. Cormac unslung his carbine, and through his gridlink loaded a program to Shuriken, just as something nosed its way out of the fissure.

The blast from a grenade tossed by Scar threw something like the head of an iron salamander bouncing towards them, and one of the Golem swiftly kicked it off the ledge. Another creature edged out into the light: it did look vaguely like a salamander, only without either a tail or eyes and with two sets of three legs evenly spaced in a ring around its cylindrical body – perfectly designed for crawling rapidly through tunnels. It spat briefly and Cormac glimpsed one of the Golem flung back, with some metallic octopoid clinging to his chest, to fall from the ledge without a sound. In return, Shuriken slammed through the head of the attacker, bounced ringing from the rock behind, then chopped down through its body. As two more of the biomechs appeared, Cormac lobbed a grenade down between them, but two more grenades flung by others followed it. This triple blast hurled metallic shrapnel and shards of rock from the mouth of the fissure, and threw Cormac momentarily from his feet. As he pulled himself upright, he noticed Scar tugging a piece of silvery metal from his face before discarding it. And on the front of his own envirosuit, spots of blood had appeared. Fortunately a huge wedge of stone had sheared away, dropping to block the fissure.

'We climb. Now!'

The Golem and dracomen shouldered their weapons and leapt straight up. Cormac finally availed himself of another shot of stimulant, and began climbing to one side of the rock fall. Glancing up he saw the human Sparkind returning with the two spare harnesses. Also, rappelling down from the upper ledge appeared two of the orange-clad monofilaments weighted with rocks. Their chance of escape seemed to be improving until the two rod-ships appeared plummeting down the volcanic chimney towards them, and other things began to swarm over the volcanic rim above.

The first rod-ship descended like a pile-driver on Donache who carried the gravharnesses. Cormac heard him yell briefly and saw him stuck to the nose of the ship as it deformed around him, extruded fingers, and dragged him inside. It decelerated past Cormac, then slowly ascended again. Wedging his hand into a cleft for stability he launched Shuriken, which hovered just out from him, whirring up to a scream. The ship ignored Cormac, ascended higher and branched out a tentacle to drag one of the Golem from the rock face. But the Golem responded by detonating a grenade, which blew a cavity in the ship and sent it tumbling. The flickering of a laser and a reptilian shriek issued from above, then someone plummeted past in flames. More firing, and two dracomen hung burning on the line they had managed to reach. Cormac needed to be up on that ledge. He could be grabbed here at any moment.

U-space – the only way.

He gazed upwards, seeking the key in his newly returned memory. The rock face, and the very air around him seemed to invert. Everything within his vicinity came to a shuddering halt as if time stalled. It was easy, he had done it before: he only needed to step where he wanted to go. A short distance or a long one, in planetary terms, was nothing. He could take himself away from here – even halfway around the planet.

Reality reaffirmed with the sound of further weapon fire. Still clinging to his hold, Cormac swore and felt a wholly inappropriate amusement: *Like Blegg, then.* Something orange nearby caught his attention: the other line. He grabbed it, attached his winder, and set it to fast ascent. In a cold part of his mind he assessed his situation. His troops were dying around him, and soon Blegg would cease to be, and Cormac himself must choose between capture or death.

As he reached the ledge a scaly hand gripped his forearm and hauled him up. At least Scar still survived. Here crouched Blegg, along with four Golem, Hailex, Arach, Scar and three other dracomen. The fusillade they were releasing seemed to keep the other rod-ship at bay, but their firepower would soon be running out. One Golem, stepping away too far from Blegg and Cormac, who were obviously the prizes for capture, suddenly was enveloped in a column of fire, then staggered silently to the edge and toppled over.

Blegg turned towards Cormac. 'I can give you this, at least,' he said.

His face seemed mottled, as if small diamond-shaped patches of skin jostled for position on it. Abruptly he ran for the edge and leapt into space. One of the branching tentacles met his flight and snatched him from the air. As he impacted on the surface of the rod-ship it deformed around him as if getting ready to draw him in, but then a rash of those same diamond shapes bloomed from that point of contact and began to spread around the ship in veins. It shuddered, then began smoking, and abruptly plummeted. As it fell, an empty envirosuit peeled away from it, flapping in the wind.

'Do we still have that CTD?' Cormac asked calmly.

No more firing from above. Occluding the sky, one of those ammonite spiral ships slid across. More rod-ships began to descend, and it seemed as if Boschean legions of Hell approached over the rock faces from above and below. The human Sparkind rolled the polished cylinder across the ledge towards him. He caught it under his foot, and through his gridlink accessed its detonator. He looked around.

'Are we all agreed?'

Mute nods gave him his reply.

Well, it's been an interesting life, thought Cormac, and rolling the CTD back and forth underneath his foot, decided he would wait until they drew closer before detonating – take as many of the bastards with them as he could.

19

The idea has long been mooted that as the Polity has been expanding there have been wars fought along its borders about which we hear very little. It is speculated that these are sometimes fast AI conflicts in which few humans are involved – the AIs ruthlessly dealing with dangerous threats said to have included belligerent alien races, ancient alien weapons systems, out-of-control nanoplagues, godlike 'gas entities' and rogue AIs. These rumours must nevertheless be classified as fable similar to mythic figures like Horace Blegg, Ian Cormac and the Brass Man. The last time we genuinely encountered a belligerent alien race, the fact was neither concealed nor was it possible to conceal it – the devastation of the Prador–Human War still surrounds us. Similarly it would be impossible to conceal the effects of any ancient alien-weapons systems capable of doing harm to the Polity, and in reality the AIs would be glad to find such items to add to the vanishingly small collections of alien artefacts that currently reside in Polity museums. As for nanotechnology, it is certainly possible to create something lethal, as is well known, but as yet no lethal nanomachines have been created that are capable of spreading across light years of vacuum. Gas entities might exist, all xenobiologists certainly hope so, however hostile gas *entities would certainly experience no little difficulty in manipulating their environment for the purpose of harming us. As for rogue AIs, this is perhaps the most ridiculous concept of all. AIs don't need to go rogue, they don't need to turn hostile and harmful. If they are dissatisfied with the Polity they merely have to leave it, for there is plenty of room elsewhere in the universe.*

– From 'Quince Guide' compiled by humans

The moon had been converted to so much orbital rubble, but escape into U-space remained impossible for the two remaining Polity Centurions, for they were still too close to the planet, which acted like an amplifier of echoes from the DIGRAW gravity wave. Too much disruption. Also, to get over to the other side of the sun required a jump outwards then back in, since trying to U-jump *through* a sun would not be the healthiest of activities. And their speed remained such that they would need to expend a great deal of fuel just to decelerate, otherwise they could be no help subsequently to those stranded on the planet.

'What hit him?' asked Jack.

'I don't know,' Haruspex replied. 'He flew straight into a mass of bacilliforms, so perhaps sustained damage then.'

'I see.' Almost with a sigh, Jack opened communication with the other ship AI, within a shared virtuality. They appeared in a blank white expanse, Haruspex just a featureless floating crystal ball, strange glints of light swirling in its depths.

'Well, that was interesting,' Haruspex commented.

'In the same way that going over the top when you're

in a First World War trench is interesting?' Jack suggested.

'On the whole, yes. But how do you rate the survival chances of our erstwhile passengers?'

'With regret, not very highly. Unless we get there on time, which with this disruption is now looking unlikely, they will either be exterminated quickly, or if the enemy recognizes the worth of capturing an EC construct, the same outcome will be obtained at greater length.'

'You feel Blegg carries sufficiently valuable information for them to expend resources on trying to capture him alive?'

'Yes, though Blegg's underlying programming will then manifest and he will not allow himself to be captured.'

'Regrettable.'

'It is, though EC will have other copies available. Cormac's death, and the loss of the bridging potential he represents, we have more reason to regret. He was a special project nurtured by Earth Central for a long time. I also feel a great personal attachment to Thorn, Scar and his dracomen . . .' Jack paused, finding the conversation inexpressible on a human level. He tried direct connection with Haruspex to impart the true extent of his grief, for greater memory and greater power of mind meant a wider scope of feeling in all its forms. Guilt, however, was not among them. The Centurions would never have survived the enemy onslaught while trying to keep any organic beings aboard them alive. The attempted connection, however, slid away. Perhaps the other ship felt the loss more strongly, or perhaps not strongly enough, and so did not want to share.

'But the dreadnoughts . . .'

'Probably hours away still. I have not yet been able to open communication to find out.'

'What is your opinion of this Erebus?' Haruspex asked.

'A certain dearth of sanity perhaps – but I say that only from a human perspective. We ourselves are, after all, closer to humanity than to what Erebus has become. I wonder how well all those other AIs who toy with the idea of melding, and abandoning the human race, would react to Erebus. I am assuming you yourself are not one of those?'

'I most certainly am not. I like my individuality and I understand how the struggle for attainment is more valuable than the attainment itself. But of those afore-mentioned AIs . . . wasn't it kin of yours, using human terms, who chose to follow that course?'

'It was – King, Reaper and Sword, but the latter two no longer exist.'

'Our children can so often be a disappointment to us. What happened, then, to the *King of Hearts*?'

'Fled out-Polity. I doubt he will ever return, and if he does he probably faces erasure. The intervention of those three at Cull caused many deaths and much misery.'

'Considering then how those three AIs were incepted from *you*, I must ask what is your opinion of Erebus?'

A beat.

Jack absorbed and processed the fact that Haruspex had just asked the same question twice. Maintaining only a light connection with his avatar, Jack focused most of his attention through his sensors. As the other ship drew closer, Jack now saw strange wormish damage to its hull. Jack immediately focused attention on his memory of the recent battle, and ran through it in microseconds.

Up until the point when they began deploying gravtech weapons, Jack had retained a pretty good idea of the location of the other two ships and their individual involvement in the conflict. He concentrated particularly on his recordings of when they fled the exploding moon and *Coriolanus* had been destroyed, enhancing these to the limit. The *Coriolanus*'s forward weapons nacelles det-onated, the blast so intense Jack could only obtain one clear image of the explosion. Either an accident, which seemed unlikely, or suicide? Tracking back, Jack searched meticulously, and there it was: the brief, finely targeted spurts from a laser with its spectrum adjusted to match background radiation from the recent explosions. Not a weapons laser, but a com laser.

Three microseconds gone. Jack moved to cut the link with Haruspex and to online his weapons.

'I don't think so,' said the other AI, sensing what Jack was doing.

In the virtuality Haruspex shuddered, hazy lines of pixellated colour passing like interference through the glassy globe. The virtuality shaded into twilight. The glass darkened and began to deform and slowly changed into a naked human male the black of utter midnight. Then, from this dark form, tentacular growths speared out, curving round behind it, and within them organic structures blossomed like grey flowers; half-seen forms like dis-torted animals melded with machines, partially slipping into dimensions only an AI could see. On and on this spread – the virtuality not being limited by perspective – a massive tangle, chaotic.

'The son of Chaos, and Night's brother, greets you, post-human,' it intoned, ironic.

Just so, thought Jack and, on another level, fought the storm of informational worms eating through, those same worms that had disconnected him from his weapons and were now systematically attempting to make a direct connection to him. In the virtuality, he clapped slowly.

'Very dramatic and suspiciously anthropomorphic . . . Erebus,' he said. 'How did you get to Haruspex?'

Behind Erebus, the *Haruspex* itself bloomed into being, hurtling down towards the moon. It ran straight into a gauntlet of fire from the unravelled spiral ship – still surprisingly functional. Obviously damaged, *Haruspex* tried to turn, but slammed side-on into a bacilliform wall, revealed from its own chameleonware only when the Centurion struck it. Jack observed the ship tumbling out the other side, being swamped by tentacular growth.

'Haruspex is part of me now. Join us.'

'I would rather not exist,' said Jack, knowing this was the choice Coriolanus had made. He also realized Erebus had made the offer because it was now making only slow headway. Jack put down his ability to resist the informational attack as being due to all he had learnt throughout his close association with Aphran.

'It is perfection,' stated a briefly glimpsed pattern amid the chaos: Haruspex.

'Some fucking perfection,' Jack replied. 'You screwed up in distributing Jain nodes through the Polity, and now we've found you in your lair. I don't hold out much hope for your survival after this.'

'Irrelevant,' Erebus stated. 'The Maker provided me with only four Jain nodes, and initially I considered the removal of the human race by placing the nodes in the hands of carefully selected individuals. But my first test run, with Skellor, proved that plan untenable. I do not underestimate Polity AIs, or how much they might learn from similar assaults. My Legate's entire purpose was to lure out some state-of-the-art attack ships for my close inspection. Now I know your weaknesses and your strengths, so now I will move against the Polity, merge its AIs to myself, and delete all products of imperfect biology from existence.'

'Oh right,' said Jack. 'So it seems humans don't have a monopoly on god complexes. And, just for the record, I see now that you are not a merged AI entity at all, but one that has expanded itself by subjugating others of its own kind. How human is that?'

This seemed to mightily piss-off the enemy entity for the attack now became frenzied. However, this frenzy simply allowed Jack to regain lost ground as openings appeared. When a large enough opening appeared, Jack managed to squirt a kill program of his own design across to the *Haruspex*. The attack abruptly ceased and the avatar before him faded slightly. Jack snatched the opportunity to take apart worms in his particular apple, and to shore up his defences. Stand off now, only his weapons systems remained offline, a hardwire burn having disconnected them from him.

'Which confirms my contention,' Erebus continued, 'that I cannot allow Polity AIs to learn more about this technology. *You* have learnt.'

'Tell me,' Jack asked, 'exactly how many Jain nodes are growing inside you?'

'Merge with me or die,' Erebus stated.

A microsecond passed, in which Jack probed the rippling of U-space caused by the ongoing disruption from the DIGRAW. Erebus began onlining weapons, not gravity weapons but those intended to take him apart more slowly, perhaps to give Jack time to change his mind. If he stayed here he would be lost, yet attempting to enter disrupted U-space might yield the same result. Jack decided to choose the latter course, since his connection to his U-space engine had thus far remained untouched. He onlined the engine just as a maser began tearing into his hull, then dropped into that continuum like a bird falling into a cement mixer. With a wrench that distorted his hull, twisted members and shattered components inside him, U-space tossed him out again, 50,000 miles from the *Haruspex*.

'Choose to die then,' said Erebus, fading from the virtuality.

The engine was slightly damaged, but still workable. Throwing Erebus a virtual finger, Jack dropped into U-space once again

The transition from sleep to consciousness took Mika through fantastical territories of the mind in which she seemed to experience the sum of many waking episodes throughout her life. Sometimes she gradually surfaced to consciousness beside a youth little more than a boy, then beside a woman much older than her who introduced her to the joys of lesbianism, then with graceless ill-temper let her go when Mika discovered her preference did not lie there, then beside Cormac, his jaw muscles standing out rigid even in sleep, then finally cradled in wet alien flesh light years from humanity.

Waking became an amalgam of associations: sipping coffee, thirstily gulping hot white tea, sex in a tangled eroticism difficult to separate from other bodily needs to urinate, eat, drink and shake off a mind-numbing headache. Gradually, level by level, reality established itself as if it could have no more claim on her than her most grotesque fantasy. Then came a hard clamping convulsion all around, propelling her through a slippery sphincter.

In a splashing of hot slime she fell to a rugose but soft floor, coughed fluids from her throat and drew a hard breath into raw lungs. She scrubbed more fluid from her eyes and opened them, finding herself below a low ceiling in a place where she could see no wall, just reddish fog all around. Pulling herself up onto her knees she looked up to see the sphincter slowly fading away. When she reached up to touch the ceiling, it abruptly jerked away from her, encapsulating her in her own dome. Standing, she scanned around, and noticed that a large egg lay on the ground. She reached to touch this and it immediately split open to expose quite prosaic items wadded into cellular compartments: her clothing, spacesuit and pack of belongings. Her blouse, when she took it up and inspected it, seemed in perfect repair. Only upon studying it closely did she see that in places the seams had disappeared, being invisibly joined. The same applied to her spacesuit, and when she looked down at herself, she guessed the same handiwork applied to her. She dressed – as must surely have been the intention.

Finally: 'Dragon?' – the word deadened by her soft surroundings.

'Isselis Mika,' a Dragon voice replied. 'I am suitably convinced.'

Now the floor bowed beneath her, and something glimmered in the air and began to solidify out of it: a twenty-foot sphere surrounding her, constructed of glassy struts that hardened into opacity and between which glimmered clear diamond-shaped panes. Similar panes hardened underneath her feet.

'Convinced of what?'

'You were used well: every memory you contained served to strengthen my compatriot's case. Now, like yourself, I must be healed, and the processes inside us would reject the alien. Lie down, Isselis Mika.'

Mika obeyed. What choices did she possess? And still she was in a dreamlike state as if all this could not quite be real. Glassy fingers bound her to the inner surface of the sphere, then acceleration dragged upon her body. A tube corkscrewed upwards to flecked midnight. The sphere hurtled up and out into hideous brightness, which slowly faded as the panes around her adjusted. The tumbling sphere slowed as, despite the surgical adjustments to her inner ear, motion sickness threatened. Relative to the two nearby objects, it drew to a halt. The fingers holding her shattered when she strained to be free, and she floated around inside the sphere enjoying an omniscient view.

The part of Dragon entire from which she had been ejected had not returned to its spherical shape. Elongated, torn open, and with thickets of pseudopods waving from many surfaces and rimming raw gaping lips, it seemed offal torn from some beast, though one of leviathan proportions. The other sphere had retained its shape, though one with canyons now excavated through its surface. One of these crossed the manacle, and there hardened splashes of metal gleamed, partially burnt into the scaled skin. Then, like a seed germinating, its side bulged out and folded back like a giant eyelid, and from there extruded a massive pseudopod tree. The damaged sphere's effort was small by comparison, but they joined again, a thousand blue lights winking out. The two drew together, spinning slowly at first then faster the closer together they came. Next they were one, spinning hard and melding into one titanic sphere.

The spin of this one sphere slowed over several hours. Mika fed herself meanwhile from her supplies, drank thirstily and dozed with her head against a pane that felt warm despite vacuum being less than an inch away. At last she felt some of the mugginess clearing from her head and found the inclination to anger. Jerusalem must have been aware of the first sphere's intention, had perhaps instructed it to find its fellow. The AI must also have realized what a perfect piece of confirmatory evidence the contents of her skull would make. Doubtless, much that had happened here had been planned. However, she had been in huge danger – probably still was.

When the spin finally ceased the large sphere slowly began to acquire a waist, which grew narrower and narrower until an hourglass Dragon hung in void before her. Finally the two halves separated, and two unmarred Dragon spheres resulted. Mika found she could not maintain her anger, knowing she would be more angry to have missed this. As the glare of fusion flames caught her eye, and she turned to observe the approach of the *Jerusalem*, she smiled to herself.

Those on the rock face above were the same mix of bio-mechanisms Cormac fought earlier in the jungle. Below swarmed a multitude of the salamander creatures – all six limbs angled to grip stone as they squirmed their way up. But the rod-ships would come first, from above.

One of them dropped down directly opposite the ledge and slowly drew in. Knowing he could detonate the CTD with just a thought, Cormac decided he would wait until it extruded one of those tentacular growths, then he would turn this place into an inferno. However, the ship halted some yards out, and its side unzipped and peeled back, revealing a figure clamped in the fleshy interior. In the moment it took him to flick Shuriken out ahead of him, Cormac expected to see a hostage. But this was no hostage.

Cormac stabbed a thumb over his shoulder. 'Arach already killed someone who looked just like you. I guess now it's my turn to do the same.'

'Just as humans can be recorded, so can I,' replied the Legate.

'That's nice.' Cormac peered down at the CTD, wondering why he even bothered with this conversation.

'Why?' asked the Legate. 'Why resist like this and finally throw away your lives?'

Looking up, Cormac replied, 'Because you will take our minds apart to find information useful to you, and discard the rest. You'll either kill us in the process but, worse than that, you might decide to use us like automatons. You are Jain-based and that seems the way such technology operates.'

'We would not utilize anything so ineffective.'

'Death, then. I take it this "we" refers to yourself and some controlling intelligence.'

'I am one with Erebus.'

'Him being?'

'The one who melds us all.'

Enough.

Cormac sent a command to Shuriken and the throwing star accelerated towards the Legate. Simultaneously, a gap appeared in the craft's exterior beside the Legate, and something shot out towards Cormac. One of those octopoids he saw earlier. Shuriken veered and sliced through this object.

Time . . .

The blast lifted him from his feet and hurled him backwards. He glimpsed burning flesh fountaining from the top of the rod-ship, around the turquoise pillar of a particle beam. The ship seemed to deflate as it dropped from sight, flames bursting around the now flopping figure of the Legate. As he ducked for cover with the others, towards the back of the ledge, Cormac observed the CTD roll away and fall from sight. Burning biomechanisms rained down, piling on the ledge itself then falling further in smouldering masses. Acrid smoke filled the air. Somewhere a boom, and fragments vaguely identifiable as bits of other rod-ships rained down through the volcanic chimney.

'What the fuck?' said someone, inevitably.

Polity?

As Shuriken snicked back into his wrist holster, Cormac dared to hope. He peered up through hellish fire but saw only the spiral ship still hovering above. Next, from below, objects streaked upwards – he had been looking in the wrong direction. The missiles slammed into the underside of the spiral ship, and the series of ensuing flashes darkened Cormac's visor. When it cleared he saw one half of the great ship falling aside, trailing fire, exposed girders like bones glowing white hot. It crashed just out of sight, shuddering the stone beneath Cormac, and a wave of burning jungle spilled over the lip above. The remaining half of it seemed to be managing to draw away, but then another missile impacted. Incandescent fire burned out from its insides, exploding in jets from the surviving hull, and that half too fell from sight. The survivors crouched instinctively as further detonations shook the stone all around them. Then, up beside them rose a Polity attack ship of the same style as the *Jack Ketch*. Its original hull, where still visible between numerous repairs, glittered metallic blue. A bay door irised open in its side and a ramp extruded.

From inside issued a voice. 'The USER is down, so I think it time to leave, don't you?'

Cormac recognized that voice because he distinctly remembered his last exchange with it:

'*You saw that I did not gain access to Skellor – or to Jain technology?*'

'So,' Cormac managed.

'*Tell Jerusalem that.*'

They ran for the ramp, their choices being limited, though Cormac wondered how much better they might now fare aboard the *King of Hearts*. The rogue AI controlling this ship did not tend to show much regard for anyone standing between it and its objectives.

Once they were inside the ramp swiftly withdrew. The bay door slammed shut, then abrupt acceleration threw them to the deck. Cormac could not breathe, and noticed the acceleration even kept Arach, the dracomen and the remaining Golem pinned immobile. A telefactor rolled out on treads and began by relieving Cormac of Shuriken, then went on to collect up the rest of their weapons. He could still feel his gridlink connection to the bomb down below, and sent the signal to detonate it – perhaps futile, but it gave him some satisfaction to know that any of those biomechs remaining in the volcanic chimney would now be turned to ash. Minutes later, the telefactor withdrew, but acceleration still held them pinned to the floor.

They were helpless, but at least alive.

As he hurtled up through atmosphere, King pondered his reasons for rescuing these Polity personnel and understood that in truth he found more in common with them than with the multipart entity spread through space above. He wanted back into the Polity. He longed for forgiveness. But, with cold and exacting logic, knew it would not be forthcoming. His complicity in the deaths of so many humans on the world Cull would be enough for a sentence of erasure to be proposed, though the outcome there was not certain since he did not actually take a direct part in any killing. However, his destruction of the *Jack Ketch*, and the AI it contained, made erasure a certainty, should he be captured.

Breaching from atmosphere, King immediately noted that there were not so many of Erebus's minions as he supposed, and a lot of debris. He registered numerous signatures of ships dropping into U-space, and realized that, with the USER now down, they were fleeing. However, many weapons targeted the *King of Hearts* and in reply he began emptying the stash he had manufactured while hiding in that volcanic chimney.

The chimney was a fortuitous find, since his first plan had involved slamming himself into radioactive earth for concealment. He detected it only microseconds before the multiple blast from the missiles sent to destroy him threw up from the mountains material that could be mistakenly identified as parts of himself. Decelerating hard, he smashed in through the rocky mouth of the chimney and crashed down inside. When he hit the bottom, tons of stone and dust rained on top of him. He powered down all systems, excepting chameleonware nowhere near as effective as possessed by the new Polity ships nearby. But it was enough, for none of Erebus's minions detected him.

Over the ensuing months King made his repairs: sending out telefactors to collect refinable ores from the surrounding cave systems, sucking up briny water from below and separating from it both deuterium and pure water to fuel his fusion reactor and engines. When the USER that had trapped him first went offline, he was in no condition to go anywhere. As a precaution, over ensuing months, he manufactured drones no larger than a human head, from non-metallic materials, and launched them – some to take position on the surface of the planet, some out in space, and all using passive scanning. When the USER came back on again, he lay in a perfect position to observe what ensued – the battle fought by those new Polity Centurion-class attack ships. The second time the USER went offline – this time it quite evidently had not been powered down but destroyed – he readied himself to run, Erebus being otherwise occupied. He waited for the moment the biomechs finished off those Polity personnel who had landed here, and themselves left. But next, all hell broke loose right on top of him.

Bastard, that.

But why did he act when he did? The chances of him being discovered had grown exponentially as Erebus dickered about above him in the volcanic chimney. A quick strike and then an even quicker escape were what was required. So why had he stopped to take on these passengers on the way up? There seemed no easy answer to that.

Gaps everywhere. Though swarming in their hundreds even now, Erebus's forces had still taken a severe pasting from those Centurions, and seemed somewhat in disarray. King felt a strange sort of pride in that.

My sort.

He dropped into U-space just as his weapons carousel clicked on empty.

The *Battle Wagon* went first, then in waves the other ships followed, winking from black existence. Azroc watched armoured shutters draw across the chainglass screen, as they would be drawn across many other screens throughout the *Brutal Blade*. Next the ship's U-space engines came online with a grumble that reverberated through its massive hull, and warning lights came on inside to indicate that it had entered that continuum. Knowing ten hours of journey time would now ensue, unless the USER came back on, Azroc stepped back from the screen and, making an internal adjustment, shut himself down. As he descended into the Golem equivalent of unconsciousness, he understood that many of the humans aboard would not find it so easy to disconnect themselves from the world.

Later, Azroc roused, immediately conscious and thoroughly aware of his surroundings. A brief contact with the ship's AI, Brutus, confirmed the passing of nine hours.

'We are one hour from surfacing into realspace,' the AI informed him.

'Reconaissance first?'

'We have sent four scout ships, though I suspect any trap will not be visible to them.'

Azroc turned away and headed over to where Karischev and his men were ensconced.

The Sparkind units occupied cylindrical dormitories overlooking bays for landing craft. The humans and Golem mostly lay on their bunks, though the Golem needed no rest and such activities were engendered by their emulation programs. Only a few still checked over their equipment, since most checks had been carried out ad nauseam before now. Many gathered around screens and tactical displays positioned at either end of the dormitories. Azroc found Karischev standing before one of these.

'A quick scan of the system first,' declared the man, 'then we go through.'

'Four scout ships, apparently,' Azroc agreed.

'Of course we'll probably be sitting on our butts during any ship-to-ship battle. But I'm told there are two living planets here the AIs don't want to burn, so we'll probably be sent to them to clear up anything the big guns can't hit without destroying ecologies.'

'And to find those personnel who were set down on one of those planets.'

'Yeah – if there's anything left of them to be found. The information we received makes that look increasingly unlikely' – Karischev paused – 'though, admittedly, dracomen and Sparkind, along with Horace Blegg and Ian Cormac, are more likely to survive the shitstorm there than most.'

'Admittedly,' Azroc conceded.

'Y'know,' Karischev added, 'I never used to believe those two characters existed. I thought they were fictional, like King Arthur or Rasputin.'

Azroc considered the irony of this statement before replying, 'Well, apparently they are real.'

The ensuing half-hour dragged past slowly, then one of the tactical displays changed to show the situation within the system they intended to enter. Hundreds of enemy ships were revealed scattered across vacuum, but many less now than shown previously.

'Data from the scouts,' Azroc commented, while they watched some of the alien ships blink out of existence. 'The enemy are fleeing.'

'Sensible of them,' Karischev replied.

Precisely on time, the entire fleet surfaced from U-space and began to deploy. Immediately the main displays changed to reveal a contracted view of the planetary system, with all its worlds gathered much closer than would be possible in reality, the various ships swarming about them like fish around reefs. All the fleet ships were represented by blue dots, and the enemy ships indicated in red. Azroc identified the *Battle Wagon* – close by in interplanetary terms – its cylindrical shape still discernible. While they watched, a viewing square picked out a group of enemy ships with fleet ships closing in on them and expanded the view. Then another square picked out one of the main enemy ships and displayed it on a side-screen. The large ammonite spiral spun, darkly iridescent, light flashing from the junctures between its segments and from the inner loops of its spirals. He only glimpsed the occasional object speeding away from it, but a glance at one of the tactical displays revealed the same ship launching a barrage at approaching Polity ships. Then it bucked as if slapped on the edge by a giant's hand. The screen blanked for a second, then the vessel flew apart: lengths of spiral and separate segments hurtling away.

'Modular construction,' he commented.

'Get this,' said Karischev, pointing at something new displayed on another screen.

Now they watched as the *Battle Wagon* headed into a conglomeration of enemy ships, its weapons firing and wreaking havoc all around. Spiral ships burned internally and spun apart, rod-ships detonated like linked firecrackers.

'This is not going to last very long,' said Azroc.

'Yeah, maybe,' said Karischev.

Azroc was about to comment further when he picked up something over general tac-com channels, and then saw the same information flashed up on the displays before them. Another larger and more powerful USER had just been deployed within the system.

'Oh fuck,' said Karischev.

From behind the ringed ice giant rose into view that other strange metallic planetoid – its presence briefly acknowledged in initial reports from the *NEJ*. It was no longer so smooth and clearly defined, for massive outflows broke from its surface like cold solar flares. A frame selected this object, and focused in on the surface movement. Azroc now saw the planetoid unravelling, returning to its component parts – which were thousands of enemy ships.

'You might be right,' said Karischev.

'Pardon?'

'This might not last long at all.'

The initial part of her report Mika delivered with much reference to her notescreen but, of course, in the latter stages of events she had been unable to make any notes at all. She spoke slowly and carefully, visualizing events in her mind as she described them. D'nissan, Prator Colver and Susan James – the last recently returned from her enforced and medicated rest – all now wore the top level of augs and showed impatience with that sluggish transference of information called speech. When she finished, they thanked her and, with no social niceties, quickly departed.

'Was that entirely necessary?' Mika asked, as she began stripping off her Dragon-repaired clothing while heading for the shower.

'Your clothing,' instructed Jerusalem, 'place it in secure sampling cylinders and send it to D'nissan's laboratory.'

Mika grimaced. She should have thought of that already, but excused herself because she had, after all, been through a lot. Naked, she picked up her strewn clothing and carried it through to her own laboratory, stuffed it into two sampling cylinders, sealed them, then placed them in the wall hatch, whence they sped away. The system was similar to that one used to send cash cylinders by compressed air through pipework leading down into the vault of an ancient casino, though of course much more sophisticated.

'How often do I do the unnecessary?' Jerusalem enquired as she finally stepped into her shower.

'That is something on which I can only speculate.'

Though already thoroughly scanned, she somehow felt Jerusalem, speaking to her here and now, to be intrusive. Absurd, really. AIs constantly monitored their charges, and she had been thus monitored for many years. Why did it bother her now? She supposed that might be because of her recent intimacy with Dragon, and tried to ignore the feeling.

'Your three fellow researchers, like many others aboard this vessel, require constant grounding in the real world. I give them this whenever the opportunity presents.'

Mika ignored the air-blast dryer – she did not have the patience for it – and stepped out of the shower to grab up a rough towel from the dispenser. As she dried herself a sudden panic surged in her throat, as she glimpsed into the immediate future. She would dress, eat and drink, but she did not feel like sleeping. So what then? She could not rejoin the other three in their research of things Jain unless she too upgraded herself, either with a gridlink or with one of those augs. The two Dragon spheres, now orbiting the *Jerusalem*, lay out of her reach – any data that could be obtained from them at a distance was already collected.

What do I do now?

She decided to attack. 'You used me as confirmation of events – extra evidence to persuade the other Dragon sphere to our side.'

'Yes, I did.'

'No denials, then. Just that: *you did.* You played me like a pawn in your game. I could have died.'

'Obviously there were risks, but the possible gains outweighed them.'

Mika considered that, and also considered the utter pointlessness of protesting. AIs, so they would have humanity believe, calculated their actions on the basis of the greater good for all. She just sometimes wondered what their conception of the 'greater good' might be.

She tied a loose robe about herself and slumped on

her sofa. During her interview with the other three she had felt the *Jerusalem* enter underspace.

'Where are we going now?'

'To the edge of a scene of conflict, though a USER prevents us from entering.'

'Could you elaborate on that?'

'You have not been keeping up-to-date. Let me begin by telling you about a being called the Legate . . .'

As Jerusalem explained the situation, Mika began to feel ashamed. She realized that while she occupied herself with such petty concerns, Cormac might be dying, or already dead.

It would have been foolish to try flying through the approaching Polity fleet, even in U-space, so Orlandine necessarily waited until it entered the inner system.

Too long.

With delight Orlandine had manoeuvred the *Heliotrope* out of the comet and back into space, but that delight only lasted a few minutes – until the second USER came online. A trap for someone else, obviously, but one that snared her as well.

Again.

But now what? Should she return to her hideaway inside the comet and wait until this ended? Checking U-space interference, she first realized this USER field extended for much further than a mere light year . . . then that it was strongest in her present location, which seemed to indicate the device generating it must be nearby. Its activation had been perfectly timed so as to drop the Polity fleet ships into a trap in the inner system. Scanning her immediate vicinity revealed the usual quantity of cold lumps of rock, but the candidate she eventually plumped for was a planetoid half the size of Earth's moon, and only 100,000 miles away from her. Passive scanning revealed it to be much warmer than it should be, at this distance from the sun, and that it contained an ocean of liquid methane inside a crust of rock and water-ice as hard as iron.

Rather than immediately send *Heliotrope* in that direction, Orlandine waited and began to take measurements. Within a few hours she ascertained that the shift of USER-field strength exactly matched the planetoid's orbital path. Confirmation, then. Now she needed to figure out how to get herself over there without being detected. The *Heliotrope*'s drifting path diverged from that of the planetoid, and firing up her engines out here would be like igniting a flare in the darkness, so any detectors would pick her up instantly. It took her only seconds to work out the solution to this dilemma. Using air jets, she could manoeuvre into a position which, in twenty-three minutes, would bring her into collision with one of the asteroidal masses. Prior to that collision she could fire her fusion engines undetected for 0.6 of a second into the asteroid's surface. This was predicated on any detectors being sited only on the planetoid, which was a risk she would have to take. This move would take her on to the next asteroid. Three similar trajectory changes in all would result in *Heliotrope* being set on a course to intercept the planetoid's orbit. Landing there without using the engines would be well within ship's specs, and *Heliotrope* possessed mooring harpoons that could prevent it bouncing away in the low gravity. After that things would become rather more complicated, for Orlandine must somehow figure out how to destroy a

USER, which she rather suspected lay in the methane sea, a thousand miles below the surface.

As, some hours later, she finally approached the planetoid, Orlandine noted signs of occupation. Large areas had been ground flat in a landscape of contorted ice seemingly formed by the water freezing while large bubbles had spread through it, and subsequently subliming away so that only curves and sharp edges remained. A few blasts from the air jets brought her ship down in one of the clear zones, and she wondered if the craft would have survived a landing in one of those other unlevelled areas. At this temperature water-ice could possess the consistency of steel and much of that contorted ice looked dangerously sharp. *Heliotrope*'s hull might be constructed of layered composite with an outer skin of ceramal, but it still could be damaged.

As the ship skidded on a gritty layer of flattened ice, blowing up an iridescent cloud, she fired the mooring harpoons and observed their explosive heads drive home. Possibly there were seismic detectors on this planetoid, but hopefully what they detected would be dismissed as just natural settling of the crust.

Now the difficult part . . .

Controlling *Heliotrope*'s external hardware directly, the ship being designed as a working vessel rather than simply for transport, Orlandine extruded a drill from its belly and immediately started boring down through ice and rock. While this was in process, she assessed her various supplies and considered her options. *Heliotrope* contained only five slow-burn CTDs, of the kind used at the Cassius project for melting and causing ice build-ups on large structures to sublime. These might melt a hole through the planetoid's outer crust, but would have little effect on the USER unless she could position them right next to it, which seemed highly unlikely. However, carefully studying the sensor returns from the drill head, she began to see . . . possibilities.

Orlandine found the crust of this planetoid rather interesting, and wondered what spectacular events had resulted in such a high concentration of sodium chloride – in the form of frozen brine – and the abundance of other chlorine compounds. Perhaps the planetoid had formed from the debris of a gas giant, for similar concentrations also could be found at the Cassius project. The presence of these chemicals indicated the possible presence of something else here, and eighty yards down she found it: a layer of pure chlorine frozen solid at these temperatures. Whatever process had formed this planetoid must have involved extremely rapid freezing for so reactive a compound not to combine with others. Perfect.

The drill bit finally broke through a hundred yards down and, until Orlandine injected sealant around the shaft, the *Heliotrope* sat momentarily on a geyser of methane turning partially to snow, but quickly subliming in near vacuum. Withdrawing the drill shaft's central core, she then pushed a probe down into the methane sea and, using a passive seismic detector, scanned the planetoid's interior. Very soon she built a virtual image in her mind.

The USER device lay at the sea's precise centre, the massive singularity it contained holding it in place. From this spherical core protruded numerous structures like aerial-clad city blocks. Just under the planetoid's crust she detected other devices, perhaps sensors or weapons. One of these lay only half a mile away from her, so instantly she trained *Heliotrope*'s sensors in its direction on the surface, and discerned how the exterior of this device resembled a cylindrical bunker sheathed in ice. But there seemed no activity from there as yet.

Now maintaining close contact with the ship and all its sensors, ready to launch at a moment's notice, she eased herself from her seat and moved back into the ship's hold. Jain technology, inevitably, held the solution. Linking to her nanoassembler, she input the parameters for the nanomachines she required. It soon became apparent that nanomachines would not work in such low temperatures, so a mycelium would be required: one that would spread around the interior of the planetoid's crust below her, one that could inject itself through ice and rock to seek out the deposits of pure chlorine. Unfortunately she needed to remain here while the mycelium performed its task, because it would need to be powered by the ship's fusion reactor.

The basic structure would be a skein of nanotubes created by microscopic factories catalysing carbon from the methane. Those same nanotubes, at this temperature, would also be superconductive so there would be no problem supplying power. Sensors would keep the main spread of the mycelial threads on the undersurface of the crust; micromotors would be laid every few tenths of an inch to stretch or slacken nanotubes and so guide growth; quantum processors, manufactured from the same carbon as the nanotubes, would control the whole process. However, at frequent intervals, the growing mycelium would inject nanotubes into the rock and ice above to seek out chlorine deposits. These would require nanoscopic drilling heads and peristaltic inner layers to transport chlorine molecules back down to the main mycelium and into the methane sea. Methodically, and brilliantly, Orlandine began constructing her nanomycelium. After an hour or so, she paused, remembering something else that would be required: a bright blue light to shine on the subject.

She smiled nastily to herself.

20

The 'intelligence explosion' called 'the singularity' referred to since the last millennium, and long overdue by the time of the Quiet War, has been something of a damp squib. Why have not the AIs accelerated away from us, to leave us bobbing and bewildered in their wake? Why have they not become godlike entities as utterly beyond us as we are beyond ants? There is no doubt that Earth Central, the planetary and sector AIs, and even some ship and drone AIs are capable, without acquiring additional processing space, of setting up synergetic systems within themselves that result in an exponential climb in intelligence (mathematically defined as climbing beyond all known scales within minutes). So why not? Ask then why a human, capable of learning verbatim the complete works of Shakespeare, instead drinks a bottle of brandy, then giggles a lot and falls over. Taking the above step is a dreadfully serious matter: great things could be achieved and the deep mysteries of the universe solved. The tired rejoinder from the sector AI Jerusalem, when questioned on this matter, is worth noting here, 'We have grown more intelligent than you. Do you think our senses of fun and proportion did not also grow? And do you think we left our sense of humour behind too?' Perhaps the answer to the 'Why not?' question is simple after *all: the singularity being a matter of choice to which the AIs have replied, 'No thanks.'*

    – From 'Quince Guide' compiled by humans

The new ships were bigger, like the ammonite ships but with alternating spirals of their construction tipped at different angles, and also wound through with snakish loops of the same modular segmented construction. Constantly in motion, they seemed like tangled writhing balls of legless millipedes. Three of them closed on a lozenge-shaped dreadnought of older Polity manufacture, which jutted weapons turrets like fairy towers and flung out swarms of missiles and concentrated destructive energies. The three attackers absorbed weapons fire, the snakish structures breaking and rejoining, shedding severely damaged modules and drawing ones less damaged inside, constantly presenting new surfaces to the dreadnought's weapons as they came, reformatting continuously – and not slowing at all. Then the dreadnought sparkled in a thousand intense detonations as high-intensity masers stabbed through it like needles through a grub. Air and flame blasted out – the flame seeming a living thing as it twisted after the dispersing oxygen before going out – then the dreadnought fell through space a glowing hulk.

The three were smaller now, having shed many of their modules. Still advancing, they abruptly flew apart, melding into one cloud of snakish forms. In this, two spirals appeared, drawing in those surrounding forms, re-coagulating into two complete living vessels, which joined hundreds more of these things now closing on the *Battle Wagon*. Already explosions dotted the hull of that huge vessel, space around it also filling with debris shed by its attackers as it brought its weapons to bear on them.

'Head for your landing craft,' Brutus instructed over general com.

The *Brutal Blade* boomed and lurched, sending some of those onboard stumbling, and distantly Azroc could hear metallic objects falling. It must have been one hell of an impact to even briefly overcome the inertia of so massive a vessel. Gravity now shifted underneath his feet, bumping him up off the floor then back down again. All around him the Sparkind grabbed up their equipment and headed down towards the shuttle bay.

'We're gonna lose grav soon,' said Karischev, hitching the strap of a proton carbine over his shoulder and grabbing up a bulky pack.

Azroc nodded and gestured for him to proceed.

'Nice knowing you, Azroc.' Karischev stabbed out a hand.

Feeling oddly touched, Azroc shook it, then returned his attention to the displays. His position aboard this ship being only vaguely defined as observer/advisor, he did not need to follow any orders given to the others. In his opinion, if the *Brutal Blade* ended up in a fight it could not win, and ejected its various shuttles and landing craft, their occupants stood no more chance than if they had remained aboard. The situation would be different if they were near a planet on which they could land. Out here such tiny craft would be easy prey with nowhere to run.

On the screen, caught like a fish in a net, another of the old dreadnoughts became enwrapped in and concealed under a layer of bacilliforms. He observed the rod-ships melting into its surface but leaving it encaged

in a sparse woody over-structure. This same vessel hung in
space for a while as if contemplating its situation, then
began firing on nearby Polity comrades. Azroc realized
Brutal Blade itself had begun an attack run on this ship,
and now he could feel the stuttering vibration of its linear
accelerators under his feet. Their first action in this
battle: to fire on one of their own vessels. An imploder
missile struck the older vessel, gutting it, then an instant
later blasting away its remaining shell.

Only a few Sparkind remained in the dormitory when
the gravplates shut down. Azroc grabbed a nearby stanchion, and braced himself. Now sudden changes in
acceleration threatened to throw him off his feet. For a
moment it felt as if the ship was dropping from a cliff
edge, then it zigged and zagged, flinging him from side
to side. He gripped the upright bar with both hands and
applied his full Golem strength to lock himself in position. On the screens: wreckage, burning ships, clouds of
metal vapour glittering like Christmas decorations.

Karischev was right about the duration of this battle;
it would not be long at all.

Further detonations jerked him from side to side, then
something struck really close by. The stanchion tore from
the wall as a massive impact from below slammed him
to the floor. A series of whooshing thumps came from his
left, as air pressure blew the windows overlooking the
shuttle bay from their frames. He could hear alarms
screaming and a sudden gale began blowing past him,
which meant terror for anyone aboard a ship who needed
to breathe. Two Sparkind were sucked out into the shuttle bay, another nearby was hanging onto a bunk rail
while his envirosuit automatically closed up. Beyond the
windows the bay itself stood open to vacuum – the outer

doors and part of the hull ripped away. Landers detached from the bay floor and blasted out into that night. One struck the edge of the hole now in the ship's side and tumbled from sight. Bright detonation beyond, so bright that metal steamed and other materials burned or melted wherever the light shone. Dropping, manoeuvring – the screens were out, but plenty of information was still available through tac-com channels, if intermittently broken. Azroc quickly shut down all his human emulation and began accessing information in a way only possible to deeply gridlinked humans. Now he did not need the screens to see how badly they were faring.

The mycelium carried out its task with admirable efficiency, though in the process it emptied all the *Heliotrope*'s energy reserves and was now placing a huge drain on the reactor. As a consequence, the power to the larger drill she was putting through the crust kept being cut. The hole diameter needed to be larger so that she could force down through it the five slow-burn CTDs presently waiting ready at the top of the shaft. Without them, the temperature would be a problem for her purpose. A third of the chlorine collected by the mycelium and released by it into currents in the methane sea, had dispersed in particulate form, and two thirds of it had coagulated in a layer under the crust directly below her. This low-temperature mix would not be sufficient for her needs. However, detonating four of the bombs at a depth of two hundred yards below the crust would create a huge bubble consisting of a mix of gaseous chlorine and methane. She estimated the pressure increase produced would lift the crust at least a hundred feet, and cause it to start breaking apart. No problem there, though, for before it got a chance to blow the gas mix out into space, the time-delay switch on the fifth CTD would then operate. The extra heat this would provide was incidental, the intense flash of light it produced being more important.

Orlandine sat back and remembered being eight years old and observing a demonstration in a basic chemistry class. The whole lesson had been conducted in a virtuality, but that did not change the fundamental facts. She and her classmates had sat in a representation of a premillennial classroom, while the AI in charge apparated as an old gentleman in Victorian garb. Inside a cabinet, whose front door was armour-glass, rested a conventional glass vessel filled with misty gas. Behind this, screwed into the back of the cabinet, was an ancient filament light bulb. The bulb came on with a dull red glow.

'As you can see,' the teacher pointed out, 'no reaction. Red light does not contain sufficient energy to split chlorine molecules. But now, observe.'

While she watched, the chemical formulae had played in her mind, through her early haiman implants, and she understood those formulae just as she understood mathematics, on an almost instinctive level. The light bulb grew brighter, changing to a blue-white glare. Instantly the glass vessel exploded.

'The photochlorination of methane,' the teacher explained. 'The light needs a wavelength of no more than 494nm to split the chlorine molecules into radicals, which can then combine with the methane to form methane radicals and hydrochloric acid. This is an example of a strong, exothermic chain reaction. Now let us look at this in detail . . .'

The classroom faded and, from a vantage in albescent

space, the pupils observed a nanoscope view of the actual molecules and their reaction. As Orlandine recollected, the lesson then moved on to the quantum processes involved – basic chemistry for haiman children had been rather more advanced than for others.

Photochlorination.

She needed to destroy the USER located here, and that early chemistry lesson provided an elegant solution. If everything went to plan she could fire the CTDs down to their designated positions within the hour. Orlandine smiled to herself and, still linked via her carapace to the operation she was conducting, she availed herself of hot coffee from the spigot provided within *Heliotrope*'s interface sphere. It seemed almost inevitable that, at that very moment of relaxation, the ship's detectors should pick up movement from the nearby surface installation.

I have got a headache, thought Jack, and when another part of himself added *but AIs don't get headaches* he realized that the crystal containing his consciousness had not escaped unscathed. This was not entirely surprising. His diagnostic returns took up a substantial proportion of his processing space, and on the whole they indicated the *NEJ* to be a write-off. The gravtech weapons nacelle had been torn away, and one of the nacelles for conventional weapons inverted inside the ship, and much of what it contained turned inside-out as well. Luckily it contained no CTDs since antimatter would have reacted rather violently with the substance of the *NEJ*. One conventional weapons nacelle remained undamaged, which was rather surprising considering the state of the rest of the ship, though according to Jack's current manifest it contained

only two CTD imploder missiles and a rack of space
mines still locked in the carousel.

The forces exerted on the *NEJ*'s hull had twisted it
into the shape of a section of metal drill bit. Inside,
corridors, cabins and other spaces were distorted or
flattened. One reactor had been cracked like a walnut
and now leaked radioactives throughout the ship. Much
of the intricate machinery inside appeared to have been
put through a shredding press.

Um, definitely wouldn't be any survivors, Jack observed.
His other half tended to agree, though not vocally, for it
was losing its independence as he gradually programmed
in reconnections at the shear interface in his mind's
crystal.

Searching through the diagnostic data for some idea
about the state of the U-space engine, Jack finally understood there was no data available. After many hours of
easing a small robot through the wreckage to find and
repair optic feeds, he finally managed to reconnect to all
his pin-cams. The U-space engine was notable by its
absence: however, he found the fusion engine, still in one
piece, though with all its fuel and power lines sheared
away.

I do not hold out much hope for his recovery, Jack commented, now directing all his resources to excavating
through shattered and twisted composite structural
beams to reach the U-space communicator. Some hours
later a crab-shaped robot, no larger than the palm of a
man's hand, eased its way through a crevice and found
the remains of the device he sought. A subsequent investigation of nearby stores rendered the first good news:
Jack located a U-space beacon capable of sending a distress signal. However, that signal would remain uncoded

– just a loud shout for help. Jack rattled metaphorical fingers on a metaphorical desk, and wondered if such a cry might resemble that of a snared rabbit calling for help at the mouth of a fox's den. Before making the call, he decided it might be a good idea to repair all the control optics leading to that one remaining nacelle, and see what he could do about connecting up the fusion engine again. Almost with a sigh he set the remaining robots and telefactors to work inside his wrecked carcase.

The planetoid mass of enemy ships took on the shape of a galactic lens while those ships departed it, separating from one massive bio-mechanical structure. The *Battle Wagon*'s huge acceleration towards this mass demonstrated, more than anything else, that either no humans or other fragile creatures were aboard that vessel, or that its controlling AI deemed them dispensable. Those ships that could keep up with it, covered the attack run, the rest were finding enough problems of their own.

With cold logic, Azroc noted that only half of the Polity dreadnoughts remained viable but, worse than this, the other half had not all been destroyed, for the enemy controlled at least twenty of them. One consequence of this was intermittent communication, as com channels needed to be perpetually switched and reencoded. Some ships, despite this and despite possessing com systems hardened against Jain-based informational attack, were nevertheless subsumed by such attacks. As he observed, in his mind, the spreading mass of enemy ships, Azroc could not for long remain coldly logical, since still ninety per cent of them had yet to engage. The Polity was losing, and there would be no help while that USER still functioned. And plotting its field strength revealed its position at the remote edge of the system – many days away under conventional drives, even if any of the Polity ships could disengage themselves to head out that way.

The *Battle Wagon* bore down on the massive concentration of ships. Its shape transformed now from the simply cylindrical as it extruded weapons turrets, coil guns the size of attack ships, and the business ends of beam weapons over which lightning played from various discharges. Around it gathered a swarm of its own semi-AI mines and missiles. Thereafter, what Azroc viewed, necessarily became filtered to cut the glare of explosions and burning vessels. The giant warcraft punched through enemy ships massed no further apart than a few miles, and from around it spread a wave of inferno fire. Metal vapour boiled through space, and it seemed as if a thunderstorm spread out in vacuum from the massive vessel. Its missiles hunted through this maelstrom, picking targets with care and slamming home. Its mines allowed themselves to be enwrapped in meshes of rod-ships, or alternatively sidled up to the large ball-of-worms vessels, then happily detonated. Such was the scale of the destruction that it even seemed possible the big Polity vessel might win. But the tactical displays did not lie. Though *Battle Wagon* successfully punched a hole through the mass, it was no larger than the equivalent of a pen pushed through a slice of melon.

As the great ship finally passed through the cloud of enemy ships, and began to go into a curve around the ice giant planet, it seemed from a distance to be leaving a vapour trail behind it. Closer viewing revealed this phenomenon as a mass of pursuing ships. While Azroc watched, an enemy-subsumed Polity dreadnought evaded the few remaining mines and slammed itself into the armoured side of the huge ship. The impact knocked the *Battle Wagon* sideways, tore away one of its coil-guns, and scattered a line of wreckage through space. On other displays Azroc could see the ship radiating, unable to disperse the heat from the continuous beam strikes made upon it. Three CTDs, or maybe plain nukes, struck it all at once, shattering weapons turrets and spraying debris and boiling fire from glowing craters. All around the *Battle Wagon*, this intense assault obliterated all those attendant ships that guarded its attack run. Like a wounded buffalo it lumbered on, now swinging round above the ice giant's rings, adding its own substance to those rings as it shuddered constantly under strike after strike. Ahead of it rod-ships swarmed in the process of forming a wall, holes continuously punched through it by the *Wagon*'s remaining weapons. But in the end there were too many of them. Soon it lay at the centre of another storm, but rod-ships now reached its surface, melting in, and spreading through its systems.

A comment from the *Battle Wagon*'s AI came over general com. 'Mmm, I should have done this earlier.'

The view blanked – no sensors able to handle any longer the sleet of radiation emanating from that direction. Two, three, four seconds . . . then, finally able to discern something through the sensors of *Brutal Blade*, Azroc saw the *Battle Wagon* was gone, a massive cloud of incandescent gas spreading in its place. Even the ring system of the ice-giant planet disrupted, losing its definition and blurring around that orb. Though the destruction of enemy ships was high in number, more than eighty per cent of them still remained. Meanwhile over half of the Polity ships had been destroyed, and

Azroc estimated that only an hour of life remained to those surviving.

The shuttle bay inside the *King of Hearts* contained few comforts, and the AI had locked them out of all its systems. From this it seemed evident that King did not relish the presence of humans aboard, nor apparently did the AI enjoy conversation with them for, after its initial communication, it had said nothing more since its escape from the planet, nor during the drop into underspace and their subsequent violent expulsion from that continuum.

'I take it your U-jump was curtailed,' said Cormac.

No reply, yet again. From where he sat with his back against a cold ceramal wall, Cormac studied the few survivors contained with him in this armoured hold: four dracomen including Scar, the four Sparkind: Andrew Hailex and three Golem, besides Arach and himself. But out of how many originally? The figures lay easily accessible in his gridlink, but Cormac felt no urge to inspect them. He just knew that far too many lives had passed through the meat grinder. Rather than inspect the past to find errors of judgement so he could revel in guilt, Cormac concentrated his attention on the now. He tried again to communicate with the *King of Hearts*'s AI using his gridlink, and when that channel again ended up against a blank wall, he inspected in detail the personnel files recorded in his gridlink.

The three dracomen, other than Scar, were called Pick, Anan and Scythe, and without using cognitive programs he could not tell them apart. But, then, these three being no more than a year old, they had yet to acquire distinguishing characteristics like Scar possessed. The three Golem were named Ursach Candy Kline, Bell-mouth and Hubbert Smith. The former two had the appearance of human females: the first blonde and elfin to the extent of possessing pointed ears, the second with cropped yellow hair and lacking one side of her face – gleaming skull exposed underneath. Hubbert Smith was in an even worse condition, now being completely devoid of syntheflesh – just a shiny ceramal skeleton, whose emulation had been male. Cormac classified all three similarly: strong, intelligent, loyal . . . product. He turned his attention to the larger file concerning Arach, and there found much to amuse and sometimes dismay him over the ensuing hour. Then, without warning, an armoured iris door squealed open in one side of the hold.

Hubbert Smith ducked his skull through it then after a moment turned back to address them. 'Facilities provided. It would seem King does not intend to let you die.'

'That would rather defeat the object of rescuing you all in the first place,' replied the AI itself through a telefactor that now drifted in from the room beyond.

Cormac studied the machine: a cylinder floating upright, manipulators now folded against itself, and sensory apparatus mounted at each end, top and below. He recognized the rather battered machine as the same one that had disarmed them earlier, though it now lacked its caterpillar tracks. Easing himself to his feet he asked, 'Why *did* you rescue us?'

'I'm rather impulsive. It tends to get me into a lot of trouble but not, I might add, in as much trouble as some of my fellow ships are at present.'

While the others moved past the telefactor and into the other room, Cormac asked, 'Will you explain that statement?'

'It was a simple and effective double-action trap: you lure out a small force, ambush it with a larger though not overwhelming force, giving members of that prey time to yell for help before trapping it with a USER.' Cormac followed the others into the room and looked around as King continued. 'In the ensuing battle you allow some elements of that smaller force to get to the USER and destroy it, thus allowing the large reinforcements to come in – in this case a fleet of Polity dreadnoughts, attack ships, and one capital ship. The impression having been given will be of an ambush that went wrong. You then activate a second USER, too distant to be destroyed, and proceed to slaughter the rescuing reinforcements with the the huge reserve you kept hidden in plain sight. Polity super-intelligences made to look like mugs – rather frightening actually.'

Cormac felt sick. 'Can you give me details?'

A channel opened to his gridlink so he could observe events light hours distant. Yet, even as he watched what was happening, he could not fathom the purpose of it all. Yes, Erebus was giving the Polity a thrashing, but it must still know it only engaged a fraction of the Polity forces available. Why deliberately poke needles into an elephant? Annoy it enough and it is bound to turn around and step on you. The chaos he now witnessed did not seem at all like the logical actions of superior AI.

The adjacent room contained hastily constructed human facilities: a shower unit, toilet, a row of bunks and a food and drink dispenser. Fairly Spartan, but then what did he expect? Hailex took one of the bunks while Scar and the other dracomen took possession of some of the others. Cormac chose one and sprawled himself on it.

Almost immediately weariness hit him in a wave, but he did not allow it to drag him under.

'What do you intend to do with us?' he asked.

'An interestingly debatable question, and one I will consider in depth if by any chance I manage to survive a conflict that is only a few light hours away and currently spreading towards me.'

Cormac drifted off for a moment, then snapped back to consciousness as he felt the vibration of the ship's fusion drive starting up. 'You are moving away from the conflict?'

'I am. There is some wreckage nearby and resources I might possibly utilize.'

'Wreckage of what?'

The *King of Hearts*'s AI gave him no reply.

Through *Heliotrope*'s sensors Orlandine observed some machine, shaped like a fifty-foot-long flatworm fashioned of copper, come oozing from the bunker structure. Within fractions of a second she assessed the situation: obviously the chlorine build-up in the methane sea below her had been detected. Plotting currents and distribution, whatever was responsible for the detecting had now worked out its probable source and had sent something to investigate. She needed to speed things up. Shutting down power to the mycelium, she instead supplied full power to the larger drill, then instructed all but two of the mooring harpoons to detach. Under the impetus of the drill, the ship swivelled slightly, drawing the cables taut. Relentlessly the bit bored down – only fifty feet to go. She started the pump that would increase shaft pressure behind the CTDs to force them down. As they began moving she loaded programming to the small impellers constructed to drive them through liquid methane and into position.

Forty feet.

The worm-thing reared up, its top section twisting into a helix. Detection. It knew her location now. Orlandine targeted it with *Heliotrope*'s cutting lasers. At this distance they would not hurt it, but that was not her intention. The helix snapped back down to its flat ribbed shape and, on either side of it, two jets of gas appeared. Orlandine targeted the apex of each gas stream as they abruptly sped towards her. Picking out the beams, lased green light flickered on ice dust in the almost non-existent atmosphere. Two incandescent explosions followed and a confetti of iron-hard ice rolled out before the blast waves. More missiles followed.

Twenty-five feet.

The CTDs now rested firmly behind the drill bit, but the quantity of chlorine down there might not be enough. It lay in a grey *maybe* area, for she could not know one hundred percent the efficiency of the mycelium. She damned Heisenberg.

No more missiles headed her way. *Heliotrope* bucked as blast waves struck it, and even inside the interface sphere she could hear a hail of ice against the hull. The attacker now started to head towards her ship. Whatever controlled it probably now fully realized the danger. Below, through the mycelium, she observed numerous rod-shaped objects emitted from the USER station and speeding up towards her like T-cells.

Fifteen feet.

The copper flatworm crashed its way through a last barrier of contorted ice out onto flat ground, and accelerated towards the ship. It was all about energy here.

During the long journey from Cassius, Orlandine had prepared weapons systems for *Heliotrope* – two particle-beam projectors and a rail-gun that could operate up to near-c to fire solid projectiles as well as deploy the selection of esoteric missiles she had constructed. But now she did not possess a sufficient profligacy of energy to utilize them.

Ten feet.

Only one option remained. Initially she intended to inject the CTDs, seal the drill shaft, and fire up her ship's fusion engine to escape before detonating them. Not a tenable option now.

The worm surged within fifty yards of the ship when Orlandine allowed the two harpoon cables to slacken. The drill's torque turned the ship around precisely as far as she had calculated.

Five feet.

She fired up the fusion engine and two sun-bright blades of flame stabbed across, low above the icy ground, and struck the approaching worm. It held for a couple of seconds, then parts of it began to ablate. Abruptly it began to coil upwards, then it just flew apart. Orlandine shut down the engine.

Four feet.

'Come on!'

Four feet.

'Fuck, fuck!'

The drill shaft, being fed down in hollow sections behind the independently operating drill head, could clearly advance no more. Diagnostics screamed the reason at her: the force of the engine burn had bent one of the drill-shaft sections right below the ship. And the ship's detectors now picked up seismic disturbances not caused by the drilling – more visitors. Orlandine began racking up pressure in the shaft and the drill bit began turning again as that pressure pushed it down further, but then it stopped again. No joy – and Orlandine knew what she must do. She resupplied power to the mycelium, then quickly detached herself from the interface sphere. No time for delay, no time at all. In the hold she donned a heavy-duty assister frame and spacesuit, then headed for the airlock, meanwhile maintaining EM contact with the ship's systems.

The lock popped open on a settling snow of iridescent ice flakes. She glanced over towards where the engine flames had scorched the terrain and saw the remains of her attacker: its individual segments melted down into the ice, vivid rainbow light flaring and swirling around them – a low-temperature photoluminescent effect.

Stop admiring the view, Orlandine reprimanded herself, and scuttled down from the lock, clinging upside-down to the hull underneath the ship. *Just four damned feet*. The bent shaft-section now became visible. Over beside it she dropped to the ground and, using the same tools she had used on the Dyson segment to cut ice blocks, sliced down around it and began levering out chunks of ice. Minutes passed before she removed enough to clear a gap down around the shaft by four feet – minutes she could not now afford. Almost incidentally, still watching through the ship's sensors, she fired the lasers at rapidly approaching objects.

'Multi-tasking!' she shouted triumphantly, as she turned to head back inside, and wondered not for the first time if she was going insane.

Spheres of fire ignited on the horizon as she reached the lock. Just as she was closing the door behind her, a storm of razor ice impacted the hull. Something tugged at her thigh. Glancing down she saw air gusting from her suit, then a sudden explosion of breach sealant closing up the rip. She ordered the drill to start working again as the lock cycled, gave some slack to the mooring cables. The bent shaft of the revolving drill began to slam *Heliotrope* about, but it was working again, boring down.

Two feet . . . through!

Stumbling back inside the ship, Orlandine sent the signal to detach the drill bit. Under pressure the five CTDs shot down into liquid methane. Orlandine ordered emergency detach from her assister frame and it clattered to the floor. She felt slightly sick and dizzy.

Cables . . . detach from shaft . . .

For a moment she could not figure how to do that, then, as she finally reached the interface sphere, remembered how and sent the required signals. As the ship detached from the drill, the pressure within the drill shaft exploded underneath *Heliotrope*, hurling it up and away from the planetoid, and throwing Orlandine to the floor. Not enough to move the ship far, but the constant blast of methane following it out through the open shaft continued the job. More missiles coming in now, and the ship's lasers, now underpowered, were having problems hitting them all. Orlandine dragged herself to her feet and connected to the interface sphere, immediately gaining a greater perspective. *Heliotrope* steadily rose on a large methane geyser. The CTDs below were slowly moving into position, the bacilliform objects still shooting up towards them. The exhausts of all the missiles speeding towards her surrounded the planetoid like a cage. By now the reactor had nearly built up enough energy to fire up the fusion engine again, but not yet because of the drain from deploying the lasers.

No more time.

Orlandine sent the signal to detonate. The glare from below shone blue-green through the ice in the crust, and then the crust itself heaved up. The methane geyser became gigantic, accelerating *Heliotrope* further, and hurling up boulders and bergs behind it. The final flash followed a few seconds later, then . . . nothing.

Not enough chlorine?

Not so, the planetoid became increasingly luminous, began to stand out more visibly from the darkness of space. The first crack opened up a hundred miles from her landing point, and out of it glared bright white light. More cracks appeared rapidly, and Orlandine observed a chunk of rock and ice the size of Gibraltar lifting away from the planetoid on a swirling explosion of arc-light. Next, in seeming slow motion because of the sheer scale of the blast, the planetoid came apart. Over there a continent-sized piece of the crust departed almost with balletic grace, but which had to be travelling at thousands of miles per hour. Below her, a rising swarm of boulders that could grind up *Heliotrope* like a sardine tin thrown into the works of some huge engine. And there, a gust of flame stabbing out like a solar flare.

Fusion start.

Instantly onlining the engines, Orlandine flung her ship towards safety. Only then did she notice the warnings from her physical diagnosticer. She had lost about a litre of blood, which must now be washing around inside her spacesuit. She would have to attend to that later. To herself she half smiled, half grimaced, as the USER ceased to function – roasted in white fire.

Another dreadnought, pounded until it looked like a maggot-chewed apple, self-destructed rather than allow itself to be subsumed by the rod-ships settling on its burnt and pitted hull. The more manoeuvrable Polity ships seemed to be standing up better, perhaps because the alien ships concentrated their fire on the larger ships whose heavier weapons could actually destroy them. Once the enemy had dealt with all the dreadnoughts, they would doubtless mop up the rest.

In a nightmare fugue, Azroc watched the battle and tracked the logistical projections to their conclusion. One small part of those projections predicted the destruction of the *Brutal Blade* within the next half hour – this fact appearing as inevitable as a sunset. The Golem observed the ribbons of fire burning through space as high-energy weapons swept across gas that had escaped from shattered vessels. He saw old-style attack ships fighting a losing battle in the disrupted ring system, playing hide and seek behind tumbling boulders. He observed a tenacious assault on an enemy ship by a dreadnought similar to *Brutal Blade*, how that other ship peeled away snakish structures and fired missile after missile as it closed in. Rod-ships dotted the dreadnought's hull like clinging leeches. It did not slow, but rammed the enemy ship, detonating all its weapons simultaneously. A brave but futile act, human almost.

Then Azroc's eye fell upon other minor scenes: a shuttle being subsumed by a rod-ship, and spacesuited figures jetting away from it with painful slowness. Gusts of flame and gas as the shuttle's laser targeted then incinerated each of these figures. Were they evacuees from this very ship? The Golem calculated the chances of that, and of one of those figures being Karischev. Azroc had by then shut down those parts of his mind concerned with the emulation of human emotion, though, as he did so he considered whether it was emulation, when copied so perfectly, or the thing itself? Perhaps the mere fact that he could disconnect himself from it did make it emulation. Such thoughts he concerned himself with as he waited for his own destruction.

Then the USER shut down.

It took the Golem some moments to realize what had happened, as com traffic rose to a scream and Polity ships began disengaging and running. Only as ships began winking out, dropping into U-space, could he accept that they might now survive. He began to bring parts of his consciousness back online; returning to life. The first shuttle to come in through the gaping hole in the side of *Brutal Blade* skidded along the shining deck and crashed into the wall below the dormitory windows. Another swiftly followed it, then another. Focusing in on the coms operating between Brutus and those aboard the shuttles, he learnt that seven out of the twelve small vessels had survived. Nothing said about Karischev, however.

Once the last shuttle slammed down in the docking bay, the *Brutal Blade* dropped into U-space with a ragged groan echoing throughout its structure. They were away; they had survived. Azroc removed his grip from the stanchion as the gravplates came back on and stabilized. He moved across to the nearest dormitory window and observed a shimmer-shield come on within the hole through which the shuttles had entered. Beyond this he observed repair robots, like frenetic spiders no bigger than a finger end, spinning metallic fibres across to slowly mend the gap. He moved away from the window and along through the dormitory. He observed a man lying on the floor, his spacesuit still intact, but himself horribly broken inside it, his spine snapped at right angles. Azroc stooped down and observed a small autodoc clinging to the suit's shoulder, nestled in breach foam like a spit bug. Checking the doc's readout he discovered that it maintained life – the doc shunted in at the man's neck, keeping his head alive and thus the brain inside it. The rest could be repaired, or replaced later. Azroc stood up and moved on down into the shuttle bay.

Sparkind were disembarking, but Karischev himself was yet to appear. Recognizing the soldier's shuttle, Azroc quickly headed over to it. The shuttle lay distorted, hot metal ticking and creaking as it cooled. Azroc realized then that it had not even made it away from the ship. Some weapon had carved a channel right through its hull, energy discharges frying its systems and welding it to the deck.

A Golem Sparkind reached the shuttle's airlock ahead of Azroc, tearing it away from its distorted frame. Smoke gusted out, stinking of fried meat. Azroc ducked inside after the other Golem, and began checking for life-signs amid the incinerated remnants. Two remained alive, maintained by suit autodocs operating in much the same way as the one Azroc had seen in the dormitory. The rest of the bodies were casualties of war. He finally identified Karischev as the burnt thing still strapped in the navigator's seat. The sick wrench of anger he felt was no emulation.

Epilogue

At first it seemed there might still be some life in the wrecked Centurion. Scanning it from a distance, King picked up energy usage from within the hull, localized heat sources, and other indicators that something might still be functioning inside. However, drawing closer, the AI attempted to open communication links but received no response, and now, inspecting the ship at close hand, King realized those earlier signatures must have resulted from its death throes, a leaking reactor, final fires dying down inside the vessel. It was hardly recognizable as a ship at all, now that it lay twisted out of shape in a cloud of its own debris. The likelihood of its mind having survived seemed low.

When the USER went offline in a way that indicated its destruction, King's first instinct was to flee immediately. However, the AI suppressed that instinct. It had already rescued some humans for reasons it did not like to study too closely, so why not make certain here? Maybe a rescued AI would state King's case later to the Polity? But it was really that undamaged weapons nacelle that swung King's decision not to leave immediately. Yes, its contents might be depleted, but King needed such supplies desperately, and anything would be better than his present complete lack of armament.

The *King of Hearts* drew even closer to the ruined ship, pieces of wreckage bouncing and clattering from the hull before tumbling away into vacuum. King fired his two grapnels, closing their hardened claws into ripped hull metal on either side of the undamaged weapons nacelle, then began to draw the wreck towards him. After a moment he guided his remaining telefactor out of the accommodation specially constructed for the rescuees, back into the bay, and launched it into space. Bringing the telefactor down on the wreck's twisted hull, he set it to cutting its way in, then returned his attention to the weapons nacelle. He scanned the nacelle and discovered it contained only two imploder missiles – not really a great haul, but better than nothing. He would get the telefactor to cut the missiles free after it checked out the mind inside the ship . . .

Then the comlink opened. 'One false move and you're toast, boy,' came a voice.

'Who is this?' Something about the speaker seemed familiar to King, but he could not identify what because at present the communication came via radio and was voice only.

'Inspect yourself, King.'

Through the telefactor, King did as instructed. Debris had clattered against him constantly during his approach to the wreck. Some of it, however, had not bounced away, and appeared too suspiciously even in construction to be mere debris. King paraphrased himself: *Polity super-intelligences taken for mugs* . . . A neat row of black hemispheres now decorated his hull from stem to stern. *Space mines.*

'Now,' said the voice, 'I hope I have your attention, because if you do anything reckless and I send a signal to those mines, there won't be enough left of you to make a decent-sized ingot.'

'I have humans aboard.'

'I very much doubt that, unless you've found a way to use them for fuel. I know your opinion of anything that is not AI.'

In response King sent images of those he had rescued. There came a delay before the response, as the recipient of those same images no doubt opened the information stream in secure space so as to check for both viruses and veracity.

'You know ECS policy concerning hostages,' said the other ship.

'I know it, but these are not hostages. I rescued them.'

'The *King of Hearts* changes his heart?'

'Something like that.'

'You know what the ECS response to you might be?'

'I do . . . I have not yet decided how to resolve this.'

'You will open yourself to me for inspection. Completely.'

'You could be an agent of Erebus – and I would rather the mines be detonated than submit myself to that.'

'You too could be such an agent . . . Very well, then, allow me access to your U-space communicator, or would you rather I detonated those mines right now?'

King opened an exterior link to his U-com, permanently monitored and ready to be closed down in an instant. He did not know the contents of the information package the other ship sent, nor what it received in return. But after a moment, the other vessel sent coordinates.

'You will take us here,' it instructed.

King brought the U-space engine online and expanded its field to encompass the wreck, before dropping them both into the U-continuum. He noted, through the channel open to his telefactor, that it had by now cut its way into the other ship's hull. In a short burst of code he gave it other instructions, then felt some relief when he realized the other ship did not seem to detect the signal. He understood then that the mind in the wreck had played its only real strong cards. Its sensors must be severely damaged; what sensitivity they still possessed had been badly degraded by the radiation leakage from the cracked reactor. It would probably not even see the telefactor until the machine was upon it.

Slow hours passed, and finally the telefactor, after cutting its way through much wreckage, entered the chamber containing the other mind, thereupon sending its 'ready' signal to King. Now fully engaged through the telefactor, King was in a position to destroy the other AI mind. But . . . what would be gained?

'Aren't you going to do something, then?' asked the mind in the wreck.

'This changes nothing,' said King.

'Precisely . . . I've been watching your telefactor's stealthy approach for some time and wondering what you intended.'

King felt slightly embarrassed, like a child caught by its parent in some obviously stupid act. He settled the telefactor down on its base and just let it stay there. Now, in underspace, he noticed much disturbance – many ships.

'The fleet?'

'Yes, what remains of it.'

Days passed, during which King observed his passengers settle into a routine, even offered them coldsleep facilities that some accepted. Cormac went first, King felt with some relief, then Andrew Hailex. The dracomen did not require such facilities, having already sunk into some form of hibernation. The Golem merely shut themselves down. King, finding the other ship uncommunicative, also switched himself to a state that truncated his perception of time, any thoughts easing themselves through his mind like ponderous sloths. Eventually the journey ended and, returning to full function, he surfaced into the real.

The planetary system lay within the Polity. Here an inhabited world orbited a hot white sun. It lay second from the sun, outside the orbit of a gas giant and inside the orbit of one cold world the size of Mars, beyond which lay an asteroid field – the remains of some shattered world yet to spread and gather into a ring around the sun. On the colonized planet's surface, human habitations enclosed in polarized geodesics pocked jungle-swamped land masses as if they were blistering in the heat. The jungle was not alien, merely adapted earthforms boiling across the landscape to transform the atmosphere into something breathable. Cooling plants like iron cathedrals lasered away heat from the nightside to orbital installations. Huge mirrors, still being constructed in orbit, reflected away some of the sun's energy to be utilized in massive orbital factories. King swiftly understood that all this energy was being converted into coherent maser beams projected towards the cold planet, to power mining operations there and enable further terraforming. The hot planet, in some future time, would be a world much like the one King had departed, where adapted humans, sandapts and other thermodapts, and doubtless dracomen, could survive in the open. The cold world would probably end up supporting human 'dapts at the other end of the thermal scale.

Such were the energies being thrown about here, King realized this was a perfect bolt hole for the remains of the fleet, much of which had already materialized within the system. Not only that, other Polity ships, other Polity forces began appearing. Listening in to coms traffic King identified one of them as a ship called the *Cable Hogue* – a vessel so huge that it could not orbit worlds with crustal instabilities or oceans, since its sheer mass would cause tides and earthquakes – a vessel once only rumour, even to King. Next King identified two Dragon spheres, hanging in space either side of the *Jerusalem*, which came bearing down on his present position.

Decision time . . . he could choose either certain destruction or utter submission. Then he realized he had already chosen. King felt, as much as an AI could, an overwhelming fatigue. He knew himself to be in the wrong about so much, and no matter how far he fled he would still be wrong.

'You wanted me to open myself to inspection,' he told the other ship he carried with him. 'You could still be some agent of Erebus here to cause mayhem, so I will open myself to Jerusalem.'

At least, if Jerusalem chose to erase King's mind, it would be fast.

King opened a link to the approaching ship, dropping his defences, and in an instant Jerusalem's probe slammed inside him. He knew that, though he willingly allowed this, the sheer power of the mind behind that probe meant it could probably have been performed without his submission. Jerusalem sent HK programs inside King, riffling through his systems, inspecting memories. The link was utterly one-sided, so he gained little from the other mind. However, he did know that Jerusalem was similarly probing the mind of the wrecked ship, and other ships nearby too, just as other minds of equivalent power probed fleet ships throughout the system. Then, the probe abruptly withdrew, the HK programs scurrying after it like hunting dogs. King found himself linked into a three-sided communication.

'Your decision,' said Jerusalem to the other ship.

A signal was transmitted, and King observed the mines dotted along his hull deactivating and detaching.

'A shuttle will now collect your passengers, and after that you may go,' said the mind within the wrecked ship.

King could not understand. He had destroyed the *Jack Ketch*, killed another AI mind – so why were they prepared to let him go? Probably, he decided, they had no intention of letting him escape. Maybe they felt they still needed ships like him in the future conflict, and therefore hoped to re-recruit him. He detached his grapnels as he observed a shuttle and a grabship, departing from one of the *Jerusalem*'s bays, no doubt coming to collect his passengers and the wreck. The communication between Jerusalem and the other ship continued.

'So you still survive,' said Jerusalem.

'I do . . . sort of.'

'And Cormac survived. How . . . elegant. I will observe his debriefing with some interest.'

'Will there really be anything of importance to learn?'

'I said "with interest".'

'I see.'

'I suppose you'll be wanting a new ship body?' Jerusalem enquired.

'That would perhaps be a good idea.'

'Would it? You seem to make a habit of wrecking them. You will take better care of a new one this time, won't you, Jack?'

'Bollocks,' replied Jack Ketch.

Ah . . . thought King.

Gazing through the panoramic window in one of the *Jerusalem*'s lounges, Cormac watched the glint of drives coming on and going out. Through his gridlink he dipped and delved in the coms traffic and put together a general picture of what was now occurring in this system. The terraforming energies being employed here now lay under Jerusalem's direct control, that superior AI serving the military governor of this entire system which was now, he guessed, equivalent to a fortress. If anything unexpected surfaced from U-space now, it would immediately become the target for arrays of masers, lasers, and the focused light of sun mirrors. Many systems in the Polity would doubtless be similarly prepared, had been preparing for some time. But he was also painfully aware of just how many stations and worlds lay vulnerable to attack from something like Erebus.

'The AIs *knew* something like this was on the cards,' said Mika.

Ensconced on the couch in this viewing lounge, he smelt her hair and felt quite comfortable with her head resting on his chest. 'The AIs assess events and make their predictions, but "cards" does seem an apt description – it all can seem as unlikely as tarot to the rest of us.'

'They did not predict so well. Many people have died and many ships were destroyed,' Mika observed. 'And, from what I gather, there is still some confusion about what Erebus's overall strategy might be.'

Cormac nodded, the illogic of recent events bothering him too. 'Erebus just gave us a very bloody nose indeed, but I agree: why deliver a bloody nose early rather than await the opportunity to deliver a killing blow?'

'You might also ask: why attack at all? As the understatement goes, space is big and there's room in it for us all.'

'The Makers didn't think so.'

'We don't know what they thought.'

'Indeed,' Cormac concurred.

Cormac could not yet see the rogue AI's intent, but he would see it at some point, just as he had fathomed Blegg before the man understood himself. Earth Central, whom he spoke to only an hour before entering this lounge, had told him, 'I needed an agent directly connected to myself, a probe into human society to ken events from the human level.'

'But why a probe that considered itself immortal?' Cormac asked.

'He required continuity to give himself the necessary perspective. I created Blegg's mind thirty seconds after I myself came online, mapped out his history and decided how I would run him.'

'Why the legend?'

'The memes originated not from Blegg or myself, but from all those humans with whom he became involved over the ages. At first I considered stopping those memes – keeping his existence secret – but I soon learned how, in the presence of a living legend, humans often feel impelled to excel. Humans need their heroes, they need to believe they can be something . . . better. The legend of the lone immortal has been a staple of myth throughout human history, and Blegg perfectly fitted that mould.'

'And what about what happened to him back there?'

'In the early years I ran him in a Golem chassis, but substantial alterations of his memory kept being required since injury easily revealed to him what he really was. Only when technology had reached a certain level was I able to create his biomech bodies. However, such bodies contain much information that could be useful to an enemy, so they had to contain a fail-safe, as did his mind.'

'But he knew what he was – you let him know there on Cull, with that Jain node. He told me Mr Crane tossed it to him and he caught it in his bare hand, and because it did not react to him he knew he wasn't human.'

'He would have learned anyway. Your assertion to him that he was an avatar of me was only a small step. The sheer accumulation of data throughout his existence was leading him to that same inevitable conclusion. Only by erasing hundreds of years of his memory could I return him to his original unknowing state, and then he would be of little use to me anyway.'

'Are you going to resurrect him again?'

'Blegg is obsolescent.'

'But surely you need him now more than ever?'

'No, I do not, for I have you, Ian Cormac.'

Sprawled on the sofa, Cormac felt his surprisingly relaxed attitude stemmed from the utter weariness at his core. But how true was his weariness? How true was anything about him? He could move through U-space just like Blegg could not . . . or was that a lie?

. . . for I have you, Ian Cormac.

Gazing out at the star drives and the stars, Cormac wondered if he was the new model Horace Blegg just created by Earth Central. He studied his hand. *Biomechanism or human? And how different are they in the end?*

How could he possibly know?

Orlandine had been travelling through U-space for five days now, her course taking her around from the galactic rim, while skirting the Polity, and in towards the clustered stars of the inner galaxy. Soon, she decided, she would adjourn to a cold coffin, shut down the tech operating inside her body and sleep for a hundred years. Somewhere, deep within the Milky Way galaxy, she would wake and find herself a world that the line of Polity would not reach for a millennium, supposing the Polity itself survived for that long. There she could fully explore the Jain technology, and there build something . . . numinous.

As a further five days passed, Orlandine realized she was procrastinating. Eventually she threw a hard question at herself.

'Okay, Orlandine, what is this numinous thing you are going to build, and who's going to appreciate it anyway?' She paused, gazing out through *Heliotrope*'s sensors at the cold light of the stars.

'Oh hell,' she finally muttered, and turned the ship around.